In Light of Moon and Sun

In Light of Moon and Sun

The Wanderer's Path

Gavin Cash Brown

San Diego

Dedication

In memory of my dad,
R. Brown

Acknowledgements

To Nathan and Chris, your continued support and feedback have made me a more thoughtful writer.

To David and Fartoon, your patience and support help keep me grounded.

Table of Contents

The Known World ~ West

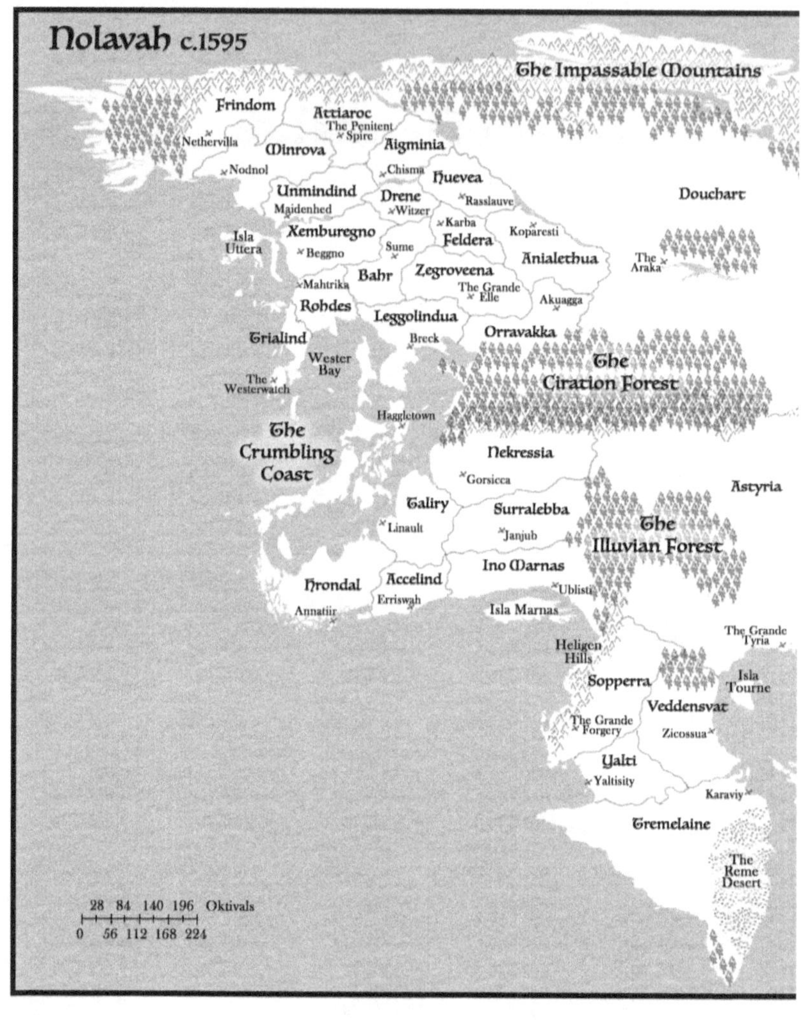

The Known World ~ East

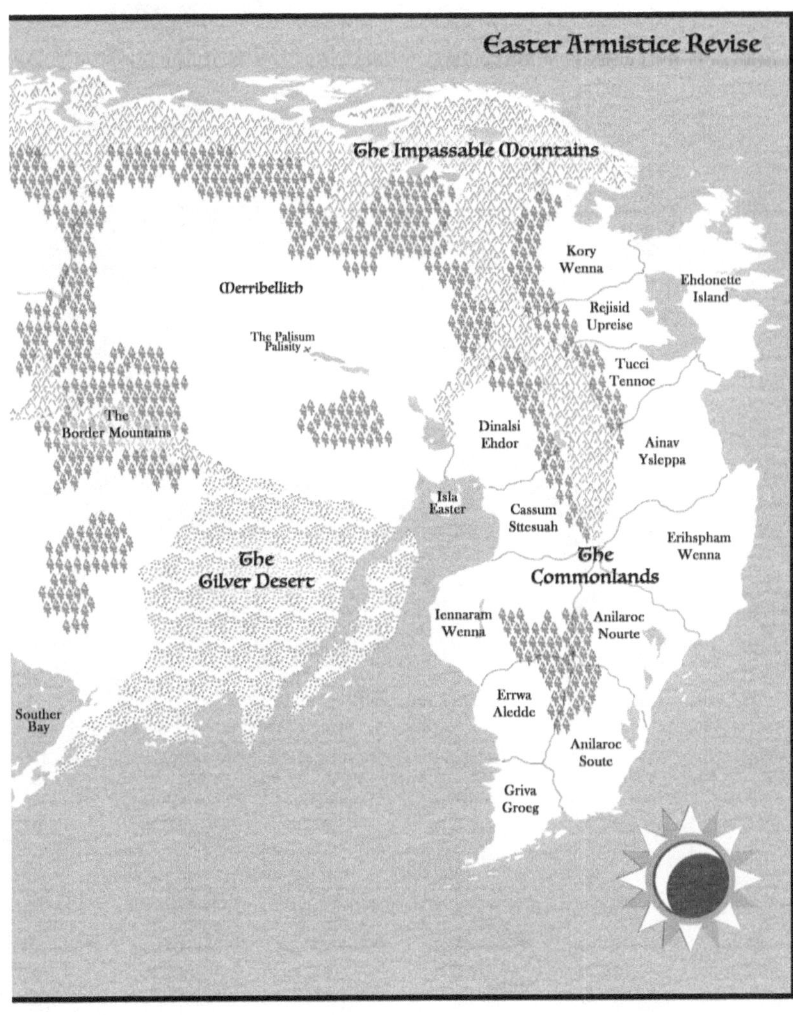

1   The Starlight's Traverse

She was once the pride of the Merribellith flotilla, built a hundred blooms after the Great Reformation. For more than the two hundred blooms since, the second-generation steamrunner had both seen and made history. She weathered the Easter War, mounting one successful sortie after another until the Commonland invaders had finally been pushed back into their provinces. But those glory days were long behind her, and modern advances had made her age apparent. Now, skirting through the clouds on outstretched sails filled with heligen, the *Starlight's Traverse* maintained duty as transport and training vessel for new recruits. On this occasion, she transported several passengers.

Journeymin Lonn was one of them, beaming brightly and standing at the bow with one sure foot planted on the sprit. He leaned forward and gazed out at the landscape all around. His eyes, green and wide, took it all in as the wind whipped through his sunkissed locks and flapped at his white tunic. The lush violet forests of norther Astyria rushed beneath them like a strong river current, and he could see the Border Mountains in the distance leading back to Merribellith. For him, the journey had been too brief and so bogged down with duties he had little time to really see the world beyond his home at the Palisum. "Soreign! Come look! You can see so far from here!"

"Fine right where I am." His older and more worldly

taskmaster lounged along the bulwark of the foredeck wearing a loosely flowing satilk tunic and fine gower-leather striders with his well-worn riding boots propped high on the railing. His calloused fingers ran along his freshly shorn white hair before scratching the back of his neck. His lips curled to one side as his brow creased in concentration. It accentuated the scars etched along his cheek and chin, the result of a shaving accident, or so he claimed. He turned the page of the latest edition of *The Knight's Procession*.

Upon its cover illustration, a knight with curly black hair and a broad, toothy smile stood in full regalia, holding his helmet under his arm with the captions surrounding him.

"Beneath the Breastplate with Sir Merriment."

"Tip of the cycle to get that armor sparkling."

"What Knightly Knight are you? Take the quest!"

Lonn turned to him. "But the view is spectacular."

"Seen it plenty of times." The taskmaster took up a shiny fountain pen and marked the page.

"Well, I haven't. Never seen anything like this before."

"You'll get over it."

"Coming in to Astyria was so turbulent… and we trained below deck the rest of the time, which is where you'd prefer to be now, I'm sure."

"A good knight always knows when it's time to train and when it's time to rest." He raised a brow and marked the page again with a faint grumble, "I'm resting."

"During that last run, I thought you'd be unmounted. Are your injuries still bothering you?"

"Nothing to worry about. Just a bit sore. Sir Kinimer is

a good knight, but his aim is never quite as true as mine. Barely even grazed my shield during last Verlith Bloom's Celebration Tourney, so he's improving at least." He folded down the top of his magazine and set his eyes on Lonn. "And what of you? Took a few good blows during your bout."

"Glancing blows. Bruises mostly. Nothing you didn't prepare me for." He stood taller with a huff of his chest. "And I gave plenty back in return."

The taskmaster smiled and gave a faint nod. "That you did."

"Don't think I've ever seen you take up one of those," he observed, settling against the bulwark. "Didn't you tell me once they were beneath my time?"

"The local rubbish is. This…" He cleared his throat, "Always important to gather foreign knowledge. Insights into their philosophy on the Knightly Order, for instance. Vital for battlefield strategies."

"But Astyria's an ally."

"Be prepared. Always. Never know when…" His gaze trailed along the Border Mountains west to the kingdom of Douchart, and his hand swiped along his chin. "They might know something we don't. Or they might be lacking. Knowing strengths and weaknesses is always good for any situation. Makes us all stronger in the end." He let out a sigh, "But this…"

"So?" Lonn asked with a grin. "What kind of knight are you?"

"Absurd, really." Soreign grimaced and gave a shake of his head. "Alright. Take this, for instance: 'Crossing a bridge, a knight blocks your path, blade drawn. During the fight, you get the upper hand and knock nim over the edge. The weight of nis armor causes nim to sink to the bottom. Do you let nim drown or rescue nim?'"

"You let nim drown," he eyed his taskmaster with a quiver of amusement on his lips, "didn't you?"

"Course I did. We were just fighting, so dead is dead. This way just saves a lot of mess." He set his gaze on the young journeymin. "You'd rescue nim?"

Lonn scrunched his brow in contemplation. "Isn't that… a code of the Knightly Order? To be honorable and help the helpless?"

"It is. But, that's not the kind of helpless they meant."

"Isn't it? Might it turn an enemy into an ally?"

"Nhe'd probably just betray you when you least expect it, but it's possible, I suppose."

"There you go, Soreign, always thinking the worst of mins."

"Comes from experience, lad. You'll learn from it too, one day."

"True, I haven't had much." He tugged on his tunic and leaned closer. "So, what's another?"

Soreign scanned the page and grinned. "Try this one. 'In single combat, a slash of your sword rips away your opponent's armor, revealing that you are fighting a knightly lady. Do you allow her to cover her immodesty or capitalize on her embarrassment and press your advantage?'"

Blinking, eyes shifting left and right, Lonn sat in uncomfortable silence for a long moment. "Soreign… when would we fight a lady?"

"Steamer battles. Boarding assaults. You know we have many in the flotilla just like the other kingdoms. Usually sign up if they try for the Order and wash out. It happens."

"They… try out for the Knightly Order?"

"Some do. Not many ladies can make it through training. Rare, but it has happened. And we can't expect other kingdoms to have our standards, so… you never know."

"There were no ladies in the tourney."

"There were a few. Just didn't realize it. Armor covers a lot, you know." The journeymin's taskmaster eyed him patiently. "And your answer?"

"I'm… not sure. Never been in that situation."

"Well… I suppose that's one good reason for quests like these," Soreign perked up. "Gives you scenarios to think over so you can be better prepared. That way, you act and don't hesitate."

"And bad things happen when we hesitate." Lonn rubbed his shoulder subconsciously, "Gotten plenty of lumps from you over the blooms to prove that." Looking past the knight, he gasped and sat straighter, "And speaking of ladies, Miku's coming."

"That's Second Midsteamin Arilona to you, My… hummm… Lord."

"Of course." The young journeymin grinned. "My apologies… Sir Soreign."

Dressed in the standard blue uniform of the Merribellith flotilla, the second midsteamin strutted steadily up the steep, creaking steps to the foredeck. Her heavy jacket showed little weathering, buttoned tightly about her waist, and her pressed striders disappeared under the straps of her shiny black boots. Yellow piping trailed down the outer seams of her arms and legs. Strapped about her hips rested an off-kilter belt from which her saber dangled on one side and a dagger sheathed on the other. She had bound her long, auburn hair back tightly to keep it from fluttering in the wind. Her smile was subdued and gentle as she stood before the two passengers. "My Lord, Sir Soreign, now that we're heading home, the captain is——"

Eyes wide and excited, Lonn lurched forward, "He's agreed?"

"Yes, he has, My Lord. A full tour of the steamer."

He bounded to the steps, pausing with a glance at his taskmaster. "Aren't you coming, Soreign… sir?"

The knight rolled up his magazine before rising to his feet with a faint groan, "Coming, My Lord."

As Lonn slid down the steep railings to the mideck, Second Midsteamin Arilona's smile widened. "My. He's so full of energy. I expected he'd be exhausted after the tourney."

Soreign shook his head. "If only such a thing were possible."

"I only wish I'd been closer in the stands to offer him a favor. He performed quite well."

"Don't let My Lord hear that. It'll go straight to his head." The old knight lingered. "Ah, but none for me? Saw you in the front row at mine."

"It's My Lord's first," she laughed, glancing over her shoulder, "Besides, Sir Knight, I know full well the favors you'd prefer. Mine could hardly measure up." She dropped down the steps, strolling across the mideck ahead of a pink-faced Soreign. His color faded to normal once they reached Lonn waiting anxiously near the steps leading to the bridge. Passing him by, she flashed a warm smile and strutted up the steps, yanking the bridge hatch open. "Please, My Lord. Sir Knight."

The sudden shift from the bright deck to the dimly lit confines caused the young journeymin to blink a few times as he adjusted. The first thing he saw was Captain Terasant, an imposing figure built up from blooms in the service, standing beside the central pilot's station. His black hair was tied back, but loose strands fell over the shoulder of his long blue coat, which swept at his knees as he turned toward them. His grip was strong as he took Lonn's hand and then Soreign's. "Oh, welcome to you both! It's a pleasure to finally offer you a proper tour. So unfortunate the bad weather we struck coming into Astyria. Not unexpected this time of the bloom, but it prevented me from accommodating you sooner!" His smile warm and broad, he laid a heavy hand on the journeymin's shoulder. "And I must congratulate you on your success in your debut tourncy, My Lord! First prize in your division, and at such a fine young age! Quite an accomplishment."

"Thank you, captain. Though, I owe much to Sir Soreign's diligent training."

"Well said!" Terasant appreciated the humble acknowledgement. "I'm sure you must be pleased having such a fine young min finally of age to journey for you, you old war woolg!"

Soreign reached out, mussing Lonn's hair. "Make a fine member of the Knightly Order when he comes to proper age."

"And so to the tour." Terasant stretched his arms wide. "Here, of course, is the bridge."

Lonn perked up, motioning around to the stations. "May I?"

"Certainly. Just, please, My Lord, don't press anything." The journeymin maneuvered along the bridge with wide-eyed enthusiasm, looking over the shoulders of the cadets at the controls of the pilot station. Aside from the massive wheel the pilot gripped in one hand, there was a confusing chaos of levers, buttons, and dials along the side panels. "Cadets Nimme and Terasant here are currently handling navigation and piloting duties," the captain explained.

Cadet Nimme swept back strands of sunkissed hair matching his own and glanced up from her chart. "Have you never been aboard a steamrunner before, My Lord?"

Lonn nodded faintly. "Once, yes, but not on active duty. I toured the *Sojourner* with my father when he was decommissioned."

Captain Terasant cut in. "Ah, such a fine vessel in his

time, that one. First second-generation off the line. Fought alongside us during the Battle of Easter Bay. Remember that riot, Soreign? Those blasted Commonlanders. Gave us both a desperate beating, but we pulled through on all fronts and showed them what's what."

Soreign frowned faintly. "I remember."

"Unfortunate that deck-weary steamer couldn't even be retrofitted for lighter service like the *Starlight's Traverse*."

Lonn glanced at the captain, surprised. "Lighter service?"

"These days, she's a training vessel first and foremost, with fifteen cadets out of twenty aboard. And we're one of the few steamers in the flotilla actively running while the others are being upgraded. A low-risk venture like this is the perfect opportunity for this lot to gain more experience before being officially assigned."

At the navigation chart spread out on a long table beside the pilot station, Cadet Nimme lined their course to the Border Mountains and made a slight adjustment toward Merribellith Pass before calling out, "Point five siehd."

"Adjusting point five siehd," Cadet Terasant responded, turning the wheel. The *Starlight's Traverse* tilted ever so slightly until the bowsprit pointed more decisively toward the mountain pass.

Lonn eyed the two as they concentrated on their controls, stepping back to the captain's side. "So, you haven't been upgraded yet?"

"No. She's non-combat. Low priority. One of the last on the Palisum's list. And even when she is... won't match a third generation. Still be good for training."

Cadet Nimme leaned closer to the pilot station. "I hear they translated a whole section out of the *Aeleophinium* on... automatic piloting, I think they're calling it. Have it even easier, Wyn."

Cadet Terasant grinned. "Sounds nice."

The captain laughed. "Ah, cadets. They're always interested in the new advancements that will supposedly make their workload lighter. Doesn't always turn out that way, my daughter." He patted the pilot's seat. "But come. There's much more to see. This way, if you will." Down the companionway, they arrived on the quardeck, the section Lonn was most familiar with since their quarters were towards the rear, near the captain's own. There was little to tell about the officer's cabins as the captain led them further down.

The lowdeck was a bustle of activity along the narrow corridors. Several crew rushed from galley to mess balancing filled trays and pots while preparing the evening meal. The deck sergeant barked orders over a high-pitched whistle to a few recruits in the gunnery room. "Load! Pressurize! Aim! Fire!" There was a distinct *poomph* and a quiet before the sergeant called out, "Again! Faster now!"

The captain stood in the doorway, watching for a moment before giving a satisfactory nod. "Yes. All good. Sergeant Frauncis there is a taskmaster akin to Sir Soreign here."

Lonn peered in with interest, watching them load the steam cannons with training rounds. They shrilled as the steam spewed from the building pressure while the cadets aimed for a target. He plugged his fingers in his ears until they fired off. "Louder than I expected!"

"Yes, My Lord! Listening to that all day'll make your ears ring for a lifetime. I know from experience. They do have ear protection now. Never had that in the war." He trailed off down the corridor. "And here is the *Traverse*'s true heart."

They entered the engine room, a sprawling room that constantly reverberated with the dual propellers rotating below them. Chief Engineer Uirvey, a slender figure, stood at the center of the room wearing a grease-spattered uniform and soot rimmed goggles atop his head. Overseeing the cadets' work as they replaced a row of pipes lined against the hull, he shouted, "No! Check those fittings. This one goes there. That one here."

Lonn stepped out of the way and was about to lean on a bulkhead when Uirvey pointed directly at him and gave a stern shout. "You! Careful there! That's the maintenance hatch. Can't have you opening that by accident."

"Oh!" Face flushed with embarrassment, the journeymin jerked away. "Sorry! Didn't realize."

"Not a problem, My Lord," the captain cut in. "Chief Uirvey is very diligent in his duties. Perhaps overly cautious. It's well sealed."

"So… if that opened during flight…"

Uirvey jumped close, spreading his arms wide. "*Whoosh!* We'd all get sucked into the props. Not pretty."

"He's perhaps being overly dramatic." The captain laughed, resting his hand on Lonn's shoulder. "No need to put the scare into Our Lord, chief."

The engineer shrugged, "True. There's an emergency seal," and motioned to the hook straps lined along the deck. "And if you're hooked in, you'll be fine. Like being in a bad windstorm."

"Any questions for our engineer, My Lord?"

Lonn perked up, glancing around, before settling to the back of the room. "Oh. I did." His eyes focused on the large black stone resting between two boiler tanks. "Is that it? The Wolk Stone?"

"That's it," the engineer responded.

"It's bigger than I expected," he commented, stepping closer to its housing. "How fresh is it?"

"Brand new. Replaced our old one just before we set

out for Astyria."

"And how long will it last?"

"Depends how much we tax it." He patted the stone. "Got a good sealant on it, so… might get this one to last four… five more cycles."

Lonn looked down at the gear housing holding the stone in place. It was on the third and most distant setting between the two tanks. "So the closer the position, the faster she'll go?"

"That's right. It'll increase the boiler pressure in the tanks and give us more to work with." The engineer scratched the top of his head. "Of course, that'll degrade the stone faster, too. You can already see a bit of ash in the bottom catch there just from our trip to Astyria." Lonn leaned in, but the chief held him back. "Not too close, My Lord. Don't wanna breathe that in."

The journeymin pulled back with a nod. "And what's her top speed?"

"Oh…" The chief thought for a moment. "Not as fast as the third gens coming off the line now, but I got her to twenty-four oktivals once."

"Impressive." Lonn appraised the Wolk array curiously. "And, this also keeps us afloat?"

"No. Just for the props… cannons. And plumbing, of course." The chief motioned to another series of tanks resting horizontally along the bulkhead. "Those are the heligen tanks that keep us in the air. I've run them in parallel for the siehd and elch sails."

Lonn leaned close, interested in the engineer's alterations. "Is that unusual?"

"Well, it's a modification I made a while back after hitting a bad squall. Tore the elch sail, and we lost pressure in the siehd sail as a result. Almost flipped us. No desire to go through that again. And it also gives us more maneuverability." Uirvey straightened up with a grin. "I hear they've even adapted it into the third generations."

The captain cleared his throat, "Well, we can't take up much more of the chief's time, much as he loves a good ego stroking for all his hard work," and led them down the corridor to the mess. "Now, my Lord, I was hoping you and Sir Soreign would join me for the evening meal. I'd be happy to answer any other—" The vessel trembled around them, and a klaxon soon screamed above the noise on the deck. Terasant glanced around, concerned. "What in the—"

Soreign pressed closer to Lonn, the concern in his face matching that of Terasant's. "This another of your drills, captain?"

"No. I didn't schedule anything for…" he trailed off and huffed with determination down the corridor. He snatched up a receiver on the intercom. "Captain. Bridge. Report."

There was too long a pause before Second Midsteamin Arilona's voice came through. "Bridge. Captain. We're… under attack!"

"Captain. All hands. Combat stations." Slamming the receiver down, he pointed toward the companionway to the quardeck. "My Lord, Sir Soreign, best if you return to your cabin and bar the door. We'll make short work of this." The captain rushed off as the steamer shuddered and groaned.

"Heard him." The knight pushed Lonn toward the companionway. "Back to the cabin."

The young journeymin grasped the railing tight as the steamer rocked. "Can't we—" An unprepared cadet tumbled into him, cutting him off with a grunt.

Soreign braced them both from falling back, setting them on their feet again. The cadet's face filled with panic.

"Wh-what do I do? Attack? What—"

Soreign gripped the cadet by the collar. "Snap to and remember your training. To your duty station, cadet!"

"Yes… yes sir!" The cadet nodded and ran off while Lonn looked around.

"Soreign, can't we help?"

"Course we can." Soreign slapped Lonn's hip. "But not without our blades."

Suddenly remembering they had left their sword belts in their cabin, his face shaded. "Of course."

They raced along the corridor to their quarters as Arilona's voice echoed through the speakers once more. "Bridge. Sergeant Frauncis. Mideck! Repel boarders!"

"Blasted! Actually being boarded?" The taskmaster grimaced.

"Soreign?" Lonn entered their cabin, snatching up his belt.

"Never trained you for this. Just keep a mind on your footing."

"But…" He hesitated. "Our armor?"

"Stowed in the hold." The high-pitched shrill and the subsequent volleys of steam cannons firing live rounds forced him to yell. "No time to search out the luggage!"

"Where should we go?!"

"As the lady said! Best help on the mideck!"

They found the sergeant at the hatch marshaling a group of six, light-armored and armed cadets onto the deck. "Defend the bridge! Don't let a single one through!" She trailed behind the last of them, and Lonn and Soreign followed.

In the orange haze of sunfall, a weathered old steamraider with black and green-fringed sails flew along their elch. It angled steeply in a turn, its siehd sail swiping dangerously close. The raiders slid along its length and landed on the foredeck, blades brandished and ready. That alone was enough to unnerve even the old knight and sergeant as much as it did the cadets. Soreign gripped the young journeymin's shoulder. "Steady on and sword up. Can't let them bloody raiders unbalance you."

Lonn took a deep breath and nodded curtly. "What's the plan?"

The sergeant glanced back, tightening her grip on her saber. "We hold the line, of course!" She eyed the cadets, sabers in wavering hands. "Tighten up fast! Remember your training!"

The cadets tensed, holding their line as the raiders yelled, charging at them across the mideck. They did their best to keep the invaders at bay, but bunched up, found little room to maneuver against the raiders' fury. Soreign saw the aelfin-forged blades they brandished and instantly knew fear. "Those are— fin! Fin blades!" He tried his best to tune out the sound of the first saber shattering and the subsequent scream from the slashed cadet. It was a familiar sound from his past. Despite their disadvantage, the cadets did their best to hold firm. But even the old knight knew they were un-prepared for an assault against raiders of such caliber.

Lonn, to his credit, buffered a number of blows. His sword, like Soreign's, was a better match against their opponents and withstood the clashing metal. He kept his footing well, difficult as that was with the rocking deck and blood spilling from the bodies that fell beside him. He also felt the fear, but Soreign had taught him to push it down. Turn it. Use it. And he did, pushing into the raiders' onslaught in his own way with swift slashes and thrusts that forced his attackers back.

The two soon found themselves very much alone on the mideck, penned in by a defensive line of raiders while others made it below decks and up to the bridge. Soreign grit his teeth, "Looks like we've had it, lad," and lunged forward, cutting into a raider who got too close. He gave an agonized cry as the knight's blade tore down his front from shoulder to hip.

It drew the attention of a cloaked figure who watched the two with interest from aboard the raiding steamer.

As raiders grouped to push against the weaker journeymin, a moment opened, and one slipped in from behind, sliding his sword into the old knight's back. He cried out from the sudden pain as Lonn jerked, offering a startled cry, "Soreign!" The journeymin leaped over his fallen taskmaster and dug his sword into the raider's stomach. Standing over the fallen knight, he swiped his blade from one side to the other, desperately keeping the raiders back.

Lying on the deck, Soreign clutched at his wound, trying to stop the blood flow, and knew it was bad. He took one last look at Lonn as a shadow fell over them. "I… I've failed you, My… heh… Lord."

"Soreign! No!" His journeymin reflexively looked down, fearing the worst.

"A lord?"

With tears welling in his eyes, Lonn swung around at the sudden sound of the subdued voice so close behind him. He carried through with a sword strike, his blade arcing tightly, and brought it to a swift stop just before landing its mark.

Standing over him was a slender figure wearing a thick brown cloak covering a vested, cream tunic and weathered beige striders. Hands on her hips. Face in shadows under her upturned hood. "Your thrust was true, little lord. Why stop?"

Lonn faltered, seeing not a sword or any weapon displayed to defend herself. "I… I cannot assault a lady so unarmed."

She took a faint breath. "Truly."

Lonn sensed movement and realized too late she had distracted him as one of the crew swept in. The young journeymin lunged forward, closing the distance and preventing the raider from swinging a lethal strike. Instead, he bashed Lonn with the hilt of his sword, knocking him off his feet. "Little whelp botherin ya, cap?"

"No." The raider reared back to strike, but the captain moved with swift grace and efficiency, blocking his sword with a small dart dagger. "Alive, Grauler. I want this one. Alive. Unspoiled."

Grauler hesitated a moment before giving the journeymin a swift strike with his fist. Lonn slumped, unconscious at the captain's feet as the grizzled raider flexed his fingers and rose to his feet. "Almost feel sorry for im if you've takin an interest."

The captain ignored his comment and eyed the mideck covered in blood and bodies. "What news?"

"Ran through most a the seasoned crew. Rest're young. Barely a deck-firm foot among em."

"And the hold?"

"Good haul," Grauler grinned. "Fortunate we got both top purse winners in one place."

The captain turned her attention to the steamraider as it pulled along side the *Starlight's Traverse*, interlinking their sails to form a bridge. "Move quick, then. Remember to pull the heligen tanks last."

"Know my business, cap. No remindin needed." On the mideck, several raiders rounded up the steamrunner's few survivors while the rest hauled loot crates across. "And them?" There was a look in his eyes.

The captain knew it well. "Do as your wretched kind does."

Grauler's lips twisted in a wicked grin, "With pleasure."

Wandering toward the survivors, he barked orders to the others, "Work fast! Strip the binch clean! Get that haul stowed below! And get those zorba in the hold slaughtered and down to Flum. Cook us up somethin fresh for once." His gaze lingered over the huddled group.

Chief Uirvey and Cadets Nimme and Terasant remained uninjured from the battle. "Shackle and cage them three." Another cadet slumped on the deck, moaning and bleeding from his stomach. Second Midsteamin Arilona threw herself over him, but Grauler shoved her away and slashed the cadet's neck. "Wouldn't even survive the night. But you… got a little fire left." He slipped his weathered fingers through her hair and pulled her head back roughly. Her face was scratched, and there were jagged tears along her bloodied jacket from numerous slashes and stab wounds. "Damaged goods. But still… can have real fun with a filly like you." He ran his tongue along his cracked lips. "Hear that, boys?! Some entertainment, too! Now move!"

The captain watched silently from a distance before glancing down at Lonn. "poor little lord. a… lady… you called me," she whispered, running her fingers through his sunkissed hair before lifting him into her arms and carrying him back to the steamraider.

2   The Virgin Devourer

The steamraider was a first-generation with a long and winding history between owners stretching long before the Revolt. The current captain had survived the two previous ones and remembered when she was something quite different. But that seemed so long ago, lost in distant memory best forgotten. As they veered away from their latest victim, she stood on the mideck and watched the *Starlight's Traverse* sink down into the sprawling forests of Astyria. Her ears twitched from the sound of cracking trushes and the buckling hull.

She looked back at the moonrise eclipsing sunfall on the easter horizon, the third brighmoon of First Rain. Upon its mostly hazy white surface, a speckled ring of yellow and brown spread out from a darkened center like an eye, the color matching her own. "Don't look at me like that." She cast her head down and stepped onto the bridge.

The growing riot from the lowdeck assaulted her ears as soon as she entered. Amid stories of close calls, notable killings, and looted finds, the surviving crew guzzled their mog, draining the first barrel dry. And then… she knew what would happen then.

Only Mikwit kept his station, piloting the steamer. He was a figure of small stature who, due to an old injury, could not participate in the events occurring below deck. But if he felt excluded, he did not show it. His hand slipped from the wheel and sipped from a mug of mog, choking when he noticed her. She hovered behind him, giving a quick glance at the controls.

He tugged the linen wrap from off his head, wiping at his mouth anxiously. Always nervous, but more so around her, he scrunched down in his seat, one small hand tugging at his striders. "O-on course f-for Alisard, cap."

"Alisard." It was not unexpected.

"J-just like Grauler s-said. Th-that's the order, r-right, cap?"

"It... is." She had not given it, but there was little point in fighting what was to come. "I'll..." her voice was faint as her hand went to her chest fingering her tunic, "be in my cabin."

Mikwit rose up in his seat with a relieved sigh, swiping at the mog stains on his dirty tunic as he straightened it out. "Very g-good, cap."

She turned away and descended the quardeck companionway. Sealing her cabin door and blocking out the sounds of the riot beyond, she found some respite. But no matter how hard she tried to push those thoughts away, her mind dwelled on what came next. It made her hands tremble, and there was only one remedy for that.

Surrounded in darkness, Lonn jerked awake to an aching jaw. He started to rise to his feet until his head slammed into cold metal. Groaning, he plopped down and reached out, his hands batting against metal bars surrounding him on all sides. A cage. He could hear things in the darkness as well. A loud riot from the deck above. And closer by, a faint whimpering. "Is..." his voice caught in his throat, "is someone out there?"

A familiar voice asked, "Who's that?"

He perked up. "Chief Uirvey?"

"I… we didn't think anyone else survived. Who are you?"

"Lonn You— remember? I was a passenger."

"Oh! My Lord, yes!" It was another familiar voice.

"Shush!" Uirvey's voice cut in sharply, "don't let *them* hear *that*!"

"S-sorry, Kiran! You're right, of course."

The journeymin leaned toward the voices to hear them better over the racket from above. "Who else is with you?"

"Cadets Nimme and Terasant."

"No one else made it?" Lonn felt crushed.

Cadet Terasant's voice trembled, "Second Midsteamin Arilona, but she… she's…" and cracked with a sob.

Nimme's voice tried to be strong and reassuring, "It's okay, Wyn."

"Nothing about it's okay, Ysari! They're—"

"Barreling her. I know."

Lonn felt useless and naive as he asked, "What's… barreling?"

There was a long silence in the dark.

Uirvey's voice was hoarse when he answered, "Nothing pleasant. But she's strong. We can only hope she endures until they're too drunk and… wear themselves out."

"Then it'll be our turn," Terasant's voice hissed.

Uirvey grunted, "You don't know that, cadet."

"I— I can't go through that! They should've let me die along side my father," she sobbed, "Ysari, just strangle me first. Can you reach?"

"You shush that, Wyn!"

Lonn felt along the bars of his cage, rattling them. "There must be some means of escape."

Uirvey sighed, "We've tried. I'd swear these cages're fin-forged."

"Same as their weapons."

"Indeed." Uirvey agreed with his observation. "Odd for raiders to have so much of it. Or even be able to keep an original steamer like this flying. No telling how old she is. Impeccably maintained."

Wyn Terasant sobbed, "H-how can either of you talk about that at a time like this?!"

The chief's voice deepened, "We're evaluating our situation, cadet. Keeping our minds focused on the immediate problem. It's painful, but there's nothing we can do for the midsteamin. Focus on what we can do for ourselves."

To that end, Lonn fumbled around for the lock and keyhole. "Don't suppose any of you have any slender metal you could use to force your lock?"

"Thought of that already. They checked us before shoving us in here… thoroughly."

"Us more'n you," Nimme spat, "Can still feel that raider scum's fingers pawing at my nethers."

"So…" the journeymin faltered, not wanting to think about that. "Are we all in separate cages?"

"Afraid so," Uirvey grunted.

Terasant hissed, "What's that even matter?"

"It matters, cadet," the chief chastised, "This crew isn't sloppy. Can't gang up on them. So we have to pay attention. Look for mistakes they make. Seize our moment and maybe get—"

He fell silent as a light streamed down into the far end of the hold. With the hatch open, Lonn clearly heard the riot above. Voices shouted in drunken jubilation, but the one called Grauler came through loudest. "And once more over the barrel she goes! This soppin ginny's suckin me right in! Might just be joyin this much as me!" There were whimpers and grunts as the beam of light wavered. Heavy foot falls stumbled down the steep steps.

"They— they're coming for us!" Terasant cried out in panic.

Nimme hissed, "Shush up!"

As the light grew brighter, Lonn saw the fear in his companions' faces. "Whatever happens, I swear we'll get out of this." But those words felt increasingly hollow as the lantern light flared across the first three cages.

The leathery old raider burped through his cracked lips and squinted in the darkness, deepening the scars etched across his face. The light lingered on the two cadets, and the raider shifted it away with disgust. "Pheh. More fillies." He spied Uirvey and hovered, scratching at his patched striders. "Hmm. Older an I like." And then the light settled on Lonn, and the old raider sighed, "Oh. But, yer a tasty boy," and, swinging his tattered green coat behind him, crouched beside the cage. "That filly up dere... now she can hold er mog, give er dat. Gone an done da crew... some twice over. Leaves ol Zaude ere axin... why settle? Sure... she's got a bung... but... jus ain't da same."

Lonn glared at him. "Vile beast."

"Got dat right, boy," Zaude gave a raspy laugh as the journeymin strained back against the stench of alcohol. "Might get worse. Hear cap's got er eye for ya. And I's heard horrible cries from out er cabin at night. Likes flictin pain, dat one. Don't call er the Virgin Devourer for nuttin. Add ya to er collection. But... she ain't intrested in yer bung, right? Won't notice if ol Zaude's had a go. And I do love me a beautiful brown boy such as yerself. A sunkissed one at dat." The old raider's hand wavered and fished a key from his belt.

Heart pounding, Lonn braced, ready to make his move. It was his best chance as the drunken raider unlocked the cage. He pushed through, swinging hard, but the raider expected it. All his fist struck was firm bone. Zaude gave a swing in turn, right to the gut. The journeymin slumped and wheezed as the raider took him under his arm with a laugh, "Oh, gettin me stiff already. Ol Zaude loves da feisty ones."

Uirvey rattled his cage, shouting, "Leave him alone!"

The other cadets joined in, making as much noise as possible. The raider trudged by, ignoring them. "Take ya where it's jus us two. Get nice an quainted."

Even as the journeymin struggled to recover, the riot became clear as Zaude hauled him up the companionway. And the crew's voices sent shivers through him. "Filly needs another drink fore goin over again!" Grauler shouted. "Flip a coin! Ginny? Bung?" There was a roar. "On edge! Mouth it is! Take er like she's roastin on a spit! Who's swelled an ready?" There was coughing and sputtering.

Another voice, quiet but insistent, rumbled. "Flum want turn. Flum wait like told. Flum make girlie feel good."

"Ahh…" There was reluctance in Grauler's voice. "We's all, about had it anyway. Already sucked my sack dry. Most others too. Fine. Jus… get rid of er when yer done. *Not* for the stew, understand? Overboard. Don't need the place stinking like week-old pollounder fillets. Ripe nough in ere as is."

Lonn heard the chilling scream in the corridor and tried again to free himself from Zaude's vice grip. The raider's hand clamped his jaw tight and covered his mouth, muffling any noise as he cried out. "Nonna dat now, my beauty. If Flum Three Leg's havin is go, the filly's finished. Don't mean nuttin by it. Jus how he is. Ain't right in da head, dat one. Probly cause his mum an da were bro an sis… or was it… nah! Don rightly member. Finish er up fore stuffin er in er barrel. Toss er overboard. Cravens'll get a good meal on what's left."

Zaude pushed a door open, and Lonn blearily eyed their surroundings through welling tears. The engine room. "Do nicely, dis. If ya scream… good. Do love screamers, and none'll hear ya. So, no holdin back while we scratch sacks." The raider threw him down against the rumbling bulkhead, but the young journeymin scrambled for the door.

"Told ya da filly's done!" Zaude grabbed his collar and threw him over a supply barrel strapped against the bulkhead. "All ya can do is help ol Zaude." Lonn gasped, eyes searching frantically. Behind him, the raider tugged his striders loose. Feeling the fear rising up in him, he squashed it down and remembered where he was. Despite the trembling in his hands, he bent over the barrel, clutching it tightly with one arm.

"Datta boy. Hol it nice an tight," he laughed while tugging at Lonn's striders, but in that moment, the journeymin made his move, swinging the maintenance hatch handle down with all his weight. Too late, the raider saw what he had done and pulled his dagger from his belt. As he stabbed it down, the hatch blew inward, dragging him back by his coattails. The blade missed its mark by a fraction of an okt, digging deep into the wooden barrel. The wind's howl drowned Zaude's cursing as the old raider gripped the hatchway frame, muscles straining, knuckles white.

With the airflow stifled, Lonn clawed his way along the bulkhead to the emergency hatch and pushed it closed with all his strength while Zaude tried to grab at him, a last desperate bid to take the journeymin with him. But that move loosened his grip, and the air current sucked him into the chamber.

Lonn did not see Zaude's final demise, dashed upon the

winding propellers, but the steamer did give a stutter as the blades tore him through. The journeymin locked the emergency hatch down and slumped tiredly against the barrel, gasping, "That's… one."

When his pounding heart slowed its pace, he swiped his disheveled hair from his face. There beside him was Zaude's dagger, embedded in the wooden barrel. "And all I got… this bloody dagger." He tugged it free and looked around the engine room, fully aware he had little idea how any of it worked. "Wonder if there's a manual," he sighed, tapping the dagger against the deck. It was possible to hinder the raiders. Or even dash them on the ground by accident.

If only he knew more.

Hardly any of the controls were labeled, and those that were… so badly faded they were barely legible. And those he could make out… all in aelfin. He knew nothing of the old language, reminding him of what Chief Uirvey pondered about just how old the steamraider was, but that hardly addressed his situation. Even if there were a manual, it would no doubt be useless.

Clutching the dagger, the journeymin made for the door only to skitter hastily away when he heard commotion from beyond. Frantic, he searched the room for a safe hiding place, finding the only refuge behind one of the steaming water tanks. Wedged against the bulkhead, he strained to avoid getting burned.

A half-drunken raider stumbled in followed by another. "tellin ya, ain't never seen a filly practically drink old Grauler under the table like that. Most're too weak-gutted. Not that one."

The other huffed. "Too bad she didn't last. Woulda been keen to keep er round."

"That's Flum for ya. Selfish gard. Blame is mutter."

"Doncha mean sisser?"

He laughed. "Same thing." Listening to them, Lonn felt the anger rise up in him, but common sense took over. He barely managed against one and doubted a favorable outcome with just a dagger. "Go pull the Wolk Stone back. No reason to run her hot now."

Fighting through the drunken haze, the raider stumbled to the gearbox and switched the half-used stone back to the furthest position. He never saw the journeymin pressed into the corner or heard his sigh of relief as the air around the tanks cooled, if only just a little. The raider turned away, tugging at his striders. "Ah, but she wiped me out, too. Gotta sleep this off."

The other nodded. "Right with ya."

Lonn peered out from behind the tank and realized they would sleep right there, with two hammocks hanging along the far bulkhead. It did not take them long to fall asleep, snoring loudly. Gripping Zaude's dagger propped in his belt, he felt the rage building in him. What held him back was the same thing that prevented him from dashing the engine controls.

He was a journeymin. In all his training and the tales that had ever been told, destroying a steamer while there were still prisoners aboard or slitting the throat of a sleeping raider would never lead to an honorable knighthood. It was an act of last resort, if the others were tragically lost and it was the only path to ruining their plans. He'd make the honorary list to the Knightly Order if nothing else.

A noble sacrifice.

But the journeymin was hardly dead yet, and if he was to honor the memory of his late taskmaster, there had to be another way. And as it happened while looking around, he found one in an air vent set high into the bulkhead, just large enough for him to fit. Glancing at the raiders and having no idea just how many more there were aboard, he took to the task of quietly prying the panel open until it dangled from a single screw.

Lonn pulled himself up and crawled arm over arm through the narrow pipes that crisscrossed the length of the steamraider hoping to get back to the hold and free the others. It was hard work, made worse by the occasional discharge of hot, wet air as the water tanks relieved pressure. Sweat dripped down the side of his face and forehead, stinging his eyes. In all that, despite the size of the steamer, he suddenly realized his mistake when he became well and truly lost.

As the journeymin pondered, he realized going straight to the hold would do him little good. It was unfortunate the fight… if he could even call it that… with Zaude had gone the way it had. The wretched raider took his keys with him as the propellers sucked him into the blades. But there had to be other copies. He just had to find them. So, slow and steady, he pressed on through the maze of pipes, hoping to eventually get his bearings.

With the chief and the cadets freed, they could actually gain control of the steamer. Uirvey had the knowledge to bring it down. Even older, first-generation steamers maintained similar designs. Or, if they could get the cadets to the bridge, they could learn where they were and fly her to the local authorities. Unless they were heading into Douchart. Merribellith did not have good ties with its wester neighbor. In fact, he would hardly have been surprised if that was their destination, to be sold and ransomed.

Soreign had told stories of attempts to do just that during the lengthy standoff between their two kingdoms. He tried to remember if any had a heroic conclusion, but none came to mind. Most ended with the prisoners nobly sacrificing themselves so they would not be used in such cowardly fashion. It was not a position he desired for himself or the others.

Pausing to wipe the sweat from his face onto his tunic sleeve, his attention was drawn to a faint and distinct sound.

~krakk~

He grew still and tilted his head, hoping to get a better sense of where it came from.

~krakk~

His pulse throbbed as he crawled with greater purpose until he was huffing. Between each was nothing but silence, and his racing mind filled the void. Another of his companions being barreled? Or had the raiders already discovered his absence and were punishing them… trying to learn of his whereabouts? What Zaude had done was against the captain's wishes. And if she found him missing? The vile raider made it clear she would be very displeased and had a penchant for violence.

~krakk~

The Virgin Devourer. A chill ran down his spine despite the heat. Lonn hardly expected the captain of a steamraider to be a… she was… he could hardly describe her from their brief confrontation. But she was certainly confident and seemed entirely unconcerned by his near-fatal thrust. That alone caused him great consternation.

~krakk~

It grew louder. And between the strikes, he started to hear something else. Someone cried out, "forgive me."

~krakk~

"please."

~krakk~

It was a voice he did not recognize, and a new rage

welled within him. Another prisoner. Another survivor. At the end of the duct, he pushed the vent panel off its mounting and slid it aside as quietly as possible. Hot. Sweaty. Joints aching from being in such cramped confines. None of that mattered as he crouched low and drew Zaude's dagger.

~krakk~

He flinched, the sound so loud it left a sharp ring in his ears.

"please forgive me." The voice was quiet, quivering.

The air whistled again. Stifling any trembles and determined to never let another lash strike the Devourer's victim, Lonn charged out from cover with the dagger tight in his hand. "Stop! Release—" his voice caught in the back of his throat with a gulp, "her."

The whip flying over the Virgin Devourer's shoulder went limp.

The brighmoon shimmered through a large viewport, casting the captain in shadows. She knelt naked, her skin moon-pale, save the crisscross of bloody streaks torn across her back. Even from where he stood, stunned and uncertain, he saw beneath the fresh strikes. Some of her scars were old and very deep.

With tears rolling down her cheek from her red-rimmed eyes, she shifted her gaze toward him and focused on the dagger held firm in his hand. A slight smile crossed her lips. She moved effortlessly, dropping the whip and drawing herself to her feet. "Finally come to your senses, my poor little lord?" she asked, striding toward him.

Long trails of dark green hair draped over her breasts and down to her slender hips. He watched them sway with one step toward him after another until the blade tip pressed into the flesh of her bare chest. It was then he noticed she was not entirely naked. A jagged, clear crystal dangled about her neck and tapped at the blade. "Well?" she asked, stretching her arms wide, "I am once again at your mercy. Will you plunge your blade deep into me now? Or will you just stand there and… stare?"

No matter his rage at the others, he felt as conflicted as the first time she confronted him. Only this time, she was well beyond being unarmed. His hand fell to his side, dropping the dagger at his feet.

Her lips twitched, frowning ever so slightly, "So, you're just going to stare." They then rose into a faint smirk, "Or do you have another dagger in mind to pierce me with?"

His upward gaze focused on her face… pale… smooth. The gentle slope to her nose. Her lips slender and shaded pink. He wondered if the rest of her was so pleasing to look at and found it difficult to keep his eyes from wandering, being so close. But, he resisted temptation, turning his head away with a cough, cheeks flushed with embarrassment, averting his gaze entirely with a few blinks. "Forgive me."

"For what?" She reached out, the tips of her slender fingers grazing his cheek and turning his face back to her. "I like how you stare at me." Her hand fell away. "Honestly, my poor little lord, you act as though you've never set your eyes upon a… lady… so disrobed before. Never pried a peek on the handmaidens while they bathed? Never plied a parry and thrust upon them? A pretty lord like you? Some might not mind at all."

"Th-that wouldn't—" he stammered, being so close to her, "be polite."

"My! Such an honorable little lord." She turned away with a laugh, "If you won't stab or stare, then do fetch my robe," and pointed with a wave of her hand. Made of red satilk, it draped over the top of a privacy screen behind him.

Lonn retrieved it and turned back, seeing her stoop and swipe up the slender whip, its length stained in fresh and old blood. Feeling the heat in the room and his quickening pulse, he stared at her. Blood still dripped down her back. "D-do you have healing salves?"

"Injure yourself during your daring escape?" She never even turned her head as she pointed with a lazy wave of her finger to the desk sitting off to the corner. "Top drawer." She tucked the whip away in a hidden alcove beside the rear viewport and closed the loose wall panel.

Lonn found the small bottle and scooped the pasty ointment onto his fingers. She stiffened as he stepped up behind her and gently ran his fingers along the bleeding strips of torn flesh. "These need to be treated." A faint glow pulsed from the ointment as it absorbed into her skin and slowly mended her injuries.

Her lips trembled, "Y-you… show me too much kindness, little lord. More than I deserve."

When finished, he draped her robe over her shoulders and drew her hair back. In that moment, he exposed one long, angular ear and gasped, "Oh! You— you're an aelfin!"

Her brow creased as she reared back, smacking his hand away and self-consciously adjusting her hair to cover her ear once more. "Don't ever call me that! I'm nothing like them!" She rose up, tugging her robe tightly about her.

Lonn saw her flash of anger and grew embarrassed. "I — forgive me. I… meant no offense."

Seeing the earnestness in his face, she composed herself with a deep sigh, "I suppose you didn't."

"It's just… well… I've never met any before."

She eyed him curiously. "Never? Not one?"

"No. I mean… my mother read me stories."

"Stories?" She wandered to her bed and sat, draping one long leg over the other. "What stories?"

"Let me…" He scratched at his ear and then embarrassingly dropped his hand to his side as he tried to remember. "Oh! *The Tales of Corvaelia.*"

"My…" she gazed down, her lips a wistful frown, "my father read me those when I was a child," and cleared her throat. "Barely remember them. Surprised a humin would bother," she sighed. "So… what's your name, my poor little lord?"

He stared at the ceiling as the moonlight faded from the room. "Lonn."

"So, Lord Lonn, do you know who I am?"

"You're the… Virgin… Devourer."

"Ah… yes," her lips twitched, "My reputation proceeds me."

"Will…" he grew uncomfortable, asking in a low voice, "you devour me?"

"I'll…" she smiled deviously, "consider it in the morning. But, it has been a long day for us both. I trust you won't stab me in my sleep. Not with a blade, anyway." Motioning to the couch, she asked, "Would you take that? Or…" and then patted the bed beside her, "would you prefer to bed with me?"

Lonn studied her with a quick gaze, trailing from her head to her long leg stretched out from under her robe, and turned toward the couch to hide the heat rising in his face. "I'll take the couch, thank you."

"Suit yourself," she shrugged, appearing indifferent, and tossed over a pillow along with a blanket before lying back and draping the bed sheets over her. Even as Lonn settled down, he could feel her eyes upon him. "And don't force my decision by trying to escape."

He hesitated, considering his options. Aelfins were rumored to have better hearing than humins. It was doubtful he could make it to the door let alone sneak around to find the cage keys without alerting her. Besides, Soreign always said a knight needed sleep. It was best to get it when possible. And he did feel exhausted. "Very well."

"Sleep soundly and keep warm, my poor little Lord Lonn."

"And you also, Virgin Devourer." He watched her fall asleep, a smile on her lips, until his own eyes were so heavy that he soon joined her.

The light of sunrise warmed the captain's cabin through the rear portal. Lonn breathed softly and watched the Devourer from his vantage. Restless, she woke him several times during the night, muttering odd words he could only surmise were aelfin and tossing about so violently, she kicked off her covers and loosened her robe. As much as he tried, he could not avert his eyes. The view of her in bed made his morning rise painful even after adjusting his striders.

She rolled over once more, and blinked against the brightening light. Her ears twitched from a faint, constant tapping at her door until it became a rhythmic thumping. The pounding would not let up. Sliding from bed in a huff, "Bloody raiders…" she drew her fingers through her hair and tugged her robe tight before stomping across her cabin. Resting her hand upon the hilt of her sword, sheathed in a belt dangling from a hook on the wall, she unbolted her door and pulled it wide by a sliver. "What's all the noise, Grauler?"

The gnarled raider wavered in his boots, still sobering up from the night's excessive riot. "Trouble," he burped, forcing her to tilt her head away was a groan. "A bit sluggish. Listin to the elch."

"Disturbed me for that?" Her annoyance etched in her tone.

"Well… old Zaude's gone missin. And tha boy yer interested in, too. They're probly—"

"My boy? Missing?" She turned, deliberately parting the door wider. "Right where I left him."

"Been here all night?" Grauler pressed closer, squinting to see Lonn lying on the long couch, one leg draped over the edge. "Shoulda told—"

"Don't tell you nothing you don't need to know," the Devourer cut him off and narrowed the door opening to a sliver once more.

"Fine," the gruff raider grunted. "Still the question of Zaude."

"Took another, didn't you? Probably stabbing his dagger in him."

"Already thought a that. With the other two. Where I left em."

"Don't know what to tell you, Grauler. Maybe he fell overboard feck drunk after what you all did to that… lady. Don't really care. And don't disturb me again until I'm on the deck."

"Oh! Well! Sorry ta interr—"

The Devourer closed the door on him and bolted it again, releasing her grip from the sword-hilt with a faint sigh. Heading to her dresser, she swept the dagger from off the floor where Lonn had dropped it, letting it dangle disdainfully from the tips of her nails. "Old Zaude's dagger." She eyed Lonn briefly as she passed by. "So, my poor little lord? What happened to that vile backstabber?"

The journeymin sat up, tense, uncertain of her reaction. "He's… dead."

"Clearly." She set it beside the bottle of healing salve in the top drawer. "Did you just hide his body somewhere? Or, did you have enough sense to toss him overboard?"

"Oh, he's… definitely overboard," his voice wavered, "Well, bits of him are, I suppose."

"What?" She glanced over her shoulder, brow creased in confusion. "Bits?"

"He… took me to the engine room, you see. To hide the noise."

"Certainly does. But that—"

"I released the maintenance hatch."

"In…" she stared, wide-eyed, momentarily stunned, "mid-flight?" Her lips trembled, and Lonn tensed, prepared for an angry outburst. But all that came was laughter. "Well, that's certainly one way to go!"

"You're…" he drew a slow breath, surprised by her reaction, "Not angry?"

"Over that raider scum?" Pulling him up by his soiled tunic, she kissed his cheek. "Very impressive, my little lord. You did him first. And in such a fashion!" He gasped as she pulled away, feeling the wave of heat wash over his face. "As for the dagger… I'd let you keep it. Victor's spoils and all that raider nonsense… but they'd see it on you, and we'd both have a problem."

Lonn stared at her in confused surprise. "You're not going to tell them?"

"No, my little lord." Her gaze shifted to the rear viewport where the bloodstained whip was hidden. "And now we both hold secrets between us." She shrugged off her robe and rifled through her dresser, searching for a fresh pair of brown striders and a clean, white tunic. She tossed a light blue one to him as well. "Wear this. That one…" Smiling, she appraised his, dirty and spattered with stains from his long crawl through the vents. "Well, it certainly looks like I devoured you last night. And you put in some proper effort."

The Devourer did not turn away as he drew it off and slipped into the new one. "And will you?"

"I'm…" she trailed off, buttoning her red vest and fluffing out her hair, "considering it."

For a raider captain, she was hardly what he expected. "Why do this… this whole ruse? You're clearly not like them. It's obvious you hate it."

"My little lord, look around. You think that matters?" she asked, "You know what they are as well as me. What they do… how they treat… ladies." The frustration grew in her voice. "I wasn't born into this life. Didn't want it! Didn't ask for it! I was forced to it! And I do what I must so it's not *me* bent over a bloody barrel! Won't apologize for that. But…" she breathed in sharply, "doesn't mean I don't deserve punishment."

Lonn turned his gaze to the panel and the secret beyond, "So you punish yourself," and wrapped his arms around her, hugging her tightly. "I'm sorry, Virgin Devourer."

She froze, surprised by his embrace, and softened with a sigh, "So am I, my sweet little lord," stroking her fingers through his sunkissed locks. "Caetriona." Her cheeks flushed red. "My name… is… Caetriona. Hardly a proper… lady… but you can call me either. I'd… like that better."

Life aboard the steamraider was much the same as on any other steamer. The crew carried their duties with determination, even if there was a bit of sluggishness, a lingering reminder of the drunken riot and the painful events of the previous night. They lived a life that caused them to do horrible violence between long bouts of quiet. And in that quiet space, there was much to do. Most of them carried on like nothing was out of the ordinary, the horrors lost in the haze left by heavy drink. Their minds focused else-where after a night's sleep.

Lonn was not so fortunate. He kept out of their way, observing them with a great deal of curiosity from the steps leading to the bridge. Two groups of four assembled along each side of the mideck, and there was a brief exchange among them as they paired off to play several rounds of eight-fingers, throwing out fingers while shouting numbers. The losers of each pair faced each other while the winners did the same.

It was all in an attempt to avoid the unenviable position of being wedged against the bulwark and gain the outer most station as they took up two large cranks jutting out on both sides. Lonn never saw such a rig on either the *Sojourner* or the *Starlight's Traverse*, leaving him to wonder if it was a feature of first generations, but his thoughts were over shad-owed by a question from Cottage, a thick-chested raider who had secured his outermost position on the crank. "Who's gettin us started?"

Another of them shouted, "Petrovey! Give us a shanty, will ya?"

Petrovey, a sullen min who once had dreams of being a minstrel before raiders pressed him into service and con-stantly goaded him, was just then mopping blood from off the deck. "Fine! Something even you gards know good and well." He gave a shout to get everyone in unison, "On the steady, now!" His voice rang out, deep and resonant, and the others soon joined, a wavering chorus to help keep their rhythm.

Singing was the last thing the young journeymin had expected from a bunch of surly raiders. But as they began, he doubted any would actually call it that.

Eight mugs of mog!
Drunk as a skog!
Over a barrel she goes!
He~va~ho!

On each "ho," the groups twisted the cranks by a full rotation. Ten rounds each they went until the cranks strained tight, and they locked the handles down. Though it stung Lonn to hear it, the song itself was divorced from recent events for them. And once they were done, they disbanded to attend other duties. Scrubbing away on the decks. Mending damaged panels along the hull from the battle. Even bogging out the plumbing.

He remained mindful of what Uirvey had said about them and found it quite true. They were diligent when it came to maintaining the steamraider. Understandable, as it was their home and their only means of livelihood. That passing thought brought up another sore reminder. It came along with guilt, knowing that somewhere below, the chief and his companions were imprisoned in cages. And Caetriona made it clear she had no interest in aiding him in their release.

There was little time left before their fates were truly sealed.

But the journeymin had another immediate problem. While the crew kept one eye on their jobs, he was painfully aware their other was always watching him. None more so than Grauler, who brushed by him with a sneer as he bounded up the steps and joined the captain on the afdeck beside the bridge. "Givin the boy the run a the steamer, now? Should be in a cell like the others. Or shackles at the least."

Caetriona paid him little mind as she leaned over the bulwark checking the running board first along the elch and then the siehd. "He and I have an understanding, Grauler."

"That right?" he scoffed. "Once we're down at Alisard, he'll bolt like a chickuck at second harvest."

"Grauler!" She rose up and stared, wide-eyed. "Had no idea you were so well-versed as a farmin."

His face piqued at the insult. "Jus warnin ya. He'll run. Mark my words."

"He won't. Given his word to stay at my side." She turned her focus on Lonn. "And unlike your kind, he's the honorable sort."

"Don't like it, cap."

"Don't care."

The raider stumbled as the steamer tilted more heavily to the elch. "Care about that?"

While others grabbed for ropes and railings, she kept her footing and called into the bridge. "Mikwit! Bleed some heligen and ease back on the siehd rotor!" The steamraider leveled off as she turned back to Grauler. "It's fine. We'll make dock. And once we're grounded, have a few of the crew tighten up the elch rotor rivets. Must've taken damage during the raid."

"Need supplies, too."

"Then have the crew take stock." She gazed up with a sigh, "Got plenty to barter off. Use your most trusted. No distractions. We leave as soon as we can… by sunfall at latest."

"Spectin trouble?"

"Just want some distance, Grauler."

"And what about the special goods?"

Caetriona cast a fleeting gaze toward Lonn before looking away with an uncomfortable shrug. "Do as your kind does."

Grauler crossed his arms. "And while we're doing all the actual work, what'll ya be doing?"

"Business." She reached up to her chest where the necklace dangled under her tunic. "Don't expect to be long.

Then I'll oversee the repairs. That make you happy?"

"Fine." He looked over at Lonn. "Takin the boy with ya?"

"Asking too many questions, Grauler. Stick to your own business. Leave me to mine." She waved him off.

"Don't like it," he grumbled under his breath and pushed past Lonn to the mideck, "Not one bloody bit."

Once he stumbled further away checking on the crew, she spoke up, "You heard all that?"

Lonn nodded faintly, feeling conflicted. "I won't try to run away, and I'll stay by your side."

"Good." She stepped down to his side. "You look troubled."

"The… special goods."

"Told you," she sighed, "Nothing you can do for them."

"But you're selling them!"

Caetriona nodded. "They are, yes!"

He stiffened in protest. "But you could stop—"

"You give me too much credit!" She glared at him sternly. "My sweet little lord, I can't stop them from doing what they do. And neither can you. As much as I know you want to, you can't save them. And *they'll* kill you for trying. Even I wouldn't be able to protect you then. Their desire for coin is greater than any fear they have of me."

"But—" he leaned in, lowering his voice, "that fear is all based on a pretense."

"Oh, no, my little lord." She turned away with a huff, "They have good cause to fear me… just as I sometimes fear myself," and cleared her throat. "But that's not anything you need to dwell on. All you can do now is hope they enter the service of good masters."

"I can't accept that."

"I know, my sweet little lord, but you will have to live with it, just like I have."

The journeymin went silent as the sails lifted in preparation for docking. "Th-they're blue."

Caetriona nodded. "That they are, my little lord. Very blue."

He blinked, suddenly confused. "But not during the raid. They were…" He leaned over the bulwark, certain they had been black and green-fringed.

"You think we could dock anywhere flying those colors?" she laughed and pointed down, drawing his attention to the running board she had been so keen on checking. It was a long, black strip stretching the length of the hull.

Lonn looked at it more carefully. "Is… that what they were reeling in?" Suddenly, the purpose for the cranks became clear.

"One of my… special modification. Keeps us well-hidden."

Despite his feelings, he was impressed. "Devious."

"Necessary. The *Virgin Wanderer* was devoured by raiders and became… something… ugly. A fine, upstanding merchant vessel once. Far as anyone's concerned, still is," she cleared her throat, composing herself, "Now, while we're in the city, you stay close. Understand? It can be dangerous."

Lonn gave a curt nod. "Yes, my lady."

With a faint flush in her cheeks, she smiled and gazed off toward Alisard just coming into view. "You're a quick learner, my little lord."

"I've had good teachers."

"Yes, I'm sure." She took his hand in hers. "You could afford them."

Alisard

The dock city of Alisard stood in the wester-most province of Astyria and maintained a vital role in trade with the surrounding kingdoms. Within the city walls, the numerous merchant guilds held sway over the various wards circling Lady Aradore's citadel. Finding ways to curry favor were paramount for the guild heads, and tensions between them often led to conflicts for power, prestige, or territory.

While most battles were waged through duplicitous means, open conflict did occur and was often quickly squashed by the heavy hand of the city protectorate. Alisard's patron lady had no desire for any distractions or disruptions in trade. It was for the common good and, more importantly, the favors provided to her personally.

Lonn knew only some of this as he leaned on the bulwark, staring out at the sky ahead of the steamraider. It was a bustle of activity with steamrunners from many corners of Nolavah crossing in all directions. The red and yellow colors of Astyria flew most dominantly, but also the yellow and green of Hrondal, a minor kingdom in the southwest, the solid yellow of Douchart to the north, the blue and red of Tremelaine, his mother's homeland, as well as the independent colors of the various merchantry guilds, which held no affiliations but their own, free to wander as they pleased.

In the midst of all that, the *Virgin Wanderer*, with blue sails raised high, became just another steamer using the city for rest and trade. Maneuvering solely with her sideboard propellers, the steamraider settled onto an empty dock nearest the large Barter Guild station. Much like the Healers Guild, they separated themselves from the internal and external politics of the other kingdoms and guilds, as they served all without reservation or question. It was as close to neutral territory as they could get.

Caetriona nodded approvingly as she looked beyond the dock to the courtyard and the bustle of merchants and patrons. "Fortunate to find a spot here." She glanced down at Lonn as she draped a brown, sheot-fur cloak over his shoulders. She had one herself, with the hood bundled about her shoulders. "Mind what I told you."

"I'll stay close." She took his hand and led him down the gangplank as the journeymin looked around, avidly curious by all the new sights and experiences of the various steamers resting on nearby platforms spread before him.

The air was thick with the scent of engine grease, and the dock planks were stained black and tacky from constant use. Workmin in worn red coveralls unloaded large crates from the hold of a nearby steamer while others hooked in thick tubes to vent out the plumbing waste or top up heligen levels. One group swapped out a bent rotor on the siehd navigation propellor.

The heavy-set dockmaster, wearing a fur cap and thick, oil-stained coveralls, trundled toward them. There was a docket in her hand and a wide smile on her lips. "Ahh, Captain Caetriona… been a while since we've seen the old Wanderer in these parts." She pulled a fountain pen from her pocket, splotched with leaking black ink. "Formalities. So… nature of your visit?"

"Resupply, Juleea. And… repair."

The dockmaster blinked in surprise. "Run into trouble?" she asked with a shade of hope in her tone.

"Elch rotor's been sluggish." She glared. "Don't get too excited. My crew'll handle the work."

Juleea sighed. "Still won't let me get a good look at the old girl, huh? Always wonder how you keep a first-gennie like her flying like you do." She laughed, "Fine. Fine. Keep your secrets. How long'll you be grounded?"

"If all goes well, just until sunfall."

"Short stay."

"Time-sensitive goods."

"I hear you." She flipped the docket around. "Just need your sign off. And then there's the matter of—" Caetriona dropped a handful of gilvers onto the page before taking up the pen. The dockmaster grinned widely. "That's what I've always liked about you. Never skimp the fees. Saves me a lot a trouble." She took the pen back and pocketed the gilvers. "Right, then! That's all the formalities. Except… enjoy your visit in Alisard, the finest dock city this side of Astyria."

"It's the only dock city this side of Astyria, Juleea."

She trundled off, waving her docket. "That don't make it no less true!"

Seeing Grauler and his hand-selected group come down the gangplank, Caetriona gripped Lonn's hand firmly and led him off the docks. The journeymin shifted his attention this way and that, seeing the throngs go about their business. There were heated debates as barter deals were negotiated and both the jubilant and sullen looks of those who were successful and those who were not. So distracted was he that he barely noticed his companion stop until his arm strained.

Grauler stood at a posting board. "Gone up since last time." He motioned to a piece of fresh parchment pinned prominently in the center.

WANTED!
Steamraider flying black and green-trimmed sails!
3000 gilver reward for a successful capture!
Speak to your local protectorate office today!

The grizzled raider scratched the back of his neck, eyeing the captain. "Notice they dropped the 'successful destruction' bit?"

"Doesn't concern us." Caetriona shrugged casually. "See to your business, and we'll return shortly."

As the two disappeared into the crowd, Grauler lingered. The boards were always good sources of information that could lead to raiding opportunities. It was one such board that announced a tourney and provided their most recent success. This one listed nothing of interest save a few warrants best left to the head merchants. He turned to join his crewmates but stopped and looked at the last, also freshly printed. There was a rough sketch of a nondescript boy, brown skin, sunkissed hair.

WANTED!
Journeymin Lonn!
2000 gilver reward for a successful capture!
Speak to your local protectorate office today!

He snatched it off the board and crumpled it into his pocket. "That what yer up too?" A number of thoughts rattled his mind, none of them good.

And he was hardly the only one who noticed a distinct similarity between the sketch and the captain's companion. Across the courtyard, a figure held another copy in his hands and silently motioned to his associates before pointing in the direction of the lower ward.

Further along the bustling street, Caetriona led Lonn through the open market, past clothiers, jewelers, and numerous food vendors. Despite all the new sights, Lonn's eyes remained focused, still curious about the posting board. "What was that back there?"

"A bounty notice. Someone alerted the protectorate about… that steamraider."

"You mean…" the journeymin gasped, pulling on her hand. "There were survivors?"

She looked around, uncertain who might be listening, and leaned in to whisper, "if you believe the rumors, that raider doesn't leave any. you… shouldn't get your hopes up."

"But…" He squeezed her hand. "Please, Caetriona. My lady. I have to know."

"Of course you do." She fingered the necklace under her tunic, staring down at the anxious journeymin at her side, and gave a faint huff, "there… may be a way. And that's if she even lets you in. There's no guarantee. And if she does… it'll be dangerous."

Lonn straightened up. "I'll take that risk."

"Of course you will." Clutching her necklace, she followed a winding trail through the darkening streets as the buildings pressed tighter together and fell further into disrepair. She groaned faintly, her nose wrinkling in disgust. "Why'd it have to be down here in the gutter ward?"

Lonn wondered what she meant, but then he remembered her senses were keener than his own. The air grew at first musty from rotted trush wood and then sour with piles of waste and rubbish lining the streets. He clutched his hand over his mouth, but it did little to ward off the stench. "My lady… Caetriona, what're you looking for?"

"A doorway," she curtly answered, breathing shallow through her mouth.

He looked at the old buildings lining the street. "Seems there are plenty to choose from."

"Not just any doorway," she chastised gently. "Aelfin-made… from before the Revolt."

The young journeymin gave an excited gasp, "Some still stand?"

"Very few." She pulled him along behind her. "Don't linger."

Lonn closed the distance between them, pausing when an odd noise echoed from a side alley. He jerked back, crying out in surprise, when a disheveled, bleary-eyed aelfin tumbled forward to accost him. He feebly pressed the young journeymin's tunic and pockets with trembling, gnarled fingers. His voice was strained, insistent, as he pleaded, "Tillup! Got tillup? Any? Even a drop? Give anything! Anything, you hear! M-my clothes! My mate! My son! He's a wee lil thing. Sweet. Sweet as tillup. Just a ta—"

"Get off, fiend!" Caetriona grabbed him by the neck and tore him away from Lonn.

He crumpled to the ground, slinking back into the darkness when she settled her hand on her sword-hilt. From the darkness of the alley, his feeble voice wavered out, "Tillup? Anyone? please?"

She glanced back at the young journeymin, still a bit shaken. "You alright?"

"Fine." He caught his breath. "What's wrong with him?"

Momentarily surprised by his question, she stared at him. "You… really have never met any aelfins before, have you?"

"No."

"It's the Scourge. Just another filthy tillup fiend." She

took his hand and pulled him away.

"Scourge? Tillup fiend?" He stared over his shoulder in confusion. "But tillup's just a medicine, isn't it?"

"For humins, maybe. Not for aelfins." She glanced back at him, somewhat surprised. "You've seriously never heard of the Scourge?"

"No," he admitted, feeling naive.

"It's how the humins defeated the aelfins during the Revolt. How do you not know that?"

"I don't know. That wasn't in the history I've read." He eyed her curiously. "Is that what you meant? About you being not like them?"

"Drop it."

"You're not a fiend like them?"

She tensed, "I said drop it!" Grabbing her necklace, she marched on a bit longer, stopping in front of a dilapidated old building that once housed a seamstress. "Finally," she sighed relief, "this is the place."

"That's the door?" It was well weathered, obscuring the once-intricate carvings. Curious, Lonn asked, "What's inside?"

"Maybe an answer to your question," she responded dubiously, "if you're still determined to see this through."

"I am."

"feck." She pulled out his hand and set a stack of gilvers into his palm. "Follow my directions. And leave these on the floor when I tell you." When he drew a questioning breath, she cut him off, "Just do as I say! Save your question for her." Placing her hand on the door handle and her other over her chest covering her necklace, she uttered the words he had heard before during her sleep.

Nei Yd Aneimun Siertham
Adnu Siertham Saeham,

Caetriona Taecouw Dea
Aeham Ameurouqatnie.

She released the handle and reached out to him. "Be brave, my sweet little lord." The door creaked inward, revealing nothing beyond but an inky blackness. Lonn nervously took her hand and followed her inside.

Grauler grumbled to himself, "Bloody binch… leavin all this to me." He had gathered the supplies, as agreed. The crew worked on the propeller, as agreed. But the captain had not yet returned. It left him in the unenviable position of putting Mikwit in charge of repairs while he took care of their special cargo. None of the others could be tasked with the job, and no one else even had the reputation built up with Balizaad to make it through the door much less get a good deal.

He huffed, pushing the large cart as it rattled along the cobbled streets. A thick tarp covered the three cages and their contents against the curious onlookers as he moved away from the barter ward and weaved along into the less travelled ward of the body merchants. At least it was during the day. After sunfall, any traveller wishing distraction and a bit of company could find a fitting match along those narrow streets.

Reaching the end of a long lane and turning down a dead-end alley, Grauler groaned as he pulled his cart to a stop by the back entrance of Balizaad's Flesh Emporium. A gruff guard wearing a shaggy grey sheot coat leaned against the wall. His hand fell from under it when the raider came into the light. "Ain't seen you round in a while."

"Ain't been round is all, Baulma"

The guard stretched out a leg, giving the door a swift kick. After a moment, it creaked open. "Watcha want now? Told ya, ain't got no snacks. Miss Ennea gobbled em all."

He jabbed his thumb outward. "Jus Grauler."

"Eh? Ah… im." He opened the door wide and waved over his shoulder. "Balizaad's up front… with a patron."

"Fine. Won't disturb em." Grauler pushed the cart inside, past the large cages that secured debtors, the indentured, and slaves alike. The emporium catered to all interests from labor in the fields and mines to the kitchen and bedroom. He noticed even a few fit for fighting.

Beyond that were the smaller cages holding animals of assorted types, some ideal for domestication and others… sport. Some were just exotic curiosities. He lingered on a fowl, its plumage glittering in blues and greens as it hopped along its rung. "Fancy thing, that." Pushing on, he stopped when he found the guild head.

Balizaad was a shrewd merchant of impeccable class, and carried herself with authority. In an ankle length purpcolored dress and a bodice that both secured and exposed her cleavage, she leaned slightly forward on the negotiating table. With a fluttering of her violet eyes and a purse of her full lips, she casually flipped her blood-red hair from off her shoulders. She gave a forced laugh at something the patron said and drew her fingers along his arm. She used all of her assets to aid in her business dealings.

Grauler watched from a distance with a smirk as she negotiated with the distinguished patron, an older fellow dressed in fine satilks. The look on her face when he finally stood and left told the raider everything. She had made a far better deal than her patron realized, intently focused as he was on anything but the transaction.

He waited for a good moment before approaching. The

guards assembled on either side of her watched him cautiously as she busied herself. Perched on the table beside her was a young girl with sunkissed hair wearing a simple red tunic that went down to her knees. "Body business' been good to you, Balizaad." He set his hand on the young girl's bare leg, sliding it upward under her tunic. "Very good." Silent, the girl glared her large blue eyes at him.

Balizaad did not even look as she stacked a row of gilvers away in the desk drawer. "Grauler. Hand."

He pulled away with a shrug. "Not on the market, then?"

"No."

"Ah, well. Shame tha. Filly reminds me of my sisser's lil one. She ain't sunkissed, though."

"Fascinating, Grauler. Really." She closed the drawer and eyed the tarp-covered cart. "This better be higher quality than that last batch you sold me."

"Them was just some orphaned micats I stumbled on. Good for the price ya paid. Got a decent return, didn't ya?"

"Along with a host of complaints. One of them was well-used goods."

"Sweet, though." Grauler laughed at the memory. "Had to have a taste, but I told ya that. And gave ya a decent discount, as I recall."

"The others broke. Easily."

He shrugged. "Can't be held for that. Buyer beware, ain't it?"

The merchant set her jaw, chastising him with a glare. "I expect better." She nodded to the cart. "Is it?"

"Better?" Grauler laughed, "Much! Taken right off a high-class steamer. Skilled labor. And pretty to look at." He untied the tarp and drew it back. "Two sweet little fillies and a fancy boy, see? High quality."

Balizaad leaned over the cages. The three were slumped

over. "They're… less energetic than I prefer."

"Couldn't cart em here while makin a fuss. Dosed em with a wee bit a tillup. Be fit and feisty in no time at all." He fished a key from his pocket and unlocked the cages in turn.

She stared at her two guards, waiting. "Boys?" They jerked into action, laying each one out on a nearby table. "Skilled labor, you say? They're wearing… what are those? Merribellith uniforms?"

"Steamer crew. What's it matter what else they are."

Balizaad quietly appraised them while the girl leaned in, poking Cadet Nimme's nose to see if she would wake. The guild head ran her fingers along Uirvey's arm, "Working hands. Seems fit," and slipped her hand under his striders. "Average. Have to see what he's like hardened up. Decent enough sack, though," she commented before moving to the black-haired Terasant and feeling her breasts. "Small but firm." When she slid her hand under the cadet's striders, she eyed Grauler. "Unspoiled?"

He waved his hand emphatically. "While we had em, nobody touched em wrong. Not nowhere. Can't speak to before we… acquired em."

Balizaad moved on to the sunkissed Nimme. Her hand lingered on her breasts. "Nice and ripe, this one." She slipped her hand under her striders and smiled when the cadet shifted and gave a slight moan. "Responsive." Pulling her hand out, she slipped her finger in her mouth and considered her options. "Syrupy, too. Hmmm. I'll offer seven hundred for her. Five for the other. Three for him. No assurance how he'll perform." She eyed Grauler. "Acceptable?"

As she waited for the inevitable protest, Baulma approached from the back. Balizaad perked up as he showed her the familiar parchment. "Gather the boys and snatch him up. Bend a few noses for me if you have to." The raider grinned faintly as the guard rushed off. He barely paid attention when Balizaad tapped her finger impatiently for his response. "That's a thousand five. Agreeable?"

He nodded absently. "Yeah. Yeah, that's fine."

She scribbled down the details with a faint grin, handing the paper slip to the girl. From the lower drawer of her table, she drew out three hefty purses. "Boys, see him out."

As they loaded his cart, Grauler eyed the merchant. "Why the rush?"

"A bit of local trouble. Those bloody head merchants again."

"Well, good luck with all that," Grauler threw the tarp over the cages and pushed the cart, grinning to the sound of jingling gilvers. "Always a pleasure, Balizaad."

Lonn stepped across the threshold feeling momentarily woozy. When he tried to breathe, there was no air. It lasted only a brief moment, leaving him gasping once he was beyond the threshold. The air inside was thick and cold with only a pressing blackness all around. Caetriona clasped his hand tight, leading him along. "Castanostrous!" Her voice rang in his ear like a muffled echo.

A moment later, their surroundings lightened to a dim violet haze that shifted around them. "Ah. The Devoured Wanderer returns," her voice pulsed with the light. "Long has it been. And you brought curious company." The formless figure circled around the young journeymin. "One both apparent and hidden."

"He…" she gazed at Lonn with an upturned, curious eye, "has a question for you."

Castanostrous appraised the journeymin, "And I may have an answer," hovering for a silent moment, "For the right price.”

Caetriona gave a curt nod, and he set the stack of gilvers at his feet. “Hmm,” she swept down, consuming the coins within her formless figure, “A little coin for a little question. Ask.”

Lonn hesitated a moment, collecting his thoughts. “We… were there any survivors from the *Starlight’s Traverse* after it crashed?”

The floating figure stopped before him. “You among five became four. This you know all too painfully well.” He felt his chest tighten at the reminder. “And one alone of sturdy stock and noble breed.”

He gasped, excited. “Oh! That must be Sir Soreign. Is—”

“You’ve bought your answer,” Caetriona cut him off, squeezing his hand tight and giving an anxious shake of her head. “Time to go.”

“Yes. I see.” The young journeymin stifled his desire to know more and turned to Castanostrous, bowing. “Thank you for answering my question.”

“Polite. For a min,” she laughed. It echoed in his ears as the blackness pressed around him and pushed him out. Caetriona followed without a word until the formless being stopped her. “Blood of my blood, you sacrificed your question for his.”

She frowned. “There’ll be another time.”

Castanostrous laughed, “Still not willing to pay my price.”

“His was more important.”

“It wasn’t. Along every path save one, he will face his answer. Yours tears at you in the black to be loosed in the light of her loving eye.”

“Unsolicited information isn’t like you.”

“I speak nothing you don’t already know, Devoured Wanderer. But, it is understandable. Difficult to confront those you have devoured."

Flipping a gilver onto the ground, she left. "For your help." The door shut behind her, and she found Lonn hunched over, trembling for breath. "Satisfied?"

He gulped, shaking his head. "There were twenty on the *Traverse*. I'm pleased Soreign is alive, but…"

"I know." Caetriona frowned. "For my part, all I can ask is your forgiveness."

He slowly rose up and huffed. "You never need ask for what I've already given, my lady."

"My sweet little lord." She smiled faintly and reached out. "Shall we go?"

Lonn's gaze lingered on the door. "Just what was that place?"

"Not sure what you'd call it. A remnant… from the Gazer who lived there."

"Gazer?" It sounded familiar, perhaps from something his mother once read to him. Lonn scratched at his neck, trying to remember. He gave up and reached for the door, opening it. The inside was ruined. Several aelfin squatters, wracked by Scourge, stared blankly from where they were sprawled out. He slowly closed the door and backed away. "Are they all like that here?"

"Here… all over. Wherever there's tillup, the fiends flock. It's all they care about. Not even worried about purges."

"Purges?" The journeymin stiffened in alarm. He had read about them, and it always filled him with sadness. "Those still happen?!"

There was sympathy in her gaze. "Oh, my sweet little lord, they never stop." She tugged on her vest and headed down the street.

Lonn rushed after her, taking her hand. "And those… doorways. Are there many?"

She shrugged, "Fewer and fewer every bloom, it seems. Most humins are quite happy to have the old aelfin homes go. And those that still exist…" Patting her chest, she sighed, "can't find them without one of these. Even then, has to be during brighmoon."

"What would've happened had I asked another question?"

She stopped and stared at him. "You'd pay in blood."

"So… a question could…" Lonn finally understood why she was so worried, "could cost a life. How would you know?" Caetriona shrugged, leaving him unnerved. "So… what now?"

"Head back. Fix up the *Wanderer* so we can get out of here. Don't need any more—" She trailed off as a figure wearing heavy black boots and faded-brown striders along with a weathered, grey longcoat came out of the darkness at the end of the street, blocking their path.

"Hold fast! No need to cross blades here." He raised a parchment in official fashion, proclaiming in a deep voice, "By order of the Alisard branch of the Head Merchants Guild, Journeymin Lonn, you are ordered to surrender yourself." Eyeing the two with a wry grin, he rolled the parchment up and tucked it away in his coat, "Not sure what you did, kid, but someone wants you back alive to answer for your crimes," and waved him over with a gloved hand. "Come with me. Now."

"Crimes?" The young journeymin reared back, confused. "Just who… are you?"

"Trouble," Caetriona finished her thought and took a firm step between him and the Head Merchant. One hand gripped her sword-hilt and the other fingered one of the loops in her belt behind her back. "He's not going anywhere with you."

The merchant stepped closer as the midsun beamed down. There were several others behind him, waiting for his signal. "So… hoping to claim the reward for yourself?"

They both jerked back, so surprised they spoke in unison, "What reward?"

"Two thousand gilvers." The merchant patted his coat. "All right here. Journeymin Lonn. Brown skin. Sunkissed hair. And he's wanted alive, so I'd prefer we avoid any… violence. But if we must… well, accidents happen. Long as he's still breathing, we get paid."

Caetriona recovered from the initial shock and laughed, "If that's all you've got…" glancing back at Lonn. "Suppose I can see the resemblance, but my boy here can't possibly be the one you're after. He's just too… honorable to commit any crime, to be sure!"

The merchant nodded. "That right?"

"Must be lots of brown boys with locks of… sunkissed… hair."

"Maybe true." He gnashed his teeth, "Now, if it's a case of mistaken identity… my sincerest apologies." He gazed at the young min, questioning, "Is it, though? I'd rather hear it from you… on your honor. Are you Journeymin Lonn?"

"On… *his*… honor?" She winced, tightening her sword grip "ah, feck,"

Lonn studied the merchant and his companions and took a half step forward. "On my honor, I am." She groaned, slumping her shoulders. "But as my lady said, I'm with her."

Caetriona perked up, glancing over her shoulder at him with a smile. "Seriously?"

"Of all the— I see how it is," the Head Merchant groaned, gazing skyward, and waved to his companions. "Keep him breathing." He focused on her as she shifted her stance. Her move was swift, flinging her hand and loosing the dart dagger she had hidden in her belt. Already too late, he caught a glint of sunlight reflected off the blade's tip and reeled back, clutching his pierced eye. "Ahh! You binch!"

Lonn stumbled back, startled by the speed at which Caetriona lunged forward. He never even saw her draw her sword as blades clashed. She met the first merchant and maneuvered him between her and his companion to fight each in turn. After dodging a few thrusts, she stepped into a sword swing, smashing her elbow into the merchant's face. There was a crunch of cartilage. Blood streamed down his face from a broken nose. As he collapsed, she was on the other, forcing him to his knees with a swift kick to the groin.

Once they were crumpled, moaning in the dirty street, she pierced the merchants' legs right through and kicked their abandoned blades aside. Hobbled, they grasped at their wounds to squelch the blood loss. She leaped back to Lonn's side, barely out of breath. "That was—" Stunned silent, the journeymin quickly understood why the raiders feared her.

She grabbed his hand, tugging him behind her. "Run!"

"But…" He eyed the discarded swords over his shoulder. "If only I had a sword, I could—"

"Get after them!" The Head Merchant shouted, glancing down at his fallen comrades. "Now! I want that boy! Alive! I want that binch's head! And…" Whimpering, he gingerly held the dagger still lodged in his eye, "Get me a bloody healer! Ah! Had to be my good eye, too!"

Lonn huffed as he kept up with Caetriona. "Doesn't sound happy with us."

She turned a corner and skittered to a halt. "And neither are they." Before them was a group of head merchants blocking the width of the street in a staggered line, weapons at the ready. Swords. Daggers. Clubs. It was too great a risk to take them all on, so she backed away only to stiffen. Coming along the other end of the street was another group, similarly armed. "feck… seems we're cut off."

Lonn eyed her, hopeful to even their odds. "Do you have another blade?"

She gave him a stern look, "You stay out of this," and pushed him back against the wall, covering him as best she could. From both directions, the two groups closed the gap between them.

But the group of head merchants stopped at the street junction, their voices raised at the sight of the opposing body merchants. "Ain't no business here for you body binches!"

Balizaad's group racked the back of their swords together with a rhythmic *cha-shink*. Baulma fingered the warrant stuffed in his belt. "Our business til the claim coin's dolled out."

"He's ours! Already shed blood!"

"Ah! Really? So happy to hear that," the body merchant guard laughed. "Feck off if ya don't want more."

"Feck off? You feck off, body merchant scum!"

"Scum?" Baulma rose up, grinning wide. "Looks like we're bendin some noses after all!"

Caetriona and Lonn, forgotten in the war of words, pressed tighter against the wall. The two groups crossed into the street junction and met in the middle with a clash of blades and the resounding *thunk* of clubs. In the mass of bodies, there were screams and howls. Blood splattered the ground, and streams splashed the walls beside them. She clutched the journeymin's tunic, pulling him along until they were past the riot.

Once clear, she quickened their pace until they were running as fast as they could out of the ward. At the sound of approaching footfalls, Caetriona skittered to a stop with Lonn beside her, huffing hard. She pushed him into a doorway as the rush of steps got louder and kept her hand on her hilt. The city protectorate marched past in their red uniforms and full armor, off to quell the riot by any force necessary. When their footfalls faded in the distance, she let out a relieved sigh and took his hand, leading him back to the barter ward courtyard and the dock beyond.

4 The Devoured Wanderer

Grauler wiped the sweat from his brow and paced back and forth along the foredeck. The crew had long since finished their work and lounged down the length of the bulwarks gulping drafts of mog and eating chunks of zorba meat off the bone. After a head-count numbering thirty-seven, he determined they had lost at least fifteen during the recent battle. Those surviving each had equal portions earned save Cottage and Mikwit, who shared in one and one-half portions, and Grauler himself, indulging in a double portion, the same that was saved for the captain.

Stowed in the hold below was a full restock of supplies along with the remaining loot from the pillaged *Starlight's Traverse*. It was enough to last until they found another venture with rich pickings. And his worries of being grounded in Alisard long-term over their engine troubles turned to be unfounded.

Mikwit and his crew had seen to that, tightening the elch rotor bolts as instructed. But the root cause… it was fortunate their pilot was so small or they would have never made the discovery. At least he had been discreet, so as not to alarm the crew. Even then, it sat stashed away on the bridge in a soiled sack and raised larger concerns only the captain could answer for. And she was still nowhere to be seen.

It had been too long already.

He pounded his fist on the bowsprit. "Can't be that hard

to dump the little whelp off, get paid, and get your bung back here." He debated the best response, but that depended on what happened once the captain returned.

With little to do but eat and drink, he tore off a thick chunk of zorba hind and chomped it down. It was rare to get anything fresh, and he savored it while it lasted before having to return to their usual fare of salted herrerel. The gruff raider paused mid-bite and scanned the courtyard beyond the dock.

Two rows of city protectorate hefting shields and blunt spears marched toward the lower ward. The sight brought a gnarled grin to his lips, "Good riddance to im." He expected any trouble would finally knock some sense back into her, and they would get on to business as usual.

His mind filled with possible ventures, striking along the scattered wester kingdoms where few even had standing flotillas, let alone steamrunners, and crossing the borders quickly meant little chance of pursuit after a raid. He liked the prospect of quick strikes and even quicker evasions. From there, it was an easy trip to Haggletown and the guild homes scattered about the Crumbling Coast. Turn their ill-gotten goods into gilvers with no questions asked. Spend some in the taverns on good food, decent drink, and plenty a young brothmaiden to share his bed for a time.

He lifted the bone to take another bite and froze at the sight of the captain crossing the dock. "Finally! At least she's —" Journeymin Lonn stepped out from behind her. "Blast that binch!" With a grunt, he threw down his food and stomped across the foredeck.

Caetriona huffed up the gangplank and stepped onto the mideck. With the crew lingering, it was clear the work had been done while she was away. "See the loading went well. Mikwit, ready to get underway?"

He made himself small as the captain passed him by. "S-sure thing, cap."

She turned to Grauler as he approached. "Business took longer than expected, but seems you have everything under control here."

"Did our jobs. Yeah," he grunted, eyeing Lonn as he came up the gangplank behind her, "Have trouble?"

"No." She shook her head. "No trouble. Why?"

"City protectorate's swarming the lower ward."

"Must be some local trouble. No business of ours." Caetriona shrugged away. "I'll double-check the repair work, and we'll be——"

Grauler raised his fist and thumped the back of her neck as hard as he could. She slumped to the ground, much to the surprise of the stunned crew. Even Lonn was momentarily shocked.

Mikwit stared at his feet where the captain fell unconscious. "Wh-what've you done? Sh-sh-she'll tear you to p-pieces when sh-sh-she comes to."

"Seems mad. A risk, ta be sure, I know. But this ain't no mutiny! Ain't lookin to replace er. Jus hear me out!" the grizzled raider shouted, raising his hands up, hoping to calm any open rebellion, especially from Cottage.

"Why should we?" The burly raider was on his feet, a drawn dagger wavering in his hand. "Didn't take no vote fer this!"

"The cap's been good for us til now. Coffers full. Never gone hungry. But somethin's been wrong since we hit that steamer. We all know it. Got distracted by that ferocious little filly. We all forned her good and well. Cept Mikwit, being half-a-min and all."

"You're a b-bung, Grauler."

"Yeah, yeah. But where was the cap? And what happened to old Zaude?" He marched up to the quardeck hatch and stabbed the warrant into it with his dagger. "Ben holdin out on us! All on account a this boy! Now, ya know I sold the others. Balizaad's always been fair. Got a thousand five hundred gilvers for the lot. And to each here, a fair portion earned. This one?"

A hush settled about the crew as they looked from Lonn to the warrant. "That's right. Two thousand for im alone! And did she do the right thing? Turn im over and spread the wealth?" He pointed. "Answer's standin right here! Messed with her head much as her ginny."

Lonn felt the raiders' eyes set on him as they pressed in. He backed away and swiped the dagger from the hatch. The parchment fluttered to the deck.

Grauler reached out, and Cottage set his own dagger in the raider's hand. "Lucky we need you livin, boy. Collect all those coins." He jabbed low for the limbs, but Lonn was quick, throwing off the blows. He tried to land his own, but all he met was metal upon his own. They circled, each striking to disable. The gruff raider feinted, anticipating the coming parry. He slit into the journeymin's arm, shedding blood, but it was not enough to get him to drop the dagger.

Lonn pushed in close, hoping to make Grauler's subsequent blows ineffective. They struggled, but even he had to concede the raider was stronger. And the journeymin understood just how unfair a fight it was when the grizzled raider pressed close and kneed his groin. As he doubled over in light-headed agony, Grauler slammed the hilt of his blade down, knocking him to the deck beside the captain.

"She'll be thinkin straight once the little whelp's gone." The gruff raider leaned on the bulwark, huffing to catch his breath, "Best to—" but trailed off, his attention drawn to a growing tide of yells and screams coming from beyond the dock.

The city protectorate staggered and defensively retreated from the lower ward into the courtyard. Both body and head merchants eagerly fought back against a foe they hated even more than each other. Food splattered the ground from over-turned stalls. The two groups snatched up what remained and hurled them at the protectorate as they fell back, shields raised against the assault of culinary projectiles. Crowds of patrons and merchants scattered every which way to escape the growing riot. From the upper ward, reinforcements arrived and entered the scrap.

"Bloody..." Grauler stared out for a long moment, weighing his options, before turning his glare on the crew. "Stations! Now! Get us in the air."

The crew rose up, hesitant. Cottage was the first to question, "Wha bout that bounty ya bragged of?"

"Look a that, Cottage." Grauller pointed back. "Wanna try gettin the boy to the city protectorate office safe through all that riot?" He motioned over his shoulder with a shake of his head, "Dump im off at a border station." He saw their reluctance a grinned. "Bet they'll even raise that bounty after this fiasco. Specially since they want im alive."

Cottage crossed his arms and nodded. "Fine. Have it yer way."

The crew considered that intently before moving to their stations leaving Grauler breathing relief at securing his position and gaining some safety. "Get them two in the cages below. Have words with er once she's calmed some."

As they prepped to launch, other steamrunners rose up along the dock, all seeking safety in the air to avoid the growing riot. The *Virgin Wanderer* lurched off her landing struts as he hopped up to the bridge. "The wester border, Mikwit."

"But, th-those stations d-don't have docks," he protested.

"N-not for merchants"

While normally they avoided crossing near a border station, here they were actively seeking one out. Grauler groaned inwardly, "Just get as close as ya can! Easy nough for ya. Sooner we get that burden gone, the better." He peered out the portal, seeing another steamer fly along a similar course. "An keep an eye on that one. Don't need no trouble right now." Swiping up the soiled sack, he trundled down the companionway to his cabin on the quardeck.

Lonn jerked awake and found himself once again surrounded in darkness. He absently rubbed the back of his head and felt the sickening ache in his groin. "Ugh. Hardly a fair fight."

In a cage nearby, Caetriona laughed, "Rarely is, my sweet little lord."

"It's not like that in tourney."

"No doubt because everyone there plays by the same honorable rules. Just have to remember one thing out here."

"And what's that, my lady?"

"There are no rules, of course." She quietly stared at him through the bars for a long moment. "Lonn… why didn't you go with the head merchants?"

"Why should I? Still don't understand." It had torn at him since the street riot. "How'd I even get a warrant placed on my head? What'd I do?"

"That's easy enough to answer," she laughed. "Nothing but politics. Some Astyrian official no doubt's trying to spare the kingdom any embarrassment of paying an official ransom to get you back. Heard of it happening. Sometimes even works out."

"Sometimes?" He groaned, "Oh, I certainly hope that

wasn't Soreign's idea."

"They'd've turned you over for their reward, and you'd probably be on your way home by now."

"Would I?" It might have been worse for him had he been caught in that riot. Without her at his side.

She smiled. "Well, at least you don't trust easily."

"I'm… learning."

"Suppose those expensive teachers of yours never taught you about any of this."

"No," he laughed halfheartedly, "Definitely neglected my education in many things." He leaned back as best he could in his cage and loosened his striders. Sliding his hand under, he tenderly adjusted himself to ease the roiling pain. Caetriona stifled a sympathetic chuckle as he groaned in relief. "What's so funny?"

"It— it's something." Unable to avert her eyes, she felt the heat rising in her cheeks. "Lonn, why… why'd you stay with me? Could've run at any time. I… wouldn't've stopped you. And, I'd've understood. I'm the one who thrust you into the deep dark of all this."

"Were you?" Lonn fell silent for a long moment. "Haven't threatened to hurt me, or kill me, or even toss me over a barrel."

She laughed, "Devouring doesn't count?"

"I… didn't think you were serious about that."

"Hmm." She bit her lip with a wry grin. "Still considering it."

"Besides. I… gave you my word."

"Oh… Lonn," Caetriona groaned, "My sweet, foolish lord."

He felt the heat rise in his cheeks. "And… what about you?"

She perked up. "What about me?"

"Could've handed me over. Claimed the warrant for yourself." He drummed his fingers along the bars. "Wouldn't've ended up like this."

"Thought about it. For a moment, perhaps. Just a moment," she sighed, "I just—" and fell silent as the hatch creaked open.

Grauler's heavy boots thrummed down the steep steps to the hold. They both blinked against the glare as he swung the lantern around, "Ah, good. Both wake," and hunched down, keeping out of reach of Caetriona's cage. "Truly sorry for the headache, cap, but ya left me little choice."

"Pretty bold having a go at me like this. Considering what you risk…"

"Maybe true. Needed ta remind ya of yer proper place. Make sure ya ain't gettin no mad ideas." He swung his arm around and tossed the soiled sack next to her cage. "Wanna betray others… lie… cheat… steal… all fine and good. Don't care so long it's not one a us! Not *me!*"

Caetriona leaned back with a huff, "Grauler, what are you going on about?"

"Mikwit found tha during the repairs… wedged in the rotor hub. Cause of our problems."

"Oh?" Curious, she leaned in, peering at a severed arm stump and the mangled hand inside. "Yep. Looks like someone had an accident."

"Old Zaude's."

"Suppose it is," she agreed, "Still don't know what this has to do with me being in here."

The grizzled raider hissed through his teeth. "Ya lied ta me!"

"Told you I didn't care what happened to him. Still don't."

He smacked the bars with the back of his hand. "Zaude was killed! No accident. If ya went down ta have yer boy for a lil fun— found im having a go instead. Killed im. I'd'a understood that. Ya'd've been straight with me. Zaude went after the boy, sure… but ya didn't know. Ya didn't kill im. Too busy flappin yer flog." Grauler swiped his thumb toward Lonn. "Wasn't with ya all night like ya said!"

"So what if he wasn't?" She glanced at Lonn. "Like him better than I did Zaude."

"Think tha matters? Should know better afer all this time." He lurched back on his heels and rose up. "He'll be well gone soon nough, an that'll end it."

She glared at him through the bars. "Oh, this isn't over between us, Grauler. Count on it."

He shook his head. "Need ya, cap. We all do. In shackles and…" He debated threatening her with the thing she feared most, but the *Virgin Wanderer* rumbled, knocking him off balance. "What the bloody—" He turned back, grasping his way along the cargo crates to the companionway. "Give ya plenty time ta think on yer situation." The steamraider jolted sharply as he clambered up the steps and disappeared, leaving them in the dark again.

Worried, Lonn looked toward Caetriona. "What was that?"

She grunted as a jarring impact knocked her into the cell bars. "Cannon shot," she laughed. "Seems we were followed."

The crew scrambled to their duty stations on the low deck as Grauler pushed through. He passed the engine room where the raiders latched themselves into the deck runners. Further along, Cottage shouted to the gunnery crews as they loaded the cannons. "Get them pipes steamin ready! Ain't but firing warnin shots, so hold til you hear the orders!" All were deck-firm and patient. They knew the drill well.

It all came down to him as he hauled himself up the companionway and onto the mideck. The steamrunner that had followed the *Virgin Wanderer* out of Alisard flew along her siehd and fired off another round across her bow. The raider scrambled up to the aft sideboard and took up the horn, shouting across the distance, "Wha's with the bloody warning shots, ya feck?!"

Aboard the *Barking Binch*, the Head Merchant, sporting a fresh patch over his once good eye, stood on the narrow afdeck beside the bridge. His boot perched on the bulwark as he leaned in and tapped his horn. "This working? Gonna try this again. See if you might be more reasonable. I hold a warrant for a head you've got aboard. Take him off your hands, him and his binch, and you can be on your way."

Grauler glared across the gap, hardly believing the demand. "Arrogant feck! No right to cut my business and demand a claim I hold! Much less anything more!" Curiosity, however, got the better of him. "Watcha want the binch fer anyway?"

The Head Merchant flipped up his patch. "Nothing but an eye."

"Real shame, that," Grauler laughed, "Sure looks better on ya than it would on er."

"I want that boy!" the Head Merchant sneered. "And that bloody binch! Now pull over!"

"Pull… what? Over?" Grauler laughed harder, "Wha's that even mean?"

"It—" the Head Merchant reared back, "It's an expression!" He glanced to his crew, questioningly, "Does that only work for zorba-drawn carriages?" and turned back to the horn with an impatient shake of head. "You know what I meant! You're on a decrepit steamerchant. Outgunned. No match for us. Do the right thing here and save yourselves a lot of trouble."

"Trouble?" The gruff raider shook his head with a

chuckle. "Don't know the meanin!" He called down, "Heard im, boys! Save ourselves a lotta trouble!"

The Head Merchant's face grew pale as the *Wanderer*'s siehd sail angled upward, altering her cant, and hidden slats along the lowdeck were thrown wide. "Ah. Unexpected." Six screaming steam cannons emerged from the dark interior and fired in quick succession. The *Barking Binch* jostled from the impacts as the hull splintered. He shouted down over the sounds of his screaming crew pierced by shrapnel, "Bang back hard!"

The *Binch* only had four cannons on her elch side, but they were larger bore. It should have been an even match as they fired, but the raider's hull was old and thick. Pelting from their first volley only left dents and fractures. The Head Merchant leaned into the bridge, shouting in fury. "Close the gap!"

Aboard the *Wanderer*, Grauler braced himself against the bulwark. There was little he needed to shout to the crew. They knew their jobs full well and worked to disable the opposing steamer. Until then, they flew along, each firing volleys across the narrowing distance. The hulls shuddered and swayed against the impacts. Even their angled sails scraped at each other. He only wished they had the main sails out to more easily puncture the other and destabilize their flight.

Each hoped to gain any advantage possible with a vital strike. Taking out the navigation propellors was a challenge but always preferred. A volley to the main rotors if they could get in their wake. A burst sail or sack... even the heligen tanks themselves to throw off their aim. While the raiders were more experienced in bringing a vessel to a standstill, there was always the chance of a lucky strike.

The *Virgin Wanderer* shuddered. Even from the mideck, Grauler heard the insistent shrill of a punctured water tank.

He leaned over the bulwark, seeing not only steam spewing through the damaged hull of the engine room but a spewing haze from one of the heligen sacks.

Cottage had been thrown out, hovering at the end of his safety line, hands gripping his throat and looking yellowish, clear signs of heligen inhalation. He floated for only a moment as he gasped and wheezed the gas from his lungs before falling into the darkness below.

"Bloody…" Grauler shook his head hard, pushing that sight away, and called up to Mikwit. "Turn! Can't take another strike on the aft siehd!"

Mikwit braced against the control panel, pulling the wheel hard to keep the steamer on course, but without pressure, the propellers sputtered, sending them into a spiral. "Can't hold er! Need the cap down there!" They exchanged panicked looks before Grauler grit his teeth.

"Blast that bloody binch!" As he scrambled down the companionway and along the narrow corridors, the crew rushed to the elch cannons as well as the two fore and aft, firing as they came about. The high pitch screech from the remaining tank and the rumble through the deck planks when the cannons fired followed him down to the hold.

Caetriona sat in her cage, arms crossing her chest. Each impact brought an unexpected growing sense of relief. When the light cast down from the open hatch, with the raider grumbling and stumbling his way toward them through the dark, there was a wistful smile on her lips. The keys on his link rattled as he searched for the right one. "What's wrong, Grauler?" She eyed him defiantly. "Hardly captain for day and already in trouble?"

"Trouble ya caused. Trouble yer gonna fix. Get yer binchy bung down to the engine fore we head to a crash."

She braced as another impact tore through the hull.

The screams from those caught in the barrage echoed through the decks. She tilted her head and took a deep breath, "No."

His hand wavered, fingering the key to release her. "Whatcha sayin?"

"No." She said again with a growing smile on her lips. "I'm done with it, Grauler. All of it."

"Bein with that boy really done yer head in."

She gazed across the gap to Lonn. "Yep. Finally doing the right thing for once in my miserable life."

From above, Mikwit called down. "Grauler! Th-that last hit t-two heligen tanks! W-we're grounding!"

The older raider grit his teeth. "Drop lines! Abandon steamer!"

"But… Grauler, w-we're——"

"Heard what I said!" He glared at her. "Guess yer miserable life won't last much longer."

Caetriona shrugged faintly. "Does seem that way."

With a grunt, he rushed back to the companionway, leaving the two behind.

Lonn gripped the bars. "What do we do?"

She set her feet against the far end of the cage and lowered her head between her knees, covering her neck with laced fingers. "Brace tight, my sweet little lord."

The journeymin matched her stance while waiting for the inevitable and met her gaze in the dimly lit hold. As the long branches of the forest scratched and tore at the hull, he realized there were things he wanted to say, but all he could do was wonder why she smiled so brightly even as tears streamed down her cheeks.

5 The Forest

The sun was out, hidden through the dense violet foliage of the surrounding forest, when Lonn awoke with a jerk and felt his head pounding. "Becoming a bad habit, this." He blinked through his blurry vision and found himself covered in a jagged section of sailcloth. The lingering warmth of a smoldering fire nearby wafted across his face. He turned his head, fighting through the lingering pain, when a blade drove down into the dirt beside him. It took him a moment to recognize it. "Old Zaude's dagger."

"So, you're finally awake, my sweet little lord?"

He rolled over and saw the wreckage of the *Virgin Wanderer*. Caetriona dropped down from a gaping hole in her hull and crouched beside him, running her fingers gently through his hair. As she fingered his wound, he groaned, "My lady?"

"Easy now. Took a nasty thump during the crash." She scooped out a dollop of healing salve, rubbing his forehead.

The heat spread out, and the tension faded. "Oh. That feels better," Lonn breathed slow, gazing up at her smiling face. "Were you hurt?"

She shrugged. "Nothing but a few bruises."

The journeymin looked at the wreckage. Without heligen, the entire propdeck had been crushed nearly flat from the full weight of the upper decks and fallen trushes. "How — how'd we even survive?"

"Those bloody cages!" she laughed, "Sturdy old things…
give em that."

"How'd you get us out of them?"

She reached under her belt buckle and yanked a key
free, tossing it into the smoldering pit. "Always kept a spare
on me. Don't have a use for it now."

He stared as the key disappeared into the ash with a
puff. "You mean— you— you could've escaped any time?!"

"Not about to let myself get caged in my own cell without a way out, my little lord," she commented with an
amused smile on her lips. "Now that *would* be embarrassing."

Lonn looked at the wreckage. "But, you could've saved her."

"I… did." She drew out strips of salted herrerel from
her belt pouch. "Here. Eat this."

He sucked on the tip while studying their surroundings.
"Did anyone else survive?"

"Dead or scattered." She settled beside him with a shrug.
"Just us two when I finally dug out."

"Thank you, Caetriona."

Her cheeks flushed faintly. "It was nothing, Lonn."

He nodded faintly. "So, do you know where we are at
least?"

"Ah…" She waved her strip of meat back and forth.
"Hard to say." The *Virgin Wanderer*'s bowsprit jutted out at
an odd angle making it difficult to determine her orienta-
tion before she grounded. "Might get a better sense once I
see the sun. Until then, I'll keep searching for any supplies."

"I should help." Lonn rose until the throbbing pain
forced him down with a groan.

"Best thing you can do is rest and regain your strength,"
she insisted before clambering back into the wreckage.

He hated feeling useless, but there was little help he
could offer in his condition. When the throbbing in his head

returned, he spread on a bit more salve, wincing when he felt the raised lump. Caetriona returned some time later with a pack slung over her shoulder and… "You found your sword."

"Yours, too. Bloody heavy thing." She unslung the pack and his belt from her shoulder and lifted up his hair to check his injury. "Improving, my sweet little lord."

He eyed the pack. "That's all that's left?"

"Just the necessities. Food to last us some days. Our cloaks. Even a few coin purses. Decent amount to cover us. Best travel light." She looked up as the sun came into view. "Ahh. Seems like we were heading south across the Illuvian Forest."

"So, where would Alisard be from here?"

"Should be…" She thought about it for a moment and pointed northwest. "Roughly that direction."

"How long would it take to get there?"

"Some days, at least." He rose up with a wobble, and she grabbed his waist to help steady him. "Carefully, my little lord."

Fighting the disorientation and finding his footing, he drew a slow breath, "I'm fine, my lady." He cinched his belt tight before sliding the dagger opposite his sword. "Caetriona, would you… in Alisard, the way you moved— fought… would you teach me?"

Surprised, she eyed him hesitantly. "Lonn, you certain that's what you want? It's not like I fight honorably."

"What we've faced out here… that hasn't helped me."

"True enough," she laughed and relented with a sigh, "Fine, but you won't match my reflexes."

He grinned, determined to meet her challenge. "I will."

She laughed, hefting the pack onto her shoulder and leading the way. "We'll see about that." The two trudged northwest through the tall trushes and orange-leaved thickets for much of the day. There was little to say between them, each taking stock of recent events in their own way.

During a rest later in the day, she tended to his injury with another application of salve. The swelling, which had been quite apparent when she first dragged him unconscious from the *Wanderer*'s wreckage, was little more than a faint discoloration in his skin. "Is it still bad?" he asked.

She grinned. "Won't even notice it by tomorrow." She leaned in, kissing his cheek. "No training til then." They carried on until sunfall grew close and found a clearing to set a small camp.

That first night, the two huddled close to each other beside the fire, their thick fur cloaks pulled about them tightly, while they sucked their meat to make them last as long as possible. She glanced down at the young journeymin as he rested his head against her shoulder. "What would you be doing if you were home right now?"

"Oh. Nothing nearly as exciting as this, my lady," he laughed, "No doubt be sore and tired from a long day of training at my taskmaster's side. I'd have my evening meal with my father and mother. And the rest of my evening would be spent reading. Something historical, no doubt." He smiled, "Unless I snuck an adventure book," but fell silent as she tensed. "I said something that upset you."

"No. Nothing you said, my little lord," she sighed and turned her head away. "Just… the mention of your parents. Try not to think about my own."

"Sorry. Didn't mean to stir bad memories."

"Weren't all bad. Had a good life once. My father… he was gonna show me all the world when I grew up. Never…

got the chance."

"That must've been difficult."

"The *Wanderer* was my last connection to… them… that life. Maybe that's why a part of me could never let go. Should've… long before now."

"You're free of that burden."

"Were it that easy." She stared at the fire. "Not a merchant. Free from being a raider. Don't know what I am."

He took her hand. "Caetriona, my lady."

"That's something, I suppose. Whoever *she* is," she laughed faintly and stroked her fingers through his hair as he curled beside her. "Get some sleep, my sweet lord. Another long day ahead." Closing their eyes, finally, they slept.

How long it was, she could not say, but she awoke some time in the night, ears twitching. The fire embers dimmed to a low glow, but the hazy moonlight through the trushes was enough that she could peer out at their surroundings. There were noises, faint movement in the forest. Certainly not the wind, which was only a faint breeze. It kept her awake and alert even as the trushes grew quiet and still once more. All the while, Lonn slept pressed against her, head resting on her chest, arm draped across her waist. His breath came in gentle sighs she found calming.

Moonfall came, eclipsing the sun for a brief time. When the sky brightened, their quiet moment together had to end, and the first challenge of the day began. True to her word, there was a task she had agreed to. She lowered her head and shifted herself around, whispering in his ear, "Lonn…" He grumbled. "Lonn, wake up. We're under attack."

His eyes sprung open. "We are?" He fought through the fog and rolled over, hand searching for his sword. She was on her feet before him, her sword out. He joined her, searching through the dim morning light. "Where?"

"Here!" She swung her sword toward him. The blade whistled, slicing air, and he circled around barely in time to block her blow. It forced him back, on the defensive too quickly as she pressed in.

It took him a moment to recover and hold her advance steady. "You're as bad as my old taskmaster, my lady!" But the tension in his blade revealed her blows were off. "You're holding back!" He pressed forward in an offensive stance.

"Fair enough." She grinned, stepping in and swiping his blow to the side. A kick at his shin threw him off balance. As she twisted his sword away, he stumbled and lost his grip. "Must do better, my lord," she advised as his blade flung to the ground.

"I don't understand it," he huffed, snatching it up. "I won every competition in my division at tourney. And lost every one against the raiders."

Caetriona nodded, sympathetic to his frustration. "Not surprising. You all trained in the same manner. Know all the rules. And for honor's sake, you follow them." She slipped her sword into its sheath and stood before him. "Lonn, where are your eyes? Where's your focus of attention?"

"On my opponent's sword hands."

"And because of that, you'll lose every time. Drilled so much, probably know the strikes by heart, so you know what to expect from someone following the same rules. It doesn't work that way out here." She smacked her chest. "This is where your eyes should be. The shoulders. Stomach. Hips. Every move your opponent makes, starts here. A tightness. A twist. Gives you a moment's warning… if you're attentive enough."

"Soreign mentioned something about that," the journeymin recalled. "Must've been working up to it."

"Can't afford to wait." She reached out with her foot,

stomping down the last embers of the fire. "Did you sense I would do that? Did you see it in how my stomach tightened? How my hips twisted, preparing for my leg to move? For now..." she gathered their supplies and tossed the pack to his feet. There was a faint smile on her lips. "Trail behind me. Pay close attention to my movements and your own. Anticipate."

Lonn hefted the pack up. "So, you want me to spend the rest of the day..." The corner of his lip curled upward. "Staring at you, my lady?"

"Study." She shrugged, "Or stare... if that's how my sweet little lord wants to phrase it." She led them northwest, throwing a quick glance over her shoulder,. "Don't get distracted, now."

Watching and trying to anticipate her movements, the journeymin trailed behind her. A shift in her shoulder to push a branch from their path or a longer stride to avoid stepping in some animal's excrement left unburied as a territorial sign. He watched until his eyes wandered lower to the sway of her hips. The way her striders—

She smacked his arm with the back of her hand.

He jerked his gaze to her face, her features set in a silent chastising, and felt the heat flooding his cheeks. "Sorry. Got... distracted."

"I noticed." She turned back, increasing the distance between them and changing up her movements to keep them from becoming routine. As they reached midsun, he was getting better at anticipating what she would do. So much so, that his sword met hers when she drew and thrust it behind her. She smiled as their metal clashed. "Better, my little lord."

Feeling more confident, Lonn kept his focus, able to hold his position and not give ground, despite the weight of the pack wearing him down. Caetriona thrust and swung, hardly winded. He saw the sway in her hips and blocked the coming kick with his leg, pressing to get the upper hand. As he focused on sweeping her off her feet and swung hard, she twisted away and elbowed his nose. His head whipped back, blood spurting out, as he tumbled to the ground. She laughed. "But overconfident. And still not fast enough."

He caught his breath. "You baited me."

"And you fell for it." She crouched beside him, wiping off the blood from his upper lip with her thumb. "Not broken."

"I lasted longer."

She kissed his cheek. "Only just."

"You're still able to keep me off balance."

She bit her lower lip. "Because you're still thinking like a brute." Lonn's brow creased, hurt by her depiction. "Oh, don't look at me like that, my sweet little lord. Just the way you were taught," she huffed, pulling him to his feet. "Focused on overpowering your opponent. Beat them down. Bash shields. Bend armor. Break swords." She held hers out. "Take mine up."

He lifted it, eyes raised in surprise at the difference. "It's so light."

"Yours is so bloody heavy, once you commit, momentum carries you through. While I remain light on my feet." She placed her hand over his. "And stop being so tight. Loosen up a little." When his hand and arm eased up, she nodded approvingly, "That's it," and stepped back. "Come at me now. Feel the difference."

He took a deep breath and swung at her with overcommitted strikes. She nimbly twisted away, gently grasping his wrist, and tugged him off balance. He went tumbling to the ground once more and cried out when the back of his head struck a moss covered stone. "Ow!"

"Oh!" Even Caetriona winced at the unexpected landing. "Sorry, my little lord!" She helped him up and stroked the back of his head, relieved there was no blood. "You alright?"

He rubbed his head. "I'm used to it, my lady." He pushed against the stone to regain his footing, faltering as his fingers grasped its unnatural shape. "This…" The stone was angular, chiseled. Its edge disappeared into the depths of the surrounding thicket. "Don't think this is natural." His face strained red as he dragged it out and wiped away the layers of dirt and entwined vines. His voice grew excited, "Perhaps an old ruin?!"

"Ruins? Not in the Illuvian." She perked up as she considered it. "Oh! Perhaps an old waymark." She glanced around hoping for an easier path north. "Might just be an old trade-route around here."

Lonn lifted it up with a groan, setting it back on its end. "I… don't…" The more he saw, the less he became convinced. Scratching the back of his head, he appraised their discovery and asked, "What do you make of this, Caetriona?"

She circled around and felt an ill wave churning her stomach. It was a worn carving of a large-eyed creature, gnarled and fat, with prominent cheeks, large and jagged ears, and bared fangs. A tuft of long, wispy hair rose from the top of its head. From head to toe across its naked form, a dark crimson streak marred the stone surface. The blood drained from her face. "ah… feck. not a waymark. it's… a… warning."

He saw the fear in her eyes, the rapid rise and fall of her chest. "we're not in the Illuvian Forest, are we?"

"oh, no, Lonn. far from it."

Among the conflicts between aelfins and humins, the Ciration Forest was never the cause. It was a rare point of agreement even among the kingdoms. None claimed it. None wanted it. None fought over it. It had been long established since the War of Ciration, when the aelfins sought to conquer the territory and unify the norther and souther segments of their growing republic, that any who entered into the forest came out in pieces, if they came out at all.

Little was known of the forest's inhabitants, the ravenous and fiercely territorial troblytes. Much had been made of them since. In myth, legend, and folk tales, they embodied something to be feared. And it was this fear that caused Caetriona to clutch Lonn's hand tightly, pulling him along behind, running as fast as she could. They were both tired. Muscles aching with a dull burn. Hearts pounding. Gasping for air. But they could hardly afford to slow down.

Ever since they had found the blood stained marker and dragged it into the light, the forest had come alive with a howling. All around them, the creatures clawed their way along the branches as the dense foliage rustled and swayed. The air filled with such a riot, Lonn never heard the faint whistle of darts fired at them as they fled. She did and dragged him to the ground, rolling them both through the thickets as the darts pierced dirt and wood alike. A sap oozed along the tips, and neither wanted to know what would happen if they were struck.

"can't… keep this… up," he gasped.

She knew full well. "they— they won't follow us beyond the forest."

"and… just… where is… that?"

They had been steadily traveling northwest, believing they would reach the Astyrian plains and the city of Alisard. Little did they realize the *Virgin Wanderer* had careened in circles during the crash and landed with her bowsprit pointing south, towards their destination instead of away from it. So, the two wayward travelers had been going steadily deeper into troblyte territory.

And now, with the souther path cut off, their only choice was to continue north. How far to the forest's edge, she had no idea. Too many days to keep up such a heavy pace. "blast that fool, Grauler. what was he thinking?" In all her travels as both merchant and raider, it was widely accepted that no steamer— no matter how desperate— crossed the Ciration Forest severing the borders of Astyria and Douchart.

He crawled as quietly as possible arm over arm through the thickets, thankful for the momentary respite. It reminded him of his time fumbling through the stifling hot vents aboard the steamraider and forced an exhausted laugh.

Caetriona eyed him with concern, hoping he was not going mad in panic. "Lonn?"

"sorry. nothing, my lady. just… a stray memory." He peered through the thick brush and pointed. "some dense trush cover that way."

She pressed her head close to his, following his gaze, and gave a curt nod. "ready?"

"when you are."

Grasping around, she found a sizable stone and tossed it as far as she could. It crashed down into the distant thickets, drawing the troblytes. Taking advantage of the distraction, they scrambled toward the dense copse of trushes in their desperate charge north. But the forest creatures soon discovered the ruse and gave swift chase. She pulled his head down, ducking them both low. A series of darts spattered the trushes as they weaved between them. "Getting closer!"

The journeymin thought about the situation in spattering moments. It took a while, but as sunfall approached and

the forest grew dark, it finally came to him. "should've…
overwhelmed us… by now."

Though she had refused to voice it sooner out of concern it would overly worry the young journeymin, the same
troubling thought had filled her mind, too. It had helped
them stay focused, but she hardly had time to respond when
another volley of darts sailed down from above. These were
even closer still. She felt one graze her arm. The sap spattered her skin as a barb sailed passed, causing half her arm
to go numb almost instantly. "feck! paralytic."

"so… not trying… to kill us." It was an ominous revelation that drove him to run faster despite the agony sear-
ing through his chest and legs.

"No. They— they've been herding us." The unfamiliar
path before them through the thickets and trushes revealed
nothing. Anything could have been a trap. Dangling vines.
Oddly angled branches or ones pulled exceedingly tight.
She did not know what to look for. So when the trap was
sprung, it was most unexpected. All she felt was a sinking
feeling as the ground about her gave out. Momentarily
shocked and disoriented with weightlessness, she hit the
hard ground with a groan. She rolled over just as Lonn fell
on top of her. "ooph!!"

"Caetriona? you alright?"

"could be better. of all the… fecky leaf trap?!" She gazed
down where he lay, hands firmly pressing upon her breasts.
"not that I mind, Lonn, but… now? hardly the time or place."

He gained his breath and jerked back. "Oh!" His face
flushed a crimson even she could see in the dark. "I— so
sorry, my lady!"

She could hardly help herself from smiling at his em-
barassment. "highly doubt that, my sweet little lord. unless… that's your sword-hilt pressing into my—"

"Yes!" He tugged it from between her legs and rolled away, letting her finally breathe again. "Sorry." A quick glance around caused him to laugh, "Well, at least there weren't any of those spikes I've read about. Could've been skewered right through."

From above, she heard the forest creatures' cautious advances, but they finally ventured close, staring into their trap with bulbous eyes as she sat up with a huff, "Might just live long enough to wish there had been." They chattered among themselves. One hissed, gnashing its fangs at another.

Lonn perked up, curious. "What do you think they're saying?"

Her lips wavered and let out a faint sigh, "No idea, but if they're debating when to kill us, I'd prefer now."

He frowned. "Caetriona, you don't have to keep punishing yourself."

"Oh, my sweet little lord, I'm not." She reached out, caressing his cheek. From above, the troblytes fired their darts. The two winced against the assault as the barbs pierced their clothes and skin. Her words slurred as she lost feeling, "I… jush… dunt…wunna… beh…"

It took only a moment before they went entirely limp.

The creatures descended upon them with howls and hisses. The largest among them grabbed at Lonn's arms, squeezing them, before poking at his chest and legs. It hissed in apparent displeasure before prying one of his eyes wide. The creature appraised it with a lick of its lips. It hissed, and the others began to arduous task of dragging them from the pit. They were soon tied to spits and dragged deeper into the forest.

The troblyte hunters transported their captured prey

some distance north, chattering and hissing amongst each other as they marched through the night. At midmoon, they stopped. With his head drooped limply back, Lonn saw the world upside down and noticed that their captives took a sudden interest in something they had found on the ground. Their chatter went low, muffled by hisses.

There was a flurry of activity among them as they settled their captives at the base of a large trush. He grew concerned when they bared their stubby fingers wide, all ending in sharp talons. Wondering if this was the end, he was surprised when one of them swung out and dug its talons into the trush trunk over his head, scrambling up into the foliage.

As they rested there, he regained some feeling across his extremities, but not enough to fight against the ropes that started chafing his wrists. His eyes darted around. "Whut ur hey gun do wi uth?"

Caetriona was beside him but said nothing, still paralyzed. No matter how hard she tried, her lips refused to part. After a moment, however, she did not want to speak. Or make any noise. The low howl coming from the foliage above made her want to hide. She knew that sound, having heard it many times before in the quiet of the night when the propellers were running soft and they were over the wilderness. The howl of the woolg.

The troblytes mimicked it well from the trush tops. And they had been left as bait, their scent, and the goading howls meant to lure in the local pack. A threat to their territory they had to defend against.

None of this she could convey to the young journeymin. But after a moment, she realized how unnecessary it was. From the darkness came a low howl, an instinctive challenge against the preceived invading pack. It came again, a more insistent warning. The troblytes kept howling, drawing the pack closer.

She saw the first one break through the thicket. A muscular frame hidden under dark fur. Its four paws padded near-silently toward them. Its snout curled back, sniffing the air. It grunted low, a signal. Two others pushed through the brush and advanced on them. Their muscles tightened, bodies reared back, preparing to pounce. It was then that the troblytes attacked, but they did not rely on their darts.

They fell on the beasts from above, three or four troblytes for each woolg. It was hard for her to keep track of the riot in the darkness. But then she did not want to watch. They both did their best to avert their eyes as the animals howled in agony. The troblytes tore into their fur with tooth and talon, gorging themselves on jagged strips of meat. They slurped at the blood, sending a shiver down Lonn's spine. Caetriona wanted to flinch with each loud crack of bone as the creatures gorged on organs and fat until they had their fill.

Most of the ravenous creatures seemed satisfied with what they could get for themselves, but there was one prize worth fighting over as one young troblyte twisted and wrenched the head of a woolg from its spine with a snap and crunch. The largest among them saw this and hissed a warning, baring its talons and knocking the prize out of smaller one's hands. The two tangled against each other, a riot of fur and dirt until the young one whimpered in defeat and limped off to nurse its wounds. The dominant troblyte took up the head with a howl and brought it to its mouth, sucking out each eye in turn.

When nothing but fur, gristle, and bone remained, the troblyte hunters slept in a huddled circle, with the dominant ones in the warm center and the youngest on the cold, outer rim. Despite their condition, both Lonn and Caetriona slept as well. But it did not last long. He awoke to a bitter odor and the sound of splashing as a troblyte relieved itself along the base of the trush beside him. Its mouth stretched wide with a yawn as it shook itself off and burped, a noxious smell considering their recent meal.

The young journeymin turned his head and retched. It was only then that he realized he could move much easier than the night before. "Caetriona, are you…" He stretched his mouth out, trying to rid himself of the ache his muscles felt from their long paralysis. "Are you well?"

"Not really. No." She stared at the remains of the woolgs as the hunting group drew themselves off the muddied fur skins.

"Finally able to move. You?"

"A bit."

"What do you think they'll do with us?"

She was silent for a while. "Imagine, same as them."

"Oh," he gasped, "But they'd've done that already if that was their intent."

She tried to glare at him. So young. So naive. So curious. "If these things have intent, my little lord… you should be more worried."

"Of course I am, my lady. Heard stories growing up… just as you did, I'm sure." A troblyte took up his rope binding and lashed him back on the spit. In the light of day, each had a hue that easily blended with the forest. And he was surprised by their strength, considering the tallest among them stood no higher than his waist. "Where… do you think they're taking us?"

Another took up Caetriona's rope and bound her tight so they could carry them both once more. "Home to feed their young, no doubt."

"That's…" he trailed off, silent for a moment, "not a pleasant thought, my lady."

"Wasn't supposed to be."

"Is it true that the aelfin—" The group lurched to a stop and stared at him, hissing and growling in low gutturals. It was clear they wanted to hear nothing of their ancient enemy.

"Lonn…" Exasperated, with head drooped low, she sighed, "Don't say *that* word around the troblytes."

"Oh… of course. Sorry." He fell silent for a long time as the dominant hunter stood over him baring its talons and snarling in warning. When it appeared satisfied their captive would not speak the offensive word again, it turned away and grunted to the others. Once again, the two were dragged roughly along while the group marched on. Hoping she would hear him, he lowered his voice, "didn't think they'd understand."

"probably not. but… *that* word…"

"so, it is true? they tried to conquer the troblytes and actually retreated?"

"that's what the stories say." She thought it over for a moment. "after seeing the results of last night, can you blame *them?*"

"no. suppose not," he responded, considering the annals of humin history he had read. "I just wonder what would've changed had *they* succeeded."

"not much, Lonn. still would've expanded east. your people still would've been conquered and enslaved. if *they* had troblytes under their control, it would've been uglier… a lot messier. might've prevented the Revolt, though, and… the Scourge."

The young journeymin blinked, a shiver running along his spine. "oh. hadn't… thought of that."

"no point dwelling, my little lord." She cleared her throat with a sniff. "happened the way it happened."

They both fell silent, saving their energy for whatever future was to come.

6   The Grande Sink

They appeared to reach their destination at a quarter to midsun. From his inverted vantage, Lonn saw an outcropping rising steep out of the ground in a small field cleared of trushes. The rock face was weathered and pitted, but his focus rested on a gaping black maw at the base and leading underground.

The chatter increased among the troblytes, excited to be home. As they got closer, the journeymin grew concerned, wondering if they would even fit. But it seemed the creatures were quite determined as one took up his spit at the front and another at the rear, pushing him into the darkness. He expected a cave, but it was a tunnel. Long and narrow. Clawed out by the creatures over time.

Somewhat closer in size to the troblytes themselves, he had little problem with the tight confines. Caetriona was not so fortunate as she grunted each time her head scraped along the jagged ceiling. Dirt knocked loose and fell into the corners of her eyes. The dust overwhelmed her, forcing her to shake her head constantly while coughing and sputtering. Fortunately for them both, the tunnel was fairly straight and angled slightly upward. He hardly wanted to consider how they would have handled a sharp turn.

The effort dragging the two captives became apparent as the creatures grunted and strained with their burden. They were still quite determined to see the venture through, to such an extent that they all, captors and captives alike, breathed relief as they emerged from the tunnel into a massive sinkhole surrounding a central, large trush. Its widespread foliage allowed filtered light through the gaping hole far above, and purp vines entwined its roots and trunk. Recesses all around the edges of the Grande Sink led to chambers where many troblytes peered out, appraising the new captives with interest.

The hunting party pressed in around the two, obscuring Lonn's already limited view, as they unlashed the captives from their spits and forced them toward a recess covered by a lattice of hastily bound trush branches. It was a rudimentary cell. They were thrown inside, with the cell door lashed tight behind them by more of the same vines that grew prominently about the trush. The creatures did not even bother untying Lonn and Caetriona's wrists as they trundled off.

The two looked at each other in the dimly lit cell, a silent nod between them to acknowledge they were mostly unharmed. He skittered to the door, surprised to find that they had been left unguarded. And the rudimentary construction — he eyed it, somewhat confused. "Do they really think this'll hold us in?" The cell door appeared easy enough to break open with just the vines sealing it. He reached to push it open, but something grabbed him from behind and pulled him back.

"Don't try it, lad! Ain't no scaping that way."

Caetriona tensed, prepared to leap to Lonn's defense, but held back when she recognized the wavering voice. "Petrovey?"

"Cap."

"You the only one who made it?"

The raider did not reply for a long moment. "Only one

left. Four or five of us made it off and into the forest. Only Mikwit and me survived the ambush. Got us both in here. Thought he was small enough to slip out, escape. Trust me. Don't wanna make a run for it." The raider leaned into the light. Blood stained the side of his face from where one of his eyes had been. "The chief… vile little beast… scooped it out and sucked it down like a good little treat."

Frowning, she settled down and leaned back against the wall. "Sorry."

"Yeah. Lotsa that goin round."

"So, we're stuck here." Lonn looked through the cell door. In all the recorded documents from the eight-bloom War of Ciration, nothing had been written about troblytes beyond physical characteristics. Whether that was because none had attempted to learn about their culture or those who did never survived the encounter, he could not say, but he kept himself busy by studying them carefully. It was unclear if that would be of any help in securing their release, but there was nothing else to do.

His only useful observation was where the hunting party had deposited their gear. He watched the one carrying his sword study it for a moment, curious. It quickly learned that the sword could be withdrawn, but it sliced its fingers in the attempt. With a screaming hiss, it threw the weapon down and scurried off, dripping blood in its path, leaving one of the others to snatch it up. They went into a chamber inset along the sinkhole wall across from their cell, returning moments later empty handed.

The first morning of their imprisonment, they awoke abruptly as a group of troblytes descended on them. There was much jabbering and chattering among them as they once again squeezed each of the captive's arms and poked them. And, much attention was on prying their eyes wide. When the group left, closing the cell door firmly behind them, Caetriona leaned close to Lonn, clearly shaken. "Thought that was the end."

He nodded and glanced at Petrovey. "Any idea what that's about?"

"Waiting…" his voiced quivered, "til we're just the way they like us."

"Not a pleasant thought." With a shiver, she leaned back and rested her head on Lonn's shoulder. He agreed with her, but it did give them time, a luxury they desperately needed. Peering through the cell door, he kept vigil with an intense scrutiny.

While primitive, they were less so than either aelfins or humins believed, with a distinct social hierarchy. That was apparent in the conflict between the dominant and young hunters, and that was over the mere possession of the woolg's eyes. He glanced at their fellow captive. Eyes were clearly a coveted delicacy, worth fighting and dying over.

But that conflict over dominance seemed to apply to all aspects of troblyte culture. While the vast majority went about naked, he did see some wearing furs. A few of the most prominent members, such as the chief, even decorated themselves in aelfin jewelry, spoils left behind from the war more than a thousand blooms before. And considering they still held animosity toward their aelfin foe, it made him wonder just how old the creatures lived normally.

The highest ranks in troblyte society also had first choice of mates, with some males accumulating numerous females to have at their disposal. Similarly, a few well-garbed females had a number of male escorts ready for service. Courting for the lower ranks was an open affair, with the suitor, whether male or female, beating its chest and baring fangs, showing its strength to their potential mate. Riots were a nightly occurrence, with fierce contests between rivals that often proved fatal. When the victor did kill its opponent, it presented the head of the slain to the female, offering its eyes to her. The rest, they consumed together, often while fornicating.

Those that were too old or injured to defend themselves were set upon by a group, as their ravenous appetite and lack of resources hardly permitted any too weak to fight back to remain. This behavior was unlike any others Lonn observed, as they took up an odd, serrated blade, slicing away the creature's hair in a final act of humiliation before tearing into it and gorging on the remains.

Regarding the sick, Lonn could hardly see that they had any. In fact, dealing with the afflicted was the only time troblytes did not consume the dead. They clearly had the sense to know that an illness would spread, and the bodies were quickly removed from the Grande Sink, disposed of in some manner he never discerned.

He also noted that it was equally rare to see a female without child. On one occasion, a troblyte trundled by carrying a child in each arm as they suckled, and her belly was already swelled from childish. Surprisingly, the young maintained a diet of purp berries gathered from the vines growing about the Grande Sink and central trush as well as copious amounts of breast milk. And the mothers themselves showed no particular preference to their own offspring. One milking mother was as good as any other as far as feeding their young was concerned. He wondered when the preference for meat took hold.

As time passed, Lonn quickly realized that their interest in food was one-sided, as the captives had been afforded little, even as their stomachs began to growl. The creatures came in a group each morning to check on their deterioration, never offering food or water. It ran contrary to his expectations, as he thought the creatures would be intent on fattening them up as much as possible before consuming them. Considering their normal diet, they were not absent of food stock. It grimly confirmed Petrovey's belief that they were considered something of a delicacy, worth savoring for the right time and conditions.

Fortunately, they were not entirely without food. About the best they got was an assault of purp berries that the children took delight in flicking through the bars. Lonn sat, accepting the daily pelting when it came, gathering the berries in the hem of his tunic. It was a curious moment when they watched him eat a few. The children laughed, but the adults simply stared. He wondered if, in their eyes, that made him and the others appear childish as he shared the tart berries with Caetriona and Petrovey. It staved off the worst of the hunger pains, but it was hardly sustaining. They each knew they had to manage an escape before they grew too weak.

They remained imprisoned for several days, and their opening came in the most unexpected of times. The light from the sinkhole dimmed as clouds covered the sun. An approaching storm. Lonn watched intently as the troblytes cleared the area surrounding the trush, always a bustle of activity, and the chamber grew unusually quiet. When the rain came, two things grew apparent. Trenches carved around the trush and along the Grande Sink floor, which he had dismissed as simply decorative, funneled water toward the tunnels to prevent flooding. And troblytes appeared none-too-fond of water.

It was a singular opportunity they could not afford to miss.

He looked to his companions. "have to go. now!" Caetriona was at his side, but Petrovey was understandably reluctant. The journeymin had no time to explain, tearing at the vines and shoving the cell door aside. With a quick check to ensure no troblytes were standing guard elsewhere, he scuttled as quietly as possible across the courtyard with her close behind. When they reached the supply room, they found piles of old aelfin relics. Swords. Armor. Various trinkets and keepsakes the creatures had no real use for. He reluctantly ignored it all as he grabbed their pack and belts and drew Zaude's blade, cutting Caetriona's bonds.

She did the same for him before tugging on her belt and rubbing her sore wrists. "you sure about this, Lonn?"

"best chance we've got." he replied as they skirted back along the tunnel to the Grande Sink.

Petrovey lingered at the opening of the cell, still reluctant even as they waved him over. Finally, he bolted into the opening, nervously looking all around, and stumbled over one of the rain trenches. Sputtering to the ground, he cried out, "Knew this was a bad idea!"

Caetriona stiffened as a troblyte howled out, alerting the others to their escape. "Bloody fool!"

He scrambled awkwardly to his feet as troblytes streamed from the recessed caves to give chase. "Don't leave me behind!"

The chattering and howling grew louder as Lonn searched for the nearest outlet, swiping his sword and cutting those down who got too close. Caetriona guarded their flank as Petrovey caught up. Further along the wall of the sink, the journeymin saw a stream bubbling down one of the tunnels. "This way!"

As the creatures circled around out of reach of their swords, hopping over the trenches and keeping to the dry areas, Lonn led the way to the tunnel. When Caetriona risked a glance over her shoulder, she pulled back in resistance. "We'll get trapped in there."

He gave a confident grin, "They won't follow." At least, that was his hope, which was reinforced as the troblytes gathered at the mouth of the tunnel, chattering angrily. But none went near the outlet as the water streamed to the outside.

Just like the tunnel the troblytes had dragged them through to reach the Grande Sink, this one was equally long and dark. It sloped downward to allow quick water drainage just like the other, but he had not expected it to be quite so muddy. He clutched at the stone walls to keep his balance and avoid slipping. The others behind him did the same, but Caetriona occasionally bumped into him, struggling with having to crouch down to avoid constantly hitting her head against the low ceiling. "Hate this! Can't see a bloody thing."

He tried to be reassuring. "Just keep going straight."

At the rear, Petrovey constantly faltered, looking over his shoulder and expecting pursuit. "Hope ya know what yer doing."

"Can always go back and make a meal for them," she groaned through grit teeth, "Got another eye to spare, don't you?"

"No need ta rub it in." He stumbled, splashing in a muddy puddle. "Don't even know where this lets out, do ya?"

Caetriona shook her head. "Always were a worrier."

He stumbled, pressing into her back with his bound hands. "So, you gonna cut me loose?"

"Once we're out. Might end up slittin your wrists… by accident."

"So, lad," he grumbled as he fumbled along behind them, "how'd ya know they weren't gonna follow?"

"Before the rain, they cleared out the Sink. Never did that any other time, not even at night. Figured they didn't like the water."

Petrovey blanched. "That's it?! Riskin our necks on a hunch?!"

"Stop complaining, Petrovey." Caetriona smiled. "Panned out so far."

"How ya figure that?"

"We aren't dead yet." She glanced back. "And if you'd stuck with us, they wouldn't even know we were gone til the rain stopped."

"So, yer sayin this is my fault?"

"Don't see anyone else to blame, do—"

"Enough of that," Lonn chastised as the tunnel leveled out. "Light ahead." The two looked over the journeymin's shoulder and sighed relief.

The torrential rain provided welcome cover as the three emerged from the tunnel and escaped into a small clearing. Caetriona shook her head, swiping the dirt from her hair, unsure of their course, "Can't see the bloody sun in this storm."

Petrovey held his bound hands out. "Little help here?"

Pulling the dagger from Lonn's belt, she slit the raider's bonds with a huff, "There."

"Thanks kindly, cap." The raider wiped at the blood staining the side of his face with a sigh, "No idea how much that's been itchin me."

"Who dare?"

The three froze in the rain to the question, muffled by the rain, and searched for its source. Caetriona pointed, spying a cell further along the cliff-face. "Someone there?"

"Sommin… here?"

She tensed, recognizing the voice as it grew louder. "That couldn't be…"

"Who'd'a thought?" Petrovey perked up, surprised. "Them beasts caught Flum Three Leg!"

The young journeymin looked between them, a shiver of anger running down his spine. "Flum?"

With a frown on her face, she eyed him sympathetically. "I know, Lonn. But…" With a grimace, she held out the dagger to Petrovey. "You were on good terms, right? Cut him loose."

"Sure," he huffed hesitantly, taking up the blade. "Suppose we were at that."

As he went off, she glanced around, debating which course was best, "North is…" and pointed, "That way… make for the Douchart border." Lonn winced, reluctant to go there of all places, but she pressed, "Reckon it's our best… only… option." Exasperated, she shook her head. "Petrovey! Haven't you freed him yet?"

"Workin on it! Tied this down tight. There!" He wrenched the cell door aside and peered into the darkness. "Hey, Flum? That you? Let's get ya free."

"Flum free?"

"Right. Flum go free."

"Who dat?"

"Petrovey. Remember? Good friend Petrovey."

"Pet-rov-ey." The giant raider, dressed in a patchwork of tattered rags, crawled from the dark cave, and Lonn soon saw why they called him Three Leg. His loose loincloth did little to hide his lengthy phallus as it dragged along the ground. He remained hunched down, crawling along as he had in the cramped confines of the *Virgin Wanderer*. Flum reached out, his wrists actually not bound at all. He gripped Petrovey by the neck and squeezed. "Not good friend. Left Flum."

"Not… by… choi—" the raider gurgled and dropped

the dagger, pounding and struggling in Flum's tightening grip until his spine crunched, and he went limp.

From above, there was a massive chattering of excitement. Troblytes looked down at them from numerous openings along the cliff-face, where rocky overhangs protected them from the rain. Among the chattering came something else. It sent a cold shiver down Lonn's spine. Just as they despised the word aelfin, they had learned another word, one they celebrated. "Flum! Flum! Flum!"

The giant ripped away one of Petrovey's arms from the rest of his body and flung it wide. One of the troblytes snatched it as it splattered against the wall and tore into it eagerly. The troblytes above chanted and cheered him on. Flum did that again and again, twisting and snapping bones, until there was nothing left of the former raider except his head, which the giant tossed to the chief for the other eye.

Lonn wondered if once again the forest creatures had outmaneuvered them but could hardly focus his attention on that as Flum turned his attention to Caetriona. His head tilted to one side as his bloody fingers scratched the top of his head. "Hel-lo. Girlie."

She took a quivering breath, "Hello… Flum. Remember… me? Remember your… captain?"

"Member. Captain girlie. Pretty girlie."

"That… that's good— and kind of you to say… Flum." She glanced around nervously. "W—we just wanna escape. You… you can escape with us too. Would you like that?"

"Scape? Like?" Rising up, Flum's lips curled in agony. His knees cricked loudly and his spine crackled as they straightened, and his shoulders popped one after the other. He towered to his full height, almost twice as tall as Caetriona herself, and drew a trembling breath. "No scape for Flum. Flum like here. Like… captain." His loincloth rose up, dangling and waving in the air as his phallus swelled toward her. "Make captain girlie feel good."

Her gaze fixated on that while her head shook nervously. "Oh… no. No, Flum."

"Flum make lotsa girlies feel good."

She stumbled back with dread. "No, Flum. You didn't make those girls feel good. You… you killed them, Flum! Do you understand? You… killed them! And… I… let you."

"Kill? Flum no kill!" Furious, he lunged at her, faster than expected, and knocked her off her feet with a swipe of his arm. "Captain lie!" She tumbled to the ground, gasping as the wind blew out of her. "Captain like others. Make fun of Flum. Chop Flum. Mash Flum. Make food Flum. Flum sneak food and Flum punished! But Flum so… hungry! Only good time Flum have with girlies. Girlies have good time."

He lumbered toward her as she staggered to her feet. "I'm… sorry, Flum. For what they did. What I did. But, none of those girls had a good time. Not one! They died, Flum! I know you didn't mean it, but you killed them!"

"Captain lie! Lies bad!" He lashed out again, knocking her off her feet once more. She flew back against the cliff-face, the jagged rocks scratching up her arms and legs. A cut over her eye oozed blood. He lumbered forward, rearing his hand back. Caetriona braced for another strike, but it never came. She sat up, wiping the blood from her brow, and stared.

Flum slowly turned his head to one side and gave a faint grunt. Lonn was on him, Zaude's dagger digging deep into his shoulder. The troblytes went silent as the giant reared back and swiped the journeymin away, sending him into the mud. He splashed down, digging his fingers deep to slow down and get himself back on his feet as Flum charged after him. In that silence, Lonn breathed deep and yelled out, baring his teeth and pounding his chest, an act the troblytes understood as he mimicked them, before drawing his sword. The labored silence broke as the creatures howled out, taking great delight in the spectacle below.

The giant swiped out, deceptively fast, but the journeymin slid away, drawing his blade along Flum's arm. He gave a wail in pain as the blood streamed down his arm. Even the troblytes were surprised, but it only made them hiss and howl more.

The journeymin kept moving, making it difficult for his larger opponent to land a strike. But it was not easy. He felt the waft of air as Flum's hand swiped too close. And both the cold rain and muddy terrain made it more challenging to keep his footing. The cumbersome sword made it more difficult to remain agile, too, so when he found Zaude's dagger in the mud, he snatched it up.

Rolling away once more from Flum's swiping arms, he suddenly found himself between the giant's legs and jabbed the dagger upward. Flum moaned in agony as his sack split open. Three testicles spilled from the jagged wound and tangled around his legs as he flailed his hands one way then another to get at the smaller opponent.

In that frantic moment, the journeymin severed the giant's hamstrings, sending him crumpling to his knees. All Lonn heard through his gasping was the rain as the troblytes went silent and still in their alcoves. The giant whimpered and cried, "Flum… hurt… Flum. Make hurt… stop."

Staring down at the miserable giant, Lonn took the dagger up once more and jabbed it hard into the back of his neck. "I'll… make it quick." He gave the blade a sharp twist, and the giant slumped down in the mud with a sighing gasp, finally still. Standing over the body, the young journeymin slid his dagger back into his belt and caught his breath.

When one of the troblyte's barber blades splashed into the mud beside him, he took it up hesitantly while the troblytes chattered excitedly above. He knew what they expected and was happy to disappoint them, stepping over Flum's body. Grasping their discarded pack and Caetriona's hand, he ran. "Time to go, my lady!"

She glanced over her shoulder, seeing their excitement turn to anger. "Think you fecked them off some, my sweet lord." He could hardly concern himself with that, focused on the path before them. They had to take advantage of the rain and gain some distance.

Sometime during the night, they slowed, exhausted and hungry, unable to maintain a heavy pace. She took the lead, better able to see their path. But they eventually had to stop for a proper rest. Pulling the pack from his shoulder, Lonn rifled through and found the rations from the *Virgin Wanderer's* stocks. "A bit wet, but it's something at least."

Caetriona chewed hers down avidly. "Better than those bloody berries." As they sat huddled under the foliage of a large trush, the rain faded to a trickle, and then there was nothing but the faint drips of rainwater off the violet leaves above. "They'll be coming after us."

The journeymin nodded faintly, flipping the barber's blade over in his hand. He was surprised how well balanced it was. "Once it's a bit dryer. Probably by morning."

"Doubt we'll be too hard to follow with all those mud tracks." She eyed his interest curiously. "Why'd they toss that thing down?"

"They… expected me to scalp him." He shrugged. "Saw them do it to others. Some sort of… ritualistic humiliation."

A faint smile grew on her lips. "Same with all that yelling and… chest pounding?"

Lonn's cheeks flushed. "No. That was… something… else." They both perked up when a howl sounded off in the distance. "Sounds like they're not waiting."

"Bloody beasts won't give us a break!" They were off again, moving as quickly as possible across the increasingly rough terrain. The howling troblyte hunters closed in from the trushes above.

The journeymin cursed himself for not considering that and grew so distracted looking upward, he bumped into her when she suddenly stopped. "My lady?"

She tilted her head. "You hear that?"

"What?" he heard nothing as she took his hand and led him west. As they got further along, the air wavered with a faint rumble. "A river!" he shouted, excited by the thought of safety.

Caetriona helped him up the final bank, but faltered when she at last saw the wide raging river swelled by the rain. She grabbed him, shouted over the thunderous roar. "On second thought… no. I… I can't cross that!"

As the clouds parted and the moon shined down, he saw the river careen over a cliff down into a lower part of the Ciration Forest. He also saw the fear in her face along with the whole forest behind them shuddering violently as the hunting party advanced. "No choice, my lady!" He grabbed her hand and pulled her in.

As she splashed into the dark cold, Caetriona cried out, "Lonn! I…" cresting the surface with a sputter, "Can't!" and went under again, her head rising just in time to see the approaching riverfall, "Swwiimm!!"

7   The River

Her hand slipped from his as they went over the cliff, and the pounding pressure pushed him down hard into the river far below. His chest burned for air as he scraped along the bottom before finding the strength to push off and claw his way to the surface. Searching around frantically, he coughed and sputtered, "Caetriona?!"

The moon shined sporadically through the parting clouds giving him fleeting glimpses of the rippling waters around him and, much to his relief, the far riverbank. His feet found solid ground and trudged from the cold waters. His cramped hands wiped his sunkissed locks from his face as he searched. "Caetriona!" There was no response in the darkness.

Shielding his eyes from the moon's glare, Lonn looked for any trace. A break in the rippling currents revealed the glare of her white sleeves. She floated face down. "Oh, feck!" Shedding both pack and belt, he dove frantically back into the river after her. She was cold and still as he flipped her onto her back and swam them both to the shore. Gasping, he dragged her to solid ground. It was clear she was not breathing. His mind raced in a panic before recalling a story.

If only he had bellows and a clothespin.

Doing the only thing that made sense, he tilted her head back. Pinching her nose and clamping his mouth over hers, he breathed deep before pushing repeatedly down on her chest with clenched fists. "Breathe, Caetriona! Breathe!"

Her whole body gave a jerk as she sputtered, the water draining from her lungs, and gasped. The young journeymin collapsed beside her, sighing relief, "That's it. Breathe slow."

"we—" Getting all the water out of her lungs, she coughed, "survived?"

"Seems that way," he laughed. "Thought I lost you there."

She fumbled, trying to sit up, but was too weak. "Almost."

"I have you, my lady." He helped her up.

"where… are we?"

"The far bank…" The sound of the riverfall hissed somewhere in the dark distance. "No telling how far down river we are, but we should be safe until morning." He retrieved their pack from further up the bank and pulled out the last of their food supplies. "Here. A bit soaked, but it's all we've got left, I'm afraid."

She took the strip of meat and sucked on the tip. "Thank you."

"It's nothing, my lady."

"It wasn't nothing, Lonn." She leaned in, salty lips pressing against his, and slowly drew back with a smile. "I've… wanted to do that for a while now."

"I…" Looking at her in the moonlight, he grew flustered. She shivered. "I… I should get a fire going. It's a cold night, and we can't risk catching fever chills."

"If you think that's a good idea." Caetriona pulled her legs against her chest, holding them tight to keep herself warm while Lonn searched the forest for dry wood. There was hardly any kindling due to the rain, but he found enough to get a small fire started.

When the orange glow flared up, warming the air, they started to feel better. But both were still soaked through. "Never get dry wearing all these wet clothes." She tugged off her vest and tunic, wringing out the water before laying them on the rocks circling the pit. "You, too, my sweet lord."

Lonn awkwardly turned away as he pulled his tunic off. She smiled, "Striders, too," and flung hers down beside her tunic. "We'll dry much faster."

"It's just…" he stammered, yanking them off one leg at a time.

"Not like you've never seen me unclothed before. You don't have to look away."

"It's not that. It's…" There was strain in his voice. "humm…"

"Lonn, look at me." He turned, face full of embarrassment with his hands covering his groin. "oh. That's what you're worried about?" She smiled sympathetically and pulled him close. He relented as she took him in her hands. "Feels nice. Firm. Warm."

"Caetriona… I…"

"Shh." She kissed him again. "No need to pound your chest, my lord." But his heart pounded. She settled back in the grass and pulled him into her with a gasp, "oh! that's…" She sighed, words lost as he pressed close. They kissed and more in the orange-white glow of the crackling fire and the midark moon overhead.

Caetriona's eyes fluttered open and stared up at the sun-lit sky. Beside her, the young journeymin rested contently, head on one breast, arm draped across her with his hand clasping the other. Their legs still tangled from the night. Feeling him pressing firm against her, she ran her fingers through his hair. "Are you awake, Lonn?"

He mumbled into her, "No. Still dreaming."

She smiled. "It's past sunrise."

Slowly opening his eyes, looking into hers, he felt different, and not just from the ache in his groin. "Is this what it feels like to be devoured?"

"Hmmm. Three times, no less." She smiled. "And hoping for a fourth, it seems."

His face flushed. "I think… that's just my morning rise, my lady. Not sure my sack has anything left. Feel drained."

"Then we should let it rest." She kissed him before sitting up, wincing at the dull ache between her own legs. "oooh. So, that's what that feels like."

Lonn sat up, looking down at himself and then her, stiffening in alarm at the splotches of blood on them both. "Caetriona, did I hurt you?"

"No. Course not," she replied with smile, "That's… normal for a first time." Finding the healing salve in their pack, she dabbed a bit on the tip of his phallus. "So energetic… you just tore your foreskin a little. It'll heal up. Just like…" She slid some between her legs and laughed. "Oh."

"What's so funny?"

"It's… gone." she sighed, "You… took it from me… for good. Virgin Devourer no more."

He looked at her, surprised by the revelation. "Then… you were a… that was… yours, too?"

"Hmm." She nodded.

"But I thought…" He considered the life she had as a raider and the delicate ruse she maintained. "Then we can both leave all that behind." Rising slow and unsteady, he wandered down to the river. "Coming?" She nodded, stepping into the cold water with a shiver to wash off their night's exertion. He took her hand, leading her out deeper. "So, how is it you never learned to swim?"

"Lived on a steamrunner all my life, Lonn," she laughed. "Just never came up."

He started to ask about that but bit his tongue, knowing she was sensitive where her parents were concerned. Instead, he floated further out. She eyed him skeptically. "We might have to do this again if the troblytes catch us up." She groaned and kept going until her feet barely touched the riverbed, reluctant to go further. "Okay. This'll be fine," he laughed. "Just lay back and relax. Kick your legs up."

She floundered, splashing in the water on her first attempt. "Don't know about this."

"Just relax." Reaching under the water, he supported her, "Tilt your head back and spread your arms out," before pulling back as she floated. "There. Just like that."

"Lonn…" Concern grew in her voice as the currents tugged at her, "I'm floating away."

He laughed as she twirled about in a semi-circle. "Swing your arms down to your sides." The momentum propelled her back to him when she did. "See? Easier once you get the hang of it."

"And how long does that take?" she asked, splashing about to regain her footing.

"Long as necessary, I suppose," he replied, helping her to shallow water. Together, they splashed back to shore. "We can keep working at it."

"That and your footwork."

"It was muddy!" The journeymin tensed, defensive, before realizing she was teasing him. "Thought I did fairly well, considering."

"You did." She kissed him. "With more practice, you can be even better." Leaning over, she wrung the water from her hair and laid back in the grass to dry out.

He collapsed beside her, looking at the distant riverfall, "Surprised that dunking pushed us so far away," and perked up. "What if we build a raft? Travel faster and offer us some protection."

"You mean…" Skeptical, she wiggled her fingers in the air. "Float? Down river? And you know how to make one?"

"Soreign showed me the basic principle."

"But you've never actually… done it?" She grew more hesitant at the idea.

"Well… no. But it's not that difficult."

Caetriona eyed him curiously. "Lonn… before… weren't you concerned about continuing north?"

Nodding faintly, he frowned. "It's just… Merribellith's not on good terms with Douchart. Could cause… problems, but it seems we have little choice."

"Then, we just won't say anything." She tugged on her clothes, "Stick to the souther border and get there through Astyria," before tossing his to him. "So, what'll we need for this raft of yours?"

"Saw some young trushes back there last night we could cut down," he pointed as he dressed. "Just need enough rope to tie them together and a long, sturdy branch for a navigation pole."

"Rope I can do." She laughed as he walked unsteadily to the forest. "Still walking a bit awkwardly there, my sweet, energetic lord."

"So are you," he smiled. "All the more reason to build a raft." She smacked his backside as he passed her and confronted the prospect of digging up deep-rooted trushes. He considered hacking at them with his sword but then realized the troblyte blade would make the work much easier with its serrated edging. It was still difficult work.

Once a decent number fell, he dragged them under his arms back to the shore and laid them out in a row nearly as long as he was tall and just about as wide. "About ten okts. Think that'll be big enough for the two of us?"

Surrounded by slivers of long blaygrass, which her fingers deftly stripped and wound together, Caetriona gave the frame a passing glance. "Hmm. Not cozy enough." He frowned, hefting up the blade and heading back into the forest until she grabbed his arm with a laugh, "It'll be fine, Lonn. Just teasing. How do you want them tied?"

He set the thickest trushes down as crossbeams before laying the others on top, tracing his fingers along and showing her the way the rope should hold the frame together in tight loops and crosses. "Curled around like that."

"Seems simple enough." She continued the work as he slipped back into the forest to gather larger leaves along with a few slender branches to build a small shelter. While he weaved them together, she tied off the first side of the raft and started on the other.

It took them a good portion of the day, but Lonn expected they would make up that time being able to travel down river both night and day. Setting the A-framed shelter into place, he glanced at her with a grin. "What do you think?"

She shrugged, dubious. "Seems… fine. But will it float?"

He pushed it into the water. After a moment's wavering, it settled, bobbing gently in the current. "Apparently."

Caetriona stepped aboard cautiously, wobbling a moment before finding her balance. "Not like a steamrunner, is it?"

Lonn leaped the distance and landed in a wide stance, holding the navigation pole firm for a long moment. Satisfied it was taking both their weight, he pushed off and settled beside her as they floated along. "Not bad for our first one, my lady.," he commented with a wide grin.

She leaned against him, kissing his cheek. "It was a good idea, my sweet lord."

The two weary travelers stretched back looking up at the darkening sky, thankful for the chance to rest. In the distance, the trushes rustled and swayed. It was not from the faint breeze. They both heard the distinctly familiar hissing and chattering. "Still hunting us."

"Imagine they'll be quite fecked with us for a time." She perked up, hearing the tones shift to a moaning howl. "Baiting woolgs again."

"Maybe that'll take their minds off us."

She rolled over, resting her head on his chest. Her hand travelled low, slipping under the hem of his striders, and fondling him gently. "Still sore?"

Lonn laughed, "Still sore," and ran his fingers through her hair. She tensed a moment as he fingered the tip of her ear.. "Sorry."

"It's… fine. Just…" she sniffed, "Not used to anyone touching me like that."

"Not even any of your previous conquests?"

"Fabled conquests," she laughed. "Not gonna let that go?"

"I just thought… well… with a reputation like yours…"

"As a vile raider, I made a habit of devouring young virgins? Honestly, the dirty things they get in their heads. Who even told you about that?"

"Old Zaude mentioned it."

"And of course, you just took his word."

"I was in a cage. Didn't seem that farfetched at the time."

"Well, yours was my first," she sighed, "I did almost lose it once… against my will. Cost my innocence, but somehow, not that."

He slid his hand along her back. "Is that when you started doing… this… to yourself?"

"I suppose it was," she cleared her throat and steered the conversation away. "But, what about you, my sweet lord?

Was I truly your first conquest?"

Lonn laughed. "You don't believe me?"

"Well… I've been to docks all over. Heard plenty from tavernmaidens about what young lords get up to. All that coin. Think they can get away with anything. And all those maidens should be grateful… even honored by the attention. But to hear it told, they're either too forceful or far too inexperienced. The worst of them are both, of course."

"Of course." He hesitated. "And… me?"

"Neither," she laughed.

"I… just… did what felt… right."

"For us both." Her cheeks flushed as she gazed up at the moon. "And I did enjoy it."

"So did I, my lady."

"I… wasn't sure I would. After all that time being around those raiders… seeing it taken relentlessly by force… the idea… it scared me. Terrified me." She hesitated a long moment before confessing, "Wasn't even sure about you at first."

Curiosity got the better of him as he asked nervously, "Caetriona, did… you really want me to kill you that day on the mideck?"

"I thought I did. Yes. But… then you spared me. You spared me, and I began to have doubts… wonder…" She laughed. "Wasn't really sure what to think, and then there you were again, standing there, dagger drawn, so determined. Finally put an end to me for all my misdeeds. Again, you dashed all my expectations and spared me."

"Thought you were whipping a prisoner."

"I know." She sighed. "Certainly wasn't expecting you to barge in on me like that. Put my mind in quite a scramble. Just happy you didn't fail my test."

Lonn perked up. "Test?"

"The couch or bed." She laughed. "Silly, really, now

that I think back on it."

He eyed her. "So… had I taken the bed?"

"I… don't know. Certainly wasn't ready for that. Prob-ably've kicked you out… back in the cage you'd go." She shook her head. "And I wouldn't even know what a horri-ble mistake I'd made."

The young journeymin laughed. "If you had any doubts, you certainly didn't show it. You just seemed so… confi-dent. But I wasn't ready either," he admitted.

"Glad we're well past all that now. No point dwelling, my sweet little lord."

"No. Happened the way it happened."

They fell silent and took turns during the night sleep-ing and keeping watch. They dared not risk the raft run-ning aground or falling prey to an attack. When sunrise came, they pulled the raft to the far bank to stretch their legs. They even returned to their previous routine of sword practice followed by swimming lessons.

Caetriona sat by the fire to dry herself off after one such session. Lonn disappeared for a short time to relieve him-self in the bushes only to return cupping a handful of berries. "More purp berries. Seems that's all that grows in these parts."

She appraised them disdainfully and plucked a few, pop-ping them in her mouth with a grimace. "Can't live on these for long." She glanced at the water. "Haven't noticed any-thing swimming along in there, have you? Nice, fat polloun-ders or herrerels?" Her stomach growled. "Even settle for a bloody gilverish."

"Nothing near the surface. Maybe deeper." He glanced into the forest. "We could risk going further from the river-bank… see if we can catch something."

She blinked, surprised at the suggestion. "Too risky. Might rile up another troblyte tribe and ruin what little safety we have."

He stamped out the fire and set the raft off. "We should move on."

She jumped aboard and settled down before he joined her. "Hopefully won't be much longer before we reach the edge of this bloody forest."

"Does seem to go on a distance." He took up the pole and pushed them along.

As their routine blurred together, Lonn and Caetriona both stopped counting the days. All their focus was spent on stopping at regular intervals to forage for berries, as there was little else to find. She sat on the riverbank after another swimming session, surprised how quickly she had taken to it. She even managed to hold her breath long enough to dive to the deeper part of the river, but there was no sign of anything edible, much to her disappointment.

"Lonn?" She glanced around, figuring he had once again retreated into the forest to relieve himself, and wondered why he did not just use the river like her. But he was gone longer than usual. "My sweet lord, where'd you get off too?" Anxious, she hastily tugged on her clothes and grabbed her sword. "Lonn?!" Finding him further along the bank, she sighed relief, "Don't scare me like that!"

"Were you calling?" He pulled himself from a blue-leaved berry bush. "Sorry. Didn't hear."

"Clearly." She eyed his cupped hand, curious. "What've you got there?"

He grinned. "Iunna berries! Makes a change from all those purps." He reached out, offering the small red berries speckled in white spots, but she jerked back. "What's wrong?"

"Get rid of them!" she gasped, "And wash your hands!"

He instantly dropped them on the ground. "What's wrong?"

"Lonn! They're poisonous!" She stared at him, alarmed. "You didn't eat any, did you?"

"No. But I was going to. Had them before, I'm sure." He trailed down to the river and washed his hands off, drying them along his striders. "Sorry. Didn't mean to frighten you."

She bit the tip of her thumb and stared at the pile of berries., "Not your fault. You didn't know." With a shake of her head, she returned to the raft. He trailed behind with a sigh, finding her hunched under the shelter when he hopped aboard and pushed them off.

Lonn remained silent, letting the moment pass. They had been in the forest too long. Fortunately, it seemed the troblytes had completely lost their trail. Neither of them had heard any sign of the creatures in days, which was a relief at least, but their growing hunger was a pressing concern. They needed a proper meal, and the ravenous creatures had clearly hunted the forest thin. It was no wonder they had turned on their own as a means to sustain themselves, but even that could not last indefinitely. His laugh jerked her from her thoughts. "What's so funny?"

"Oh." Seeing her mood brighten, he smiled. "I just realized… we actually know more about troblyte society than anyone else in all of Nolavah."

"Arretatingoc," she corrected, lying back and staring up at him. "And we might live long enough to get out of this fecky forest to speak of it. Could even write one of those travelogues that are so popular among the avid explorers."

"You think people would actually read it? It's not like anyone would dare venture here."

"The curious ones would… read it, I mean. Only the

utterly mad would come here willingly. Of course, it'll draw some of those to make the attempt now that we know it's at least possible." She smiled. "You could put a warning on the cover. 'Leave the troblytes bloody well alone!'"

Lonn took a deep breath. "Caetriona, my lady…"

"Yes, Lonn, my lord?"

"Look." She craned her neck back, looking ahead, and slowly rolled over. The forest thinned out, and a wide plain spread before them on both banks of the river. "We… made it."

8 Fizzpot

Caetriona stood on the shallow bank looking at the white stone bridge and the dusty path leading west and east. Lonn gathered their belongings, huffing across the gap from raft to shore, and eyed it one final time with a smile. "Held up better than I expected it would. Shame we have to leave it behind."

"Maybe someone'll come along and find a use for it, my sweet lord." Taking his hand, she kissed his cheek. "At least there's a path. And that means…" She craned her neck, squinting east, with her hand shading against the lowering sun, before finally pointing. "Over there!"

He followed her gaze and shook his head. "Can't see anything."

"Smoke. A farm. Maybe even a village." She pulled him along. "Hmm. Food. A bed. And…" she sighed, "A bloody nice, hot bath." Her stomach grumbled followed soon by his, leading them both to laugh. "A big meal."

Lonn hefted up one of the coin purses. "Have enough to last… for a while, anyway."

Their hunger compelled them to a quicker pace along the gravel path, but a bell ringing out in a chaotic fashion, growing louder as it neared, caused them to slow. His eyes grew large as an old farmin trudged along the curving path followed by a shaggy beast. "Never seen a rhinoxen up close before." It had a horn jutting from the bridge of its muzzle and two others curling out from the top of its long head. The bell dangled from a bright yellow ribbon wrapped around its neck as it lumbered along hauling an empty wagon.

Caetriona eyed him, surprised. "Need to get out more."

"Oh. Ho. Forgive me. Didn't see you there. Eyes not so good these days." Staring down at the path, the farmin perked up and glanced to his companion. "Make room Soochie. Let the…" They drew closer, and he blinked, seeing their dirty clothes and worn faces. "Oh, my. Well-traveled, the pair of you."

"It has been a rough road for us, good farmin," Lonn cleared his throat, "Could you perhaps tell us where we are?"

"Where you are depends on where you came from."

"We…" he hesitated a moment, "came through the forest."

Forcing a smile, Caetriona set her hand gently on his shoulder. "From Astyria."

"Through… that forest? From Astyria?" The farmin tilted his neck toward the Ciration Forest stretching along the souther border. His cheeks rose as he let out a long laugh, "Oh! You traveling jesters! Almost had me for a moment there. That's a good one, but no need to exaggerate *that* much. Make it believable at least."

Lonn's brow furrowed. "We… didn't. Just… looking for food and board."

"Sure you didn't! Sure. Don't wish to tell me, that's fine. Meant no offense." The old farmin wiped at his cheeks. "Fizzpot's just up the ways. Sall's at the tavern. Has a room or two she can put you up."

"Fizzpot?"

"That's what I said, young lad." He led Soochie along the road, "Have a good day to you both," and chuckled to himself, "heh. From the forest."

Caetriona watched as the two continued along until they

turned, out of sight. "Not very helpful. Still feels like we're lost."

He shook his head. "Why didn't he believe us?"

"Some people dwell on fears and believe things impossible." She took his hand, pulling him along. "I'm dwelling on food, and so should you, my sweet."

They carried along until the village came into view. It was a generous assessment, comprising little more than five buildings arranged in a half circle up a trail off the main path. Their angular roofs were freshly thatched with blaygrass and smoke from their hearths puffed from cobbled chimneys. Out front on the stoops were tied up hay bales along with barrels of plucked produce.

The farmins finishing their day's toils in the nearby field stopped, eyeing them curiously as they walked up the path. "Must not get a lot of travelers in these parts." Lonn scratched his head and looked at the buildings set before them. None appeared much different than the others, nor had any distinguishing markers as far as he could tell. "Which one's this tavern he spoke of?"

She had a similar moment of confusion until the door to the easter most building swiped open, and a drunken farmaiden stumbled down the steps with a burp. "Reckon that's the one." Caetriona shot the min a glare as she passed them by, lingering too long to gaze at Lonn as he hopped up the steps before scuttling off.

She stomped up the steps after him and went inside. It was cleaner than she expected, with a few farmins having an early meal. There were two at the bar guzzling down mugs of mog to ease away their labor. They were all locals and eyed the newcomers curiously for a passing moment before returning to their own interests or conversations.

Behind the bar, Sall, a stout and pique-faced keep, pulled a mug away from one of her patrons. "Tha's yer third helpin, and I's not seen no coin yet."

"Ah! Know I'm good fer it." The drunkard grinned. "Pay ya another way if ya'd like."

"Think even a quarter moon-turn shacked with you's worth three mugs? Let alone one?" She laughed, "Back to yer wife and dream, Freidol. Pry a few soppers from between her legs and pay yer tap!" She slammed the mug down on the back bar before seeing them. Her face instantly brightened with a wide smile. "Well! Don'tcha two dearies look like a couple a drowned micats."

Lonn nodded. "We… did go over a riverfall some many days back."

Caetriona frowned. "I almost drowned."

Sall laughed, slamming a large pitcher on the counter and sliding it down to the other waiting patron. "You traveling jesters! Good one, that is. Delivery needs a bit a work. No matter! What can Sall do you for?"

"Food and board for the night, keep."

Sall beamed. "Just so happens… can accommodate both. Only…" She eyed them. "Room's just a single bed."

"That's all we need." Caetriona smiled, leaning on the counter. "Is there a bath, too? Hot water?"

"Sure thing, dearie. Tank's topped. Wolk's got plenty left in her." Sall shifted her demeanor, tapping the bar. "Only a matter of…" Uncertain of the amount, Lonn slid five gilvers across the counter, and her smile quickly returned. "Lovely. More'n enough, that is," she laughed, "Happy to know I's accommodatin yer needs here."

"Would we be able to get our clothes cleaned?"

Sliding the gilvers into her pocket, Sall blinked. "Not a problem, dear. None at all. For that coin, I's offerin none but a premium service! Just set dem out. Fresh by morning. Guaranteed." She motioned. "First door. Top of the steps.

Have a meal sent up once I's cooked it."

Lonn nodded, pausing. "Sorry. One more thing. Could you tell us where we are?"

Sall stared at him blankly. "Why, Fizzpot, dear. Course."

"Of course. But..." He hesitated a moment. "Under whose banner?"

"Oh! Why that would be his right honorable Lord Barretun."

He nodded and followed Caetriona up the steps. "Very helpful. Thank you."

"Anytime, dear. Just let me know if you'll be needin anythin else. Anythin at all." She stepped around the bar and leaned down the steps to the cellar. "Weavul! Get yer cheeky bung outta my preserves and get up ere! Got work to do!" She returned to the bar, glancing down with a shake of her head as the door above closed. "Just a bad lot in life." She felt the gilvers in her pocket. "Tidy profit, though."

In the room above, Caetriona sighed relief as her gaze fixated on the large basin in the corner. "Been looking so forward to this!" She pumped the tap and smiled as it started to flow and tugged off her vest and tunic, tossing them toward the door, while Lonn set their pack down. "So, you know this Lord Barretun?"

"Only by name. Banners for King Aesinar, so definitely puts us somewhere in Douchart."

"I know you're concerned about that, but shouldn't be a problem so long as they think we're..." She pulled off her striders and dipped her hand in the basin, pulling it away sharply. "Ow! That is hot!" Perching on the basin, she waited for the water to cool some.

"Jesters," he finished her original thought, looking down

at himself. "Don't know why. We're not exactly dressed for it."

"Does it matter?"

"Suppose not. We'll just keep going east as planned."

"Oh, that's…" she finally slipped into the basin with a sigh before dunking her head under. Sputtering to the surface, she eyed him with a grin. "Room enough for us both, Lonn."

He tugged off his clothes, folding them in a neat stack along with hers before pushing them out the door. He quickly slid into the basin beside her. "That is nice."

She looked at him, cheeks flushed. "Not still sore, are you?"

"No. You?" She shook her head. He settled into her, kissing her and more as the water sloshed from one end to the other.

When the water cooled, there was a knock on the door. Caetriona sighed, "Better be our meal."

Lonn wrapped a towel about his waist and opened it. There was a small girl with frazzled black hair wearing in a simple smock standing out in the hall balancing a full tray. He took it with a smile. "Thank you, Weavul, is it?" She tilted her head with a silent nod, peering inside as the door closed.

Her stomach grumbling, Caetriona slipped out, drying herself off, "Stayed in too long. Skin's all wrinkled," and drew the towel about her as she plopped down at the table. With the tray between them, he dug into his stew and she into hers. After taking a few heaping bites, she stretched her bare foot out, rubbing it along his leg. "So, what's the first thing you plan to do when you get home?"

He wavered mid-bite as her foot slid along his thigh. "Hadn't given it much thought, honestly."

"Really?"

He grinned, "Been preoccupied."

"Have you now?"

"And I will be again in a moment if you keep that up."

"You certainly will." She smiled, avidly eating her stew as her toes wiggled into his groin.

Downstairs at moonrise, the patrons stumbled home after a long day in the field and a hot meal along with ample amounts of mog. Sall stood at the bar, cleaning up. As it grew quiet, Weavul glanced up at the thumping and muffled moans coming from above. "Loud little filly, she is." She glanced at the girl. "Pshh. Pshh. Dem piles not washin themselves. What'd I take you in fer if you ain't gonna pull yer weight?" The girl jerked back when the room grew quiet again, hunching over the washbasin as Sall dried the dishes she set on the counter.

The thumping returned as they finished the last of them. "Ah, to be so young. What's that? Second? Third time now?" She shook her head and sighed, "Well, let the poor girl have er fill." Weavul stared up with a gaping mouth and curious eyes. "Down the cellar shoot with you. No mad ideas gettin in at head a yers." The girl scrambled down the steps.

When she was gone, Sall poured a mug of hot tefee and set it on the far table in the corner. "On the house… so long's you pay what you promised." The figure sitting in the dark tapped a shiny claw against the ceramic mug several times before tossing a coin purse onto the table. Sall snatched it up and tucked it into her pocket. "In the morning. Hear? As agreed."

She did not sleep that night, nervously busying herself as best she could, and was surprised when she heard noises before sunrise. Straightening out her dress, she grew increasingly tense as footfalls came down the steps. She put on a smile when Caetriona strode up to the bar. "Morning dearie. Bet you slept well."

"I did." She straightened her tunic and buttoned her vest. "Appreciate you getting these clean."

"Ah. No problem at all." She tilted her head. "But, my. Absolutely glowin, you is. Plundered you right proper, now, he did. Them youngins. Always so full a spunk."

She settled on a stool, face red, and leaned close. "We… we weren't… too loud, were we?"

"Nuthin ta be concerned over. These poor walls've heard nough drowned sorrows." She busied herself at the back counter, "Always… heh… nice ta have a bit a vigor brighten the place," before turning and sliding a mug toward her. "Drink that up now." Caetriona did with a few gulps.

Their attention drew to Lonn as he came down the steps, pack slung over his shoulder, adjusting his belt and swiping the grit from his eyes. "Oh. Such a pretty lad hidden under all tha grime." Sall looked him over with a grin and slid the drained mug to the back counter. "Quite a catch you got there." She set another mug for him as he set his pack down and perched himself on the stool beside Caetriona. "There you go, dear. Drink up." Her lips wavered. "Such a pretty pair you make."

Caetriona looked at Sall and felt as if she were swaying. Beside her, Lonn lifted the mug to his lips, but she reached out, covering the top with her trembling hand. He glanced at her, worried. "What's wrong?"

"Sall…" She felt her stomach tighten. "What… did you… do?"

"Nuthin personal. But… I's got no choice in it," The stout keep frowned and slid a weathered parchment out from under the counter and onto the bar. They both knew exactly what it was. "And I really can use the coin."

He steadied Caetriona as she wavered on her stool. "Are you alright?"

"I… I… I feel…" She looked at him, panic in her face.

"Didn't get both, but she's the only one that mattered." They both turned as a figure stepped out from the back corner and into the light. The Head Merchant scratched at his patched eye with a metal armature glove that pressed into tatters of skin near his elbow. His metal fingers ended in taloned claws. "Been some time, Journeymin Lonn."

His brow creased. "Who're you?"

"Really?" The Head Merchant balked. "Don't recognize your handiwork back in Alisard?"

Caetriona leaned in, finding her vision blurry. "Not… without my… dagger in your eye."

"Oh. Didn't recognize you with that claw hand."

The merchant clenched his armature. "Lost it when I grounded your miserable steamer."

Lonn blinked, surprised. "How'd you even find us?"

"I…" he stammered, "I'm a head merchant. It's what I do!"

Caetriona blinked through her hazing vision with a huff, "Just… what'd you and that binch do to me?"

"After our last little bout?" The Head Merchant shrugged. "Figured… tillup would knock the fight outta you for a spell. Calm you down."

"Tillup? Calm *me* down?" Caetriona gripped Lonn by his tunic, "Run! Fast as you can! Don't look back! Go!" and pushed him toward the door, but the Head Merchant cut him off.

"Kid's not running anywhere. Collect on his warrant, and then you and me'll have some time together. Got this claw on account of you. I'll enjoy slicing you up with it. Eye for an eye. Arm for an arm."

Sall stared at him, wide-eyed. "I's not agreed to—"

"Shush up, keep!" He reached for his sword. "So, Journeymin Lonn… just you and me now. Ready to come quietly?"

Before he could even grasp his sword, Caetriona rose up, hissing through clenched teeth, "Told you before!" Her glaring eyes clouded white, leaving only red veins throbbing along the surface. "Not going anywhere with you! He's with me!"

The Head Merchant took a reflexive step back. "Ah. Unexpected."

Caetriona lunged at the Head Merchant, her head a jumble of memories old and new as the tillup surged through her. All she felt as her anger toward the Head Merchant and the old raider captain merged was an unbridled rage. She lashed out, hardly making a distinction between them. "Leave my Lonn?! My mother?! My Lonn! My mother! Alone!"

Her mind flipped between the tavern and the old cabin aboard the *Virgin Wanderer* as she grabbed her stool and swung it down, shattering it over them. They lifted their arms to defend against the assault before lashing out themselves with clenched fists. Her head whipped back, but the tillup induced rage numbed her even as she tasted blood. She ducked as they swung again, swiping out with a hooked thumb. She clawed at their face and dug deep, tearing into their eye as they cried out.

They grabbed her by the hair and punched her in the stomach, forcing the air from her as she stumbled back. Pulling a dagger, they slashed at her. The blade dragged along her arm, but if she felt the pain, she did not cry out as the blood streamed down her pale skin. They lunged in, thrusting low, but too slow. She clutched their wrist with both hands, twisting until something snapped and the dagger fell to the floor. She kicked out and felt their arm tear loose as they stumbled back. There was a cry. More blood splattered across the floor, causing her to slip.

In that distraction, they backhanded her, knocking her over a table. She tumbled to the floor but scrambled to her feet, tearing off the table leg and flinging it around like a cudgel. They doubled over, gasping. She brought the leg down again, knocking them to the floor, and tossed the weapon aside. Hooking her fingers into a nearby cabinet, she tore it loose, bringing it crashing down. They cried out, their legs crushed under the weight. Her breathing came in short rasps through clenched teeth laid bare as she drew her sword and raised it over her head. They looked up at her, faces contorted in fear.

"Stop!" The fight that seemed to stretch out had lasted only a few moments, surprising even Lonn by its rapid ferocity as he recovered and moved to put an end to it. "Caetriona, stop!"

She turned sharply and saw a flash of her mother as she brought the sword down, but the image tore apart. A flare from the sunrise burst through a window. Her eyes went wide, seeing him cast before it, with wings of sun flames stretching from his back. "Lonn?" Dropping her sword, she fell to her knees, blinking through the haze that clouded her vision and mind. "help... me."

He was at her side as she slumped to the ground, body trembling. "I've got you." Wiping the sweat from her forehead, the journeymin held her tight. "I'll always have you, my lady."

From behind the bar, Sall looked up and around. "It over?" She hefted herself off the floor, straightening her dress and adjusting her hair, and wandered around the ruined tavern in wide-eyed shock. "Bloody mess you made!" Caetriona glared, baring teeth and hissing spit and venom. The tavern keep jumped back. "Din't mean nuthin by it!"

Lonn tightened his grip. "Stop, Caetriona." She jerked her head toward him, finding his voice and gaze comforting, and breathed slower, calming down. "Better." He caressed her cheek and slipped his fingers through her disheveled hair.

It was then that Sall saw one of her ears and gasped, "Oh, bloody curses. Din't know she was…" With a shake of her head, she rushed to the door. The local farmins gathered outside, debating whether to enter or stay well clear. "Riot's drawn some attention." Turning to look at Lonn, she dug her hand deep into her pocket. "Well… I's not spectin a decent… not even a good recommendation, really, on account a all this. Not from neither of you. Can at least offer a refund ta cover my responsibilities here." She took his hand, returning their five gilvers. "Now, lad, can you carry her?"

Lonn rose up without hesitation. "I will."

"Then gather your pack there, and out the back you go."

He glanced down at the Head Merchant crushed under the cabinet. "What about him?"

"Don't you set no worries on him. Not goin nowhere soon. I'll see ta him. You see ta her," she sighed, "That why they after you?"

"No. It's a… misunderstanding."

"Some misunderstanding. Never a given her any a that if he told me she was… one a them."

Frowning, Lonn slipped his pack on and hefted Caetriona over his shoulder. "He didn't know. Nobody does."

"Well, I's not judgin that." Leading them through the back stores, Sall shook her head. "Watch er head now. Bit tight through ere." There were cabinets of fresh linens and supplies, even a few jars of preserves. She pushed open the service door. "Now run, you poor dearies. And best a luck to you." She frowned, watching him carry her, and then rushed back to the front. The Head Merchant gasped when she tapped his shoulder with her foot. "Dead, you dirty micat?"

"Wh… what'd that binch do to me this time?" He blinked through his one bad eye and saw his ruined armature scattered in pieces across the floor. "Ah! Just got that!" Reaching up with his good hand, he wiped at the blood dripping from under his eye patch. "That binch did it again?! He-healer. Need a bloody healer!"

"Not a good place to start makin demands." She stood over him, looking at the warrant notice. "This warrant even real? Or you jus usin it ta get yer revenge on at poor girl?"

"Girl?! You see what that thing did to me?! Ain't no girl! Feral beast that was!"

"Look it my place! A right wreck!" Sall kicked his shoulder. "I's a mind to let you jus stay there an bleed fer all this."

"B-but you won't." He eyed her and drew a slow breath, "You won't. Right?"

Trodding to the cellar shoot, she yelled, "Weavul! Grab a mop an bucket and get yer bloody bung up ere!" before stepping out to the front stoop. A growing number of curious farmins lingered in the courtyard. "Terribly apologetic about the riot. Had an unexpected… drunken outburst. Caused some redecorating."

She smiled wide. "Truth be told, I's needin one a you ta be so kind an fetch ol lady Narannia. Fer healin services… and whatnot." She looked around, seeing the locals eyeing each other, waiting for someone else to volunteer. "Take yer time. Sure there's no rush."

"Where's that bloody healer?!"

She ignored him, looking at the farmins. "Any a you lot?"

And while Sall waited for one of the locals to volunteer, on the far easter edge of the fields, Lonn huffed his way through the long blaygrass and up a shallow hill to a copse of trushes. He set Caetriona down against one and collapsed beside her to catch his breath. She flailed her arms out in a daze, mumbling faintly, until he held her tight. "Easy now. You're safe."

She turned toward him, her eyes slowly unclouding. Her cheeks grew clammy and puffed out as she doubled over to one side. He pulled her hair back as she vomited and retched. "Lonn?" she asked through coughing fits.

"Right here." He pulled the bottle of healing salve and swiped some along her arm and lip to mend her injuries. "These need treatment." She sat up, body trembling, as her eyes returned to normal. "Oh… looking better."

"Where…" She looked around before spotting the village in the distance. "You… carried…"

He smiled. "Of course."

Sniffing and hugging her knees, she turned away, "Don't look at me like that!" and cried. "I… I never wanted you to see me like that. Why didn't you run? Told you to run."

"Wasn't about to leave you behind." He scooted closer, but she flinched at his touch. He pulled away and leaned back against the trush. "But I had no idea tillup would do… *that*. Is that… normal?" The tillup addicts they encountered in Alisard all seemed more desperate than aggressive.

"For me, Lonn. Just me." Her body shuddered. "Don't know why."

"This happened before."

"Once." Her fingers wiped at her mouth. "Almost killed you, Lonn. Just like…"

He frowned. "Your mother."

"I didn't…" She sobbed, her head dropping on her

knees. "Oh! What I did to her was… so much worse!"

"You can tell me." He ran his fingers through her hair, trailing along her ear. "Please tell me."

"I… no!" She pulled away, refusing to be comforted. "You'll hate me… fear me. Just like the raiders."

He could hardly see that as a smile rose on his lips. "I love you."

She looked at him, shocked. "Y-you— how can you say that?! After… what I almost did?"

"Caetriona, I know you've had to do horrible things. I… can't say I understand it all." He looked around with a sigh, "There's a lot in this world I don't understand at all… but I know that wasn't you. And I know you're trying to make amends. That's all that matters."

"You don't know all of it."

"Then tell me," he insisted.

Despite being reassured by his sympathetic smile, she grew pale and sick at the thought. Having held tight the shame and pain for so long, it was hard to find the words, or even really where to begin. She took a slow breath, "My… mother…

9   Caetriona

She birthed me on the foredeck of the *Wanderer* when the brighmoon was at its highest. I asked her once, when I was old enough to understand little things, why my skin was so pale. Hers was the color of trush sapwood, while father's was darker, like charred cinders. She simply smiled, mussing my hair. "The loving eye above determines such things." She often talked like that, as if the moon was somehow… alive?

I sometimes wondered if… maybe she would've explained it when I got older.

It was just odd talk that I had little interest in. I took after my father in that regard. When she reached the point where she started mumbling, he simply smiled, humoring her mostly. Or he'd quietly slip away and busy himself in the engine room or up on the bridge. Always tinkering or fixing something. Even things that didn't really need to be fixed. I'd follow him around, always interested in what he was doing.

At times, I'd simply take it upon myself to explore, crawling through every duct… pulling open every panel. And just like him, I pulled things apart, more often than not without any idea how to put them back together. Always knew when I'd done something wrong. And he'd be there, standing over me with steamer parts spread all about, and sit by my side, pointing out my mistakes until I fixed whatever it was I'd broken in the first place.

When I was tall enough to reach the controls, he taught me how to fly. But that first time… just stood there, looking at everything, unsure of myself. "Oh, little Caet… another growth spurt?!" He humored me even though I was standing on a shipping crate. "Not out of a job yet, not until you're tall enough to see the bowsprit." Took my hand in his and placed them on the wheel, going through the motions of adjusting course by shifting the propellers to change the airflow. Even remained quite patient when I once purged the heligen from the siehd sail, and the *Wanderer* rocked so hard, we could hear mother's screams all the way from the kitchen.

Learned everything I know about steamrunners through him. "Can't trust anyone else to do the job right, little Caet," he would say, often right before bopping my nose with a greasy finger. "And if anything goes wrong, the only one to blame is yourself. As it should be."

As merchants of trade, our livelihood was in the *Wanderer*. We couldn't just ground at a dock if something went wrong. Because of his diligence, and ignoring my… many… many… mistakes, she always sailed smooth. And during the quiet times, I'd stand out on the bow gazing out at everything spread before us. Sometimes, I'd even crawl out onto the bowsprit and stare down as the world blurred below.

Until father caught me by the ankle and hauled me back.

Never mad, just cautious. He'd point out with a smile. "Someday, you'll carry on the family tradition. And you'll sail as far and wide as the horizon falls, little Caet. Hopefully even as far as the lost Corvaellum Forest itself. But that won't happen if you slip and fall overboard. Keep your feet deck-firm. Besides… can't direct our path with your head blocking my view."

Of course, he took risks himself, like the time he did a

mid-flight repair while we were hauling fresh herrerel. If you've never been set on by a flock of hungry puguuls… well, more than a few snagged in the propellers. Clogged the elch rotors so bad we were flying in lazy circles from midsun to fall. And there was father in his safety harness and goggles dangling over the edge plucking out feathers and carcasses until the rotors whirred back to life. Luckily didn't lose any fingers. Mother cooked up their best parts, though.

They left nothing to waste.

Didn't seem like it, but they made very little coin. Just enough to live on, but that was enough. We went where the trade paths were best, of course, but we always seemed to be heading west. Mother always said west was our true path. "We follow moonfall where her gaze lingers upon the great Corvaellum, and our people thrive." She was determined to find some promised land where aelfin lived free. But we seemed free enough. We had a steamrunner. Go where we wanted. Dock where we wanted.

Even though we did quite often for trade, father didn't trust the dockworkers to do anything but unload cargo. I didn't really understand it when I was that little. Now, of course, I know we were never really free. Always wary. Always concerned what the humins would do if they found out we were aelfin. The skies were dangerous enough. Didn't need problems grounded as well.

But father and mother both kept me away from all that. Even when we were set on by raiders, they both seemed to know what to do. I was ushered into a closet soon after the steam cannon fired out across the bow. It was a regular occurrence, especially over one stretch along the wester kingdoms. I heard everything from my hidden spot. The sound of our sails interlinking. The heavy bootfalls of a large figure. Even hidden away, the stench of mog was overpowering.

His name was Leandrus. Captain Leandrus the Libatious. Or the Lecherous, depending on who asked. His long, tefee-stained hair was always pulled back in a zorbatail. And he wore this old, green longcoat scarred with black stitches.

I came to know him… too well.

Chastised my father the moment he came aboard. "Aesard, Aesard, Aesard… always brings a smile to my face when I see the old *Virgin Wanderer* sail by. Until it reminds me just how light my purse is." His gruff voice softened. "Lovely to see you, though, Safrion."

"We… we don't have much."

"Never do," he laughed, raspy and thick. "Just how am I gonna protect you? All these little kingdoms and not a standing flotilla among them… draws a dangerous sort. Expensive to keep routes open for all you merchants." He gave a labored sigh. "I like you Aesard. Really do. But you know I can't cut a break. If others found out I went soft, they'll start holding back and then… well… what does that leave me and my half-starved crew?"

"I can make you stew," mother cut in.

"Safrion, I would eat anything out of your steaming cook pot." The captain grumbled after a long thought, "Alright. Fine. We'll only take a few things this time, some choice items… barely break even. Along with Safrion's enticing stew." He slammed a tankard down. "Drink to an agreement." The raider captain guzzled down half. Out of courtesy and following tradition, father drank the rest. "Agreed, then!"

Mother worked the kitchen while the captain lingered, sending his raiders below. I listened to them tearing through the hold for whatever valuables they could claim. That was the first time I ever heard Grauler's raspy voice. It sent shivers through me. "Tha's a good nough stash. Cap don't want us ta bleed er dry like the last one."

"Why? Ain't nuthin here."

The grizzled raider laughed. "Got his eye on a real prize fer certain."

Didn't know what he meant at the time. Also never learned how Leandrus discovered we were aelfin, but he'd been slipping tillup in their drink for… oh, I don't know how long. It was barely noticeable, but the results became obvious. For a while, father seemed better after one of his visits, and then he'd become lethargic, each time quicker than the last.

I was… maybe seven? the first time I really noticed something was wrong. Father started forgetting things he'd known by heart since I was little. He slipped on routine maintenance he'd taught me as far back as I could hold a tightwrench. Mother noticed it too but said nothing. Maybe for my benefit. Trying to keep appearances. I knew nothing of the Scourge back then.

But thinking back on it, it was clear she knew. Took over more and more of the trading business while father wasted away. And, I started hearing them argue, something that never happened when I was little. Always late at night, when they thought I was sound asleep. "What happened to the cronzes I gave you?"

Father's words slurred, "Dinnt giimmee nnuun."

"Spent it on tillup! Didn't you?" That was the first time I heard the word. "We made a promise we'd stay away from it, Aesard! Ever since we were youngins! By moon's light, think of little Caet?"

"pfft," he scoffed. "Shheez sslleeppiin." There was a long silence. "Ggrreeaat ssttuuf… tthhiis. Ttrry ssoomme."

I heard it ring out in my ears. She smacked him. Knocked

the tillup bottle from his hand. "Look what it's done to you! You're turning into a fiend!"

The truth was that it already had. All he ever thought about. From moonrise to sunfall. Not long after one of Leandrus' visits, we had to ground. She went out to barter while I tended the engine. He crawled after me, hovering, looking worse and worse, skin wrinkled, eyes puffed and clammy. His words were clearer, but rushed. "Hey little Caet… do your father a favor. Find tillup. Any tillup. Know where she hid it. You must!" He grabbed at me, insistent, until I knocked him away. It shocked me. Used to be so strong, but I brushed him off, a mere child. "I'd do it for you!"

But he wouldn't. Realized that soon enough. Say anything to get it. Was all he cared about. And mother… after a while, she simply stopped trying. Wherever he passed out was where she left him. It got to the point we had to lock him away when we grounded so he didn't wander off and disappear. I thought it was just so he wouldn't find any more of it and make himself worse. But she didn't want anyone discovering us, learning the family secret or falling victim to humins looking to do us harm.

Without him and his contacts, trade dried up, and there were fewer and fewer places we could find work. But that didn't stop Leandrus. In fact, the lecher counted on it.

Mother would make me disappear, hidden away, but I could still hear. Not everything. Didn't know what she was doing to keep the captain happy… not for a while. Naively thought he'd just go away and leave us alone. We didn't have the coin to pay him. Didn't realize that wasn't his interest where she was concerned. When he was with her, there was no talking. Just a lot of the same sounds mother made when she'd been with father late at night… before the tillup took him away.

It made me hate her.

I was… too young to understand. She only did what she had to.

By that point, we weren't doing much business. Coin was gone. Couldn't even afford the parts to keep the *Wanderer* in good shape. It was easy for him to find us. Same time every cycle. I'd get hidden away for a time while he had his way and then he'd leave, satisfied.

Only, he wasn't.

Came at sunfall that last time. During our meal before bedtime. She scrambled, panicked, hiding me away in the cabinet. "In here and stay quiet. Close your eyes and hands over your ears." But I couldn't bring myself to obey her. Saw it all through the slats.

She rushed up to him, tightening her robe as he pushed through the cabin door. "Captain Leandrus… it's… too soon. Barely been half a cycle."

He stared down at her before pulling her close, hands on her bung, squeezing. "Tired of hunting you down. Every steamer I see, I just want it to be yours. Tired of being parted. Can't stand it no more, Safrion." He tugged open her robe, hands pawing her all over. His mouth… I could see it on her face. Part of her liked what he did… even wanted it.

"My… mate's right there." She tugged on his arm, insistent. "Come to the bedroom."

That made me hate her even more.

"Such a pretty fletal. Too good for a fiend like him." He stroked her cheek and stood over father, slumped against the dinner table like usual, barely aware of anything. "Aesard, you in there? I'm taking your mate… well, I've taken her plenty, but now for keeps." He looked around. "And I've come to like this old steamer. Got… character. Taking the

Virgin off your hands, too." He knocked father off the table with his boot. "Hear me, Aesard? You even care?"

Father just lay there as Leandrus pulled his sword… this sword. "One of the first things I ever took from you. Beautiful craftfinship… couldn't bring myself to part with it. Saved my life… too many times. Doing you a favor and returning it. With interest." He thrust out. Mother didn't even try to stop him. In fact, all I saw on her face was… relief.

From father… not a single sound as the sword struck him through.

All I saw was his blood spilling out, staining the rug, and I knew death for the first time. "Father!" I burst out from my hiding spot, eyes blurry with tears, and fell over him as Leandrus wiped his sword off on father's striders.

He stared at me, surprised. "Safrion… Safrion… Safrion. Never told me you had a little fletal."

She tugged on his arm. "Forget her. Come to the bedroom."

He dragged me from father and lifted me up by my tunic. The way he stared brought a fear so bad I couldn't move. "And just as pretty." The stink of his breath made me retch as he licked his lips.

Mother gripped his wrist holding me. "Leave her be and do as we agreed. You… can have me. Anyway you want."

"Oh, fletal, I already have you. Every way I want." He grabbed her by the neck and kissed her roughly. "Quite the pair, you two together. Oh… I'll enjoy you both."

She kept her hand on his wrist, gripping it tightly until her knuckles went white. "Not if you want the *Virgin*. You'll never keep it flying. And she's the only one who can do that."

Leandrus considered that for a long moment. "That true, little fletal?" So scared, I couldn't even find my voice. "Got a tongue? Better have. And learn to use it proper." He grinned. "Like your mother, here."

I stammered through my anguish, "y… yes."

He considered it a moment. Felt like a whole Verlith Bloom went by. And then he set me down, hands sliding over my shoulders to straighten my crumpled tunic. "Alright. Dry your eyes. Tears're wasted on a fiend, even if he was your father. Now, little fletal… you're gonna make me a promise. You keep the *Virgin Wanderer* here in fit shape, flying strong. And I promise none of my min, not a one, will ever touch you wrong. And I won't either…" He looked at my mother. "Until your mother offers you up herself. Agreed?"

I was terrified, not really understanding what he meant, but my head nodded furiously. "a… greed."

He snatched up my cup of gower's milk from off the table and swigged down half before holding it out. Took it, hands trembling so bad I almost dropped it. Helped me get it to my mouth, and I gulped it all down quick as I could. He grinned, wiping away some that spilled down my chin. "Agreed!"

He dropped the empty cup on the table and turned to mother, forcing her over as he flipped up her robe. "Now, let's see that beautiful bung of yours."

Her face turned red. "Not in front of her!"

Leandrus simply laughed as he undid his striders. "Let her watch." It was the first time I ever saw one… his phallus stabbing into her with moans from them both. "A good lesson for when you give her to me." He gripped her hair, drawing her head up, forcing her to look at him. "And you will give her to me."

He was a monster. Red faced. Huffing and grunting. Relentless.

The look on my mother's face… some part of her enjoyed it. She… she even forgot I was there. Every uttered moan made my hate mix with disgust. But no matter how much I wanted to, I couldn't make myself look away. Stood frigid still in a puddle, warm feck dribbling down my legs, terrified that would someday be me.

Didn't move. Not while mother satisfied him. When they were done, he passed me by, laughing, "Bet you'll be just as good and twice as tight, little fletal." Even mussed my hair. Mother said nothing. Just straightened her robe and disappeared into the bedroom, leaving me alone with father.

Don't think I... no, never spoke to her again after that. Just... I just couldn't do it.

Fell to me knees and... when I woke up, Leandrus was nudging me with his boot. Some of the raiders were dragging father's body away in the bloody rug. I stared up at him from the floor. "Time to make good on your promise, little fletal. Get that old engine fixed up." Still couldn't move, bringing a wicked smile to his lips. "Reneging on our agreement already?" He tugged on the cords of his striders.

It was the only thing that got me to roll over and drag myself to my feet. While I slept, the raiders had gutted their own steamer, gravely damaged from a battle I knew nothing about. I saw them slit the sails, spilling the last of the heligen and sending it crashing to the ground. They had done a good job stripping it. Suddenly, there were parts aplenty to fix up what I hadn't been able to.

But I was broken.

Just felt numb all over. Kept dropping tools. It amused the raiders plenty, watching me stagger along the corridors. Took wagers, seeing how long I'd last. They also staked claims on who'd get what part of me after the captain broke me in. They made no secret of it. I knew exactly what each of them wanted to do to me, from my mouth to my... feet, oddly enough.

But Leandrus was feared and true to his word. Despite

the talk and bluster, none ever laid a wrong hand on me.

And I just busied myself in the *Wanderer*'s bowels fixing things, even when they didn't need fixing. Every once in a while, there'd be a demand… some need… like figuring out how to power the cannons they'd brought over from their wreck of a steamer. It was a good distraction. Kept me occupied.

But I couldn't ignore the sounds Leandrus and mother made at night. Sometimes she got so loud and enthusiastic, there was nowhere I could go to get a decent sleep except right there by the engine. Always got the crew roiled up too, and when their hands weren't good enough flogging their phalluses… there was always the raiding.

Knew that was part of it, but it didn't prepare me for my first. The high pitch of the cannons as they boiled up. The rumbling. The yelling. Even from the bridge, I could hear Leandrus barking orders down to me in the engine room. Steamer battles were such frantic things to me in those days. But those raiders… well weathered… it was so routine, they appeared bored. Just trying to get through it as quick as possible to get to the pillaging and… entertainment.

It was a relief when it was over. Everything grew so quiet. Though, Leandrus didn't let me stay hidden below. He pushed through the engine room hatch, looking around at the practical nest I'd made for myself so I never had to leave. "Get that pretty little bung of yours on deck. Scavenge everything you need before we ground that steamer for good."

Knew exactly what he'd say if I refused. But he enjoyed it, giving me some task to remind me of our agreement, knowing I'd do anything to ensure I didn't break my promise. There was a perverse pleasure in sending me among the raiders to bear witness to what they did. I was protected, skittering between them as they pillaged, ducking as they plundered, and averting my eyes as they set themselves upon those who weren't.

I could barely see anything through my tears as a girl not much older than myself at the time pleaded for them to stop. Screamed for my aid until her mouth was filled and muffled. They all had their way with her. Didn't even stop after they broke her back. Tossed her overboard when they were done. Her scream faded in the distance, drowned by them laughing.

And I… did nothing.

Stepping over bodies. Skirting around the blood. I did as I was told and mostly kept my head down. Did it so often it became normal. And I kept my promise. For so long, in fact, the raiders actually accepted me as one of their own.

There was this one who'd taken a liking to me. Not in the usual raider way. Deenauve actually saw me as something of a luck charm. Came down to the engine room, sometimes just to watch me work. "Fletal, we ain't never ben so cessful as since ya started tendin us." I was nervous when he pulled his blade, but then he flipped it around. "Fel betta if ya cun put up a fight. Teach ya this if ya teach me tha."

The others laughed when they found out, but I thought it was a fair exchange. Deenauve taught me everything about sword fighting. I tried to teach him everything I could about steamrunners. Even he admitted I was the better student.

Leandrus humored it. Long as I did as agreed, he cared little about what I got up to. Never let me anywhere near a real fight, though, even when I was good enough, which was fine by me. Needed me in the engine room, and he wanted me unspoiled.

Surprised him as much as me that mother refused to submit. In the kitchen less and less often, especially when

Flum took over cooking duties. And then she was simply…
in their room, always ready and waiting to satisfy him. And
she did in… every… way. But even after a few Verlith Blooms
passed, she still wouldn't give me to him. I only knew that
because he didn't set himself on me. But the desire to have
us both never left him. Always saw it in his eyes.

Not long into my fourth bloom as a raider…

hard to believe I was only fifteen…

Leandrus came down to the engine room, smile on his
lips. It gave me a sick feeling. But then, the way he leered
always did. "Little fletal… you should come. Your mother's
a right mess."

I was under one of the water tanks, trying my best to
ignore him. "What business is that of mine?"

"She's calling for you."

I huffed, showing my displeasure at being bothered.
"What's wrong with her?"

"Must've caught something a while back."

My heart pounded in my chest. I'd heard things… raider
talk. And considering what they did constantly, I wondered.
"Didn't catch a case of childish, did she?"

Leandrus blinked, surprised, but laughed it off. "Just
come with me, little fletal."

I knew the threats were soon to follow, so I did. Walking into that room after so long… the air was stale and
reeked from their constant forning. He closed the door behind us and leaned in close. "You know, a fin can't catch
childish from a min. But one thing they can catch…"

One look at mother sprawled out on the bed, and it was
clear she had the Scourge. He laughed even as I broke out
in a cold sweat. "I really wanted you both. Quite a prize.
But… your mother… stronger than I gave her credit, little
fletal." He kicked the bed, jarring her awake. "Tell her,

Safrion, my lovely Safrion. Tell her what you just told me? You'll love this."

My heart pounded until I could barely breathe.

Mother rolled over, a wistful smile on her lips. "You can have her… all you want… for some tillup." He flung a bottle onto the bed, and she snatched it up, slurping it down. And I found myself once again filled with fear.

He slipped under my tunic, his rough hands pawing at my bare chest. "Hear that, little fletal? Your mother finally gave you up." His tongue scraped along my ear. "Told you she would." Should've realized the lecher would cheat to get his way.

Pressed himself into me, tearing at my clothes, and… I… actually tried to fight back. So feeble, he laughed, "Little fletal's got some fire." Grabbed me by the neck and pushed me down on the bed. "Don't like my little loves too feisty, now. Hate to do this so soon…" Snatched the bottle from mother and poured what little was left down my throat. "But it'll make your first time easier… won't hurt as much when I plunder your tight little ginny." Clamped my mouth shut, forcing me to swallow.

Expected me to be docile. I was nothing of the sort. Forced his tongue in my mouth. All I felt was a sickness and his stinking breath. My vision blurred and everything became a haze. All my anger… so much rage… blooms in the making… spilled out. Bit down hard as I could, tearing his tongue from his mouth. He reeled back, screaming and gurgling blood. I tore into him. Tried to fight back, but I gouged out one of his eyes. Broke his arm before tearing it off. Slammed him over the table. Beat him with a chair. Clawed and kicked at his guts til they spilled.

And I… don't remember doing any of it.

It was the raiders bursting in that brought me to my

senses. They stopped cold, the fear in their eyes… so intense. I just stood there in his mess, half naked, drenched in his blood… devouring his severed sack.

None of them wanted to enter that room. Not even Grauler. Deenauve was the one, with a faint nod of his head, who reached in. "Sury ta botha ya, fletal." Grabbed the door and slammed it shut. It was good he did. I collapsed to my knees right then and there, heaving until my stomach quivered, utterly empty.

I knelt there… don't know how long. Cleaned myself up when I finally had the strength and found some fresh clothes. Too big for me, but it didn't matter. Too tired. Hungry. Sick. Utterly disgusted.

And what had mother been doing all that time? Dipping her fingers down the bottle, scraping up every last drop of tillup she could, and sucking them clean.

It made me so… angry.

Didn't say a thing to her as I grabbed her by the hair and dragged her behind me.

The raiders were all on the lowdeck, whispering amongst themselves, concerned in a way I'd never seen before. They all grew silent when they saw me. The fear lingered. Tense, some reached for their blades, wondering if I'd set myself on them next.

Just kicked a barrel down and threw mother over it. Swiped up a bottle of mog from one raider and a slab of meat from another. "Just have at her. Mouth to feet. Like you've always wanted. As your kind always does." Stood there for a moment, not exactly sure what would happen next.

It was Grauler who rose up. Even after all that time with them, couldn't pretend to understand their ways. But the raider code is pretty clear. "As you say, cap."

That… was my first act as captain. That was my birth

as the Virgin Devourer. A raider warning. A reminder. Then a joke. It just stuck.

All their frustration over not being able to do a thing to her or me over the blooms came out. And I… I just plopped down in the corner, feet propped on a table, chomping on that slab of meat, taking long draws from the bottle, and… and… watched.

Just been watching ever since.

Half way through the crew, she looked at me, her face covered in… their… filth… and she… smiled. I felt so angry and disgusted. I hated her so much. And when Grauler asked what he should do with her when they were finished… I… I… feck!

I had him sell her off.

Like she was nothing.

As if that would just make it go away.

There was… so much guilt… shame. Just made it worse. For her and every last one who came after.

It took a long time for me to realize the thing I was really angry and disgusted at… the thing I most hated… was… myself.

10   The Forest Once More

Hunched against the thick trush, Caetriona's shoulders trembled and her tears flowed free. "You see now, don't you, Lonn? H-how horrible I am? Don't deserve anything. Certainly not your... love."

He sat in the short grass, chin on his knee, listening to her tale, and reached out with a sympathetic sigh, "That must have been so difficult for you, Caetriona. Can't even imagine." She shied away from his touch, but he held her hand to give comfort. "But it doesn't change how I feel."

"How can you say that?!"

"Because that back there wasn't you. Over these many days, I've only just started to know you... the real you." He drew a faint breath, "And considering all that's happened... I have no idea where I'd be without you. I'm grateful for all you've done."

"Didn't do anything, Lonn. Still like that helpless, frightened child. Didn't stop the raid on the *Traverse*. Didn't hand you over to the city protectorate. Even when they were right there," she huffed, "Can't even ask Castanostrous a simple question. I'm... such a coward."

"Oh!" Lonn suddenly felt foolish and hugged her tightly. "I'm so sorry. I didn't realize."

"Thought it would've been obvious. I'm always running away."

"Not that," he sighed, "I... took your question."

She wiped at her eyes, sniffling. "It's alright, Lonn. Can't bring myself to ask it anyway."

"Next brighmoon. We'll find a door so you can ask her then."

"N-next? Are you… serious? Talking like that…" She blinked. "You really should hate me. I ripped you from your life."

"What life?" She was startled by his faint laugh, "Caetriona, you just ripped away the fantasy. Before the tourney, I didn't have a life. All I did was what I was told. I could never leave. I used to look over the Palisum ramparts at the city below and just wonder what things were like based on the stories I read. And they were nothing like being out here. This is real life. The first time I've really lived." He looked around. "And it's both brutal and… beautiful… like you."

She blinked, still baffled by his youthful innocence. "I… don't know what to say to that."

"Don't have to say anything." He shrugged up to her, rubbing her arm and the mending wound. "Feeling better?"

"A little" She nodded with a sniff and a swipe at her nose. "So, what now?"

"Head east to the border."

"You really wanna still be with me? Even after all that?"

"Of course, my lady." He took a nervous breath. "Actually, there is… something you should know before we reach Merribellith."

"Oh?" She swiped her disheveled hair from her face and peered at him, reminded of what Castanostrous had revealed. "And what's that?"

His cheeks flushed, embarrassed. "It was Soreign's idea. Being my first tourney and not really known, he thought I'd have more honest competition if nobody else knew who I really was."

"So, if not my sweet lord, then…"

"Lonn… Youta." He breathed deep, "Prince of Merri-bellith," and went stiff, thinking the worst, when she blinked and laughed.

"So, that's what you've been hiding all this time?"

"What?" He gulped, surprised. "H-how did you—"

"Castanostrous mentioned you were hiding something."

"She did? And you didn't say anything?"

"You *were* right there." She lifted a trembling hand to his cheek. "Besides, didn't feel I had the right. And if it was important, you'd tell me when you were ready."

"It doesn't… change things between us, does it?"

"Oh, my sweet Lonn, why should it? You're… good. Patient. Kind. Better than I deserve. That's all that matters." She leaned in, kissing him gently. "So, I've fallen in love with a prince."

He sat up straight. "You… you've…"

Her cheeks flushed red. "Well, you said it first."

"So I did." He smiled and was on his feet, hand out. "Still want to be with me? Even after all that?"

"I do." She took it and hugged him tight. "For now and ever, my dear, sweet prince."

He wrapped his arm about her waist, propping her up as they headed down the hill. "Take your time, my lady. No need to rush."

"But…" She glanced back at the village in the distance with concern. "What happened to the Head Merchant? I'm still a little hazy."

Lonn shrugged. "Nothing particularly pleasant."

"Did I kill him?"

"Still alive, but very much… hobbled."

Her stomach growled as they reached the road. "Unfortunate we couldn't properly resupply."

"Here." He held out a strip of salted meat. "Best I could do, I'm afraid."

"Where'd that come from?"

"Sall's stores," he responded with a slight wince, "Might've taken a handful as we left."

Her eyes grew wide. "Lonn! You…" she swiped it up, "See?!" and waved the strip toward him before slipping it in her mouth. "Picking up such bad habits. Just shows what a horrible influence I've been, my sweet prince."

"I…" he grew flustered at the thought, "considered it a… fair exchange."

"And that's just how it starts."

"Not going to resort to raiding, if that's a concern."

"We'd need a steamer for that… not that I intend to fall back on bad habits myself."

"I'm pleased to hear that, my lady." He took her hand with a smile, and together carried on to the east.

South of the dirt road, several rhinoxen grazed casually on the long blaygrass. They chomped down, intent on eating their fill, until one on the far side ruffled its head and looked up with a questioning grunt. Its ear twitched as the others followed suit, perking up, curious.

On the far side of the field near the forest edge, the echo of irobon meeting irobon rang out. Caetriona, still recovering from her ordeal in Fizzpot days before, was hardly in her usual form, breathing heavily as Lonn pressed his advantage. Her face strained with each block and parry against his thrusts. "Getting tired? Want to stop?"

"And provide you the dissatisfaction of a hollow victory, my sweet prince? Never!" She strained forward, trying to find an advantage. "This might be your best chance. At least make it a proper one."

"That's hardly fair, using that as an excuse."

"When's life fair, my love? You think a real opponent would spare you a moment to rest and catch your breath?"

It reminded him of his conversation with Soreign, one that felt so long ago now. Would he let the fallen knight drown in the river? "Are you saying no one fights fair? No one fights with honor?"

She smiled. "Only one I know even comes close." Stepping back to deflect one of his blows, she slipped in a mud puddle. His blow hit hard, knocking the sword from her hand, and she grabbed his tunic, dragging him down with her. He abandoned his own blade and landed on top, hands pressing on her breasts. "Now that wasn't fair at all."

"A win's still a win," he grinned. "Not my fault you slipped. I just… took advantage."

"And… what will you do now with your defeated foe?"

He squeezed his hands. "I… had some ideas."

"I'm sure," she grinned. "Or is that just your sword-hilt again?"

Lonn looked at their discarded swords jabbed into the soil. "Not this time."

"Oh… well… are you gonna do something about that? Or do you want me to…" She started to reach down, but fell still and silent as the long blaygrass rustled. They both looked up as the snout of a rhinoxen burst through, its mouth munching in slow half-circles as it peered at them curiously. She laughed, "Think we've disturbed the locals."

There were several that had encircled them, drawn by the noise. "We do seem to have gathered an audience."

"Let them watch." She loosened her striders. "Not like they'll tell anyone."

"Seem domesticated." He tugged at his own. "Wonder

if there's a farm nearby."

"Look for it later. Right now, I'm—"

"SINARAHH??"

Lonn looked up. "What was that?"

She drew his face back to hers and kissed him. "Nothing to do with us, my love."

"SINNAARRAAHHH!!!!!"

"Sounds like someone's in trouble." With a concerned look, he rolled away, retrieving his sword and cinching his striders tight. "Should see if we can help."

Tightening her striders, she rose to her feet with a huff, "Doesn't mean we have to, my love."

"It's the right thing to do." He returned her sword and waded through the long blaygrass.

"Ah… feck." Following after him, she shook her head, "Course it is," and guided him.

The voice called out again. "SINARAH!"

"See anything?"

There was a group huddled at the edge of the field near the forest. "Just children," she responded. Two of them ran to the edge of the forest before running back. "Probably some foolish game they're playing." She grabbed his hand. "Let's just go back and play ours instead."

But he trudged forward, finally breaking through the blaygrass and seeing the group gathered nearby. A few jerked around, suddenly cautious and concerned by the newcomers. Others ran off as quick as their legs could carry them. "Appears they've seen us." He gripped his belt and drew close to those who remained at the forest's edge. "What's going on here?"

They stammered, looking amongst each other before staring at dirt and their muddy boots. "Nuthin."

Lonn looked among them. "Nothing?"

They glanced up as Caetriona stopped by his side, hand on her hilt. "You're lying." They lingered on her sheathed blade. "Know what happens to naughty children who lie?"

One of the girls dug the tip of her boot into the dirt. "Just troblyte baiting."

"Troblyte… baiting?"

Caetriona shook her head as Lonn pressed them. "What were you calling out?"

"Sin-Sinarah. My— my sister," one of the boys stammered, pointing to the forest. "Went in. She— she's not come out."

"Of all the—" Caetriona gasped. "Told your parents?"

They grew defensive. One backed away. "No way! Ain't gettin my bung switched."

Lonn looked at Sinarah's brother. "How long's she been in there?"

He shrugged. "Since quarter to midsun, maybe. She was hoping to break the record. Expected her to run out like a scared little chickuck long ago."

"Record?" Caetriona glanced up, seeing it was near midsun. When she turned, Lonn was already striding across the field toward the forest. "Oh… feck. Can't seriously be thinking of going in after her. Remember what happened last time we riled up those bloody troblytes?"

"Hard to forget. And I'm not having that happen to an innocent child."

"No. Course not," she sighed, passing the children by with a stern glare. "Wait for me, my love."

They disappeared into the trushes, leaving the children, mouths agape. "Really going there?"

"Either brave or just mad."

"Well, I'm going back. Papa's gonna notice I'm gone." She looked at Sinarah's brother. "Coming, Tomah?"

"Can't. Get in trouble either way, so…"

"Really think they'll find her?"

He shrugged. "Dunno."

Finding themselves once again immersed in the Ciration Forest, Lonn and Caetriona trod carefully through the trushes, keeping their grips on their hilts. She tilted her head one way and then another. "Bad sign. Don't hear anything."

"I know." He also felt the unsettled stillness too.

"Lonn… she brought this on herself. Not your fault if we…"

"She's just a child who didn't know any better."

"Exactly. Let it serve as a lesson to the others not to play foolish games with things that would very much like to *eat* them. Honestly. Troblyte baiting? Have they really nothing better to do?"

He glanced back at her. "Been on the road… how many days? Seen anything better?"

"Tend rhinoxen and… forn." She grabbed his arm. "Which we could be doing right now."

"They're just… children."

"What's your point? Clearly that's what their parents've been doing. Did you see how many of them there were running around?" Lonn stopped short. She tensed. "My love?"

He stooped, shaking the leaves off of a small wooden sword, and held it out to her. "Maybe she wants a different life than that."

"Unless this belonged to some other child who was equally unlucky." She took it up dubiously, flipping it over in her hand.

"Won't believe that until we find her." He looked around. "See any tracks?"

"What? Tracks?" She eyed him with a skeptical scoff, "Lonn, I lived on a steamrunner my whole life. Wouldn't even know where to begin."

"In the stories my mother told, aelfin always had excellent perception skills."

"Suppose that's true."

"Like good hearing," he continued.

"Excellent, actually."

"And keen eyesight."

"Better in the dark," she shrugged. "But, I do have a keen sense of direction."

He laughed, "Then why'd we go north?"

"That's not fair, my love!" She smacked his shoulder. "Didn't think that fool Grauler would fly anywhere near this bloody forest. Who does that? Thought he'd have sense enough to go south. If we'd ended up in the Illuvian Forest, we'd be in Alisard right this very day waiting for transport back to Merribellith, courtesy of the Astyrian kingdom. Put us up in a nice, warm townhouse. Mugs of tefee near a roaring fire. And a big bed to forn in til midmoon… or later, knowing you."

"That does sound nice, my lady." He smiled wistfully. "Just keep your eyes open."

"They are. Still don't see what—" She pointed with a faint huff, "Well… maybe that's a foot print there. Could just as well be a trick of light."

"No. I think you're right." He squatted, peering at the ground intently before pointing. "Something went that way. See. Another imprint there. And… another. Running."

"Lonn, that's going deeper into the forest."

"Maybe she got scared and lost her sense of direction." Stepping gingerly though the dense foliage, he tried to spot the trail.

"Why'd your mother tell you stories about aelfin?" she asked, following close behind. "Didn't think that was a popular topic among humins."

"Maybe it was her way of showing a different side of them, one most humins've forgotten."

"They didn't forget, Lonn. Far as most're concerned, the Revolt happened just last Verlith Bloom. That's how they act, anyway. And they're not about to let us forget they're still angry. Honestly, you'd think they'd get over being enslaved after a few hundred blooms. You have."

"Read about it, but I just thought we'd moved past it as a people."

She shook her head. "They never let you out of that sheltered existence at all, did they?"

"This was the first time, and it took *quite* a lot of persuasion."

She frowned. "Sure must regret that decision now."

"Well, I don't." He faltered. "Except where Miku Arilona and the others are concerned."

"I know. Sorry." She cleared her throat, "Don't mind me saying, but it sounds… lonely."

"Didn't know any different at the time. Thought it was normal." He shrugged. "Now… just seems they were trying to keep a lot of things from me."

"Wanted to keep you—" Grabbing his shoulder, she pointed to a ridge topped by young trushes and reached for her sword. But it was not even half-out of its scabbard when the low foliage shuddered, and a massive woolg with bristling fur colored like the surrounding blaygrass burst through, hissing and snarling. It knocked her back, and all she could manage was to brace her forearm against its throat, holding it back as its jaw snapped, trying to tear into her.

Before Lonn could leap in to help, the leaves rustled

close by. Another woolg ducked under the low branches, fangs bared as saliva dripped from its curled lips. He drew his sword as it hunched low, muscle tense, prepared to lunge. He steadied himself, digging his boots into the muddy ground.

Worried about Caetriona in her weakened state, the young journeymin risked a glance to her. Face strained red. Arms trembling, desperate to hold the woolg back. The other took advantage of his distraction, charging forward. But he was ready, twisting away and bringing the blade down. It yelped in agony as the sword bit flesh and sliced deep. It collapsed to the ground, front paws scratching at the ground while its rear paws dragged limply behind, hardly a threat with its spine severed.

With a gasp, Lonn charged to her aid. The beast's snapping maw grew closer, almost at her throat, as her strength faded. Its eyes flared wide when his blade thrust deep into its neck. Blood splattered down her arms and across her face as it slumped with a whimper. She wiped at the blood spatters and tried to push the carcass away but soon gave up with a quivering sigh, "Oof. That's heavy."

He grabbed it by the scruff and dragged it off of her. "You hurt, my love?"

"Just my pride." She kissed him as he pulled her to her feet. "You did well." While she caught her breath, he slashed his sword into the other to put a swift end to its anguished mewling. "So, what were these two after?" She huffed her way up the ridge and peered over. "Oh, look." There was a hole dug deep into the ground. "Another troblyte trap."

He glanced high into the trushes but saw no hint of the troblytes. "Not an ambush, at least. Would've eaten those two back there."

"Got lucky on that count." She approached the edge cautiously. "Wonder if whatever tripped it is…" As they approached, her ears twitched to the faint sound of whimpering. "Yep. Still alive."

Sprawled out at the bottom of the pit was a girl in a simple beige dress, her auburn hair pulled back in a bun, face and arms dirty and bruised. When their shadow fell over her, she loosed a piercing shrill.

Caetriona clamped her hands over her ears, wincing. "Sounds like our girl!"

Lonn's eye twitched. "Sinarah? Will you—"

"Shush it!" The girl went silent, staring up at the two. "Better. Done that sooner, we'd've found you already."

"Y… you're not… troblytes?"

"See, my love?" Caetriona reared back, scoffing, "Foolish girl doesn't know what a troblyte even looks like."

Lonn helped her out of the pit and pulled the bottle of healing salve from their pack, "Got hurt a bit there," slathering some over her arms and cheek where she had been injured in the fall.

Caetriona's nose twitched. "What's that… smell?"

The girl looked down, face pink with embarrassment. "Got scared and…" Her hand swiped at the wet streak down the back of her dress, trying to hide it.

"Oh. Suppose it happens to the best of us." She gave an understanding nod and looked the girl over, "Could've been worse," before scanning the trushes. Her hand went to her belt, fingering the wooden sword Lonn had found.

"That's…" Sinarah perked up, eyes wide. "You… found my sword!"

Lonn grinned. "See, Caetriona?"

With a slight shake of her head, she handed it to the girl hilt first. "Should get a real one if you're going on adventures like… this." Her attention drew higher into the trush foliage.

The journeymin tensed his sword grip, concerned. "Hear anything?"

"Not sure. But… shouldn't linger. Scent of blood in the air… draw any troblytes if they're close by." With a faint shiver, she retraced their steps.

Sinarah lingered, staring at the two dead woolgs as they passed. "You… really did that?"

Caetriona nodded. "Lonn did."

"Are you… monster fighters?"

Lonn laughed it off, but then thought about it a moment. "In… ah… way, I suppose."

"But… weren't you afraid to come into the forest?"

"Not our first time in the Ciration Forest." She responded, slipping her sword away, "Is it, my love?"

"No. Though, I'd rather not make a habit of it."

"But—" The girl blinked between them. "The troblytes! Didn't you…"

"We know all we need to about them. Vicious. Hungry. Devious. Bloody little beasts." She motioned behind them. "That was one of their traps you tripped. Fortunate. Eat you right down to the bone, they would. And then suck out each of your delicious eyes. Chomp them down like tasty little treats."

"Caetriona!"

"She should know what she's risking, baiting them, my love."

The girl shivered, "Sounds awful."

"It is. Horrible way to go. But, Lonn's killed a few of them."

The girl looked up him, wide-eyed and impressed. "Really?"

He nodded, mussing her hair. "Really."

"Then… you're very brave monster fighters. I wish I could've been that brave."

Caetriona sighed, jostling one of the woolg carcasses with her foot. "Oh! That one's still twitching a bit. Think you can finish it off?"

Sinarah brightened. "Can I?"

Lonn smiled. "Right there at the neck."

The girl took up her sword and lunged in, pushing with all her strength until her face turned red. The dull wood broke through the tough skin, and she drew it out with a grunt, pleased with the accomplishment.

"I'm sure that finished it off for good."

She looked at them both as they started to walk away. "Um…" Lonn turned back. "Couldn't we take them with us? These… could… feed my village."

"They're pretty heav…" Caetriona eyed them each dubiously, sighing as he draped the larger of the two over his shoulders with a huff. "Always trying to do the right thing, my love."

"She's right. Shouldn't let them go to waste."

"No. Course…" she groaned and dragged the other into her arms, "not."

He looked at her, concerned. "You okay?"

"I'll… make it." Her face turned red, and her arms trembled. "If… we hurry." Sinarah shuffled close, trying her best to help her with the burden. "Thank you, Sinarah. That… helps."

As they trudged toward the edge of the forest, the girl spattered them with questions. "What other monster's have you fought?"

"Besides troblytes and woolgs? Raiders mostly," he replied.

"That… purp vine we simply… murdered." Caetriona chimed in with a scrunch of her nose. "Oh, and there was a… giant."

Sinarah eyed them both, mouth agape. "A… giant?"

"Had three testicles in its sack."

"Really?" The girl scrunched her nose at the thought. "Sounds monstrous."

"He was. And the awful thing he wanted to do to me—"

"Caetriona! Don't tell her that!"

"She's a farmin's daughter, Lonn. Knows only too well what beasts do out of habit. She can handle it." The two looked at each other and laughed, leaving him bewildered as he led the way back to the forest's edge and Sinarah's anxious brother.

Sheot Farms

Tomah stared nervously at the forest. The two strangers had disappeared and been gone too long to the point that he feared the worst for them and his sister.

"Tomah!"

And then he feared the worst for himself as his father stormed down the field path, pinching one of his friends by the ear with one hand and holding his pitchfork in the other. Sweat dripped from his brow, pulled straight from the fields. The boy eyed the long blaygrass for a lingering moment, wondering if escape was the better choice. But the looks on the others' faces, resigned to their fate, made him change his mind. "We're in so much trouble."

His father released his grip on his friend and stood over him. "Tomah, where's your sister?" He stared down at his father's muddy boots and mumbled under his breath, flinching when his father smacked his cheek lightly. "Speak up, now, boy."

"She…" he gulped, "went into the forest, father."

"And whose foolish idea was that now?"

"H-hers, father."

"Fool boy! And where were you? How's that looking after your sister?" He slapped him, harder this time, and glared at the other children. "Or any of you? I've a mind to belt you all!" Hefting his pitchfork, he marched toward the forest. "Sinarah!"

"She's… gone, father."

One of the children stared at him. "You should tell him about the—"

"Shhh!" The other children glared.

"About what?" Tomah's father glared. "About. What?!"

"St-strangers, father. Heard me calling after her. Th-they went in to… find her."

"Courageous to do what you couldn't." Frowning, he shook his head, "Deal with you all later," and marched to the forest.

Others from the village came down the path, armed with pitchforks and hoes, and gave stern looks to the children before eyeing their fellow farmin. "Ellavel! What're you doing?"

"Going to find my daughter." He froze when the trushes shuddered and gripped the pitchfork tight, ready for anything. The others behind him nervously did the same.

Lonn pushed through the forest's edge and stomped out into the field. He was tired and blood spattered with the limp woolg draped across his back. Behind him, Caetriona emerged equally soiled, her face showing the strain of the burden in her arms. Ellavel's face fell, fearing the worst. "Oh… Sinarah… no…"

Stepping to the side, the young journeymin smiled and revealed the girl, dirty from her own trials, marching along side Caetriona, face beaming. "Here, father!"

He dropped the pitchfork and ran to her, hugging her tight. "Oh, Sinarah! Foolish, strong-headed girl!"

"Sorry, father."

"You will be. Never do that again!"

"I won't father. Promise. Not until I get a real sword."

"Which'll be never," he chastised, "But… we'll… discuss your punishment later," and looked at the two newcomers, taking them each in turn and squeezing them tight. "Oh, thank you both!"

Sinarah tugged on her father's tunic. "This is Lonn and Caetriona. They're monster fighters."

"Yes. Yes, I see." He stooped in and took Caetriona's burden, "Let me, please," draping the woolg over his shoulder. "I am Ellavel. Nothing I have can truly repay you for saving my daughter, but you are both gladly welcome in my home and at my table."

"Thank you, Ellavel. Most gracious" Lonn smiled and gave a faint nod. "It's been many days without proper rest or a meal."

"Then you shall have both! Sheot Farms isn't far." He turned reassuringly to the others from the village. "Friends, let's ease their burden." They closed around with hugs as they took up the two woolgs, appraising them with enthusiasm. "Woolgs plague these parts. Knowing there are two less so close… it brings relief. Truly, your reputation must be well earned."

Sinarah rose up on the tips of her feet with a shout, "I helped, father!" and brandished her bloody sword.

"So I see."

As the group passed the children, Sinarah eyed them all with a wide grin. "Beat that record."

Lonn and Caetriona walked hand-in-hand as the curious villagers assaulted the travel-weary visitors with questions, so many that it was hard for them to keep track of each one. Ellavel stepped in, "All of you, please. Our new friends must be tired. Let's allow them some rest. Time to clean up. Plenty of opportunity for stories over a hearty meal. We have meat aplenty!"

There were cheers as they crested the ridge. Caetriona saw the village of Sheot Farms first, larger than Fizzpot, with ten family houses and several barns where herds of woolly sheots roamed in large pens. The herdsmin tended them diligently, keeping the various colored groups separate. In the outer field, rhinoxen grazed. Chickucks hopped around freely, pecking at the ground for seed and grub.

Ellavel's home was modest, like the others, with a tall roof, angled steep and newly thatched. Several farmins perked up from their meal preparations when they saw the group approach and exchanged hesitant glances. But caution turned to curiosity with the two woolgs set out on the courtyard table. Ellavel waved to a farmaiden with a smile. "Querna!"

She was large, mostly due to her bout of childish, and trundled over. "What's this, Ellavel?"

"New friends, my wife! Caetriona and Lonn. They saved Sinarah from the forest and brought us this bounty. Renowned monster fighters, they are!"

"Oh!" She hastily straightened her dress and bundled hair. "Well! Thank you both mightily!" Snatching Caetriona's hand, she tugged her behind. "But, look at you! Dreadful! Come along, dear. Get you cleaned up." Too tired to protest, she followed.

"And I'll find some clothes that'll fit you while we get yours cleaned and mended," Ellavel stated, looking Lonn over, and motioned to a small outhouse. "Get you sorted."

The young journeymin nodded. "Thank you for your hospitality."

"Nonsense! And that's the last you need to thank me."

Inside, Querna tugged at Caetriona's clothes. "A filthy mess, these. How can you stand it?"

"Just do."

Querna turned and let out a gasp at the sight of Caetriona's scarred back. "Oh, my precious! Must've been a mighty beast that did such a thing to you."

She nervously draped her hair back. "I… suppose it was."

"Well, put this on. Sure it'll fit. One of mine in my younger days…" she laughed, rubbing her belly, "Before my many bouts of childish."

"That's… a…" Caetriona blinked, appearing dubious.

Outside, Lonn found the water basin and washed down as Ellavel set a stack of clothes down. "Think we found some good ones for you… should be about your size."

"Grateful." Feeling much more refreshed after his wash, he returned to the courtyard. The villagers gathered to prepare the sunfall meal. The woolgs sat on spits, their furs draped out to dry. He sat and watched with avid curiosity, having spent little time in the kitchens. Soreign taught him the basics and told stories of his own training being left in the norther Merribellith woods, days fending for himself. He had never been allowed to do such a thing. And even through all his recent adventures, there was still so much more for him to learn.

Ellavel dropped down in the seat by him, pulling him from his thoughts with a faint wave of his hand. "Quite a fine lady you've got there. Cleans up nice."

Lonn turned and blinked, finding his breath taken from him. Caetriona approached with the farmaidens of the village and came to a stop by his side, looking down at him. "Don't you dare laugh, my love."

"Never, my lady. I just…" he smiled, "never pictured you in a… dress." It was finely woven from white sheot wool, almost matching her own pale skin, and draped over her shoulders down to her ankles. "It's… lovely on you."

Her face turned crimson, which lingered as she tried to sit down, finding her legs tangled in the flowing cloth. He stifled a laugh then, sliding over and offering the end so she could swing her legs around. She hung her head down, leaning close to him. "Well, that wasn't embarrassing at all."

"I'm sure nobody noticed."

She glanced up. "They're all staring at us."

"No," he laughed, "That might just be you."

"Don't like it. Not used to…" She shifted in her seat with a faint huff and stared down at her exposed bosom. "Don't like… drawing attention to myself like this, Lonn."

Understanding her discomfort, he took her hand reassuringly. "Just for a little while, Caetriona. You'll be perfectly safe."

As the sun slowly lowered in the sky, the villagers laid out the meal and settled at the table. Some of the children wiggled and winced, trying to find comfortable positions from their punishments. Ellavel stood at the end, motioning around the table. "Old friends! Another day has passed. And we've been spared a tragedy. Thanks to our new friends! Lonn, Caetriona, it is from you we are able to enjoy meat at our table once more. Eat well!"

And they did. Large plates set before them both heaped with produce from the farm and large slices of woolg meat. But as they cleaned and cleared their plates, the journeymin grew curious watching the herds of rhinoxen and sheots in the distance. "Ellavel, we are grateful to all of you for sharing your bounty. But… why haven't you been able to get meat?"

"We share what we can, but our herds are kept for the coming war."

"War?" he asked hesitantly.

"Surely you're aware of the easter troubles."

"I… didn't think things were so bad," he commented cautiously. "Is war truly inevitable?"

"Who can say. We have to be prepared against Merribellith's aggression," Ellavel sighed, "with a third of our crop going to our patron, Lord Barretun. Another third to the soldiers standing watch on the border. But we have enough to cloth ourselves. Like the dress your fine lady wears. Douchart has called upon us, and we will always answer."

"Of course. Such duties are important."

"And what of you? What brings monster fighters this far south?"

About to reply, he stopped when Caetriona squeezed his hand. "We're returning to Lonn's family in the east."

Ellavel shook his head. "Skirting the Ciration Forest is a dangerous path, but clearly you can handle yourselves. And fortunate for us and my dear Sinarah. Braving that place… you truly are stout fighters. Surprised, though, ones so renowned as you weren't called to service."

Lonn took a slow drink. "We… have been traveling of late."

Caetriona nodded. "Perhaps we were, and the news is just now waiting for us back home."

"If they have, we'll all be better for it. We've lived under this shadow for far too many blooms as it is. The sooner it's over with, the sooner our lives get back to normal." The stout farmin hesitated. "Don't mean to sound like I'm complaining. We grow the crops to tend us and the herds. Harvest the wool and fur. Just… leaves little room for… diversion."

"Yes…" She jabbed Lonn with her elbow. "You do have a lot of children running about."

The villagers laughed. "Oh, there's always time for that. No." Ellavel took a draught of mog, "Talking about something of the local…" and grinned, "interests."

Querna rose and scooped up the empty plates with a sigh, "Don't need to hear you drone on about that. Not tonight. Been a long day for them both. Traveling. Fighting. Set you up in the loft. Not much, but it's warm and dry."

"Grateful," Lonn smiled. "It'll make a nice change."

Ellavel nodded. "We'll continue this in the morning, then."

The villagers started dispersing, heading home after more hugs for the new comers. It left them drained as they followed Querna inside. She patted the ladder leading up to the loft. "Sinarah's given you her side for the night as a show of appreciation."

He followed Caetriona up, just in case she had a challenge navigating in her dress, but she made it to the top and plunged down in the pile of long blaygrass. "Almost like sleeping outside."

Lonn sighed, settling beside her. "But warmer."

Sinarah and her brother slept across from them, but the girl only pretended to sleep, watching them through half-closed eyes. Leaning close, Caetriona whispered, "the girl's watching us."

"curious. suppose it's only natural."

"wondering if we'll take up the… local interests?" She grinned, sliding up her dress. "don't mind getting back to where we were before her little adventure interrupted us."

"seeing you in that dress certainly makes it tempting." He kissed her. "tomorrow. when we're far from here."

She rested her head on his shoulder. "well, if you promise."

He laughed. "you do know I like to keep my word."

"I certainly do, my love." She draped her arm across his waist and closed her eyes. In the safety of Ellavel's home with the flames softly crackling in the hearth below, they both slept soundly through the whole night.

Sunlight streamed through the doors and windows below, but it was Caetriona once again mumbling the Gazer's invocation that tugged Lonn awake. "Oh. Past sunrise." He slid his fingers through her hair, teasing the tip of her ear until her lips twitched. "You awake?"

"No." She lifted her head off his chest, looking across. The children were gone, and the house was quiet. "Is the house empty?"

"Seems that way."

"Just a bit longer, my love." She dropped her head down and clutched his waist tight.

He sniffed the air. "Smell that? Morning meal."

"That's nice." She refused to move.

"Oh! You must be feeling better if the prospect of a meal doesn't get you up," he laughed, glancing over the edge of the rafters. "And they've even left our clothes out for us."

She finally rose up, tugging the laces of her bodice. "Relieved to get outta this dress."

"You look nice in it." He cleared his throat and dropped down as she glared after him.

"Barely move. Can't even kick. Hardly see the point." She leaned over as he threw her clothes up. "Sure you wouldn't want to just get out of those and into me, my love?"

"Tonight. As promised."

"Make it sound like we'd disturb the whole village. Don't make that much noise, do we?"

"You do."

After tugging on her boots and cinching them tight, she dropped down and kissed his cheek. "Can only be held partly to blame for that, now."

Lonn slung their pack over his shoulder and slipped outside, blinking against the glare of the approaching midsun. "Oh… lot later than I thought."

She tightened her belt and glanced around. Some of the farmins busied themselves fixing for the midday meal. Querna glanced at them with a smile. "Thought you'd both sleep the whole day away."

Embarrassed, Lonn winced, "Sorry."

"Nonsense! Deserve the rest after everything you've done." She toddled to the village post and rang the bell. "Be a few before they come in from the fields. Sit. Relax. Serve up a good meal in just a while." Her face flashed a moment's annoyance. "And Ellavel's insistent you get a taste of… well. You know about *males* and their… distractions."

Caetriona nodded with a frown. "A little too well."

They both sat at the table leaning back with their feet kicked out as they waited. He looked about curiously. "What do you think it could be?"

"Probably touting some local brew they've concocted."

Around them, the children mingled, more subdued than when they first saw them. "At least they've had their fill of troblyte baiting."

"Doubt it'll stop," she shrugged, "Probably still sore from a few swipes to the bung."

He shook his head. "Still can't believe anyone punishes children like that."

She eyed him for a moment before laughing, "Course, you've never been switched! Were you ever punished for anything?"

He was silent for a long moment. "Was sent to my room without supper once."

"Oh! That must've been quite the scandal. And what'd you do to deserve that?"

"Can't… rightly remember."

"See? They remember. Pain is good that way. Won't stop them, but they know exactly what they'll get for any mischief if they get caught."

"Is it always like that out here?" he asked with a sigh.

"Not always. Just most of the time. Sometimes, it has to be."

"Have to wonder about that."

She smiled sympathetically and kissed his cheek. "I know you do, my love."

"Ah! My friends! Awake at last!" Ellavel passed the two by with hearty slaps on the shoulders. "Insisted they let you sleep as long as you needed. Suspected your travels had drained you quite a bit."

"Appreciate that. We did need the rest."

"And I see you packed, ready to move on. But not after a hearty meal. And…" the farmin wagged his finger, "I have a surprise." The two exchanged cautious glances, but he slapped the journeymin's shoulder again, laughing, "But later! Later!"

The meal spread across the entire table, and the two did eat well at Ellavel's insistence, knowing it was a good number of days to the next settlement. Lonn cut through the idle villager chatter. "Do you know of any paths toward the… Astyrian border?"

"The main road." Ellavel nodded, pointing northeast. "Easier than skirting the forest boundary. Less dangerous."

"Is it far?"

Ellavel nodded, chomping through a slice of woolg meat. "On foot… you'd be there by sunfall tomorrow. But don't concern yourself about that." He grinned, "Get you there tonight," and finished off his plate before wandering from the table along with several of the other farmin.

"Already midsun." Caetriona leaned close, whispering, "what could possibly get us that far in so short a time?"

"Maybe they've got an old steamrunner hidden in the barn. Suppose we'll see." He was just as perplexed as the farmins returned to the fields to harvest or tend to their flocks. Several farmaidens cleared the table and made themselves scarce while Querna shook her head dismissively.

They were both left alone until Ellavel returned trailed by a rhinoxen. Her shaggy coat was shorn, and a padded yellow harness draped over her shoulders and stretched along her chest and back. Caetriona took a reflexive step back as she stopped beside them. "Not what I was expecting."

Lonn leaned to one side, looking along her flank where two taught straps stretched back to a cart that hardly seemed useful for any meaningful work. It only had two wheels. He looked at the farmin, curious. "What is this, Ellavel?"

He grinned, patting the rhinoxen's flank. With a shake of her head, she gave a snort. "Bizzey. Been rearing her up since she was a calf and now… she's my champion."

"Champion at… what?" Caetriona eyed him skeptically.

"Why, racing, of course!" He stared at them, shocked. "Have you never seen a race?"

They both blinked. "Racing… rhinoxen?"

"Sure! All the rage among the villages." Ellavel threw his thumb over his shoulder. "Got a whole track in the back pasture. In fact, we're hosting this bloom's championship race. Bizzey's won three blooms straight." The large beast stamped at the ground, raising a plume of dust. "Look at her! Scrapping for a fourth!" He motioned them back. "Had the lads strap her up at sunrise. Anxious to stretch her legs. Get her ready."

Caetriona looked at the cart, even more skeptical. Reigns leading from Bizzey's harness draped over the crossbar. Other straps were set along the inner rim of the cart. "And you… ride in this?"

Ellavel laughed. "How else would you do it?"

"And it's… safe?"

"Sure!"

Querna sidled by with a huff, "Except the crashes. Dismounts. Dislodged wheels. And don't get me started if the

186

rhinoxen start rutting. Unsightly mess that is."

Ellavel looked at his wife, red faced, "Well… during a race, sure! That's the challenge, dear," before turning to the two. "Wouldn't be any fun without a challenge, right?" He slapped Lonn's shoulder. "Ah! If only you could waylay your travels a short while. You'd make a great steermin, I reckon."

The young journeymin hesitated, stifling his curiosity. "We've been delayed too long already, I'm afraid."

"Certainly! I understand. We'll be off once you're ready." He trailed away to make final preparations, leaving them both standing there. Bizzey looked at them with a snort.

"Nope."

"Spare us a whole day and a half," Lonn responded.

She crossed her arms, dubious. "You believe that? It's a rhinoxen. How fast can they really go, anyway?" Bizzey stamped her foot. "No offense."

"Even if it's not as fast as he claims, saves us walking." He bit his tongue. "Give us more energy for… tonight."

"Lonn! That's cruel," she huffed. "Feck… fine! Since you put it that way."

Soon after midsun, they said their goodbyes. Sinarah hugged them both tightly. "I'll have a real sword next we meet. That's a promise."

"Just stay out of the bloody forest." Caetriona mussed her hair.

The girl lowered her gaze, foot digging into the dirt. "No promises."

Ellavel hopped onto the cart and tied himself in. "Come along. Strap in. Nice and tight. Ride's a bit bumpy in places."

Querna approached as Lonn tugged his strap tight and handed him a bundle. "For the long days ahead, dearies."

He took it with a slight bow. "You've been very gracious and hospitable. Thank you, all."

Caetriona hesitantly hopped onto the cart and wrapped the straps around her several times. Cinching them tight, she looked at him with a shrug, "Just in case."

They waved their goodbyes as Ellavel called back, "Ready now?" and snapped the reigns. "And we're off!"

Bizzey dug her hooves into the dirt and charged forward, sending Caetriona off her feet. Lonn braced her as she steadied herself against the sideboard and gripped his arm tightly. He looked over Ellavel's shoulder as the great beast tore along the path, a broad smile on his lips. She shook her head, face full of worry. "How can you enjoy this?!" her voice wavered against the jarring jerks and dips as the cart kicked up plumes of dust in their wake.

Ellavel shouted back, "And this isn't even as fast as she can go! Gotten her to ninety-five oktals at full charge! Heavier load than she's used too, this, but great for training!" The two looked around as the fields blurred by. Behind them in the distance, Sheot Farms was lost. The cart leaned into the curves as Bizzey followed the winding path.

Impressed, even Caetriona started to believe the claim.

It was past a quarter to sunfall when the cart lurched at a sharp turn, and a wide road spread before them. "This is the main road I spoke of!" Ellavel called out, "Goes all the way to the easter road! But I can only get you a little farther along!"

Lonn slapped the farmin's shoulder. "Appreciate even this much, Ellavel!"

Some distance down the road, Ellavel tugged on the reigns, and Bizzey slowed. "Easy, girl." They came to a stop, and he turned to them both with a sigh, "Well, this is the border of Lord Barretun's land. It saddens me I can't take you farther considering everything you've done," and squeezed them both into him. "You make it back to these parts, my home is yours, my friends! Always welcome!" Lonn unstrapped himself and hopped down before helping Caetriona. Ellavel turned Bizzey around and waved. "Back home, Bizzey! Safe travels, friends!"

He watched them disappear into a cloud of dust in the distance while she hunched over, hands on her trembling knees. "never. never again, my love."

"I thought it was fun," he commented, "Certainly different."

"Fun?" She took a slow breath, "Mad, they are. Utterly mad. Jesters. Racing rhinoxen. Honestly, what's wrong with this kingdom?" She rose up and tested herself with a few steps. "Now I know why father hardly ever did business here."

"The villagers were pleasant."

"Yes. At least there's that." She eyed the bundle Querna had given them. "What's that?"

Lonn opened it and smiled. "Dried woolg meat and a helping of crops."

She nodded. "Very generous."

"Just have to make it last." He reached out. "Ready to go, my lady?"

"Until moonrise." Smiling, she took his hand and glanced up. "And then you have a promise to keep, my sweet prince."

12   The Caravan

The clash of swords once again rang out as Lonn and Caetriona swiped and thrust in their morning spar. She ducked into the long blaygrass, disappearing from his view as he stood his ground, circling to the crackling sound she made while maneuvering to strike. The young journeymin anticipated even before it came, slipping his dagger behind him to block the swipe of her sword as it struck at his back.

"Well done, my love!" She laughed, "Tell me I'm not becoming too predictable."

"I considered some of those noises were you tossing another distraction."

"Have to remember that. Can't fool you too often." She leaned in, kissing him. It was only in that moment he felt the cool metal at his neck. "Got you again."

He pulled away. "That's the worst distraction you've ever made, Caetriona!"

"And the nicest one, my sweet prince."

"HOAH!" A howling came from the distance.

Lonn perked up. "Did you hear that?"

Caetriona looked around before spying a long, colorful caravan stopped along the road. A jester stood on top waving his arms. "There."

"HOAH! Hello there! Are you in dire straights? In need of aid?"

They looked at each other and laughed. Lonn swiped up their pack and sheathed his sword, wading through the blaygrass back to the road and came face-to-face with a harnessed rhinoxen. It snorted as Caetriona emerged. "Oh… feck. Not again." Two others stood at its side, ignoring them completely as they grazed on short grasses along the road.

Lonn looked at the odd caravan of multi-colored trailers. Perched in the driver's box was a portly jester with a wispy mustache that drooped toward his chin. He wore a purp-colored jacket and dark green striders. His black boots were well polished. "Heard the riot from the road. These are usually such quiet journeys. Gave us quite a start, I dare say!"

Leaning out the side of the front trailer was a slender maiden, her silvery hair bound in a zorbatail draped over her shoulder, squinting long and hard at Caetriona. "Don't like the look of em, Terric. Ruffians."

From inside, a shrill voice called out. "Ruffians, you say? Move your fat bung outta the way, Majie. Let me see!"

"Let's not be hasty now." Terric slapped the side of the trailer and leaned down to get a better look as the two approached. "Not woolgs, was it?"

"Not this time. Simply sparring. Our…" Lonn replied hesitantly, "morning practice. Didn't intend to scare you, good jesters."

Terric perked up, looking around. "I know these parts well, young min. You're nowhere near a battlefield. Nowhere near anywhere, in truth."

"My lady and I've been traveling for some many days."

Terric nodded. "Truly looks it, I dare say. But just what are you doing all the way out here?"

"We were… waylaid."

"But not by woolgs," Caetriona clarified.

"True. Those came… later."

She perked up. "By ruffians first."

Terric shook his head. "Terrible. Simply terrible. Never heard anything so outrageous. Used to be such peaceful roads, these. But all this talk of war… boils the blood and brings out the worst." He stiffened. "But where are my own manners. Terric the Terrificus, I am! And my troupe of stalwart performers, this is. Our humble goal… to spread joy!"

"A noble goal for a noble profession. I'm Lonn and this is Caetriona."

"And what, if I may ask, is your profession?" He eyed them both, noting their muddy boots, worn clothes… the swords dangling at their sides.

Lonn perked up, "Jesters ourselves."

"Monster fighters," Caetriona simultaneously stated.

They looked at each other a moment before looking up at Terric.

"And monster fighters," said Lonn

While Caetriona simultaneously said, "Also jesters."

They glanced at each other again, a silent signal, before saying in unison, "Monster fighting jesters."

Terric fell silent for a moment, staring up at the sky. A smile rose to his lips along with a bellyful laugh, "Wonderful!"

Majie scrunched her face on one side, suspicious. "No such thing."

"Quiet now. Inspired. Simply inspired! What an act that must be!" He leaned toward them. "Perhaps I can take some of your troubles away… at least for a time. Can find room in the back trailer, I'm sure."

"Terric! Can't be serious!"

"And what would you have me do?" he asked, glaring at Majie, "I'll not earn the reputation of refusing aid to fellow professionals!" and waved his finger at the two. "Now,

I'm not offering a place on the troupe, you understand. But... perhaps... we might accommodate a performance at our next stop. An act by monster fighting jesters... now that's something I'd be eager to see!"

Lonn bowed. "We thank you for your gracious hospitality." Caetriona gave a faint nod, watching Majie carefully as she followed him to the back trailer. The interior was cramped, full of trunks and piles of folded cloth. They found a seat as they heard the jester call out from the front.

"Terric's troupe is rolling on!"

She braced herself, expecting the worst as the trailer slowly swayed side to side, and finally relaxed with a sigh, "Ah. That's more like it."

Lonn laughed, "Did you expect us to be tearing up the road with just those three rhinoxen hauling all this?"

"My love, I don't know what to expect anymore from this mad kingdom." From the front trailer, a high voice rang out in song.

> Through hill and dale,
> Rhinoxen for sale!
> Little Twill went flap,
> Into the troblyte trap!
>
> Sir Ellsten swept in,
> Slinging a spear so thin!
> He dished her out,
> Gave her a bout!
>
> With childish she grew,
> And fearful he flew!
> Rutting he will do!
> A rutting he will do!

"Like that!" she flopped down into one of the cloth piles with a huff. "Not expecting us to sing like that or anything, are they? I can't sing."

"Suppose we should be happy he stopped at all to check on us and didn't move on with greater haste."

"But they expect us to… perform. Don't know the first thing about… jestering." She looked at him expectantly.

"What?" He opened the dwindling bundle from Querna and offered her the last of the meat.

"Lonn!" She swiped it up and took a bite. "We're not even real jesters. Just pretenders."

"Isn't that what jestering is?"

"Don't you know?" she asked, surprised. "You're a… well… weren't you surrounded by them back home? A performance for every meal?"

"Hardly ever," he laughed at the thought, "Maybe on some special occasions."

"And?" She waited expectantly. "What did they do?"

Lonn motioned to the front of the caravan. "Sing songs. Dance. Do card tricks. Tell stories. Juggle."

She eyed him skeptically. "Juggle?"

"Can't be that difficult, can it?"

"How can you say that?"

"Wasn't difficult back in Fizzpot. They seemed pretty convinced."

"Fizzpot?" She tensed at the thought of that place. "Weren't even trying to convince them of anything in Fizzpot. All we did was tell them what happened to us!"

"Exactly my point." He leaned beside her, smiling. "Our recent adventure's like one big joke to them."

She clasped her arms about her waist with a huff, "Still not singing."

As sunfall approached, the caravan skittered to a halt along the roadside. "Set camp!" Terric's voice rang out.

Lonn looked at Caetriona as he pulled himself from the deep pile of cloth. "Should lend a hand."

She nodded. "Suppose it's only fair."

They hopped from the back trailer and stretched their legs for a moment before trailing along the length toward the others. Terric tugged on his jacket as he looked among them. "Ah! Proper introductions in order now that you've rested, Jester Lonn, Jester Caetriona." He motioned to the shortest min of their group. "May I present Jester Puppen."

The jester paused and gave a faint nod as he hauled deadwood from the nearby trushes over his shoulder and set up a camp fire. He swiped his curling brown hair from his face. "Goods meeting." He rose up after setting the wood and drew a stick from his jacket pocket and held it out prominently before him. Giving a swish of his mouth, he spat fire, setting it alight before putting it down in the kindling.

Terric beamed. "Our dedicated arsonist."

Lonn stared for a long moment, impressed, before Caetriona nudged him. "Could've used that skill plenty in the forest. Wonder if troblytes are as frightened of fire as they are water."

"Did someone say troblytes?!" a familiar shrilling voice shouted.

Terric stiffened. "In jest, Voral. Only in jest, I'm sure." He glanced at the two. "Our resident fool. He plays the part well due to his nervous disposition, but he's anything but."

Voral was tall and lanky, wearing clothes too small for him. He gave the two a brief nod, his gaze lingering on Caetriona before nervously shifting away and sauntering off to tend to the rhinoxen with a bushel of blaygrass in hand.

"Jester Majie you've met. She's in the kitchen. And…" Terric glanced around for an anxious moment before the last two of their troupe appeared. "Ah. Jester Cirral, our re-sounding minstrel, and the lovely Jester Uffraine."

Cirral was a well-built min with long black hair pulled back in a zorbatail. He wore a simple green tunic and strid-ers, muddied up to his knees. "Just set the stockade alarm bells for the night, Terric."

"With great relief and gratitude." He took Uffraine's hand as she approached. "And what talents can I claim to Jester Uffraine here but those that range wide from sultry brothmaiden to noble queen."

She was a slender min with hair as violet as the sur-rounding trushes and dressed plainly a long brown kirtle. "Always the flatterer, Terric." She settled her gaze on Caetri-ona. "And what've you played?"

Caught off-guard, Caetriona hesitated a moment be-fore Lonn took her hand and chimed in. "From innocent virgin to vile raider."

"That's a decent range." The jester nodded. "He always speak for you?"

She coughed faintly, recovering. "I'm not… as… socia-ble as he is in… new company."

"Judge your audience." She grinned. "Can respect that. Used to be the same when I started out. You'll get over it."

Terric pat her hand. "I'm sure there's work to tend, dear Uffraine."

"Always is."

Terric watched her as she wandered off before clearing his throat. "And that is our troupe company. Small but ver-satile. A good range of talents among us."

"Certainly seems that way." Lonn nodded. "And what

can we do to earn our keep?"

"Set the tables. Feed the rhinoxen. Perhaps… yes… avoid the kitchen." Terric himself wandered off to lend his hand. "I'm sure you'll find something."

In the moment of silence that followed between them, Caetriona took a sharp breath. "Nope. No rhinoxen for me."

The young journeymin laughed. "Figured you'd say that. Can't be all that different from mucking out the zorba."

She stared, surprised considering his position. "You had to do… that?"

"All part of the… duty, as they say." He wandered off and joined Voral in the stockade to feed the large beasts while Caetriona helped Uffraine in setting the tables around the fire.

With the meal cooked, the troupe gathered together near sunfall and shared. Lonn nodded to all of them. "We appreciate you letting us join you." Between bites, he turned to Majie, who still appraised the newcomers with suspicion. "And the meal is quite good."

Terric glanced between the two and the awkward silence that followed. "Well… as I said, I could hardly stand by and allow you to continue wandering in such a state after all you've been through."

"Allegedly," Majie chimed in.

"Enough of that."

Voral blinked, offering fleeting gazes toward Caetriona. "Th-they've done nothing to wrong us, Majie."

Cirral nodded. "Well said, Voral.

Lonn perked up. "Oh! We heard your… song earlier."

Cirral frowned. "Ah. Yes. Still a work in progress, I'm afraid. *The Roast of Sir Ellsten*… in sixteen verses… so far."

Caetriona leaned toward the fire, curious. "So far?"

"Depends how many more offenses I learn about."

"Offenses?"

Puppen laughed. "Never heard of Sir Ellsten? Gots quite the reputation."

Uffraine chimed in. "Barely a village in Douchart that don't have at least one of his youngins running round. Surprised you never heard none of it."

"We've been away for a good long while." Caetriona stiffened. "Rumors haven't reached the other kingdoms."

"Not rumors!" Irritated, Cirral leaned toward the fire and spat. A hissing spark flared out. "Fecky knight of ill-repute."

"He apologizes for the outburst. Gets him riled." Puppen pat his colleague on the shoulder. "Twill's his cousin, see? Poor girl. Said he loved her. Gots her head swirling with sweet words. Forned her plenty, right until her belly swelled."

"Lecher slipped out in the middle of the night, off to spill his seed in another unsuspecting maiden. He'll make promises a plenty. And not keep a one."

Lonn looked at the jesters across the fire and frowned. "It's very troubling to hear all that. Is he of the Knightly Order?"

Puppen nodded. "Course he is. Like the lot of em. What's it matter?"

The young journeymin shook his head. "It's just… knightly knights don't conduct themselves like that."

Uffraine laughed. "Don't know many knights, then."

Caetriona took his hand as he stiffened. He collected himself with a deep breath. "Not in Douchart, that's true." Lonn recalled the lyrics. "But if I may ask… why'd your cousin go into the forest in the first place?"

"Into the forest?" Cirral shook his head, confused. "No min goes into the forest."

"Then…" Lonn grew equally confused. "How'd she fall into a troblyte trap?"

"Don't you know?" Cirral asked. "All this countryside used to be the Ciration Forest before the aelfins cut it down to make way for their empire. Forced the troblytes south. Even to this day, near a thousand blooms after their foul war, you hear stories of some poor min falling victim to one of their undiscovered traps." He sighed. "Just a pity that unknightly knight happened by. Mark my words. When they finally catch him and put him to the roast, I'll be ready. Travel right to the Araka itself. Let them all hear the truth. Every last verse, however long it takes to sing it."

Lonn nodded. "I wish you the best of luck in the endeavor."

Cirral leaned back, breathing deep to calm himself. "Appreciate you saying so."

Terric clapped. "Right! Best to clean up and settle down. We'll be off to an early start to make our next stop." The troupe took to their cleaning duties with Lonn and Caetriona lending aid where possible until sunfall and the dark moment of the eclipse struck. They settled into their trailer as moonrise came. There was little to say as they slumped into the piles of clothes and slept.

It was nearly midsun when the caravan swayed to the rhinoxen turning up the narrow path to Shakesville, a sprawling town in the southeast of Douchart attracting many business opportunities on the main trade route to Astyria. Terric tugged on the reigns, bringing them to a halt before the gatehouse. His ruddy face beamed as two members of the town protectorate, wearing bright yellow tabards over their chainmail, sauntered out and stopped beside the driver's box. "A good day to you both!" he called out.

They dug their spears into the ground and craned their neck upward to get a good look. "Nature of your business?"

the first asked.

"Business?" Terric waved his arm back. "Why… laughter, of course!"

The protectors glanced at each other with labored sighs. "More licensed jesters."

"More you say?" Terric tugged at his mustache. "Others pale in comparison, I'm sure! We perform for the people!"

Yawning, the other protector held his gloved hand out. "And this unpaled performance has permission?"

"Ah." Terric opened his jacket, hand sliding along one side and then the other. His face brightened. "Travel papers and authorization, all here."

The protector snatched it, skimming with a lazy eye, "Seems to be in order," before flapping it back in Terric's direction. "Anything to declare?"

"Declare?" Terric's face reddened as his cheeks puffed out and his hands stuffed his papers into his jacket pocket and patted it nervously. "Oh. Let me ponder."

The front window of the caravan creaked open, and Majie stuck her head out, a grin on her lips. "That'll be them two wretches you picked up on the roadside, Terric. Don't forget."

The protectors perked up, grips tightening on their spears. "Wretches?"

"No! Wretches? Certainly not!" Face flustered, Terric tugged on his mustache. "We did encounter a couple. Jesters fallen on hard times along the road. I… Terric the Terrificus… could not just abandon fellow performers in such a state, you understand."

The protectors glanced at each other. "But… they have papers?"

"Oh…" The jester stroked his chin nervously. "Not sure if they still have them. Didn't ask, you see. Not my place to pry, force them to recollect their troubles. Never humor there. Clear they lost near everything. And I simply refuse to bring the mood low."

The two protectors hefted their spears, grinning. "We'll need to speak with them."

"Ah… yes. To your duty, as they say." Terric shifted off his seat, perturbed by Majie's smirk. "We'll speak of this later." Hopping to the ground, he led the protectors to the rear trailer, "They'd been walking for days, apparently. Certainly looked the part when we found them," and gently tapped on the trailer door. "Oh, Jester Lonn? Jester Caetriona?"

The door swung open, and the young journeymin looked out. "Jester Terric?" He fell silent when he saw the protectors. "Is there a… problem?"

"Oh… certainly hope not." The portly jester glanced between him and the two protectors. "Matters of paperwork. Rather insistent… as you see."

Lonn stepped from the trailer and Caetriona joined him, their pack slung over her shoulder. The protectors looked the two up and down before fixating on the swords dangling from their belts. "Since when do jesters go around armed?"

Terric stiffened. "Why, it's their performance as… monster fighters."

The protectors looked at each other. "Monster… fighters? And you have papers for… that?"

"Yes! Papers!" Lonn ran his hand along his tunic before glancing at Caetriona. "Papers?"

She busied herself, digging through their pack before glancing up apologetically. "Seems they didn't survive, my love."

The protectors looked between the two. "Survive… what?"

Lonn nervously laughed, "Oh! Where to begin!"

"No!" The first protector held up his hand, cutting him off. "None of that. We're…"

"Not authorized!" the other cried out.

"Exactly that. Not authorized to listen to another jester tale."

"Cuts into our duties!"

"Duties! Exactly that! Have to let the main office sort this out." The first waved at Terric. "Your troupe… move on."

"Oh. Yes. Of course," Terric shifted awkwardly, looking at Lonn and Caetriona while backing away one slow step after another. "If you are able to resolve this… unfortunate situation… do find us at the town square. We'll be assembling the pavilion. Can't miss us." He tugged his mustache. "Can't wait to see what new act you'll bring to delight the crowds!"

They both watched the jester climb back to the driver's box, and the caravan slowly rolled into town. Lonn looked at the protectors. "Main office, you said?"

The protectors looked at them, smiles on their faces. "Certainly did. Have a pleasant chat. Get this all sorted."

13 Shakesville

Being one of the most frequented locations on the jester circuit, Shakesville held the distinction for the most caravan disputes in a single bloom for seven blooms running. Clashes over venues were commonplace, often leading to vandalism, sabotage, and occasional violence. It was a source of frustration for the town protectorate, one that the two travelers keenly felt as the cell slammed tight, and they found themselves once more detained.

Caetriona stood at the bars swiping her fingers along with a thrumming din. "Doesn't feel like this'll be a pleasant chat, my love."

"I got that impression." He stuffed his roughly upturned and emptied pockets down and collapsed onto the narrow bench.

She slumped onto the bench and curled up at his side. "How should we handle this?"

Lonn pondered that for a quiet moment when the jailroom door swung wide with a clatter. Wearing a tight yellow uniform and shiny black boots, Protectorate Commander Peppritch strode in followed by an attendant carrying a ledger. Standing before the cell, she appraised them both. "Searched your belongings. Didn't find any travel papers."

Lonn nodded. "Must've… lost them."

"So you say." She stared up at the ceiling. "Do you have anything to prove you're licensed jesters? Or where you're registered out of?"

"Oh… was it… or…" Caetriona shook her head sadly. "No. Hard to remember. We… move around so much."

"So…" Glancing at the formal questionnaire in the ledger, the commander gave an annoyed grunt, "How did you lose them?"

Lonn leaned forward. "We were traveling… on a steamrunner… and were… robbed."

"Robbed?" Commander Peppritch asked with a skeptical huff. "On a steamrunner? Do you know how—"

"By raiders!" Caetriona cut her off, giving Lonn a nudge. "Don't leave that out, my love. Took almost everything we had!"

Lonn nodded. "And the crash took the rest."

"Crash?" The commander glanced back at the attendant frantically scribbling everything down. "And this is documented?"

Caetriona took a slow, cautious breath. "Probably… not?"

"Not here, anyway." Lonn nudged her this time. "But… perhaps in Astyria."

"Oh. You may be right, my love. It's… possible."

"Wait," the commander stopped them. "This all happened in Astyria?"

"Oh!" Lonn cried out. "No. In the Ciration Forest."

"You… crashed… in the Ciration Forest?" the commander asked.

"Yes! A very dangerous place!" Caetriona nodded. "And then we were running for our lives, of course.

"Because of the troblytes."

"Troblytes?" The commander rubbed her hand over her mouth.

Lonn nodded enthusiastically. "They eat people! Did you know? Suck the eyes right from your skulls, they will."

"The things we saw." Caetriona stared out, eyes wide

and distant.

He nodded somberly. "That poor crew."

"And that giant! Don't forget that giant you slew, my love."

"Giant?" The commander asked with disbelief in her voice.

Caetriona leaned forward, hand to the side of her mouth intended for the commander's ears only. "Had three testicles, he did."

Stiff, Commander Peppritch tugged at her uniform collar, cheeks flushed at the thought. "Three…"

"What it planned for me… but my love beat him back. Sliced that beast's sack right open." Caetriona clutched his arm. "So very brave!"

The attendant's hand wavered on the page while shifting his stance, body shuddering at the thought. The commander looked between them. "You seriously expect—"

"Oh, and the riverfall!" Lonn cut her off.

"Rather we forgot that whole episode, my love." She shook her head. "Dragged himself right over with me in tow. Practically drowned!"

"Didn't know you couldn't swim at the time, my love."

"I did say… as we were going over." She clutched his arm tighter. "Swam for us both! So heroic!"

"So you see, anything we had left was soaked right through."

Annoyed, the commander snatched the ledger from the attendant, leaving a long black streak across the page. "So… when you came away from the raiders who robbed you… the steamrunner crash in the Ciration Forest… escaping troblytes, slicing the sack off a… three… testicled… giant, and surviving a riverfall… after all that, you didn't report your loss to your local garrison and seek replacements?"

Lonn turned to Caetriona for a moment before looking at the commander, face full of embarrassment. "We certainly would have!"

"And we were going to!"

"It's just… we didn't know where we were when we came out of the forest, you see."

"And this is the first place we've visited since that even has a protectorate posting."

"But…" Lonn laughed faintly, "we didn't know that until your protectors detained us at the gate."

"And where was that?"

"The… gate?" Caetriona eyed the commander, surprised. "It's out front. Really must get out more."

"No!" Frustrated, Commander Peppritch shoved the ledger into the attendant's hands and stepped closer to the cell. "Where did you… come out of the forest?"

"Oh!" The two glanced at each other before looking at her, saying in unison, "Fizzpot."

The commander turned to the attendant. "Fizz…" He flipped to the back of the ledger, intently studying the map. "Find it? Have a protectorate posting there?" Rolling his shoulders, he shook his head.

Caetriona looked at Lonn. "You know, my love… I don't think she believes us."

"Can see why, my love." Lonn nodded in agreement. "It's quite a mad story."

"Mad. But all true! Maybe we should go over it again."

"Yes!" Lonn grinned, "Perhaps in song!" ignoring the sudden flash of annoyance on her face as he drew a deep breath.

"No." Gripping the cell bars, the commander clenched her teeth tight, "No! Really! Not necessary!" She flipped hastily through her keys. "Here's what I'll do. Issue temporary papers until you can reregister with your home office for proper replacements."

Lonn smiled. "Well, that is most generous of you, commander."

Commander Peppritch gave a groan and yanked the cell door wide, "Let them deal with you." She led them to the main room. On a nearby table rested their pack, which had been equally turned out and thoroughly searched. She lifted the troblyte blade. "Odd things to be traveling with. Like this."

"It's a barber's blade."

"Doesn't seem very practical." The commander set it down skeptically and handed Lonn their pack.

"Seems to work for the troblytes," he commented before strapping his belt tight and repacking.

The commander snatched up a few travel cards along with a fountain pen. "Names?"

"Ah…" he blinked, "Lonn Caetriona."

She carried that along with a smile, "And Caetriona Lonn."

Commander Peppritch's hasty scribing faltered as she stared at them. "Think this is some sort of joke?"

"We…" the journeymin shrugged, "are traveling jesters."

"Monster. Fighting. Jesters," Caetriona added, pointing to the line noting their profession.

The commander again hesitated. "Is that even a real profession?"

"Oh! All the rage where we're from… I'm sure." With a faint cough, Lonn nodded enthusiastically. "Made short work of the jester fighting monsters, I'll tell you that!"

Caetriona snatched up his hand, following his lead. "Such a bloody affair, my love."

"The sight of all those fuzzy caps…" He shook his head mournfully. "Red noses… painted faces flying this way and that. The… bells. The… jangling bells… falling… silent."

"Still gives me nightmares, my love."

The commander shot a glare over her shoulder as several of the protectors chuckled. "And… where exactly are you traveling?"

They looked at each other, responding in unison. "East."

"There's nothing east from here except…" Commander Peppritch glanced up at a painted map of Douchart hanging on the wall, "the border. What possible reason would you want to risk going there?"

"Why, the garrisons, of course. Think of all those soldiers—"

"Bored soldiers," Caetriona cut in.

"Yes. Bored soldiers cut off and desperate for some respite from their toil waiting for a war that… well… let's be honest between us… might not happen for cycles—"

"Blooms even."

"Don't we owe it to them to provide proper entertainment?"

The commander eyed them suspiciously. "They've got no coin. No food to spare."

"Laughter!" Lonn stiffened. "Their laughter will be nourishment enough. Payment for a most venerable service to… our fine kingdom."

The commander shook her head, baffled. "If you're captured… I hear Merribellith soldiers shoot jesters on sight. Got no sense of humor. But, it's your heads they'll send flying."

"A risk well worth taking!" Lonn shouted, "Just think of the boost to morale in spreading joy and merriment!" Behind them, one of the protectors doubled over, red faced from laughing so hard. "That good protector there knows what I mean. Are you soldiers not the most in need of humorous antics to brighten your days?"

Scribbling faster, Commander Peppritch slid the papers across the table with a groan. "Just… please just take your papers and go! I'll… even forego the fee!"

"Are you certain? We could stay a bit longer." Lonn swiped them up. "You in particular might appreciate an epic ballad."

"No. No! Go!" The commander was on her feet, red faced, as she grabbed them both and dragged them to the door. "Just go bother someone else!" She pushed them out onto the street and slammed the door. "Bloody jesters!"

Catching his breath, one of the protectorate wiped his eyes. "Thought… they were… funny."

Commander Peppritch eyed him. "You would."

As the door slammed behind them, Caetriona smacked Lonn's shoulder hard. "That was cruel, my love!"

Lonn held out her travel papers. "It worked, didn't it?"

"Suppose I should be relieved she didn't want me to sing. Never've gotten out of that cell."

"Wouldn't stand for it by the look on her face." He patted his pocket. "At least we have these."

"Yes." Caetriona tucked hers away in her vest. "Officially monster fighting jesters."

"Should think of an act before we return to Terric's troupe."

She went stiff at the thought. "Why go back to that micat?"

"Said it yourself. Still don't know much about this place," Lonn commented with a frown. "Just doing what he had to. And it might be safer to travel with them… at least until we get closer to the border. Shouldn't be more than another day or two."

"And you can regale him with this grand plan to entertain the garrisons." She shook her head. "Where'd that even come from?

"Soreign, I guess," he sighed, "Every time he talked

about his time in the Easter War… it seemed all his focus was on the long bouts between fighting. Waiting. Said there was nothing worse than the waiting." The journeymin laughed, "I think it was his attempt to show being a knight isn't all epic battles and glory. But I knew that already considering all the time spent scrubbing and polishing armor."

She stared at him, once again surprised. "So, not only mucking zorba, but he seriously made you clean armor?"

"Oh, not just the armor. Sharpening swords. Buffing shields. All part of the… duty." He took her hand and walked along the street, but Caetriona stood stiff, staring at the posting board. "What's wrong?"

She tore away the warrant. "Bloody thing follows us everywhere."

"Seriously?" he asked, alarmed. "They're even here?"

"Head merchants don't care for borders where profit's concerned." Stuffing the warrant in their pack, she pulled him along to the more crowded main street, searching until she found it.

Tucked between two larger businesses, Wolk Supplies and Surplus was easy enough to miss. The fogged windows hid the interior, and on the door dangled a sign, "Absolutely *NO* Liquids Allowed." Inside, most of the shelves had small Wolk Stones stored in glass jars of various sizes for domestic use. Some mounting brackets. A variety of scaled water tanks. The shopkeep behind the counter was an older lady who eyed them both curiously as Caetriona pulled Lonn inside and scanned the stock. "Don't get many new comers. Welcome. And what can I help you find?"

"Looking for sealant. Grade four. And a brush."

The shopkeep sighed, "Oh. Another amateur," and waved to one shelf. "Four gilvers," she tallied as Caetriona set them on the counter.

"For grade four? Outrageous!" she complained, "Not worth even half that!"

The keep shrugged. "Best I can do with the pending war."

She reluctantly dropped the gilvers on the counter and swiped up her purchase. Lonn followed her out. "What was all that?"

She looked around cautiously before pushing him out of sight into an alley. "Bend over. Don't want this getting on your skin." She fluffed out his hair before popping the bottle, gasping at the thick chemical smell. "The real thing at least."

"What is it?" He asked, his throat quivering. "It reeks."

"Only for a moment. It's Wolk Stone sealant. Helps contain the debris. Prevents getting ash lung." She dabbed the brush and swiped it along his strands of hair. "Hate doing this… much prefer your sunkissed locks, my love… but if those postings are here…" Lonn held his breath as she applied a light coating until his hair darkened. She laughed as he stood straight, his hair stuck out stiffly, and waited for it to fully dry before patting it down. "Should avoid suspicion at least."

"It's not… permanent, is it?"

She kissed him. "It'll wash out. Eventually."

"So, what's wrong with grade four?"

"Complete feck. Just watered-down grade three sold cheap. Makes you think you're getting a deal. Doesn't hold nearly as well, but it's fine for this." She took his hand as they walked from the alley out to the street, casually perusing the merchant stalls and shop windows. In the distance, the large tent rose into place at the town square.

Still wondering what they would do once they got there, he stopped, and Caetriona turned. "My love?" His attention focused on an old tavern sign creaking in the faint breeze. The One Eyed Queen.

"Just a thought." He tugged her across the street to a fruit stall and, with a wry grin, lifted up a vermillion-shaded orapp fruit. "I know what our act is."

She eyed the round fruit suspiciously. "Not… juggling, is it?"

The blade whistled faintly in the air to its mark, impaling the orapp tightly held between Lonn's teeth down to the hilt. The audience gasped as he stepped away from the upturned table and sliced the fruit in half, taking a casual bite. Imbedded into the table behind him were Caetriona's dart daggers, tightly outlining his frame. The gathered crowd hummed with chatter and applause.

At his side, she took his hand and gave a faint bow. They both wore colorful jester costumes in shades of yellow and red, similar to the rest of the troupe as they performed, at Terric's insistence. She whispered out of the corner of her mouth, "can't believe you talked me into this, my love."

"seems to've worked out well," he whispered back.

Behind them, Voral, retrieved the daggers, yanking each free until the last, lodged so deep it would not budge. The audience laughed, thinking it was part of the act. Wiping his brow, he breathed deep and set his foot against the table for leverage. His face turned red at the effort before tumbling back, to a roar of laughter. He lifted the dagger and found the plank had pried free instead and dragged it off stage with a shake of his head. Behind him, the audience applauded.

"Wonderful! Wonderful! Masterful performance, Jester Caetriona!" Terric grabbed Lonn by the shoulders and looked him over backstage. "And not a scratch! Not a nick!

Not a trace of blood! Unsure of this new hair style." He beamed, "Still! If only we'd stumbled upon you sooner! A bit of excitement between songs and stories," and leaned back to look at the crowd. "The audience certainly enjoyed it thoroughly! A new spectacle!"

They retreated to the troupe's rest room, where a table had been set up with assorted food for them between their set pieces. Majie sat there along with other members of the troupe preparing for their final performance of the day. Cirral was already dressed as a Douchart footsoldier. Uffraine was dressed as a simple farmaiden. And Puppen, dressed in oversized blue robes, twirled an equally oversized crown around his fingers. They all swiftly got up as the two approached to prepare the stage, but Majie's face was fully irritated as she passed them by. "Couldn't've missed at least once?"

Caetriona turned after her, stopping as Lonn clutched her hand. "Ignore her, my love."

"Such a binch." She swiped a fruit and sat, glancing up as Voral approached.

"I…" he stammered, "have your daggers, J-Jester Caetriona," and set them carefully before her, hilts first, until he got to the last.

She appraised the teetering plank, "Stuck?" and slammed her fist down on the high end, dislodging the dagger. "That did it. Thank you, Jester Voral."

He stared at her, impressed, "You… you're welcome," and shuffled away, stopping every few steps to look back at her.

Lonn shook his head with a chuckle. "Seems you have an admirer."

"Fortunately for me, I'm taken." She turned to him with a smile. "Now, can we get out of these foolish clothes? Then we can watch what mad thing they'll do next."

Once changed, they slipped in with the audience as a hush settled among them. Terric took the stage tugging his jacket as he paced across the stage. "I know… we've had song! We've had scares! But we can't leave you without… story! And we all know what the best story is, don't we? The one you've all been waiting for? The one no other troupe could even conceive or… dare to perform! Terric the Terrificus proudly presents… the error of comedies… *The Easter Upset*!"

With that, and the applauding crowd, the curtains pulled aside.

ACT I
SCENE 1

Setting: A pillaged village. Upturned tables and chairs. Stuffed sacks splayed out as corpses. Red ribbons litter the floor as blood.

At Rise: Farmaiden bends over a table, her skirts bunched about her waist. Douchart Soldier thrusts his hips into her from behind.

DOUCHART SOLDIER

Travelled we did, three cycles full, along the Impassable Mountains and finally fell upon the east. Put up little fight. And this. This is all a Commonlander's good for, I tell you.
[Farmaiden lifts her finger.]
Just here to whet my spear for a spurt.
[Enter stage right Merribellith Soldier.]
[Taps Douchart Soldier's right shoulder with a huff.]
[Douchart Soldier looks left instead.]

What's that I feel?
       [Taps Douchart Soldier's left shoulder with a huff]
         [Douchart Soldier looks right instead.]
And there again!
           [Looks forward and gives a shrug.]
Just some gassy wind—

MERRIBELLITH SOLDIER

Just who do you think you're doing?

DOUCHART SOLDIER (startled)

Ah! Who's this sneaking in but an ally! And just what am I doing, he dares ask?
           [Looks down at Farmaiden.]
Why… I'm… taming this foul Commonlander into submission.
           [Farmaiden lifts her finger.]
She was… quite… unoccupied when I found her. Did I… take your spear's sheath?

MERRIBELLITH SOLDIER

Who. Not what.

DOUCHART SOLDIER

Why, I don't know. Didn't bother to get her name.

MERRIBELLITH SOLDIER

Aren't you supposed to be… in the east?

DOUCHART SOLDIER (confused)

But I am, I say! For three cycles we travelled. And here we are in the Commonlands!

MERRIBELLITH SOLDIER and FARMAIDEN

This isn't the Commonlands!

DOUCHART SOLDIER (gasps)
What is this madness! How can this not be the Commonlands?
[Aside.]
What fool does this Merribellithi take me for? When I'd happily share in this action? Perhaps he dislikes assaulting the sewer while I clearly hold firm battering the front gate.
[To Merribellith Soldier.]
We went east, I say! If you wish to spear your own Commonlander, there're plenty about well deserving a frontal flogging!

MERRIBELLITH SOLDIER (sighs)
You travelled east of Douchart. But you're not in the east.

DOUCHART SOLDIER (laughing)
How can I not be in the east if I traveled east?

MERRIBELLITH SOLDIER
You are east. But you're not east of east.

DOUCHART SOLDIER (confused)
If I am just east and not east of east… where exactly am I?

MERRIBELLITH SOLDIER and FARMAIDEN
Merribellith!

DOUCHART SOLDIER (shocked)
Ah! Then… this… isn't some Commonlander I've just commonlawed?

[Hastily pulls away.]
Quite… embarrassing.

[Merribellith Soldier chases.]
[Smacks his sword across Douchart Soldier's backside.]
I'm going! In spurts and spunk, I'm going!
[Exit stage left Douchart Soldier in a hurry.]

MERRIBELLITH SOLDIER (sadly)
And so we have chased off the foul Doucharty villains, aggrieved in our losses to land and life. Bitter is the taste of vile betrayal.
[Exit stage right Merribellith Soldier, head sunk low.]

FARMAIDEN
[Looks forward, chin resting in her palm.]
Tried to tell im, I did. Just how garded are them bloody Doucharty?
[Hikes her skirt down.]
Now where'd he go? Village ain't gonna repoplate itself, is it?
[Exit stage right Farmaiden chasing Merribellith Soldier.]

As the curtain swept closed at the end of the first scene, the crowd murmured. Some laughed. Others booed. A few questioned in hushed whispers just how to feel about the unflattering depiction of the Douchart army and the bold choice to openly challenge the prevailing narrative of the kingdom.

Amid the crowd, two were silent. Lonn hunched forward, watching with quiet concern etched in his face, disturbed by the revelation on events he thought he knew. Meanwhile, Caetriona rubbed his back and leaned close. "It's just a play, my love," she whispered, hoping to comfort him.

After a few moments, the curtains drew open again.

ACT I
SCENE 2

Setting: Douchart. The Araka throne room.

At Rise: King Aesinar lounges sideways in his throne and anxiously reads a parchment. Numerous others are scattered upon the floor surrounding him.

KING AESINAR (sadly)

Oh, but what horrid news! My forces? Lost in snow and storm. Traveling circles. Disoriented. Delayed by three cycles! Pitiable to find themselves on Merribellith's wrong side, unable to defend Youta's noble plan. And thinking they were in the Commonland, beset themselves upon the perceived enemy with valiant vigor… oh, what a misstep was made!

[Jumps to his feet and addresses the audience.]
Try passing the Impassable Mountains, and you'll know, my good and loyal subjects. But weighed low, I have but lost a friend. Dear King Youta is dead! So tragic a fate at the hands of foul Commonlanders.

[Enter stage right King Youta, crown covering his eyes.]
[Trips on his robes and stumbles blindly.]

KING YOUTA

Aesinar!

KING AESINAR

A voice calls in such dark times?

[Looks left and right, but not down.]
Imagination. Cruel tricks it plays.

KING YOUTA

[Tugs his crown up so he can see.]

Betrayer! Backstabber!

KING AESINAR

[Looks down and jumps back, shocked.]

What claims are these? And from so small a messenger?

KING YOUTA (outraged)

Messenger? pah! No messenger stands before you. I am—

[Trips on his robes.]

King Youta!

KING AESINAR

Could it be?! My dear friend survived! Miracles! But my!
How… short… you've become. Lost your legs and not your life?

[Looks at the audience with an exaggerated shrug.]

Hmm. Perhaps a fair exchange?

KING YOUTA

My father—

[Adjusting the loose crown fallen over his eyes.]

Told me of your wicked deeds before he died!

KING AESINAR (confused)

Deeds? Wicked? Oh, what a misunderstanding! I must explain so we may be friends again!

[Crouches and speaks slow.]

It. Was. An. Ac- ci- dent.

KING YOUTA (furious)

Lies! We shall never be friends while you take my land!

KING AESINAR (aside)
The young king speaks madness in his grief!
[Looks at King Youta.]
My forces returned. No land has been siezed.

KING YOUTA
More lies!
[Jumps up and down in a tantrum.]
You lie! You lie! You lie!

Hearing the laughing crowd, Caetriona grew uncomfortable and slipped her hand over Lonn's, finding it clenched fist tight, a visceral reaction to the unflattering depiction of his father. He said nothing, shaking his head sadly before pulling away and heading back to the trailer. She chased after him. "I'm so sorry, my love."

"Had… no idea that's what they thought." He went silent for a long moment, collecting his thoughts. "Is all this talk of war really just a… a misunderstanding? An accident of misfortune?"

She pulled him into the trailer and hugged him tight. "No idea. Merchants stay out of local politics. Bad for business."

"And raiders?"

She gave a faint laugh, "Even worse. They don't care. And they'll happily take full advantage of the chaos."

"But they're preparing for war. Is Merribellith the same?"

"Imagine so. They are enemies."

"These people are no one's enemy. Just want to live in peace. I have to believe that's what most people want."

She smiled, hugging him tighter. "I know you do, my love."

"The people leading the kingdoms. The problem's there."

"Take care," she chastised, "Starting to sound like one

of those Commonlanders yourself."

"Maybe they have a point."

She pulled away, staring at him in surprise. "Lonn!"

"Sorry. You're right. I…" he sighed, "not sure what to believe right now. Doesn't feel right."

"It never does." She rested her head against his. "Hopefully you'll feel better in the morning."

As they struggled to fall asleep, Majie sat by the door, intently listening in, her mind swirling with questions and concern.

The morning after the troupe's final performance in Shakesville came. "Packed up? Ready to head out?" Terric patrolled the long caravan before turning to Lonn and Caetriona. "And what of you both?"

"We'd like to travel on with you…" the journeymin hesitated, "Just to the easter road. Doubt your path lies south toward Astyria."

"That's true, but I'm tempted to have you stay on. Fresh acts… only rarely ever come about."

Caetriona nudged him. "Actually, there is another idea he could leave you with."

"Oh. Yes." He looked around cautiously. "Perhaps we can speak of it tonight."

"Such a tease, Jester Lonn." Terric smiled broadly. "Very well! You've tugged my interest." He gave one final check before climbing to the driver's box. "And this is Terric's troupe heading out!" The caravan rumbled out the gates and along the dusty path before turning east.

It swayed gently along the main road, and on the top of the last trailer, Lonn faced Caetriona, sword at the ready. He wavered on his feet while she remained steady. "How is this not bothering you? Can't get any good footing."

She smiled. "Practice. Living on a steamrunner your whole life would help, too. Forces you to get used to the shifting ground."

As their swords clashed, Cirral sat beside Terric in the driver's box constantly glancing back and flinching at every impact. "You sure that's a good idea, Terric?"

The jester beamed. "Must know what they're doing. Handling blades is their act. Have to practice, just as you do with your voice."

"Seems a bit… limited. Their performance skills, I mean."

Terric brightened. "Oh, Cirral, they have vision! Think of it. Brand new acts the likes of which audiences've never seen! And Jester Lonn has promised to inform me of another of his ideas. Exciting, isn't it?! A change is coming! I can smell it!"

"Thought that was just the pie Majie said she was baking."

But Majie was not baking at all. She had at that moment snuck into the rear trailer and rifled through the stored supplies until she found the wayward travelers' pack. "Now… what're you two ruffians hiding?" As their swords clashed overhead, she rummaged through, wincing when her finger snagged on the sharp and jagged metal of the troblyte blade. "Bloody nasty thing."

She licked her wound and dug deeper, finding one of the coin purses. "Not so broke, now, are you?" Buried near the bottom was a crumpled piece of parchment. After smoothing it out, her eyes went wide. "Two… thousand? And not a jester at all?" She crumpled the paper up again and stuffed everything back in their pack before slipping from the trailer, pondering what to do.

The caravan traveled until sunfall, when they reached the end of the souther road and made camp. The whole troupe sat around a crackling fire with Terric perched on a log across from the two. "Well, it seems our new friends will be parting company in the morning."

Lonn nodded, smiling. "It was a pleasure meeting you all. And we thank you for your hospitality." He looked across the flames. "And where will your troupe head next, Jester Terric?"

"Pulptown. A bit closer to the border than I like, but we get good crowds. A pity you can't join us. An act like yours would be simply smashing."

"It's funny you mention the border. That's actually the subject I wished to speak on."

Terric leaned closer. "Do go on, Jester Lonn."

"Seems such a missed opportunity. You visit the villages and towns, but… not the garrisons."

"No. Never go near them." The jester shook his head. "I'm sure you can understand why after experiencing all that unfortunate business coming into Shakesville."

Lonn nodded. "But, they were just doing their duty."

"And just how'd you get em to let you go?" Majie scrunched her brow in suspicion.

Caetriona responded cautiously. "We… simply explained what happened to us."

"And they believed you? All that farce on being accosted by ruffians?"

"Now, Majie," Terric held up his hand, "we all know there's plenty of truth in the absurd… or… plenty of absurd in the truth?" He shook his head. "Either way… we shouldn't doubt our new friends."

"Just have a hard time figuring how they let you go without a fuss."

Lonn shrugged. "Found them sympathetic to our plight. Even gave us temporary travel papers. Which made me think of the garrisons."

Majie looked between them. "Why're you so interested in the garrisons?"

"I was actually getting to that. Considering the mounting tensions… those soldiers must be pretty restless. Might just provide some welcome distraction if jesters performed for the soldiers."

"Perform? Just for the soldiers?" Terric coughed, shaking his head at such a dubious endeavor. "Jester Lonn, they're not like the townsfolk A bit too serious, if you ask me."

"They are," the young journeymin agreed, "But… aren't many of them conscripted from the townsfolk? Perhaps if we brought them entertainment, they'd feel more at home. I would think they'd be relieved to have something to distract them for a short while."

Majie perked up, alarmed, and slipped away even as Terric tilted his head in thought. "Ah. I hadn't considered that." He grinned. "I see where you're going, Jester Lonn. Well worth considering."

They continued on with idle chatter for a time until the air grew thick. Caetriona smelled it first before seeing black smoke billowing from the front trailer window. "Something's burning."

Terric jerked around, alarmed. "Oh! Who left the stove on?!"

Voral jumped up and bounded into the trailer, coming out a moment later with a charred lump. "Think it was the pie."

"What were you thinking, leaving it alone? Majie?" Terric peered through the darkness. "Majie! Oh, where is that blasted min?" He looked at Voral and Cirral. "Check that way. Puppen… make sure there's no damage to the trailer. Uffraine, join me."

Filled with foreboding, Caetriona grabbed Lonn's hand

and pulled him to the rear trailer. "We'll check this way." She ducked in and rummaged quickly through their pack, huffing, "Binch stole our coin purses!"

He grew worried. "And the—"

"Gone too," she frowned.

"So, she's returning to Shakesville to report me to the head—"

"No. Too far." Caetriona looked east. "No doubt making for the nearest garrison."

"Have a hard time finding it in the dark." He peered east across the fields to the forest. "Doubt she's used to rough terrain like we are. Could catch up to her."

"Then what?" she asked, looking at him cautiously. "*Silence* her?"

"No!" he shouted in alarm at the thought. "Perhaps just explain things, so she understands."

"To that binch?" She shook her head. "Not likely to listen. Already spending those gilvers in her head. Besides, if she does report us first…"

"It's just her word against ours."

"And the warrant. It's enough to make you interesting, my love. And you don't wanna end up a pawn to be bargained for in this dispute if they learn who you really are."

"Then…" he slumped his shoulders, "what do you suggest?"

Caetriona saw the others searching for Majie. "Leave now while they're occupied. Get as far east as we can before the soldiers starting hunting us."

Lonn shrugged their pack over his shoulder and took her hand. "Let's go, then." Together, they crossed the wide easter road and disappeared into the long blaygrass.

Just past midmoon, with thick clouds obscuring the light, the two reached the forest stretching north and south along Douchart's easter borderlands. Beyond that was the garrisons and the no-mins land, an oktal-wide clearing constituting the official border between the two kingdoms. While neither side had violated that stretch after the Easter Upset, it allowed each to watch for invasion. Lonn trudged forward, determined to reach it before moonfall, but the path grew more difficult the darker it got.

Taking up the lead, Caetriona sniffed the air. "Smells like water'll fall, my love."

"I know," he huffed, hunching low with her pressed beside him. Ahead, they watched brief flashes of lantern-light streaming one way and then another. "a patrol? are we… cut off?"

She squinted through the dark, silent for a long moment. "this way." Taking his hand, she led him slowly through the trushes, trying to make as little noise as possible. When the lights disappeared in the distance, they hastened their pace but hardly made it far before another patrol appeared. And they soon found their path cut off as a second patrol advanced on them. With a silent nudge, she pushed him into a nearby trush and scrambled up behind him, climbing as high as they could before the patrols converged.

"Ain't no sign of em?" One patrol commander asked the other as they conferred.

"Nuthin. Wondering if it's all just a jester prank."

The first sighed. "Skewer that jestering min if it is. Get us all riled up, specially on a night like this."

As the patrol commanders spoke, one of the soldiers wandered around the trush they were hiding in and squatted, relieving herself with a long sigh. Dangling over her head, Lonn stifled his breath and held as still as possible.

Beside him, Caetriona clung to a length of branch, head tilted, listening intently to the conversation over the sound of the soldier's relief. The soldier hiked up her striders and rushed after her patrol as the two groups parted on their routes. When Caetriona no longer heard them, she slipped down to the ground with him close behind. "that binch—"

"you were right," he grimaced, seeing the streams of lantern light speckling the dark forest. "and they've quite the vested interested."

"told them we're spies," she continued.

Lonn eyed her, alarmed. "Spies?!"

She pressed her hand over his mouth, "shush!" and groaned as the first droplets fell through the trushes, "just what we need right now." The rain fell harder, helping obscure the noise, but any hope they had that it would deter the patrols was dashed. "getting more frequent."

"how much farther, you think?"

Caetriona shrugged, silent. With the mud sucking at their boots, she worried their tracks left too obvious a trail. But it was brief. The numerous trails left by the frequent patrols would cause theirs to go unnoticed. They pressed on, cold and wet, until finally reaching the far edge of the forest.

All along the border, garrison towers stood tall as a deterrent, normally giving both sides clear views against any trespass or aggression. Lonn peered across the dark distance. "Can you see any garrisons on the other side?"

"Barely see a bloody thing in this storm."

"Seems there's no choice but to risk it. Go slow. Not make ourselves too obvious." He took her hand, assured that the falling rain would hide their crossing. "Ready, my lady?"

She smiled at his continued determination, "Always, my sweet prince," and clutched his hand. He led the way across the no-min's land from Douchart and into Merribellith.

14   The Cloud Grazer

Lonn leaned back against the cold hard stone and drummed his knuckles against the cell bars. Caetriona curled up along the bench, head resting on his thigh. "Remind me again why this keeps happening to us?" she mumbled.

Tracing his finger along her ear, he smiled. "Bad luck?"

"It's because you never got out as a child," she sighed, "Name recognition only goes so far, you know. People need to see your face."

"I did try to explain."

"You'd think it would've warranted us a more comfortable cell. Wider bench at the very least," she shivered, "A few blankets."

"I'd settle for a talk with the garrison commander," Lonn sighed, having lost count of the days since their arrival in Merribellith. It had hardly been the welcome he hoped for. They snuck across the border through the rain, still unsure where the nearest garrison stood. When Caetriona spotted the tower and colors of his homeland flying high, he breathed relief.

Cold. Tired. Hungry. They huffed up the steep hill and approached the gatehouse. The duty-watch saw them and flashed her spear down. "Who goes?"

He pulled back his hood and wiped the water from his face. "Prince Lonn Youta seeking shelter and transport back to the Palisum. Please inform the garrison commander."

After a long delay, a soldier finally came out, flashing his lantern at them both before conferring in hushed whispers with the duty-watch. They kept looking back to the point Caetriona grew uncomfortable. "Don't like this, my love."

"I'm sure it's nothing. We did arrive unannounced. Just conferring to give us an appropriate welcome."

He frowned, remembering just how inappropriate it had been. Accosted. Pockets turned outward. The duty-watch seized on their Douchart papers, and into the cells they went, branded spies. The jail guard slammed the cell door and spat. "Doucharty scum."

It hardly got better from there, as each passing guard wanted them to perform some jester feat. One of them even wanted a song before she slid their food through the bars. They refused to listen to anything Lonn tried to tell them.

He looked up through the cell window as the sky darkened. "Another storm's coming." It was about all he could look forward to as he fingered the loosening sealant in his hair. "See if we can get more of this stuff out."

"Mostly there, my love," she breathed deep. "Doesn't smell like the water'll fall this time."

"At least we're dry."

"Yes. At least there's that." A creaking echoed down the hall, and she groaned. "Wonder what new humiliation they'll press on us this time."

"Juggle," he commented, slipping her hair over her ear. She slapped his knee. "Don't even, my love."

The door to the jail room rattled open and the guard stepped in and stood stiff, waiting. From further down the hall, muffled voices approached. "...crossing the border. All they carried were Douchart travel papers. Lonn Caetriona and Caetriona Lonn. Monster Fighting Jesters," one gruff voice laughed. "And the boy presents himself at the gate as

Prince Lonn Youta like he owned the place. Madness. But that's Douchart for you. Course, the duty-watch locked em straight up. Sent the notification with the usual dispatches. Can't say I expected *this* kind of response."

"We were… in the area, Commander Linault."

The young journeymin perked up at the sound of a familiar voice. A broad smile rose on his lips as Soreign, dressed in his official Merribellith standards, stepped through the door followed by the garrison commander dressed in a well-worn uniform. "Open the cell for Sir Soreign." The jail guard hastened with the key and swung the door wide open.

The old knight stepped in and towered over the two sitting on the bench. "Hear you two make for some fecky Douchart spies."

"No worse than your pretense as a corpse," Lonn responded, cracking a wry grin.

With a hearty laugh, Soreign swiped him up, sending Caetriona's head crashing onto the bench with a *thunk*. "Ow!"

"Oh, but we feared the worst, My Prince!" he cried, hugging Lonn tight. "Alive and well!"

"And so are you, Sir Soreign!"

The guard looked at his commander, confused. "That… really is… Prince… Youta?" They both looked to the floor, embarrassed.

The knight ignored them as he continued, "And none too worse for wear, I see."

"It was close," the journeymin admitted, "On… too many occasions."

"Truly a miracle!" He shook his head in amazement and ruffled Lonn's hair, pulling his hand away and finding it flecked with sealant shards. "And what's all this?"

"Something of a… disguise. But, it's mostly out."

Soreign chuckled. "Ah! Smart lad."

"But what of you? Have you… healed from your wound?"

"Almost back to fighting fit, My Prince, but soon enough." He patted his side. "That bloody raider skewered me right through."

"I was so relieved when I learned you'd survived."

"You knew?" He eyed the young prince in surprise. "H-how?"

"Later." He patted the knight on the shoulder. "We'll speak of that later."

"Along with how you made your escape from that raider binch. On your own, no less."

"Hardly. If it wasn't for Caetriona, I wouldn't've made it this far," he commented with a faint wince.

Head resting on her arm, she let the two have their moment, but chimed in with his acknowledgement. "Thank you, Lonn."

Soreign glanced at her for the first time. "That's Prince Youta."

Lonn turned to Commander Linault. "Am I to understand my companion and I are finally free to go?"

"Hehm… of course, Your Highness." Nodding his head emphatically, the commander barely looked up. "With our sincerest… apologies."

"Much of this could have been avoided had you just met with me as requested."

The commander's face turned red, embarrassed. "I… realize that now, Your Highness."

"Ready to go, my lady?" She hopped up and took his hand, but he hesitated at the door. "Treat your prisoners more kindly, commander. They shouldn't have to perform for their meals. Provide blankets as well."

Caetriona chimed in. "And wider benches."

"I'll… take that under advisement, Your Highness."

Lonn led her out. "Come along, Soreign! Still work to do!"

Soreign looked at the guard and commander with a huff, "Perhaps best you forget this entire incident," and marched out to catch up with the young prince.

The guard glanced at his commander. "Think that could've gone worse."

Commander Linault shook his head. "All be scrubbing latrines for cycles, fool."

Down the hall, Lonn and Caetriona strapped their sword belts on and loaded their pack. Soreign eyed them both. "My Prince, who is… she?"

"My lady, Caetriona."

"You'll have to forgive me, but…" He had a vague recollection. "She looks… familiar."

"We… met. Briefly," she took a quivering breath, "I'm… that raider binch you mentioned earlier," and gave a nervous laugh, reaching her hand out. "Sorry about all that bad business before. At least it wasn't me who ran you through, right? No hard feelings?"

Her hand hung in the air while Soreign glared at her. "Got plenty."

"I… thought this might be… awkward."

"My Prince, she is *not* coming with—"

"She's coming," he cut the knight off and took her outstretched hand.

She pointed as he pulled her along. "I… go where my sweet prince goes."

Soreign shook his head with a grimace. "Bloody…"

"Come along, Soreign!" Lonn reached the door leading to the courtyard and pushed through. "I do hope you brought—" Outside, he looked up, blinking with mouth agape. "Oh. And I thought it was another storm."

Caetriona gazed upward, feeling Lonn's grip tighten.

"Different kind of storm, my love."

Hovering in the sky and shrouding the sun were military steamrunners. Nineteen in all, showing the full capabilities of the Merribellith flotilla. He counted no less than four transports, six defenders, five escorts, three patrols, and a scout. "Soreign… did you bring the entire flotilla with you?"

"If only I could. These were all I managed to secure. Twenty steamers. Five hundred footsoldiers."

Lonn stared at him, shocked. "And… just what were you planning?"

"Raze the Ciration." Soreign shrugged. "If necessary."

The young prince shook his head in disbelief. "Father… agreed to that?"

"On account of the circumstance…"

"Even at the risk of provoking King Aesinar?"

"Well, we hadn't planned on this course… not until we received the dispatch."

"But you didn't have to bring the whole flotilla *here* for that. One steamer was all you needed."

"And if it didn't come to anything? Wasted enough time as it was." Soreign stiffened. "Made the best choice I could. Now… you get an elaborate escort home."

Concerned, Lonn shook his head. "Has an emissary been dispatched to Douchart to inform King Aesinar of your intentions?"

"No. And His Highness saw no reason to." Soreign stepped close, eyeing Caetriona as he leaned in, whispering in his ear. "not even Merribellith's people know the truth of your… absence, My Prince."

"They'll think the worst," she huffed, crossing her arms.

He nodded at her assessment. "Imagine they'll be reinforcing their garrisons in short order."

"Worst?" Soreign looked between them. "Reinforcing?"

Caetriona shrugged. "We… might've left a bad impression."

"I know the feeling well where you're concerned."

Lonn looked up at the flotilla. "Which is the fastest steamer? I must speak to my father… about a number of things."

"The one I came on… the *Cloud Grazer* under Captain Iemy. Grounded at the dock."

He followed Soreign with set determination. The steam-scout, built for swift reconnaissance, sat waiting. It held a small crew, but it was fine for his needs. He huffed up the gangplank and met the captain, a stiff-shouldered min, waiting on the mideck. "Permission to come aboard, Captain Iemy?"

"Certainly. The *Cloud Grazer*'s crew welcomes you, Your Highness."

"Thank you. Once we're flying, set a direct course with all speed to the Palisum. I was told this is the fastest steamer in the flotilla. Do put that to the test."

"With pleasure, Highness! We'll make you proud." The captain hesitated. "What should I relay to the rest of the flotilla?"

"Sir Soreign will know what's best," he responded, heading to the foredeck.

"Very good, Highness."

Lonn leaned on the bow bulwark as Caetriona slipped down on the seat beside him, "I like this assertive side of you, my love," and grinned. "Can you be assertive with me later?" He smiled and stroked her cheek.

Behind them, Soreign came up to the deck, "Captain," and glanced at Lonn. "Has My Prince conveyed his orders?"

"He has to this steamer. As for the rest of the flotilla…"

"Have the captains return at their own pace." He looked

toward Douchart, feeling uncertain. "And run extensive combat drills."

The captain looked worried. "Expecting trouble?"

"Not sure." He pointed south. "Also, relay a message to Captain Pavella of the *Crimson Duress* out of Astyria. Tell him we have retrieved the journeymin alive. He'll understand."

"Very good, Sir Knight." Captain Iemy paused, looking at the bow. "And… who's she?"

Soreign grimaced, shaking his head. "Don't ask."

"Ah. Certainly, sir." He turned to carry out his duties, pausing again at the bridge hatch. "Oh. Should His Highness need rest, my quarters are at his disposal."

The *Grazer* jerked and swayed as she lifted off the dock and dropped her sails for flight, heading east at full speed. Sunfall came and went before them with the darkening eclipse and the moonrise. Caetriona spread out on the bench beside him, bent arm supporting her head. Soreign waited, giving his journeymin some time before sidling up to him. "Looks like you've got a lot on your mind, My Prince."

"Too many things, Soreign," he sighed.

"If you don't mind… what're you going to talk to His Highness about?"

"We've just gotten out of yet another cell… and I have to count ourselves fortunate. There are people we left behind in Alisard. Our people, Soreign. Sold to body merchants and now… who knows where they are."

"Ah… and you feel like you'd fail them if you don't get them home."

"Shouldn't I? And… they're not alone."

"Highness…" He winced. "I know this isn't what you'd like to hear, but they did their sworn duty. Knew the risks going in. The hardest lesson to learn… not everyone comes back."

Lonn hung his head low, eyes clenched. "Like Second Midsteamin Arilona? You… have no idea what was done to her. What the others are going through now?" He shook his head. "No, Soreign. No sworn duty should ask such a horrible price of anyone."

"Nobody asks. They follow orders and do their duty. They're willing to make that sacrifice. And we honor them the best we can for it." He rested his hand on the young prince's shoulder. "Don't know what His Highness'll say or do, but they may never be found. All we can hope is they didn't suffer."

"Hope." He sighed, "That's not good enough," and turned his gaze from the crescenbright moon to Caetriona. "Not when there's a way."

"Well, I know what His Highness'll say to that." He grumbled. "Won't like you getting mixed up in it. Especially after… all this."

"There's a lot you didn't tell me."

Soreign hung his head low. "And, I've been… facing up to that of late. All I can ask is your forgiveness. Didn't think you were ready."

"I… wasn't. Not for a lot of it. But Caetriona helped me through the worst."

"And why'd you have to get mixed up with her? Belongs in that cell back there."

"No. She's been punished enough, I think. But, I don't expect you'd understand."

The old knight eyed her for a moment. "Oh… think I understand plenty."

"We've been through a lot together. I know mistakes were made. Misdeeds. I've forgiven her. I hope you can too, in time, once you get to know her. I've come to respect her greatly and…"

He groaned, "Oh, don't say it."

"I love her, Soreign." Lonn smiled. "In a way I can't even describe."

"Bloody foolish," he sighed. "And you really think she loves you the same way?"

Caetriona twitched in annoyance and glared up at him. "Yes! Yes, I do!"

He stared down at her, face red. "Been listening in this whole time?!"

"Pretend I don't exist all you want, but I'm lying right *here!*"

"Caused us nothing but problems."

"Me cause problems? What about you?" She lashed out, pointing an accusatory finger. "Know what's caused nothing but problems for me and my sweet Lonn? That bloody warrant! None of this would've happened!"

"Not even the raid on the *Starlight's Traverse?*"

She dropped her hand, face red. "Well… no. Th-that was Grauler's idea. And they only raided the tourney winners, so… really this is still your fault for being too good. Lose next time!"

Soreign's face turned red. "And the warrant wasn't mine! Didn't even know about it til it was too late. I was in a healing bed after being skewered through by one of *your* vile raiders! So, it's your fault!"

"And I apologized for that!"

Bristling, Lonn gripped the bulwark tight. "Will you two stop?!" He glanced at Soreign, "It's your fault," then shifted to Caetriona, "And your fault," before sighing at the moon, "And my fault. Everyone's at fault. And… it doesn't matter! It's done! Leave it behind."

Soreign stiffened. "Well… I… can accept that, My Prince."

"As can I, my love," Caetriona sympathetically sighed.

Tired, Lonn slumped his shoulders. "Had something

else I wanted to discuss, but… later."

"You need proper sleep, My Prince. The captain offered his cabin."

"Most kind. Please convey my appreciation." He strode to the quardeck. "Coming, my lady?"

Caetriona rolled off the bench, but Soreign stepped close. "The captain offered that to *him*."

She frowned, staring at her feet. "Sir… Soreign… I know you're looking out for his best interests. So am I." Soreign grumbled and let her pass. "Thank you." She turned back, arms hugging her slender waist, a sly grin on her lips, "Besides, my sweet prince can't sleep without his two favorite pillows."

As she rushed after Lonn, the old taskmaster grumbled, "pillaging binch."

Halfway down to the mideck, she turned. "Heard that."

"Good!" He leaned on the bow bulwark, shaking his head. "Where'd I go wrong?"

Below decks in the captain's quarters, the young prince slumped down on the bed and pried off his boots. "Hard to believe that I'm finally heading home."

Caetriona slid her fingers through his hair. "Oh, Lonn, you're simply exhausted."

Torn, he pulled away and eyed her necklace anxiously. "I…"

Knowing his concern only too well, she kissed him. "It's okay, my love."

He gripped the crystal tightly. "No, it's… I shouldn't take your question. Not again."

"But it's my question, Lonn. I can wait. Lasted this long, and… I'm… not… even sure I'm ready for the answer. You can find them."

"Thank you, Caetriona." He tilted his head as a pressure grew in his hand and jerked away in surprise. "Huh."

"Lonn?"

"Odd, but… I… felt it pulling."

Caetriona eyed at him curiously. "Why would it do that for you?"

He blinked in surprise. "It's done that before?"

"Of course. It always pulls toward the closest door. Stronger with the coming brighmoon. But you shouldn't feel that."

"Why not?"

"Because…" she kissed him again, "You're humin."

He eyed her, certain she was holding something back. "Where did you get it?"

"It…" She frowned. "It was… mother's. And her mother's. Going all the way back to Castanostrous," and gave a faint sigh, "Found it… in her things… after… you know about all that." She pulled him down onto the bed, "Now sleep, my sweet prince. You'll need your rest for when we reach the Palisum. You'll need to be strong," and hugged him tight. "Very strong."

They fell asleep as the *Cloud Grazer* carried them eastward through the night. It was the first time in quite a while they had a real bed, and they slumbered soundly.

Soreign slept equally well in his own bunk, finally able to relax after the stress of the search eased away. Until he was jarred awake by the clinking of swords. Sunlight streamed into the cabin. "Bloody… under attack again?!" With a swipe at his eyes and a shake of his head to clear the fog, he snatched up his sword with a shout, "Knew that—" and slammed his head against the bunk beam. "Blasted binch!" Pushing through the door and wiping the blood away from the cut on his head, he burst onto the mideck, bracing for a riot, but stumbled in surprise. "What the… feck… is… this?"

Lonn and Caetriona faced each other, sparring as they did each morning. The young journeymin ducked under a swipe of her blade and came back on his feet. "Sorry, Soreign. Did we wake you?"

The knight jammed his sword into its sheath and crossed his arms, watching them. "What's she doing, My Prince? Teaching you to dance?"

Caetriona glared at him. "Just doing what you should've from the start. Teaching him to fight." She lurched back as Lonn thrust high. "Properly."

"Properly." The old knight scoffed. "With that poker you call a sword?"

She eyed his sheathed one. "Better than that butcher of yours."

"Don't give me any ideas." He focused on the young prince. "Never bested me in a match. Think you can with that dainty little thing?"

Lonn lowered his sword. "May I borrow yours, my lady?"

"Of course, my sweet prince." She handed it over along with a kiss on his cheek. "Don't be too hard on him. Still recovering from his injuries, after all."

"my lady. my sweet prince," Soreign quietly grumbled. "Don't you bloody worry about my injuries." He stepped further out on deck and was on the journeymin even as he took up her sword, raising it just in time to block the knight's blow.

Lonn thought back to every defeat. Every blow. Every knockdown. And then he did as Caetriona had taught him, focusing on the knight's chest. Being younger… faster… he wondered if Soreign had never taught him that to maintain his advantage. Countering each blow with his own, he cut out the distractions and anticipated his taskmaster's movements, throwing in a few feints to keep the knight off balance until he was winded. He then swiped in, twisting his blade around, forcing Soreign to lose his grip.

"Undisciplined. Dirty. Dishonorable," the old knight sighed, rubbing his wrist while his sword clattered across the deck. "Certainly done you no favors, My Prince."

"No favors?" Caetriona hefted up his blade. "It saved us both out there! And he just bested you, didn't he?"

He ignored her, snatching his sword away. "Have to get you retrained before going to another tourney."

"Tourney? This is real life out here!" She crossed her arms. "Old knight! You're all backwards!"

"That's Sir Old Knight to you!" he corrected, pointing at her sternly. "And I'll not be told how to train my journeymin by a—" He faltered, remembering his agreement. "Just what do you mean backwards?"

She stepped behind Lonn. "Look at the fighter you're training. He's light. Agile. You just weigh him down, fitting him to your expectations for bashing and smashing without a thought until he can't move a bloody step."

"It's what builds a knight for real combat."

"Real combat? A tourney?" she scoffed. "Not to bring up a sore point, but how'd you get run through? Want him to think everyone fights with honor and nobility. And it almost got him killed!" Her face reddened. "People fight to survive! And it's a dirty, ugly thing trying to survive out here. There's no glory in it. And it's just the survivors who get to wake up the next morning and regret the things they had to do to earn just one more day of life. Your stories… honor… glory… just a fantasy to make you feel better about yourselves and what you've done."

Soreign stood stiff, watching her wipe tears from her eyes, and laughed halfheartedly, "Well… there's the truth of it."

Lonn stared at the knight, stunned by his admission. "Soreign?"

"We'll be at the Palisum soon enough." His taskmaster slid his sword into its sheath and stomped down to the quardeck, tossing a discarding wave and disappearing below. "I'll gather your things, My Prince."

Caetriona frowned. "Did I hurt his feelings?"

"Not sure. I hope not." He kissed her and followed his taskmaster down.

The knight stood in the captain's quarters, collecting their pack, and glanced up. "No need to trouble yourself, My Prince."

"It's not, Soreign. I'm just concerned."

He patted the young journeymin's shoulder. "Perhaps I'm getting to that age."

"No. What she said upset you."

"What's that old saying? Truth hurts. And I've had to face up to my share of failings of late." He cleared his throat. "Even offered my retirement on account of my failure here."

"Soreign! You… didn't!" Lonn stared at him, shocked. "It wasn't your fault."

"It was."

"What did my father say?"

"Refused to hear me out until the matter was resolved and you were returned."

Sitting, he studied his old taskmaster for a moment before speaking up. "Perhaps you should tell me everything. I…" He hesitated and took a deep breath, "Sir Soreign, I require a full accounting of what's happened at court in my absence."

242

The knight fell silent for a moment. "Understandable, My Prince. Very well." He nodded curtly and sat on the edge of the bed. "It's…

15 Sir Soreign

Not something I've ever gotten used to… that odd sensation of cold irobon sliding into me. No matter how many times… first time it ever went right through, though. Don't recommend the experience. Just proves I'm getting too old.

Faded in and out there. Remember getting thrown about in the crash… bodies pressing into me. Might've been the thing that saved me… pressure on the wounds. Some protection from the cold.

I remember the cold.

Can't say for sure how long I was there before they found me. An Astyrian steampatroller … the *Crimson Duress*. Good crew. A fine captain. Pavella was his name. Big min. Firm grip. The solid sort you'd be glad to have at your back in a riot.

Made a thorough search of the *Starlight's Traverse* and was respectful of our fallen crew. Shrouded them well for transport back to Merribellith so they could receive full honors and have a good resting place on home soil. Made a full account and came up five short against the manifest. When he saw you were missing… a journeymin… some son of a noble… suppose it gave him cause to send out that warrant.

Didn't know anything about that. Fully in the hands of the Healers. Their Head, Ysena, was a firm lass. Seen more of me than any min and didn't shy away even when she was reaching inside places unknown to tend my wounds. Couldn't be more appreciative of those medicines they concoct. A painful burning, but at least you know it's mending things proper. She said the blade missed my lung by a fraction of an okt. Very lucky.

Didn't feel like it. Lying there in bed… nothing to do but think. With you missing, suppose I focused on every failure I could think up. Surprised by how long a list that was. Things I forgot. Things I should've done sooner. Never knew why I was selected as your taskmaster… maybe simply because I obey my orders, but… I should've pushed back harder where it really mattered. Found ways to bend the rules some. Would've seen what you're really capable of.

Made an even stronger case I'm too old for it.

The first time I was aware enough to know I'd survived, I was simply frantic, still thinking I was in that riot long since lost, shouting your name. Trying to find my feet and get back in the scrap, push through the pain tearing at my side. Healer Ysena was hovering over me, holding me down with a solid hand. Stronger than she looked, that one, being no taller than you are now. "Calmness, Sir Knight! Calmness! You'll rend your wounds open." Just felt that mist they breath out wafting over my face. Relaxed me right down. "That's it. Breathe deep."

Didn't have the strength to protest after that. She got a cup of water so I could regain my voice. "Drink this. Slowly." Slid her gloved hand under my head and propped me up. I gulped and coughed. "Slowly, Sir Knight. There are no worries upon you here."

But I had plenty of them, despite her attempt to reassure me. It was then, with Pavella sitting just beyond those sterile curtains they have, that I learned where I was and how I came to be alive. For a flotilla officer, he was blunt, which I appreciated. "Lucky to be alive from what I hear.

The rest of your crew wasn't. Why didn't you have a bloody escort?"

Thought about that myself. "Captain's call," I told him. In truth, Terasant was the only one who could answer that. Looking back, it was a foolish decision.

Pavella reported the findings of their search in short order, but I seized on the only thing that really mattered. You were unaccounted among the bodies. There was a chance. But there was information the captain desperately wanted. "It's most likely they were taken captive, so anything you could tell us about the attack would be helpful."

Easy enough to volunteer that. "Touring the lowdeck when the assault came. It was sudden. Raiders were already boarding when we got to the mideck. Never seen anything like it. Sliding down the sails as the steamraider veered around us. Knew exactly what they were doing."

"So you got a good look at her."

"Up close and personal, so to speak." I tried to pat my bound wound but had little strength at the time. "One thing I did notice… even before I was done through… their blades were fin-forged. Only the finest irobon could weather against that."

"That's… troubling. Fortunately none of the raiders we found were. Last thing we need is a bunch of bloody fin intent on revenge for the Revolt… and the blasted Scourge." Pavella's voice was full of concern. "And the steamer? Any markings? Flying colors?"

"Never saw her markings. But the sails…" I remembered those. Hard to forget. "Black. Green-fringed. She was old but didn't fly like it." Even through the curtain, I saw the captain deflate. "Not good news, then."

"That blasted steamraider! All we know of her is from sketchy rumors and the words of dying crew. She attacks suddenly. Hardly any survive. Those that do… barely live long enough to tell us much beyond what you have. No idea to her markings. All we know is that she flies with those sails and her captain might just be the foulest binch ever to take up the mantle."

I confirmed that… the last thing I remembered seeing… *her* standing over us. "No sightings at any dock towns?" I asked, hopeful.

"None. How she gets resupplied or offloads her stolen cargo… would have to be along the Crumbling Coast."

The guild homes. No fealty to any but themselves. If they'd gotten you there… would've been near impossible to track you down. "Think they mean to ransom the prisoners?"

"Crew isn't worth much, but you know that. Only one with any real potential value is your journeymin. But that's only if they discover who he is. *We're* not even sure who he really is. The steamer's manifest didn't exactly help."

Couldn't shed any light where that matter was concerned. Probably should've, if only to help the captain understand the delicate situation. If I had, perhaps things might have gone better for us all. It was after that conversation that Healer Ysena whisked him away to let me rest.

When Captain Pavella made his plans… never told me. Reckon on account of my condition and, admittedly, poor mental state. Saw it all over. My doubts. My fears. "It's not your fault."

"Course it is. His first venture. My responsibility. Doesn't know what the world is like. What the people are really like." I slumped down, wheezing against the pain, "Can't… even imagine what he's… going through right now. Vile… horrors he's enduring. Didn't… prepare him for none of that. He… he isn't ready."

Pavella crossed his arms, giving a labored sigh, "If he's

anything like his taskmaster, he'll endure it. Just as you did."

"That's different. When I was his age… it was the war. Had to grow up fast."

"We all did. And we survived. He will too… and be stronger for it."

"Will he?" Had my doubts then… so many on account of my failure. "Fear it'll change him."

"Hopefully it does. For the better." The captain kicked forward and sat up. "So, let's stay focused on getting him back."

Of course I wanted that more than anything. But in my state, just couldn't see it. That's why he waited so long to fill me in. Now, I understand why he did it. A difficult position to be in. Just wish he consulted me beforehand. But he adamantly believed it would get you back, and Astyria would save face. It put you in danger, and on top of that… I worried about a black mark on your reputation. Still couldn't tell him the whole of it.

But it did give us leads we could follow.

Then we got summoned to Alisard. Made a right bloody mess of that place, I'll tell you. The riot tore up most of the barter district. Should've seen it. Food stalls upturned. Blood splatters and smeared produce all over the courtyard. Windows smashed in. Take a good while to clean all that up. Even more to get the patrons back. Place was near empty when we got there. Nervous vendors and shopkeeps. None willing to talk.

I was at least on my feet again by then. Remember visiting the city protectorate office staring at these two big cells… head merchants in one, body merchants in the other. And their riot still wasn't done. Didn't have any weapons but barbed tongues and a few fists for anyone who dared get close enough to the other. Hadn't seen that many bruised and bloody faces in one place since the Easter War, let me tell you.

She was at least right about that… could've gotten hurt or worse.

And they were both sides laying claim to the reward even though you'd long gone. Took a good while to figure that out. Did learn you weren't alone, and hoped it was one of the others from the *Traverse*. That was dashed after giving it a thought. Would've turned yourself right in had that been the case.

No. Had to narrow the search down to all the steam-runners that made their escape during the riot. And that dockmaster of theirs… Captain Pavella got hold of her ledger and… could barely read a word of it. Horrible script, she had. "Are these… ship names?" Made my frustration clear. "What is this feck? No cargo manifests? No destination records?"

The captain knew it fell short of our needs but was more tolerant. "Doing the best she can. Know how difficult it can be. A private bunch, these merchants. Not likely to share their manifests or even let inspectors aboard. Most just run the lanes wherever they think the profit might be. Some don't even know where they're going, no plan greater than a whim."

Twenty-three in all on that list. Impressed they'd already cleared nineteen of them, leaving just four. Could've been anywhere at that point, but at least we narrowed the search down. Just had to wait. Course, you know how good I am at waiting.

Fortunately, it wasn't long. In fact, I just so happened to be on the foredeck of the *Duress* when two Astyrian steam-patrollers sailed by, towing the broken wreck of one of our quarry, the *Barking Binch*. She'd certainly put up a fight and gotten a pounding for it. The hull was speckled with cannon shot, puncture holes the size of my head. Barely flying with just two patched up navigation propellers. Looked so cobbled together, surprised she managed to get anywhere, let alone a patrol lane.

And the crew was in just as bad shape. Torn up by the shattered hull and cannon shrapnel. Some burnt from tanks bursting and the steam exhaust… so bad their skin sloughed off in chunks. Horrible thing to see. By the time I got to the dock, healers were already carting off the worst of the bunch. Screams of agony like you wouldn't believe.

They even had a few strapped down tight on stretchers. Heligen inhalation. Make sure they didn't just float away from breathing all that gas when the tanks ruptured. Horrible fate, I hear. Just… up and float away, so high that you'll freeze to death in moonlight or just… *poof*… burn to a crisp in the sun.

Now, I was itching to find the captain of that doomed steamer on account we didn't know what fate had befallen her. Made my way through the injured for even one who was still right in the head. Best I found was the First Midsteamin. The healer leading the group protested at first, but relented at my insistence. "Of— of course. Seems that's all he's been doing anyways." Really talking up quite the storm, that one.

"… and the captain, he's all like, 'I wanna kill that binch!' and we's just… that's all fine and good, but what's in it fur us? I mean, seriously no profit in revenge."

The one tending looked at me. "His injuries are minor, Sir Knight, but remain brief."

"Minor?!" The First Midsteamin lifted his arm, showing the long bloody gashes torn along the length. "These ain't minor! What's bloody wrong with yu?!"

"Just means you'll live. Looks like some of your crew

won't be so lucky," I told him. He wore a guild mark on his arm, tattered from his injury, but I could make it out well enough. "So, you're part of the head merchantry. Where's your guild head?"

"Like I just sayin,'" the First Midsteamin chuckled, "Got himself a personal grudge and… got lost in the battle. Likely dead."

"So you're in for a promotion."

He perked up at that. "Say! That's right! Hadn't thought a that."

"And the warrant you were chasing down… I need details."

"Some whelp." Slapped that insubordination right out of him with the back of my hand, I did. He rubbed his jaw. "Alright. Alright! No need tu rough me up more. A… what's it called. journeymin. Head wanted him something fierce. Him and some binch he was running with. Made off on some old steamer."

"The name," I insisted, despite the healers' protests.

"*Wanderer*… the *Virgin Wanderer*. Head, he just thought we'd run um tu pace and force the crew tu hand um over. Fired a few shots tu get their attention. Before yu know it, they had a full flank a six sideboard cannons tearing us tu pieces! And pairs on both fore and aft quarters!" he gasped, "Never seen a steamerchant armed like that. What's the world comin tu?"

Leaned closer, losing patience. "What happened?"

"We fired back's what happened! They fired! We fired! Every which way. Heligen tanks blown. Water tanks blown. Everything blown! We left um sinking. Barely had enough pressure tu run. Got a good headwind, though. Yu figure the rest."

"Didn't you go after the head?"

"How?" That reply surprised me plenty. Ruined their

whole reputation. "Look a that wreck. Couldn't pull off a capture. Besides, no way I was risking my neck. Not where they crashed. Not for all the clinkin coin in the world." I insisted he tell me where the steamer ran to ground. Might've roughed him up a bit to the displeasure of the tending healers. "The Ciration Forest! Ain't no comin outta there. Lay off now, will yu!"

I did and without hesitation made for the *Crimson Duress*, course set. Our determined search started where the patrol first encountered the *Barking Binch*, heading along the forest edge. Captain Pavella had five spotters on deck at all times investigating any sign of the *Virgin Wanderer*'s wreckage. Found her a quarter to midsun on the third day. Come to a most violent crash, as you well know. Gouged a long crescent in the forest before coming to her final resting spot, bow wedged in the dirt and piles of fallen trushes.

Grew so anxious to get grounded and begin searching, I threw down my own line, prepared to rappel the distance. Pavella protested, hoping I would wait for a more prepared expedition, but relented when two of his midsteamin, the bravest officers I could ever have at my side, threw their own lines down to join me.

Second Midsteamin Whincott was short but muscular, with keen eyes and a hawkish nose, while Third Midsteamin Kierlow was a lean figure and tall, standing almost a head over me.

We three descended into that deep dark, blades brandished as we set boots on the bent and twisted mideck. All seemed quiet and still, with just the faint sound of the navigation propellers from the *Duress* above.

But that silence shattered when beset we were so suddenly by a vile horde of troblytes! Never seen creatures so foul. Each taller than the tallest foe I ever faced in any battle. Their beady, blood-hungry eyes showed their villainous intent.

One swipe of an arm, and Kierlow was off his feet, sent sprawling into the trushes. The branches gave a violent riot as he fought the beasts off. Their agonized screams sent shudders even down my spine, I'll tell you.

But Whincott stood firm at my back with her sword at the ready as we together warded off those that surrounded us. Hacking at limbs and heads, we cut a bloody swath of violence through them until she and I were left winded, arms heavy, spattered in blood and bile.

There was no accounting for the losses they took as the survivors limped back into the forest right where they belonged to lick their wounds. Suffice to say, we gave them such a dashing they held no interest in a second attempt, and we were left unmolested to search the remainder of the wreckage.

All we found were badly mutilated bodies, by fortune none matching your size or stature. Whincott, with those trained eyes of hers, did spot a source of hope. Down in the dirt along the broken hull of the forequarter was a fire pit the likes of which those foul troblytes couldn't conceive. A clear sign of survivors.

We spread out, searching for clues. My own discovery only confirmed my suspicions about the true intent of the *Virgin Wanderer*. A torn fragment of her sails, black with green trimming. The revelation that the foul steamraider had been disguised as a distinguished merchant vessel came as a shock to us all. But it proved we were on the proper trail.

I found Whincott crouched, neck craned, squinting through the dense foliage. She pointed out at my approach. "Got tracks here, Sir Soreign." I joined her, careful not to tread heavily and ruin any revelations. When she pointed them out, they became as clear as if I had made them my-self not moments before. Her voice grew low with worry. "Heading north. Don't know why."

Studied the setting and came to the grim conclusion you'd grown disoriented from the crash and believed in earnest you were heading on a proper course. It was then that I faced the impossible decision. After such a fight, fa-tigued as we were, there was no chance we could make fur-ther progress as sunfall approached. The *Crimson Duress* was sturdy, but his crew was admittedly small.

Made my determined decision then to return to Mer-ribellith to gain a properly outfitted company of reinforce-ments. It was an anguishing choice, but even Captain Pavella agreed it was the best option. And they had the *Starlight's Traverse*'s crew to consider, honor bound to return. It was a grim course that we set.

Even wondered somberly as we left the wreck behind if any of the corpses we had found were the other captured crew, put to work during the battle. But there was no telling, and we had to give them up for losses. I also faced the ob-vious failure of returning without a true accounting of you, a stain I carried throughout the voyage and even after I set my eyes on the Palisum spires stretching into the sky.

We were met by two escorts and received at the dock by the royal protectorate.

The captain joined me on the foredeck, and I took his arm gladly. "Captain Pavella, you and your valiant crew have gone beyond your duty. A credit to your kingdom," I told him, deeply earnest, as we set down.

"Don't go telling that to your king, now! Don't need the reputation… or the promotion," he declared, causing us both to laugh heartily, before stepping up to the bow. "Astyr-ian honor-guard requesting permission to disembark!"

From below, Royal Protectorate Commander Henatore stepped forward and called up, "Merribellith respectfully welcomes the Astyrian honor-guard!"

Pavella took to my shoulder, and together we went down the gangplank.

"Sir Soreign, welcome back! We—" The commander's face fell when he saw the crew of the *Crimson Duress* trailing behind us bearing the shrouded bodies from the *Starlight's Traverse*. He cleared his throat and waved with his hand. "Protectorate! Relieve their burdens with… with honor and grace to the fallen."

It was a respectful exchange. The protectorate took up positions and bore the weight of the stretchers as the crew fell back, standing in stoic silence until the last had been delivered properly to Merribellith soil. The captain looked at the commander. "On behalf of Astyria and the honorable crew of the *Crimson Duress*, convey our deepest regrets and sympathies to the families of the fallen."

Commander Henatore stiffened. "I shall do so personally, captain."

I saw to it that the steampatroller was properly restocked and outfitted for its return to Astyria and parted from the captain and crew with nothing but respect and newfound friendship.

Once the grim business had passed, the commander escorted me to the great hall where His Majesty awaited word. I stood before the great doors as I was announced, expecting the worst. "Sir Soreign requesting an audience with His Majesty." I was almost relieved when the doors parted and found the court had been dismissed from the hall. My humiliation would be contained, at least for a while, until the rumors slipped out.

And they always do.

His Majesty and My gracious Queen sat at the far end, ready to receive me. It was still difficult to bear the shame of my failure to them alone as I made my approach. The sound of the doors sealing behind me in that silent hall never was more thunderous. I reached the steps and took to my knee, head bowed low.

His Majesty's voice rose up. "Sir Soreign! Returned at last. Gone quite a while… celebrating your magnificent victories, no doubt! What news?" There was a moment of silence. "And where's our son?! I want to see that little rascal!"

I grew pale, surprised the report issued by Captain Pavella and myself as we entered Merribellith had not reached his ears. It was left to me to break the unhappy news. Still not able to raise my head and look at either of them, I drew a slow breath, "Your Majesty… I… regret to report that I return bearing ill tidings."

His Majesty slid to the edge of his throne, worry on his face as he exchanged glances with My equally worried Queen. "Oh? Do tell."

I recounted our unfortunate tale much as I have here, concluding with my penance. "If it pleases Your Majesty, I offer my retirement from the field."

My Queen, in all her wisdom, rose up. "When there is still an incomplete quest before you?"

His Majesty nodded. "Had you your shield, I'd break it over your head for suggesting anything so outlandish."

I offered. "I could find one, Your Majesty, if it pleases you."

Again, My Queen provided wise counsel, "I doubt that's called for… nor the trouble of fixing up the old coffin." She remained pale, hands clasped tightly before her, clearly affected by my tale. "They were set upon by a superior force, My King."

"As you say." His Majesty tilted his head in deference to

My Queen. "There's enough amends to make with a successful campaign."

"But in the Ciration Forest, My King?" Her tone revealed her skepticism.

His Majesty nodded. "Yes, yes, My Queen. I know the stories. Those… fin. Spreading their tales of terror. And what are we supposed to believe? They could not conquer such a trivial territory, so how could us mere humins accomplish such a thing? But look what we accomplished in the Revolt. And look where the fin are now." He cast his gaze full upon me. "Sir Soreign, I am tasking you with preparing a plan of assault. If there are even more of those foul beasts that live within that horrendous forest like those that beset you, I want a well prepared troop to make short work of them."

My Queen offered, "The flotilla is still in disrepair."

"Still?" His Highness glanced back at My Queen and grunted, "Ah! There must be a few we can outfit quickly. Yes! Have ready a report to me…" he paused, "Tomorrow?"

My Queen shook her head. "We have that—"

"Yes, of course… that… if we must." He scratched the tip of his nose. "Two days hence." Eyes cast to the ceiling, he paused, but My Queen remained silent. "Yes. Two days."

And so that was my task, My Prince. I gathered a solid flotilla with enough footsoldiers outfitted for the task to sweep north from the *Virgin Wanderer*'s wreck in search of you. En route, we received a report of Douchart spies and your claim. Filled with hope, I diverted our course, and, with great relief, the rest, you know.

16 The Palisum

Listening to his taskmaster's tale, Lonn slowly nodded. "That was… quite the harrowing tale, Soreign. Must've been a challenge to endure that all the while you were recuperating."

"Appreciate you saying so, My Prince."

"Are you… still going to push for retirement?"

Soreign remained silent, considering it carefully. "I may have a bit more left to teach, if it pleases you to have me stay on, My Prince."

"Certainly, Soreign," he smiled. "I wouldn't like to have to break in a brand new taskmaster after all this time. I'd be grateful for your continued service."

"I… I thank you, My Prince, for saying so," the old knight choked, busying himself collecting their pack. "I'll finish here."

Lonn left Soreign to his thoughts and found Caetriona sitting on the steps leading to the bridge, settling down beside her. She rested her head against his with a laugh, "Did I hear that right? Troblytes taller that the tallest foe?"

"Shush," he chuckled, "Must've been a different tribe than the one we escaped."

"Oh, yes. That must be it, my love."

He gasped and rose to his feet. "And there it is." Stretching through the clouds, the glimmering towers of the Palisum came into view. Citrimaline gemstones embedded within the stonework provided its distinct shimmering yellow hue, a marvel of aelfin design and humin construction finished long before the Revolt. It rose out of the surrounding rock and towered over a sprawling city below, the heart of the Merribellith kingdom. "Home at last."

She pressed close, tightly wrapping her arms about him. "Yes. Home… at last."

The *Cloud Grazer* raised her sails, switching to navigation propellers for her final approach, and lurched with a great *thump* on her landing skids. Soreign emerged from the quardeck with their gear in hand and waited at the gangplank. "We should head straight to the great hall, My Prince."

Lonn hesitated, looking down at himself. "You think that's wise, Soreign?"

"Think it's not up to me. Nor you."

"Of course." Understanding fully, the young prince sighed, "They must be quite worried," and took the lead.

The dockworkers milled around the edge, waiting to provide support and services to the steamscout, but one among them, a stout figure with long curling dark hair and wearing light blue, grease-stained coveralls and goggles dangling about his neck, was not so focused on the tasks as he was on the party. In his grip dangled a tightwrench as he blocked their path. "So, Sir Knightly Knight. You're back! And sooner than you said."

Caetriona turned an amused gaze between the two min while Lonn stopped in his tracks, eyeing his taskmaster with a question, "Soreign?"

The knight faltered a step, a wash of crimson spread over his face. "Oh, bloody feck."

The dockmaster bounded up to the old knight and gripped him firmly, planting a kiss on his lips. "Thought your expedition was gonna keep you away from me for at least a cycle or more. Just couldn't wait for me to offer more of my favor, huh?"

"The… expedition met with unexpected success, my… dear Zhanne."

"Oh? So… that must be…" The dockmaster released him from his embrace and glanced down at the journeymin, offering a nervous bow. "Prince Lonn… Your Highness… so pleased my knightly knight's found you safe and well. He's been beside himself with worry these past many days."

Offering a faint nod, the young prince. "Thank you for saying so."

"Best get on with business then!" He smacked Soreign's backside and grinned. "Off my shift at a quarter to midmoon."

Soreign cleared his throat. "Provided My Prince does not need me…"

"Best not…" He hoisted his tightwrench over his shoulder and strutted across the dock toward the *Cloud Grazer*. "Least not every night."

Lonn watched the dockmaster carry on, desperate to stifle his surprise and curiosity. "Sir Soreign… it seems your account was perhaps… lacking a detail… or two?"

The knight's face reddened. "Not at all, My Prince. My account covered all except where matters of the… hem… bedchamber… are concerned."

"Ahh. You're right, of course." The young prince nodded, moving along the dock. "It's not my place to pry, but I'm happy for you."

"Appreciate you saying so, My Prince. It just… well… a knight should have something to look forward to in retirement."

"Or sooner," the young prince commented, taking Caetriona's hand.

Along the side of the dock stood a group of royal protectorate. Commander Henatore stiffened in his crisp blue uniform as they approached. "Welcome home, Prince Lonn."

"Thank you," he responded with a nod.

Quickly appraising the group, Henatore motioned. "Sir Soreign, allow my protector to unburden you."

"With thanks, commander. This can be placed in Prince Lonn's chambers." He handed over the pack.

The commander turned his gaze to Caetriona, focused on her belt and sword. "And I must ask that you relinquish your arms."

She stiffened a moment, looking between them. "And why am *I* the only one who has to give over my blade?"

Lonn frowned faintly. "Protocol, I'm afraid, my lady."

Soreign cleared his throat, "Not a knight. Not a soldier. Not one sworn to any duty or loyalty."

"Except to my sweet prince."

"And you're going to see His Majesty."

"Oh!" Surprised at the suggestion, she huffed, "But where's the trust?!"

Soreign quietly grumbled, "where you're concerned?"

She shot him a glare as Lonn squeezed her hand reassuringly. "Only temporary."

"Temporary," she sighed, unlatching her buckle. "Very well." As the protector turned to depart, she wavered on her feet, "Hold a moment," and unclasped her necklace, dropping it into their pack, as the protector faltered. "Carry on."

Lonn eyed her curiously as she returned to his side and took his hand.

Commander Henatore gave them all another look before turning. "This way, My Prince."

"If you insist on escorting, commander," he shrugged. "But, I do know the way."

"I have my orders, My Prince." He led them along the wide corridors, up the spiral towers, and across courtyards on their way to the great hall.

As they trailed down the final corridor with the great doors in view, Lonn felt resistance in his grip and glanced back, concerned. "Caetriona, are you… nervous? Your hand's trembling."

"Perhaps a bit, my sweet prince." She laughed faintly, "Must be just the thought of… meeting your parents for the first time."

"Everything'll be fine. You'll see." He eyed her, lingering on her bare neck. "And there wasn't a need to leave your necklace behind. Strange seeing you without it, I have to admit. Never seen you take it off before."

"Only… temporary, my love." She found herself wanting to say more, but could hardly find the words as they reached the doors.

"Prince Lonn and… company requesting an audience with His Majesty," the herald called out, and the large doors rattled open. At the far end, King and Queen Youta resided on their thrones, anxiously waiting, while the rest of the hall remained empty and quiet. He strode forward along the blue carpet, but Caetriona lingered, hesitant, trying to catch her breath.

Soreign stepped up behind her. "Just one foot forward. Breathe slow." Finding his voice and tone almost reassuring and sympathetic, she took one hesitant step after another trailing some paces behind Lonn with Soreign marching at the rear, still on guard. Her shoulders gave a slight jerk as the doors rattled closed behind them. "Hold here. Give them their moment." She glanced back, seeing him lower to his knee, head bowed, and awkwardly did the same.

Lonn stood straight before the raised dais, looking up

at his parents. Tired. Disheveled. Utterly unprepared for an audience. He was relieved that they had dismissed the court. King Youta rose off his throne, drawing back his long blue robes trimmed in gilver threads, and clasped his son about the shoulders. "My son! Welcome home!"

"Thank you father, mother. I hope you have both been well and not overly distressed by my absence."

Queen Youta, in a gilver dress threaded in Merribellith blue, swept down the steps, hugging him tightly with a sigh of relief, "Of course, we have been greatly worried, my dear son!" She appraised him carefully. "You haven't been hurt, have you? Clearly haven't been eating well."

"No. mother." Lonn's face grew flush with embarrassment. "Nothing serious."

"When Sir Soreign fully informed us of the situation… raiders? Riots? And troblytes?"

"Think of what you put your poor mother through! And me!" Sporting a beaming grin from beneath his bushy brown beard, the king ruffled his son's hair, "But you managed your own escape! Braving such travails… done yourself proud, my son."

He looked between them, determined. "Father, I was not the only one. We must discuss—"

"Oh, later, Lonn," the king cut him off, patting his shoulder. "Time enough for that later. Once you've cleaned yourself up." His nose twitched. "Bathed."

The queen nodded. "You're absolutely filthy from your travels."

"I'm well aware, mother, and count myself fortunate." He stiffened. "But while I do those things, others— our citizens, father— toil in far worse states. For far too long already— sold to body merchants in Alisard! I swore an oath to see them freed!"

"Others, you say?" King Youta reared up, looking past the young prince. "Sir Soreign, what others?"

The old knight glanced up. "Your Highness, based on My Prince's account, I was apparently mistaken about the fate of the *Starlight's Traverse*'s crew. Not all of them perished."

"Yes. I see. Tragic situation, that. So very tragic." The king nodded somberly. "Body merchantry in Alisard, you say… hmmm. I will send an immediate letter of inquiry to Queen Valinar to see this matter resolved."

"A letter of inquiry?" Lonn shook his head. "Father, a more substantial—"

"More substantial?" King Youta raised a finger, cutting the prince off. "No."

"But you don't fully understand the situation!"

"And you don't understand these delicate politics. No, my son! That wouldn't do."

"Delicate politics?" Lonn's face reddened. "What of those in regard to Douchart? What will King Aesinar think when he hears of the flotilla at his border?"

"Let that traitor think what he will! It has nothing to do with our dealings with Astyria. Queen Valinar is a dear friend and ally. We will do all we can… diplomatically."

The queen took her son's hand. "Far as any are concerned, Lonn, you remained in Astyria to take in the sights. Your first time in a foreign land and to celebrate your thirteenth bloom. That is all anyone need know."

"And your successful return can put this whole business behind us."

"I… see." Lonn looked between them, realizing the futility of further argument.

The queen smiled. "We thought that best, dear. No need to worry about such things anymore. Now you're home and can rest easy. Let things get back to normal."

The young prince frowned. "Normal."

"Yes!" The king smiled. "Now go get cleaned up, and over dinner, regale us with tales of your adventures."

"Adventures," he sighed.

His father slapped him on the shoulder. "I'm sure you have grand stories to tell surviving out there like that all on your own!"

"But I wasn't on my own, father." Lonn looked between his parents before turning back, his hand out. "Caetriona… my lady." Both king and queen exchanged cautious glances between them as she rose up, taking a few nervous steps and clutching his hand briefly. "I wouldn't have survived long without her at my side."

"You… made your escape with another captive?" King Youta appraised her thoughtfully. "Well, Lady Caetriona, come and present yourself. What noble family do you herald from?"

She took a deep breath and quickly embraced the young prince, whispering in his ear, "don't blame them, my love. whatever happens."

"What?' Lonn stiffened. "No! You—"

She cut him off with a shake of her head, placing her finger on his lips. With a faint smile, she turned away and approached his parents, head low. "I… am no proper lady, your grace. I hold no title, nor come from any family of nobility. My name is… Caetriona Vidula, daughter of the once honorable merchant Aesard Vidul."

"Caetriona! You don't have to—"

"But I do, my sweet prince!" She cut him off sharply, staring at the floor, wiping at her eyes. "For the harm I caused, I must."

"Harm?" Queen Youta stiffened, gazing at Caetriona standing before them pale and trembling.

King Youta huffed, "Yes. Explain yourself."

Hesitantly, she looked at them both. "As the bound captain of the former *Virgin Wanderer*, my inactions wronged you deeply. While my sweet Prince Lonn has graciously forgiven me my past deeds—"

"Stop! You've punished yourself enough!"

"Not one more outburst!" The king pointed sternly at his son. "Let. Her. Speak!"

"For my past misdeeds… all I can offer is my heartfelt regret and my deepest apologies. It will never be enough."

Queen Youta appraised her in quiet sympathy seeing honest tears drip down her cheeks. But there was something else she noticed in her pale features. Remaining silent, she turned to her husband as he huffed.

"Captain? Captain of the *Virgin Wanderer*, you say? Foolish girl!" The king looked from Caetriona to Lonn and Soreign, both tense. With a shake of his head, he cast an eye to the arching ceiling, collecting his thoughts, "You condemn yourself!" and turned back to her. "The crime of raiding brings a death sentence."

Lonn lurched forward. "You can't do that!"

The king grew red-faced. "Sir Soreign, remove the prince from these chambers!"

Soreign sighed and stepped forward, leveling a firm hand on his shoulder. "My Prince."

"They can't do this, Soreign! It's wrong!"

"You can't help her like this, My Prince. Walk out with dignity… or I carry you." Lonn glared at him a moment before turning to Caetriona. She wiped the tears away with the back of her hand and nodded. He clenched his fists and turned, stalking across the hall with Soreign trailing close behind until the doors opened and they were through.

When the doors rattled closed, the king sighed, "Where

was I?"

Queen Youta clenched her hands in her lap. "Death sentence, My King."

He nodded, looking down at the former raider. "Death sentence! Do you realize that, girl?"

"Only too well, your grace," she nodded, sniffing back tears.

He looked around the empty chamber and then eyed his queen. She tilted her head, appraising the situation thoughtfully, but gave a faint shrug when she noticed her husband's gaze. He nodded curtly. "Guard!" The doors rattled open. "Take this girl to a cell."

The guard took her in hand and led her out into the hall beyond where Lonn paced anxiously. She smiled at him as they passed. "I love you, my sweet prince. Remember that."

He charged after her, stopped once more by Soreign's firm hand. Struggling still, the young prince turned back to his father, tears in his eyes, and entered the hall once more. "How could you do that? It wasn't her fault!"

"Her confession says otherwise and left me little choice. And you brought her before us!" The king laid an accusatory eye on his son. "You knew, yet said nothing!"

"She's not like them! And she saved my life— many times over!" He wiped at his eyes. "What she was forced to do in the past doesn't matter!"

"It most certainly does, my son! And should you ever make it to the throne, you'll have to understand that." He glanced at his queen. "We'll speak again once you've calmed yourself."

Queen Youta raised her head. "Sir Soreign, our son is not permitted near the dungeons."

Soreign grimaced faintly. "As you order, My Queen." He gripped Lonn's shoulder and once again escorted him from the chamber.

When the doors rattled closed and silence set in, King Youta collapsed onto his throne with a heavy sigh, "Well, that soured the mood quickly, My Queen."

She nodded thoughtfully. "It took quite some courage to confess that."

He reached out, and she took his hand. "Certainly did."

"And how long do you plan to keep the poor girl locked away?"

"Long enough to let this blow over." He shrugged, uncertain. "Half a bloom?"

"Not three cycles?"

"You think a quarter bloom is enough?"

"So… two cycles?"

"Fine," he sighed. "A cycle then."

"That would be punishment enough… for them both."

"For both, you think?" He stared at her, shocked. "Just an infatuation. He'll get over it."

The queen eyed him, highly dubious. "That… wasn't infatuation, My King."

He perked up, surprised. "What? You think it's… love? He's too young for that."

"Is he?" She gazed down to where Caetriona's tears stained the floor. "I wonder."

He waved his hand absently. "Forced or not, a raider is a raider."

"Certainly an attractive prospect there for so young a min."

The king nodded appreciatively. "With a perky bosom."

"Surprised he didn't smother himself in his sleep."

"And those long legs."

"Leading to an enticing valley."

"You believe he explored that far?"

"Quite a few times, I should think, by the look of them," she shrugged, "as young mins are so wont to do these days."

"After only a cycle away." The king sniffed and wiped a stray tear from his eye. "Our littlest one's gone and grown up, My Queen!"

She pat his hand reassuringly. "I know, my dear. I know."

Lonn burst through his chamber door, seething in anger, pacing back and forth, and wanting to hit something with fists clenched. But the glinting metal of Caetriona's necklace drooping from the top of their pack caught his eye and gave him pause. As Soreign entered and shut the door behind him, the young prince pulled it free and appraised it with a sigh, "Knew this might… would happen. And she did it anyway." He glanced at his taskmaster. "You knew, didn't you?"

"No, My Prince. Not for sure. But…" The old knight stiffened and shook his head. "Well, she made no secret of who she was when we met. And she asked for my forgiveness. Wasn't… sure she was in earnest then, but… seeing her before our audience… clearly determined to do the right thing."

"It wasn't"

Soreign drew a long sigh, "Begging your forgiveness, My Prince, but it was. A criminal courting a prince? Doesn't matter what she's done since. What she was… did before… it was right to confess. Better than if they learned it on their own and you'd said nothing."

He glared at his taskmaster. "You knew and said nothing."

"And if His Majesty had asked me directly, I would've told him," the old knight admitted, "But I believe I was under My Prince's instruction to drop the matter."

Lonn blinked, shaking his head in embarrassment. "You're right. Forgive me. I'm… clearly in a foul mood."

He gripped the crystal tight, feeling it pull. "Oh, Soreign. If… if she's executed… she told me not to blame them, but…"

"Can't speak to the mind of His Highness, but she did put him in a difficult spot."

"She left this behind for me so her sacrifice wouldn't be in vain, but… I don't know if I can do this without her."

"Just what is that, My Prince?"

"A Gazer's Stone."

Soreign's eyes grew wide in shock. "A… Gazer? They're… real?"

The young prince nodded. "Met one. She… knew things. Told me you were alive. If I can just ask the right question… she could tell me where the others are."

"Hmmm." The old knight grimaced, uncertain. "I've heard stories… old myths… dangerous… dark. Bad sort to get mixed with."

"No choice." He slipped it around his neck and dropped it under his tunic. "How long before the next brighmoon?"

"Brighmoon? Oh… should be… tomorrow or the next."

Upturning their pack on a small side-table, he rifled through the meager belongings remaining from their journey and sighed relief, "At least she didn't steal them all." Buried at the bottom was the last coin purse Caetriona had recovered from the *Virgin Wanderer*'s wreckage.

"My Prince?"

"Majie… she… found the warrant in our pack along with our coin purses before reporting us to the Douchart garrison." He poured the pile of gilvers into his palm but was uncertain if it would meet Castanostrous' price. "Sir Soreign, your services are not required for the night. Visit your min. I need time to think."

Soreign eyed him cautiously. "You'll not do anything rash, My Prince?"

Lonn looked out the window. "Seems I can't do a bloody thing until the brighmoon."

Down in the Palisum dungeons, Caetriona sat on the narrow bench leaning against the stone wall and hugging her knees. Her ears twitched with the faint jangle of keys. The door whined open, causing her to wince. She looked up when a sack dropped on the floor, jingling from the sizable load of gilvers within. "And what's that?"

On the other side of the bars, Queen Youta stood stoic, looking at her curiously. "Three thousand gilvers. The final total on my son's warrant, so I've been told."

"So they did raise it!" She tilted her head back and laughed, "Grauler would've been so pleased with himself."

"Cut all your pretenses, raider. It's what you truly came for, isn't it? You brought him home safe. In appreciation for your efforts…" She slipped a key from the back of her belt and unlocked the cell door, swinging it wide open.

Caetriona appraised her with a faint smirk. "So, you know that trick, too."

The queen stepped back, motioning from the sack to the door. "It's yours along with your life and your freedom on condition you leave this kingdom and never return… under pain of death, of course."

"Of course." She remained seated. "Really should make these benches wider, your highness."

"They're not intended for long stays."

"Well, I'm certainly not going anywhere. You'll just have to execute me. That's the only way you'll get me to leave Lonn."

The queen lingered in the doorway. "Are you so certain?" She reached into her gown. "As a princess, I served my father mediating between the royal court of Tremelaine and the Healers Guild. I also learned some of their trade… helped in birthings. Most might not notice, but for someone who just traveled such a distance, you are quite pale."

"If you say so."

"I believe you call it the Brighmoon's Blessing. So, you know what this is." The queen pulled a bottle from her gown pocket and tapped it on the bars of the cell. Caetriona instinctively pressed back against the stone wall. "I see that you do." She nodded, her concerns proven. "Your kind desires it above all else."

"keep that away from me!"

"No reason to fight it. You'll have all the tillup you can carry. Enough to bliss away with your newfound wealth until your so-called Scourge takes you. Until you're far from this kingdom, and my son is a forgotten memory."

"G—"

"Yes?" Queen Youta held it out. "It's right here. Just reach out and take it."

Caetriona shook her head furiously. "Get that filth away from me!"

The queen drew back, impressed by her willpower. "As you wish."

"You can keep your gilvers, your grace! And your foul tillup! Nothing you do'll make me leave my Lonn!" she hissed through her clenched teeth, wiping at the tears in her eyes. "You'll have to execute me! And on that day, you'll do the most horrible thing of all! You'll break his sweet heart, and he'll *never* forgive you!"

"Hmm. We shall see." She stepped away, but stopped and set the bottle on the sack of gilvers. "I'll just leave this here for when you change your mind." Keeping the cell door swung wide open, the queen departed.

17 The Gazer's Path

Soreign rummaged through his old chest, pulling trinkets and souvenirs from campaigns long past, and felt the nostalgia set in. They filled his thoughts increasingly over the past cycle as he placed them carefully aside so not to wake Zhanne lying sprawled out and disheveled in his bed.

Finally, he uncovered his old journeymin's armor and checked it over, from helm to sabatons. Complete and in good condition. It had been his plan to use them in Lonn's advanced training, when the journeymin was finally ready for that step, but recent events proved that he had delayed far too long. He slid each piece into a large sack and hoisted it over his shoulder with a faint chuckle to himself.

It was light compared to how it felt when he was Lonn's age. As uncertain as he was of the young prince's plans, he was determined to do everything possible in the time that remained. Casually striding along the Palisum corridors, there was no hurry in his steps and no pressing need to irritate his still mending wound. It bothered him on occasion, but the pain had fallen to a dull throb.

At his passing, servants skirted to the side, heads bowed as they made way for him and his burden. All but one. Philla maintained a different standing among the servants on account of her position as the queen's handmaiden. She was a slender, unassuming girl. On this occasion, she wore a green satilk kirtle and a matching fabric coif that kept her flowing brown hair draped down her back and out of her face as she went about her daily tasks. So focused was she that she did not see Soreign until he was almost upon her.

He leaned over, perusing the serving tray she carried and plucked away one iunna berry. She gasped, startled by the interruption of her thoughts. "Where are your manners!" She looked up and realized her error as her cheeks turned crimson. "Apologies, Sir Soreign. Still…"

He looked down at her, smiling. "Just one?" He popped it in his mouth.

"One. The rest is not for you."

Soreign eyed the tray again. "Ah. I thought My Queen had finished, and you were going back to the kitchens. A bit spare if you're coming, isn't it?" He leaned closer, his voice lower. "or is Her Highness… slimming down?"

"Certainly not!" Philla stiffened, pulling away with a huff. "And no business of yours if she were! Do act your station, sir!"

"Always a pleasure, Philla." Soreign smiled, watching her continue down the corridor before carrying on across the lower courtyards towards the royal residence.

"Do you need assistance, Sir Soreign?"

He turned abruptly and saw two of the younger knights at the far end heading toward the docks. "I can handle my business, Sir Malvek." The strapping knight carried his helm under one arm, letting his long, silvery hair flow free. Sir Torain marched along beside him, of similar disposition only with curling auburn locks. The two were hardly ever parted from each other's company.

"Are you handling yours?" the old knight asked. "Ready for another round on the docks?" Ever since his experiences aboard the disastrous final voyage of the *Starlight's Traverse* and his preparation for the expedition into the Ciration Forest, he had instructed the knights to train the flotilla cadets and even the officers in better sword fighting techniques.

There was a flash of hesitance in the young knight's brow, revealing things were not going smoothly. "Oh… yes!"

Sir Torain joined in. "Another day, sir!"

"On the docks."

"Absolutely, sir."

Soreign grinned. "Very good! You'll whip those cadets into shape, I'm sure."

Malvek paused before continuing on the path. "Won't you be joining us?"

Soreign hesitated, uncertain. "Perhaps later. Once I see to my journeymin."

Torain perked up. "Oh! So, it's no rumor, sir? Prince Lonn has finally returned from tourney?"

The knight nodded. "He has."

Malvek smiled. "That is good news! It's been odd to see you stalking the Palisum halls without his company these past many days."

They returned to their duties with a wave, and Soreign continued on his course towards Lonn's chambers, finding the young prince standing on his tiptoes awkwardly rifling through one of the tall cabinets. There was heaviness in his gaze along with precarious footing that exposed his restlessness. Setting the sack by the door, he quickly propped his journeymin up before he toppled backward. "Steady on, My Prince. Did you get any sleep last night?"

"Is it sunrise already?" Lonn jerked, suddenly realizing Soreign's presence.

"Well past."

"Suppose not. Not much. Grown so used to having her at my side, Soreign," he laughed faintly. "Isn't that odd?"

"To be expected, I think." He looked up. "What're you

after?”

“Goblets. The nice ones.”

Soreign reached up high and drew two down made from solid gilver. “These the ones?”

The young prince snatched them up. “Thank you.”

“Expecting company?

Setting them beside the coin purse, Lonn eyed his taskmaster for a quiet moment. “Not exactly.”

“Ah… this is to do with the Gazers. You’re still intent on…” The concern in his voice was evident. “Just what *are* you intent on doing?”

Resting his hand over his chest, Lonn hesitated. “Suppose it all depends on if I can even get past the door.”

“Door, huh? And where is that?”

“Not sure. But I have the four days of brighmoon to find it.”

“And if you do get through?”

“Thought about my question all night.” He looked at the offerings. “Just not sure what it’ll cost me.”

“Well, you’ve got quite a stack of gilvers there. And those goblets are worth a fair bit.”

Lonn nodded but could not tell his taskmaster the full extent of the Gazer’s price. Feeling the jagged crystal press more insistently against his chest, the time was getting close. He pulled on some fresh clothes and reached for Caetriona’s belt dangling over the back of the chair.

Soreign appraised the other. “Not taking yours?”

“No.” It felt right as he strapped it tight. Perhaps just one more thing to keep her close to him. “Just the dagger.”

Soreign drew it out, appraising the well weathered hilt. “Interesting blade.”

“Belonged to Old Zaude.” After all the time in his possession, he never considered it thoughtfully. “He… had quite the reputation as a… backstabber.”

Tossing it on the table, Soreign grew pale, "Could've warned me of that sooner." He hastily wiped his hands along his striders. "Didn't try to—"

"Tried." Lonn drew it up and slid it into her belt. "Killed him before he could."

"Ah! That's… good!" The old knight nodded approvingly, "That's alright, then." It was then that he saw the troblyte blade. "Now, that's a right nasty looking thing." Hesitating a moment until the journeymin nodded, he took it up and flipped it over in his hand. "Good balance, though."

"Got it when we were escaping the troblytes."

The knight perked up. "Oh… well… if those that came after me'd had these… now that would've been a fight worthy of song."

"It's just a barber's blade, Soreign."

"Really?" The old knight wavered a moment. "So… must've seen quite a few. How… tall you recon were the ones you fought?"

"Oh…" Lonn held his hand flat out near her belt, "Perhaps about…" but saw the look in Soreign's eye and slowly lifted his hand up until his arm stretched high. "This tall at least."

"That's about right, My Prince." Soreign grinned. "So you do have stories to tell! If you'd just stuck with that yesterday—"

"Only ones that end in a lot of bloodshed," he commented, collecting his payment and letting the crystal guide him out the door.

"But… My Prince…" Soreign chased after him. "Those're the best kind!"

Down in the dungeons, Caetriona stretched out uncomfortably on the narrow bench facing the stone wall. Her ears twitched from the whining door and approaching footfalls. There was a gasp and a clatter. Turning, she jerked off the weight of a hand on her shoulder. She blinked in surprise, expecting the queen. She saw a stranger instead. "Who're you?"

"Philla!" The handmaiden stumbled back, gasping hard and appearing quite pale from fright. "I— so sorry if I startled you!"

"Seems like I startled you enough for us both." She looked the young, nicely dressed min over. "Take it you're not another prisoner sent down to keep me company."

"Prisoner?!" Philla stared at her with wide, brown eyes. "Perish the thought! I'm Her Highness' handmaiden."

"What're you doing down here, then?"

"Brought a meal, as Her Highness instructed." She motioned back to the tray sitting on the floor beside the sack. "But… the cell door's open."

Caetriona slowly sat up and stretched out her legs, peering past Philla at the offerings. "So?"

"The guards only do that if… if a prisoner is… is dead."

"I'm sure that would greatly please her grace," she laughed.

Philla looked at her, brow furrowed in confusion. "But… you could leave at any time."

"And her grace would very much like if I did. Not giving her that satisfaction either."

"I… don't understand."

"Don't expect you to… Philla, was it?" She motioned to the tray, reluctant to even get close to the queen's supposed temptations. "Mind sliding that my way?"

Philla jerked, embarrassed. "Oh! Of course."

"Surprised her grace bothered. But she's clearly not providing any good offerings to the prisoners." She faltered, plucking out a small red berry and eyeing its white spots suspiciously. "But poison's not off the table, I see."

"P-poison?!" The handmaiden grew stiff, face crimson. "H-how dare you suggest—"

"These *are* iunna berries, right?"

She blinked. "Of course."

Caetriona remembered back to the Ciration Forest when Lonn found some. He hardly seemed concerned either. "You… actually eat these?"

"All the time."

She flicked the berry at Philla, landing it in the folds of her kirtle. "Well, go on then."

The young handmaiden shrugged and popped it in her mouth. "They really are quite tasty. You should try them since you've never had them before judging them so harshly."

Leaning in, Caetriona watched intently for any reaction. But none came. "Perhaps built a tolerance?" She plucked out the purp berries, her nose wrinkling from their tartness. "Thought I'd had the last of these horrid things. But you can have the others."

Philla hesitated before slipping a few iunna berries into her mouth. "I'll leave a few in case you change your mind." She rose up and lingered at the door. "I have other duties to attend, but I… don't have a key. Did you want this opened or closed?"

"Doesn't matter, Philla. Thank you for the meal, though. Meat next time?"

"Prisoners only get that for their final."

"Oh. Blanket, then? That would be nice."

"So…" The handmaiden tilted her head. "You're really just going to stay down here?"

"That's right. You can tell her grace I'm still not going anywhere."

Clutched in Lonn's firm grip, the Gazer's Stone pulled insistently first one way and then another, guiding his path forward. He remembered what Caetriona had told him and wondered if the door might even be found within the Palisum itself. But any such hope was dashed when he stood on the furthest terrace overlooking the city below. Soreign glanced over the young prince's shoulder with an upturned eye. "Not allowed down in Palisity. You know that."

"Not a child anymore. Afraid of what I'll see?"

"For starters," his taskmaster replied. "Best hope His Majesty doesn't learn of this. Or My Queen. Break two shields over my head. Fix the old coffin up and lay me out for a right dishonorable funeral roast. Might even be songs of my misdeeds."

"What're you on about, Soreign?" Lonn asked, heading for the main gates.

"Just considering all the ways this could end badly, My Prince," the old knight replied, rushing after him. "How about you tell me one of those stories. Take my mind off the fact I'm disobeying orders."

With the crystal leading him, Lonn figured there was little else to do until they reached their destination and told Soreign as much of their journey as possible once they were beyond the gatehouse. While he had never been down in the city proper, his focus was not on exploration the new sights but on following his insistent guide. It was some time before the pressure exerted by the crystal changed.

Soreign trailed close, face wrinkled in revulsion. "Three? Th-that— that's just unnatural."

"Zaude suggested his parents were… closely related. It left the wretched figure deformed and… confused. And being tormented by the crew only made him worse."

"I've heard of such things. Still…" He shook his head with a shiver and grabbed at his striders. "To slice any min's sack open like that. Not a decent thing at all."

"It was… it was the only weapon he had. And he'd used it before…" Lonn stopped in his tracks and looked up as the brighmoon crested over the buildings. "Miku Arilona. She… died… because of it."

"I'm sorry, My Prince. Know how fond you were of her." The old knight frowned. "So, it was revenge."

"Won't deny… that was part of it." The journeymin grew embarrassed, knowing it was hardly the honorable path, but… "You're right. It wasn't decent. Should've… acted better."

"Heat of battle does that. Can't let it overwhelm you."

"I'm learning that. At the time, I thought my only concern was for Caetriona. Couldn't let him do the same to her." He shook his head. "Once he was hobbled… such a miserable creature. So confused. In so much pain. I… ended it quickly. He'd already suffered enough in life."

"For the best, I suppose." Soreign followed as Lonn picked up the path again, winding through the streets until he stopped the young prince from heading down a narrow alley. "Not down there!"

"What are you so concerned about?" he asked, undeterred. "It's this way."

"You've… never been down to these parts before." He peered nervously into the darkness. "No good'll come of it."

Lonn stopped near an alcove, drawn to a familiar sound. A trembling aelfin hunched against the stonework, body ravaged by the Scourge. "Is this why?" he asked sadly. "Is this what you and everyone else up there have tried to keep me from?" He shook his head. There was nothing he could do for the aelfin. "Saw poor wretches like him in Alisard. To know we've allowed such things to happen even in our own kingdom—"

"You were young. My Queen wished you to be kept from away from it all. And forgive my saying, but she was right."

"It's disgraceful." He stared at his taskmaster. "And just how long has this been going on? How long has father allowed such things as… as this?"

"Before his time… before your grandfather's time. It goes all the way back to the Revolt, using the only weapon we had at a time when our people were nothing but enslaved chattel under the fin empire's fist. It's better this way."

"Shameful so many think like that," the young prince lamented.

"Better than if they regain their senses and rise up… cause us real problems… try to return things back the way they were."

"You really think they'd want that? After all this time? Just want to be left alone. Live in peace like the rest of us."

"Some… perhaps. But enough would want back what they think was taken from them."

"I suppose I can see why." Lonn glanced around at the surrounding buildings. "Look at everything they accomplished. Think of what we could accomplish together."

"Begging your pardon, but this *is* what we accomplished together. Mins built this. All of it. While subjugated under whips and chains. This is our labor. And we've got more right to it than them. Our ancestors did what they thought best."

"But to resort to such a foul thing as addicting them to tillup… while we claim to stand on our… honor?" Following the alley, he gave an exasperated sigh. "Could've risen above such pettiness. All we did was do to them what they did to us."

"You're right," Soreign agreed. "No better than them on that count. We exploited their weakness long ago, just as they once exploited ours. Nothing much to be done about it now."

"Considering everything I've seen, I have to believe you're wrong."

Soreign smiled sympathetically. "I know you do."

Disappointed seeing the same problems had taken root in the heart of his own home, Lonn carried on for a while in silence, collecting his thoughts. He wondered if there was anything he could do about it, but those thoughts faded when the crystal in his hand gave a final forceful pull and went still. "I think… this is it."

The old building was not a dilapidated hovel like the one Caetriona had taken him to in Alisard. It was a quaint old bakery with empty trays lining the window, ready for the morning. Even the scent from fresh baking lingered in the air.

"This place? You sure?" The old knight crossed the stoop and jiggled the door engraved in ornate vines and berries. "Locked up for the night. I could wake the baker to let us in."

"No. No need to disturb them," Lonn reached for the handle but hesitated, glancing at his taskmaster. "Soreign… it's best if—"

"I'll remain at your side, My Prince," his taskmaster cut in, resting his hand on his sword-hilt out of habit.

"Best you say nothing," he continued. "And… don't draw your blade."

"Oh. Yes. Of course, I can do that," Soreign winced, taking his hand from his sword. "What now?"

"I suppose we'll find out." Lonn reached out again, nervously gripping the handle and placing his other hand over his chest. With a deep breath, he uttered the words that she so often muttered in her sleep,

> Nei Yd Aneimun Siertham
> Adnu Siertham Saeham,
> Caetriona Taecouw Dea
> Aeham Ameurouqatnie

He stepped back, hoping he had it right, and gasped when the door swung wide. With a mix of shock and anxiousness, he stared at the black realm of the Gazers. "It… worked, Soreign."

"Can see that." The knight shifted nervously on his feet. "What now?"

"Hold your breath until you're well inside. It'll spare you some… unpleasantness."

"I'll do my best."

Lonn breathed deep as he crossed the threshold with Soreign following anxiously behind him. On the far side, they found themselves surrounded by stifling cold. The young prince called out, "Are—" and instantly clamped his mouth shut, shaking his head for his foolishness. "Castanostrous!" His muffled voice echoed throughout the dark realm.

As before, the formless figure appeared in a violet haze. "Oh, ho! Back again so soon, the apparent… hidden… now revealed one. But the devoured wanderer remained behind. How interesting," She floated around him in swirls before turning her focus on Soreign. "Oh, and here is the answer to your question. Sturdy breed and noble stock, indeed."

"I have another question."

"Ho, but of course you do. It has weighed heavily on your mind this long cycle. And I may have an answer." She floated back to him, patiently waiting.

Lonn pulled the purse and poured the gilvers onto the floor at his feet. "I have coin." He placed one of the goblets beside them and drew his dagger across his palm. Behind him, Soreign stiffened but kept his senses enough to remain silent as the goblet filled. "And I have blood."

"Oh, ho! Eager to meet my price," Castanostrous chuckled and swirled down, snatching the gilvers up. "A modest sum for the question you have." Descending on the goblet, she drained it dry and went still. "Tasted the blood of my blood. Now, that is a curious thing. And explains much." Finally, she turned to him. "Ask your question."

Lonn had considered it thoughtfully for a long time and finally posed it. "Aboard the *Virgin Wanderer* were Chief Engineer Kiran Uirvey, Cadet Wyn Terasant, Cadet Ysari Nimme… and… Merchant Safrion Vidula. Where can I find those four?"

"Where indeed." Castanostrous fluttered in waves of violet around his head. "Those who were sold were in turn sold. Ah! But, this you know," she laughed. "There! Bookends within a small convergence, you can find those four. In flickering flames. In flowing gilver threads. In hands of black. On bended knee among the clouds, touching neither land nor sky. Nothing more need I tell you."

He bowed his head, his brow creased with confusion, "Thank you for… your answer," and turned to leave.

"Young prince…"

"Castanostrous," he paused, turning back.

"This goblet is but one of a pair, and as a pair you came… without her."

"This is true." Lonn hesitated a moment before drawing the other goblet along with his dagger and holding them out to Soreign. "Sorry. I didn't know."

The old knight snatched it up and gave a quick slice

across his hand, letting his blood drip into the goblet. Castanostrous was there in an instant, sucking up the offering. "Hmm. Well worth a taste. I'd have paid well to add a min like you to my house servants. Private quarters." Her light flickered as she laughed.

Soreign's face turned red as Lonn gasped, cutting him off before he could say anything. "Thank you! Castanostrous. Until… next time. May it not be too soon." Lonn stepped away and felt the darkness tug at him until he was forced across the threshold. Finding himself standing before the closed bakery door, he blinked, waiting expectantly, but the wave of nausea that had so affected him before was absent.

Soreign was not so lucky, doubled over and retching in the street gutter. "Ah… foul place got my insides all tangled."

He frowned in sympathy. "My first experience was like that."

"Handled it well, My Prince. Bloody thing sent chills right through me."

Lonn appraised his hand and the throbbing wound. "I didn't think she'd ask a price of you, too."

"Not to worry. Had worse. Important thing, you got your answer." The knight wiped his mouth with the back of his hand and glanced at his journeymin dubiously. "But… just how helpful was it?"

"That is the question." Lonn scrunched up his brow. "She was… less cryptic before. But I was more aware of the situation. This… bookends and a convergence. Four people. Four leads."

Soreign shook his head, perplexed. "You'd think she could've been more straightforward. Like one of those blasted riddles."

"Take it as a place to start. Just have to dig deeper."

"Hmm. And when you have something, My Prince?"

Looking up to the tall spires stretching into the sky, Lonn responded, "Free Caetriona and go after them."

"His Majesty'll have something to say about that, I'm sure."

"I'm sure he will. But if he's unwilling to listen…"

"Forgive me, My Prince, but I'm staying well out of that one, if you don't mind." With a faint huff, Soreign rose to his feet, "Getting over that finally," and glanced down at Lonn. "Keep my mind off this queasy feeling. Give us another tale."

"Oh. Let me…" The young prince laughed, considering where he left off and purposefully skipped the events of Fizzpot. "We encountered a group of children in Douchart playing near the Ciration Forest, and…" His tale continued as they strolled across the city back to the Palisum.

18 Training Grounds

Lonn awoke from a restless sleep but, staring at the hastily scribbled words on a scrap of parchment, at least felt a renewed sense of purpose. The Gazer's riddle perplexed him greatly. Flickering flames… anything related to fire. Hands of black… possibly associated with the Pounders Guild. Wolk Stone extractors, always in need of labor, were often known by their black hands. Gilver threads… the most skilled weavers were known to wind slender coils of gilver into expensive clothes. The last… he had not a thought of what could kneel among the clouds while touching neither land nor sky.

He pondered all these while readying himself for the day, until he tripped on the large sack. It took him a moment to remember that Soreign had brought it and left it behind. Filled with curiosity, he tugged it open and found his taskmaster's note: "Journeymin, wear this now."

Looking at the plated armor pieces, he laughed, struggling to get them all on and feeling heavy and unbalanced once he did. "Must be joking. Just how am I supposed to do anything in this?" Lonn walked in weaves, trying his best to maintain some level of dignity as the Palisum attendants skirted to the edges of the corridors to clear a wide path. All but one.

He almost stumbled into Philla carrying off some unknowable task for his mother. She stopped him. "Your Highness! What have you gotten yourself into?"

"Sir Soreign instructed I wear this. All part of my training as a journeymin, Philla."

"Did he not give proper instruction on how to fit it? Honestly." With an exasperated sigh, she set her tray to the side and went about tightening buckles and setting his armor into a better position. "Begging your forgiveness, but you cannot simply dress yourself in armor alone, Your Highness."

When she finished, he did feel more balanced. "Thank you, Philla."

She curtsied with cheeks flushed. "Certainly, Your Highness."

"Actually, would you happen to know where Sir Soreign is?"

"Oh…" She gave it some thought. "No. Not at all. Ever since he returned on an Astyrian steamrunner— still unclear why he didn't just return on the *Starlight's Traverse*, unless they experienced some problems on their voyage."

Lonn blinked. "It's… possible."

"Oh! How forward! Of course, you would know better than me of such matters. On his return, spent quite some time in the library as well as the docks… oh! And has certainly been keeping the forges busy of late. He was dividing his time between them, but I don't believe he's been to the library recently. Reviewing old maps of the Ciration Forest from the time of that aelfin war, though why anyone would wish to go into that awful place is beyond me. Not even in our own lands." She paused, her face flushed with embarrassment. "Oh, but it's not my place to judge, Your Highness."

Lonn nodded. "So… the docks or forges, then?"

"Oh, yes! I know he's been intent on overseeing the flotilla cadets in sword techniques, but I don't believe it's gone well. That could be part of it. And of course he's also spending time there because Dockmaster Zhanne works day shifts. But he's not the sort to let any personal liaisons interfere with his knightly duties." The handmaiden stiffened. "Oh! Perhaps the less said on that the better."

"It's fine, Philla. Thank you."

"I'm sorry I couldn't be more helpful, Your Highness." She retrieved her tray and curtsied again before continuing on with her duties, leaving Lonn to stomp his way down to the docks, pleased to be walking straight after Philla's adjustments.

The docks themselves were a bustle of activity with the upgrades and refits in full production. Dockmaster Zhanne shouted orders as crews made adjustments on one steamrunner before moving to the next. Each station had its own duties, and the workers had singular tasks they repeated time and again to perfection. Considering the size of Merribellith's flotilla, that was no small feat.

Keeping out of the way, Lonn circled around until he heard Soreign's booming voice. "Keep that sword up! Watch that footing there!" It came from the mideck of a moored steamrunner. The knight leaned over the bulwark, looking down at the dock crew, "Put your backs into it down there! Can barely feel any sway here!" Glancing up, he gave a shout, "Ah, My Prince!" and waved for his journeymin to join him.

It was some effort to get up the gangplank, but he did make it, red faced and huffing. On the mideck, Sirs Malvek and Torain stood with the cadets. "Good day, Your Highness!" Torain's lips trembled, stifling a laugh.

Malvek shook his head. "You're putting him through that torment already, Sir Soreign? Sure His Highness can handle it?"

"More'n you at that age, guarantee it."

"Well, it's good to see things getting back to the normal routine."

"Yes! Very good, sir," Torain chimed in.

Soreign frowned. "Nothing normal down the road we're heading."

Both knights glanced at the taskmaster. "Sir?"

"Nothing." He waved them off. "Get back to that."

The cadets swung heavy swords through familiar routines, reminding Lonn only too well of the fight on the *Traverse*. "Soreign, is this the result of…" he whispered, cautious and still unsure what was known and what remained secret, "everything that happened?"

The old knight nodded. "Just preparing for possibilities."

"And this?" he asked, motioning to his armor.

"My old training armor. Figured it was time to change up the routine. Get you better prepared for… well… whatever comes."

"And you expect me wear this all the time?"

His taskmaster beamed. "From sunrise to fall."

"I can barely move."

"You'll get used to it."

Lonn looked at the cadets as they sparred, lumbering and slow, like he used to be. "Hate to point this out, Soreign… but…"

The knight stiffened, anticipating what he was going to say, "I know. Blast her! I know!" and turned to the knights, grumbling. "Sir Malvek… check the stores. Put a raider blade in every one of their hands by midsun. Confiscated plenty over the blooms. Should have enough. Expect you'll see progress then."

The two knights eyed him curiously before nodding. "We'll see it's done, Sir Soreign."

"Satisfied, My Prince?" his taskmaster asked with a huff.

"Yes. I'm sure it'll help them just as it did me."

The old knight eyed the young prince cautiously. "Now… you finally ready to talk about what's been nagging your mind?"

"With everything that's happened these last few days… it keeps slipping away. Never got the chance," he sighed. "I need to know about the war."

Soreign laughed dismissively, "Told you plenty about that."

"Stories, yes. But not the actual… politics."

"This about all that time you spent in Douchart?"

"They're all preparing for war, Soreign. As if it's inevitable."

"And we show up with a flotilla…" he nodded, seeing the dilemma. "Ah. That's what has you concerned."

"But the way they see us…" Leaning against the bulwark, Lonn looked out across the dock. "We traveled with a group of jesters for a short time."

His taskmaster snorted laughter, "Jesters?"

"They're an important part of Douchart culture, Soreign."

He nodded his head, stifling his amusement. "Course. Of course. Apologies, My Prince. Smart of you to play along." His lips trembled, "You didn't… did you actually perform?"

"We did."

"What was it? Fire breathing? Disappearing coins? Juggling? Now that'd be something worth seeing."

"None of that," the young prince chuckled, "Our act was… different. Played to our strengths. And the audience seemed to enjoy it well enough," but his lips fell to a frown. "But after… since I was small, I heard the story. King Aesinar betrayed the Allied Kingdoms during the last campaign of the Easter War."

"Imagine they tell a different tune there."

"The troupe put on a play. *The Easter Upset*. Terric called it an Error of Comedies. The Douchart army headed east as planned and lost their way. Thought they were in the Commonlands when they attacked, only it was Merribellith instead. They insist it was an accident."

Soreign considered events carefully and leaned closer. "I was a journeymin myself at the start of it… not much older than you are now. I know what the boiling blood can do. And there were plenty of times in the heat of the riot where I didn't know which way was which or which side I was on. All just blurs together. So… I can believe it. If they say they got all turned around… so be it."

The old knight shook his head. "You asked about the politics, so here it is. Here's what I can't believe. Not just as a knight, but as a civilized humin. No acceptance of responsibility. No apology. No recompense for the dead. Not to the kingdom and certainly not to those families. King Aesinar reneged on his oath and insulted the young King Youta. Didn't matter he was still mourning the loss of his father… your grandfather."

Soreign sighed, "Have to understand, My Prince. Five villages were sacked. Sixty-two Merribellith citizens were slaughtered. And they were elders… farmaidens… and children. You've been out there now. Seen things true. So… don't need me telling you what else those poor wretches endured. King Aesinar thought he could escape paying his debt for that because of your father's youth and inexperience. There's no start to mending the alliance until that happens at the *very* least."

Lonn remained silent and thoughtful before responding, "Thank you for being so direct."

He leaned even closer. "Now don't you dare let My Queen know I told you anything like that of the sort. But…

ah! Don't need shielding anymore. Not after everything you've been through."

"I appreciate you saying so, Soreign."

"As for what happened with the flotilla… that was on me. Not thinking straight on account of how bad things were. Still, I was in command and… made a judgement. If it wasn't the right one, so be it. But if they've reinforced their garrisons expecting an attack, it won't come. Not from us. Increase tensions some, but that always happens. Dies down over time. Always does."

"I do hope you're right."

"In the meantime…" He stood stiff. "Journeymin, I didn't get you in that armor so you could just lounge about all day. On your feet. Five full laps around the docks. No scamping."

Lonn slumped. "Seriously? In this armor?"

"In that armor," the old taskmaster laughed as his journeymin rose to his feet and rattled off.

Caetriona stretched out on her stomach, her face turned to the stone wall, and absently rubbed the palm of her hand. With nothing better to do, she stared at the weathered holes in the masonry, wondering if any of the previous tenants had made them, slowly chipping their way to an escape. It was easier for her. All she had to do was walk out of the cell, but if she did that, the queen won, and she would never be with Lonn again. She could not face such a dismal future.

So, she was thankful for the distraction when the door whined open. "Mealtime already, Philla?" She glanced over her shoulder and saw Queen Youta standing at the cell door. "Another personal visit, your grace? People may start to talk."

The queen gazed down at the aelfin, lingering on where

her tunic had pulled free from her striders revealing the scars trailing up her back. "It has been some days." The sack of gilvers sat where she had left it along with the tillup bottle. "And you've resisted temptation. Stronger than I gave you credit."

"Not a very effective temptation when I've got something better to live for."

"And just what is it about my son that makes you so determined to stay by him?"

Studying the queen, she sat up, "Oh… his smile. His laugh. The way he makes me want to laugh," and smiled wistfully. "His optimism. His comfort. The way he makes me feel when he strokes my ear," She leaned forward. "And that wonderful feeling of him being inside me. I miss it."

The queen glared, appraising her suspiciously for a long moment of silence. Her lips twitched and her face softened as she laughed, "Oh, you are a shrewd one."

"As are you, your grace."

"I think we understand each other better now." She stepped into the cell and sat on the far end of the bench. "So, let us speak plainly as min and fin, just the two of us."

Caetriona leaned back. "That would be refreshing."

"Are you holding out hope for the power the throne affords?"

"Power?" she laughed, "Like the sack over there and the tillup. It's not what I want."

"Still, capturing and seducing a prince must have been quite a boon."

"So…" she grinned, "That's something even *you* didn't know."

Queen Youta raised an eyebrow, surprised at being caught off-guard. "Have I missed a detail? Do tell."

"Lonn didn't go to the tourney as a prince. Nobody

knew. I didn't even know… until he told me. Just a little lord. And even that didn't matter… not to me. Still doesn't."

"So, this is about the kind of min he is."

"Suppose so. Still be in this cell even if he'd been a pauper's son. Only… I'd've been executed by now, wouldn't I? What royals care for the feelings of their lowly subjects compared to the weight of my crimes?"

The queen considered that carefully. "And that's all it took? You don't strike me as the kind to trust so easily."

"Considering everything I've gone through… no. Certainly not." She shook her head. "First time I set my eyes on him, Lonn fought so bravely. And he almost killed me when we met."

"Why didn't he?"

"His honor. Thought I was unarmed and spared my life." She smiled, wiping at her eyes. "Didn't see me as a raider. Not a butcher or monster. He… called me a… lady. Treated me like one, even when I didn't deserve it. Looked at me and saw something I couldn't even see in myself. And it didn't change. Not when he discovered I'm aelfin. Not even after I confessed my crimes. Lonn saved my life. In so many ways."

"He claims you saved his."

She laughed, "Suppose we have been taking turns."

"And just why did you confess your crimes when you came before us? You could have remained silent."

"Oh, your grace…" Caetriona leaned her head back and sighed, "Don't expect you to understand. Never been trapped… forced to do… horrible things… to ensure you aren't killed… or… worse. Been a timid child hiding away in closets and corners so long, just grown used to being a coward. Being silent. Good at not taking any responsibility… for anything. But I have to. I deserve punishment," she sighed.

"Lonn…" she smiled, "doesn't understand it either… so quick to forgive. And I love him dearly, but it's hard to forgive myself. He wants me to *so* badly, but I don't know how. All I can do is try to right *this* wrong… start making amends somehow… even if it's small. And when I am executed… at least I know I… tried."

Queen Youta considered her words thoughtfully and appraised the bench as she rose to her feet. "It is quite narrow."

Wiping at her eyes, she chuckled, "It really is."

Closing the cell door behind her, the queen lingered. "Be glad you didn't confess before the court. You'd have been held to proper judgement regardless of your feelings… or ours."

Caetriona studied her carefully. "So, you're not going to execute me?"

"That's not my decision to make."

"But it is a decision a shrewd min might influence."

The queen nodded as she left. "Perhaps a shrewd enough min might."

Red-face and panting, Lonn finished his final lap and dragged himself slowly up the gangplank. Soreign looked him over. "So, how're you getting used to it?"

"Why's it… so… heavy?"

"Heavy as it needs to be." He drew his sword. "Come on. Out with it."

"Now? You… expect me to… fight?"

"That's right." The old taskmaster grinned. "Now I expect you to fight."

Lonn eyed him suspiciously. "Did you… do all that to… get back at me for… finally… besting you?"

"Oh, you won't be fighting me." Soreign laughed and nodded over his shoulder where Sir Malvek and Torain waited. "And they won't go easy on you just because you're a prince."

"One… or both?" he asked, taking up her blade.

Soreign shrugged. "Not up to me. And it's not up to you."

"Such as in life." The journeymin nodded curtly and advanced on the knights slowly, pacing himself and remaining mindful of Caetriona's lessons. Malvek came at him first, forcing him to parry. The added weight made him sluggish. As Malvek kept him occupied, Torain swept in. Too slow to respond, Lonn clattered to the deck. With a grunt, he pushed to his feet and tried again.

It reminded him of his earliest days of training, still barely able to hold the full weight of a sword. He fell, each time faster than before. Stumbling to his taskmaster's side, Lonn shook his head to get the sweat out of his burning eyes.

"Hold." The two knights fell back when Soreign lifted his hand and appraised his young journeymin, red faced and gasping. "You look tired. Now, you've actually been out there. Know the truth of it. Think a real opponent would care? Or even stop?"

"Take any… advantage… they can," he admitted.

"Rightly so. And just what're you gonna do about that? Now, I'll grant she taught you things to help. But here's the thing she doesn't understand. Can't rely on reflexes alone. At some point, you're gonna get cut."

"I know that," Lonn huffed.

Soreign pat the young journeymin's shoulder. "This armor's not just about protection. We wear it to strengthen our bodies. Keep wearing it until you can move in it as if you weren't. It'll help when you're caught without it. That's what comes from proper training. And if you don't mind me saying, she could do with a bit of that herself. It's a good way to live… and keep living. You'd both be better for it."

Lonn considered his taskmaster thoughtfully. "So… why didn't you… have me do this… sooner?"

"I…" he winced, "didn't think you were ready for it. Begging your forgiveness, My Prince, but His Majesty and My Queen never allowed me to test you properly. I never saw what you're capable of. The test is always out there. And you proved you could survive it."

"Not without help," he sighed.

"Oh, My Prince… that's the hardest and most important test of all. Can't expect to do everything on your own."

"Like putting on this armor."

"Like putting on that armor," Soreign laughed, "But enough of this for now. I'm sure you've got other interests to pursue."

"Speaking of help, I do." Lonn rose sluggishly. "Off to the library."

"To make sense of that riddle? Yes! Vesire there might offer insights. Provided he's in a good enough mood."

"That's what I'm hoping."

The library filled the top floor of the tallest spire of the Palisum, its angled windows taking full advantage of the sun's light as it crossed the sky. Lonn had visited it often as a child to read stories of the outside world, its history, its people. Having experienced those now first hand, the accounts were not always accurate or entirely honest. But much as it was with Castanostrous, perhaps it all came down to asking the right question. With that in mind, he entered and found it in an absolute state of disrepair compared to his last visit. Books scattered across tabletops and stacked on the floor. Some had toppled over.

Vesire, the elder archivist, slumped at his desk, head cradled in the palm of his hand. "Come to ruin more of my…" he trailed off, appraising the approaching journeymin suspiciously. "A bit short for a knight."

"Prince Lonn, Archivist Vesire. We've… met before, but it has been some time."

"Oh! Your Highness. Didn't recognize you in… that."

"Part of my journeymin training."

"I see." He glanced down at the top of his desk, shuffling papers. "And what can I do for you?"

"I've been presented recently with a… riddle of sorts. Was hoping I might appeal to your learned wisdom in deciphering it."

"Appears I've got nothing better to do." Vesire frowned, looking around until he found a crumpled piece of parchment. "A riddle, you say? Let's hear it."

"Bookends within a small convergence, you can find those four. In flickering flames. In flowing gilver threads. In hands of black. On bended knee among the clouds, touching neither land nor sky."

The old archivist scribbled and blinked. "And just where'd you hear this from?"

"A… Gazer," the young prince admitted.

"Children these days!" Baffled, the old archivist shook his head. "Playing with powers you don't understand. But, fine! You went and did it. Don't even tell me what you paid."

"You know about them?" he asked, surprised.

"Somewhat. A mad bunch, Gazers. Always in the jumble of the ever-present. As to your… riddle…" the elder archivist coughed, "Hmm. More like a forecast. First part… easy enough if you work backward. These four things you're questing after all converged in a single place…" and cleared his throat. "But the bookends. Books. The end of a book. Something written... recorded?"

Lonn stiffened, feeling foolish for not considering it sooner. "Like... a business ledger?"

The archivist nodded. "Could be just that."

"And the rest?"

Vesire scratched his head. "Need more context. Probably from the book."

Lonn thought back. Even if he had not asked his first question, he would have learned of Soreign's fate eventually. "Are their answers predetermined?"

"Interesting question, Your Highness." Vesire blinked in surprise. "Not necessarily. I don't think so, anyway. My understanding is they read the ever-present threads when you ask your question and determine a potential outcome. Should events change drastically between the asking and the outcome... their prediction could prove false."

"So..." Lonn grew anxious at the thought, "The longer I wait... the less likely it becomes?"

The elder archivist shrugged. "Possibly. But as I said, I'm no expert."

Wishing for more time, the journeymin sighed, "You've given me a place to start at least. Thank you," and turned to the chaotic mess. "I also need to look at some maps. The most detailed you have of all the kingdoms. And reference material on territories. I... don't expect I'll have much luck finding them on my own."

"Maps you say?" Vesire slowly got up. "Follow me. Think that's the one section *they* haven't touched." He led Lonn through the stacks, weaving among the strewn book piles. "Had a system. Everything in its proper place. A mess right now with all the fuss over those steamrunners. No point cleaning up until *they're* done." He stopped at one corridor.

"Yes, here we are."

Lonn looked at the tidy shelves of numerous books and countless rolls of maps. "All of this?" The old archivist waddled off back to his desk, leaving the young prince scratching his head. "Might take longer than expected." He perused each shelf, pulling anything that might help him. With rolls of old maps tucked under his arm and precariously balancing a tall stack of books, he passed the archivist. "Need to borrow these."

The old archivist frowned, looking around at the piles of misplaced books and scattered documents. "All I've been hearing of late, Your Highness. Can't wait for this blasted so-called refit to be done. Had everything organized. Once."

Sympathetic, Lonn nodded, "Understanding ancient aelfin is hard work. Saw some myself a while back and couldn't make any sense of it."

The old archivist eyed the young prince skeptically with a huff, "Could've just asked, but no. Has to be so very secret."

Remembering the excited cadets' conversation about the newly deciphered advancements from the *Aeleophinium*, the seminal work on steamrunner construction, along with the growing risk of war with Douchart, he frowned, "Well, I suppose it has to be that way for now," and hoisted the stack. "Thank you. I'll return these once I'm through."

The old archivist slumped at his desk. "Been hearing that of late, too."

Lonn pushed through his chamber door and set the books down before sliding the maps from under his arm. Gazing down at himself, he gasped and took to the task of undoing his armor until it came to the unreachable buckles. About to call a porter, he turned and saw his mother standing in the doorway. She looked at him sympathetically, "Allow me," and slowly undid the straps of his breastplate. "Used to do this all the time for your father."

"Thank you, mother."

"Of course, Lonn. You haven't spoken a word to us in the many days since all that unpleasantness. I was concerned it might become a permanent rift."

"What's there to speak of?" he asked with a frown. "I hoped for support to right an injustice only to find indifference. You and father clearly have your priorities… sending out the flotilla to raze a forest and risk war, but not to rescue your own people lost to misfortune." As the armor came off, he stood straighter. "And then there's—"

"They were military," she cut him off, "Did their duty and were tragically lost. Your father sent inquiry, and we received a response, not that you were there to hear it yourself. Queen Valinar investigated your claim and found no Merribellith citizens in the city of Alisard."

He gave an exasperated huff, "Because they'd already been sold, mother."

"So, they are lost. I don't know how you expect to remedy that."

"If there's anything I've leaned in my time away… the lost can be found and brought home."

"Not just speaking of them, of course." The queen stiffened. "You're speaking about… her."

"Yes, mother. I'm speaking about Caetriona."

"Can she be trusted, Lonn?"

He looked at her, confident. "With my life."

"And… your heart?"

He closed his eyes and reached up, hand over the Gazer's Stone. "Certainly that, too."

"Is that wise?" She reached into her gown and set a bottle by the stack of books and rolled up maps. "She hides what she is quite well."

He stared at the tillup bottle for a long moment, silent, before shaking his head. "So… you know. Doesn't change anything."

"Lonn! It changes everything! What were you thinking getting involved with an aelfin fiend?"

"Don't!" He drew a sharp breath, face red with anger, and turned on her with a pointed finger. "Don't ever talk of her like that, mother!"

"And just how long has she been addicted? How long before it's all she cares about? How long before she… breaks your heart?"

"She won't."

"But she *has* taken it. That much is evident. It's in her… that need. It will never leave her. I've seen it before… too often to count. It will break her just like it's broken all her kind."

"It won't! She's… not like them!" Tightening her belt and slipping on his cloak, Lonn sighed and headed for the door. "You… just don't understand."

"I do. Better than you. Think of your position. Your reputation. If you're so concerned how the other kingdoms will respond to our actions, think of what yours will do if word gets out you consort with… an aelfin. Did you think it would be fine so long as she kept her ears covered?"

He froze, "Position. Reputation," and turned sharply. "What about honor? Respect? Love? I don't care what others think of me. Considering the way they treat aelfins… even here in our own kingdom, mother… it's unconscionable!" Gripping the door, his knuckles went white. "And I like her ears! I understand why she has to hide them. Only wish she didn't have to without fearing judgement… without getting lynched in the streets! But…" he sighed, "we don't live in that world," and slammed the door behind him, leaving the queen standing stoic.

Looking at the stack of books on the table, she flipped open the cover of the first, *The Territories of the Easterlinds*, and appraised it thoughtfully. "Not your typical choice." Stepping to the window, she watched Lonn stomp across the courtyard. "No. Not a simple infatuation at all."

19 Palisity

Despite the long day of training and researching, Lonn hardly felt tired. It was the adrenaline coursing through him, still piqued from the altercation with his mother. Upturning the sheet-furred hood, he slipped past the gatehouse and away from the Palisum. The bustle of the city as sunfall came, with patrons purchasing their final items before heading home and shopkeeps eager to close up for the night, was energetic and oddly calming.

Wandering along the main street, he wondered if any among them held larger concerns, but their sparse conversations held little focus regarding their wester neighbor. Even the publications on the proclamation stand revealed no concerns over the prospect of war, at least not with Douchart. Their focus was on the easter border conflicts with the Commonlands, touting one victorious stand after another thanks to the Easter Guard. All was apparently quiet and peaceful in Merribellith.

Lonn was quite uncertain whether to be comforted or unnerved by such a stark contrast compared to the concerns he found in Douchart. And still his mother's words lingered. He was greatly concerned by the actions of Merribellith and how they could be perceived. If King Aesinar reinforced his garrisons… all it would take was one careless mistake leading to a disastrous war. But did his own actions have the same weighty significance?

Growing up in isolation, the idea that he could sway larger opinion seemed laughable. Even as his feelings for Caetriona grew, he never considered the ramifications. As a child, the Revolt seemed so far remote from everyday life. But the consequences were evident all around, constant reminders in every back alley and abandoned building. It was clear the attitudes many had. And having any good relations with aelfins was seen as traitorous. Could that just as easily lead to a war? He had no easy answer, but it did give him pause as the streets grew quiet and his only company was his own thoughts.

The brighcrescent moon of Stem hung overhead, casting his path in a hazy glow, as he wandered aimlessly. A few lights streamed down onto the streets from behind shaded windows, but they were few and far between, mostly with families settling for a late meal or sorting children for their beds. About the only sound he heard was the faint murmur of voices coming from off the main street.

He followed it to a tavern still lively with business both inside and out. Several young maidens lingered on the stoop, leaning against the stone wall, spending their idle time with gossip. They wore simple half-kirtles, the bodices of their low-slung chemises left exposed. At his approach, one of them nudged the youngest, a fair-haired maiden with a rounded face. She put on a smile, leaning on the balustrade. "Heya." She reached out and drew his hood down. "My... such a sweet youngin." The others behind her giggled.

Giving a faint nod, Lonn glanced up at her and then the others. "Good night, ladies."

The oldest eyed him with interest. "A real gentle... must be fresh."

The youngest pouted as he drew his hood over his head. "Oh, sweetie... don't you wanna spend some time together?

Must see something here you like." She leaned toward him, letting her bodice droop low. "Since you're fresh, I'll even offer a discount."

Suddenly realizing what she was offering, the heat rose in his cheeks but he was spared from a response. The tavern doors burst wide, and a portly figure, piqued about the face from drink, toppled down the steps.

Another min stepped out after him, tall and thick about the arms, fuming angry as he wiped mog from the front of his elaborately embroidered satilk tunic. "Feck-faced oaf! Spill your drink and cheat me outta recompense, will ya? This the finest satilk ya ruined. Mog don't come outta it."

"I— I said—" the drunken patron burped, "sorry, good keep!"

"Sorry?" The keep stepped down to the street, drawing his sword. "More an sorry after I stick ya full a holes."

The portly drunk scrambled down the street as the keep gave chase, swiping at him with his sword. On the stoop, the brothmaidens watched. One yawned. "There he goes again."

"Tellin you, he does it on purpose. Spot one an oktal away." She gave shiver. "Good fer us. Nuthin worse dan forning a slop, specially when dey don't pay."

The keep returned a moment later, face beaming and laughing heartily. "Faster an he looked, that one. Almost got him. Funny to watch the bloated slops scurry like mi-cats." He slipped his sword into its scabbard and hopped up the steps. "Sorry if I interrupted you fillies."

"Just tryin ta pick up some fresh business. Hard ta do with you going off like that."

"Oh? Really?" Appraising Lonn, the keep leaned closer. "Did she offer the discount?"

Lonn coughed, finding his voice. "It's a kindness—"

"Well, if you're looking for a good piece of bung to settle your dagger in for a spurt—" The youngest one lurched forward with a moan and bit her lower lip as he slapped her backside. "Got the best this side of the Crumbling Coast right here! Whinnies like a zorba, this one! Especially mounted from behind."

"Teach you the moves if you don't know em!" she pouted, "Go real slow. Treat you real good, I will."

"I have a few stout brothmin if that's more your thing," the keep added.

"But I have a lady waiting for me," Lonn continued.

The keep reached out, slapping his shoulder. "Not so fresh after-all! Good for you, lad! A faithful filly's hard to find! A faithful min as a result… rare indeed!" He stepped back and drew off his tunic. "Now, will one of you unfaithful fillies put your talents to this before that mog really does set in? Love this tunic."

The brothmaidens watched Lonn as he pulled his hood up and continued down the street. "Well, that's a right shame, ain't it," the oldest said before snatching the tunic the keep dangled before them insistently. "Just use witzer on it, ya gard."

Lonn left their conversation behind along with their business, surprised to find any willing to sell themselves in such a fashion. But the more he gave it thought, perhaps it should not have come as much of a surprise. There seemed to be a market for anything and everything if the patron had enough gilvers to pay. And just as many to make the patron lords and ladies feign ignorance.

He shook his head, confused by such thinking unduly influenced by the nefarious mindset. Spending even a short amount of time in the raiders' company had deeply affected him. It had certainly woken him up. But he could do little about it all except stay true to himself, regardless of the consequences.

Feeling more confident, he turned has path back to the Palisum. It was fortunate the spires rose so tall and glimmered at night. The last thing he wanted was to lose his bearings and get lost in the sprawling unfamiliar cityscape. As it turned out, retracing his path grew difficult enough. Several wrong turns amid the tight corners and narrowing streets found him passing by one unfamiliar building after another. As they pressed in around him, the muffled sounds of nightlife became all too prominent even through the stone walls.

The occasional moaning through a window sent his mind lingering on Caetriona's absence. The odd jovial riot as groups gathered in small celebrations, recounting the adventures of the day or retelling old tales. At one window, there was a different sound of faint whimpering and groaning. He tensed as a faint cry rang out followed by sobbing.

A moment later, a basement window lit with lantern light. "Oh… what's the matter, little fletal?"

He saw a girl curled up on her bed wearing a soiled chemise from night sweats. She hugged her knees and wiped at her eyes, sniffling, "Th-they're after me again, papi!"

"Curse those cousins for fillin your head." He set the lantern on the bedside table and sat beside her, drawing his fingers through her dark hair. "Just a mad dream is all." He bent low, looking under the bed. "Nope. No troblytes there."

The girl pointed, voice trembling, "Closet?"

"Ahh!" Her father creeped up and flung the door wide, ruffling through clothes and folded linens. "Nope. None here, neither." He sat back down tugging at her toes poking out from under her chemise. "They only come after the naughty children. And you ain't been naughty, have you, fletal?"

The girl shook her head adamantly. "No, papi!"

"Then you ain't got nothing to worry about." He tucked her into bed and kissed the top of her head. "Now back to bed. And no more mad dreams." The light faded from the room as the door closed, leaving Lonn once again in darkness.

Despite his recent experiences, he could hardly ignore the good along with the bad. In their travels, they had found both. The brutal and the beautiful. He was determined not to let one overshadow the other, certainly not within himself. A difficult challenge considering his chosen path.

Moving on, he was surprised how cramped the city felt. Buildings buttressed against others, leaving no space, no feeling of privacy. A fleeting memory of Alisard came to him. Caetriona called the worst and darkest part the gutter ward. There was some truth to that even here as the alleys grew darker, cluttered with rubbish and muck. In the air, there was a lingering odor and the echoes of a faint riot ahead. Gripping the hilt of her sword, he advanced cautiously.

The mumbling voices grew clearer, and he needed little aid in filling the gaps. "Come on, old timer. Bottle's right here. Just crawl through all that feck and beg for it."

"tillup… just… a…"

Lonn lingered in the shadows feeling the anger build as two young nobles, dark and fair-haired, stood over a Scourge ravaged aelfin. Scratching at the ground, he dragged himself on his belly toward them. The fair-haired one dangled a slender bottle just out of reach. "Just me, or these things getting boring? Don't even put up a fight no more." The young noble rose up. "Where'd the other one go? Told you we'd've had more fun with that one."

The dark-haired chuckled, "This fiend wouldn't even care what we did to it. Just guzzle tillup."

"If we even had any. Bottle's empty. Not gonna waste good tillup on a fiend anyway."

"Better use for it. Knocked that noble's daughter right out. Didn't even know who got into her when she woke the next morning," the other laughed.

"Just complained of being a bit stomach-sore," the fair-haired laughed and drew his sword, "Yeah. Let's put this one down and get the other."

Unable to restrain himself further, Lonn stepped forward. "Sheath that blade and leave."

The dark-haired jerked back, "Who's that little feck?"

The fair-haired stiffened. "Think it's that fin lover?"

"That you?" The other swung his sword to face Lonn. "Little fin lover?"

"There's a reward out, right?"

Lonn drew her blade. "Told you both to leave."

With a gasp, the fair-haired stared at it shimmering in the faint light. "Using a blade like that? Really are a fin lover," He advanced, sword ready. "And you think you can take two on at once?"

They lunged at him, both clumsy in their slashes and easily deflected. He put them on the defensive, forcing them to the end of the alley, hoping they would take the hint and leave. When they refused, he disarmed the dark-haired and drove the tip of her blade into one leg. Crumpling to the ground, the noble cried out, "Ah! Feck! You know who I am? Who my father is?"

"Don't care." Lonn stepped back, giving the other a chance to reconsider. "You can help your friend and leave with your lives. Your choice."

The anger grew and the fair-haired charged, swinging wildly. "Get you! Fin loving scum!"

The journeymin parried the frantic assault and pinned the young noble in, knocking the blade away with a swift strike. He stumbled back to join his friend as the young prince advanced. "Giving you your lives. Do something better with them."

"Fine! Fin loving feck!" The young noble relented with a huff and lifted up his companion. Together, they hobbled down the alley.

When they were some distance away, Lonn turned back to help the aelfin out of the muck. His withered face looked up at the young prince. "Tillup?"

"No. That won't help—" He turned sharply to the sound of clattering, sword at the ready, but drew back when a young girl pulled herself from her hiding spot in a drainage inlet. She wore a ragged dress and eyed him cautiously. "Not going to hurt you," he comforted with a smile and reached to the small belt pouch, wondering.

There were a few slivers of woolg meat left that Caetriona had tucked away. He offered one to the girl. "Not much, but a bit of meat." The girl lurched forward, snatching it up and sucking on it. "One for you, too." The other aelfin refused at first, interested only in tillup, but finally relented.

It was then that a sharp cry echoed down the alley. Lonn was on his feet, sword ready. The girl scrambled behind him, clutching at his cloak. A dark figure stepped into the alley wearing black striders and a red sheot-furred cloak. "You let those two ignoble lechers live." The voice was faint and firm.

"That's right. They were hobbled. Disarmed. Not a threat. No one had to die here. And they could've learned from what happened."

"Until they healed. Until they got better blades. Until they came back. Revenge. That's what they'd learn… what they'd want… on whoever they find. Won't make things better down here, kid. Should've killed them. Save me the trouble."

Lonn frowned. "Wasn't right what they were doing.

What you did wasn't either."

"Not gonna lose any sleep over *that*." The hooded figure shifted, peering at the young aelfin hiding behind him. "But at least you found those two. Slipped out on me. Didn't you, Petra? Should know better by now."

The girl clutched Lonn's cloak. "She didn't tell me her name."

"No. She wouldn't. She can't. Lechers like them back there had their fun with her. Cut her tongue out when they got tired of her screams." The hood tilted. "Takes a lot to earn her trust."

"Just gave her some food."

The voice laughed, "That's a lot."

Lonn glanced down. "Is it really that bad down here?"

"Must be new, kid. Got no idea. Just look around."

"In a way…" he sighed, "Guess I am."

The shrouded figure glanced back. "Not like this where you come from? There's actually a place where these poor wretches aren't treated badly?"

"Used to think so, but now… not so sure."

"You're very odd. Know that?"

He chuckled, "Suppose so."

"Got a name?"

"Lonn." He glanced at her hesitantly. "And you?"

"Just call me Tilli… Tilli the Rouge… on account of the…" She tugged on her cloak, similar in color to his own.

"They thought I was you."

"Can see why. Imitation's the best flattery… that how it goes? Pretty foolish to imitate me, if you ask."

"Wasn't trying to. Don't know anything about you."

She stretched her arms out. "And here I am… all over the wanted boards."

"Know how that feels," he nodded sympathetically.

"Have a warrant myself."

"Really?" Tilli lurched back, surprised. "And how much're *you* going for?"

"Two thousand gilvers," he replied with a shrug.

"And just what'd you do to get *that*?!" Tilli gasped.

Lonn laughed, "Nothing but politics."

"Well, I'm not wanted that badly, yet. Worth a pittance by comparison… just two hundred soppers." Tilli pulled the aelfin over her shoulder. "Follow me. Best get off the streets. Riot probably disturbed a few people's sleep. Protectorate'll be down here eventually, and it's best if they just find those two back there. Let em think they killed each other."

Taking Petra's hand, he followed her through the dirty streets until she stooped down and yanked up a grating. "The… sewers?" he asked, hesitating.

"Only place nobody wants to search."

"How can they allow this?" He glanced at the Palisum spires stretching high above them.

"Asking the wrong person, kid."

He followed her down. Once in more familiar territory, Petra pulled her hand free and charged ahead of them all. "Will she be okay?"

"She's fine. Knows the way." Further along, flickering light wavered along the wall through a wide gap in the mortar. "Well… this is… home."

Lonn pulled himself through and found the other side gave him a familiar sense. It was laid out much like the troblyte den, with a large open space in the center and numerous rooms set off in recesses all along the edges. Instead of a large trush, the room was taken up by a number of cots, mostly filled, with aelfins in various stages of the Scourge. Candlelight cast the white walls in an orange hue. "What is this place?"

"The old Healer's Hall… before they built that big clinic of theirs."

She set the aelfin down on a cot and flipped back her hood, revealing tightly braided black hair and dark skin. Much to his surprise, she was… "Humin?"

Tilli eyed at him curiously. "Thought I was aelfin?"

His face shaded, embarrassed. "Sorry. Just haven't met any others who… treat them well."

"Suppose not. Aren't many of us. And we aren't popular."

Lonn glanced around. "How did you even find this place?"

"Found records of it before… well… before I was outcast." She drew off her cloak revealing a scar on her bare arm where the guild-mark had been cut away.

"You were a member of the Healers Guild?" he asked, even more surprised, considering she had killed the young nobles. "I thought you took oaths to do no harm."

"Why do you think I'm an outcast?" Tilli shrugged, "Look, Lonn… you should understand. I was… in the lower ward during the last purge. It was…" and shook her head sadly. "Had helpless patients, and those butchers went from one bed to another checking ears and slitting open any aelfin they found."

"That's… awful." He stifled his anger, confused. "When was that?"

"Ten blooms back," she sighed, "but still feels like yesterday."

"Ten?" Lonn gasped, "I… had no idea," shocked knowing anything so horrible had happened right beneath his very feet as a young child. "It… must've been difficult."

"Not really. Killing's surprisingly easy. We're trained to fix injuries, but that also means we know how to cause them. Of course, my superiors didn't agree with my actions. Should've just stood back and not gotten involved… let them all get killed. And provide aid to any purger who got injured, of course… on principle."

"That's horrible!"

"Well, that's why I'm here."

Lonn wandered to the chamber door Petra disappeared through and found her slipping into a small cot along with other children. "Are they all aelfin here?"

"Every one." Tilli nodded. "Most're children… abandoned… orphaned. Expect some of their parents're still alive, but… the Scourge made them forget… or not care. Do our best to get them off the streets, but don't always find them in time before… well… things like what happened to Petra there."

"Will they all get the Scourge?"

"It's in them," she sighed tiredly, "all born to addicts. Sometimes I see the trembles right out of the womb. All we can do is try our best to keep them away from it. If they're never exposed again… they might have something of a life."

But the stark reality was etched in her frowning face. "Down here. Hiding in the shadows. Maybe they can pass above… for a short time. But one slip is all it takes. It's really not much of a life, Lonn."

"Has no one tried to… find a cure?"

"No cure. It's an addiction. But treatments?" She waved her arm. "Not exactly abundant with resources. Hard enough just to find food."

Lonn hesitated a moment but had to ask, "Have… any of the children… or any aelfin… had a different reaction to tillup?"

"Different?" She looked confused. "In what way?"

"White clouding in the eyes?"

She shook her head, confounded. "Think I'd remember something that unusual. No. Where's that coming from?"

"Something I… heard about."

"Just another made-up story, if you ask me," Tilli laughed bitterly. "Anything to make them more like beasts to justify what's done to them."

"Is there anyone else you know who might know more about cures… treatments?"

She eyed him cautiously. "Why're you so keen on that?"

"I…" he hesitated, uncertain how much to share, "An aelfin saved me. Saved my life, and I… I don't…" There was so little they understood about why Caetriona reacted differently. "Just don't want anything like this happening to her."

"Saved you? And she's older?" She considered it with a shake of her head. "Hard to believe that. Must have some strong will."

"She's been… able to stay away from it. But like you said… just takes one slip."

"So… where is she now?"

Lonn glanced at the ceiling. "Up there. In the Palisum dungeon."

"That's…" she whistled, "rough."

"Just waiting for the right time to get her out."

Tilli gave an incredulous laugh, "Well, good luck with that! Sounds as impossible a feat as finding food." She sighed, "As for someone who might just be working on a treatment…" and fell silent, hesitant to continue.

Lonn picked up on her reluctance. "A trade. Food for a name."

"Food first," she stated firmly.

The young journeymin nodded. "Fair enough."

20 The Healers

The Healer's Guild academy was a sprawling complex of white stone buildings where trainees learned their craft and skilled trainers and researchers carried on the work of advancing the healing arts. But the front facing building was the clinic where patrons attended from all across Palisity to cure their ailments and mend their injuries.

Having never before been inside, Lonn had only ever heard tales told to him by his mother of her experiences working within the clinic in Tremelaine. It gave him an image, but the reality was quite different as he entered. Sanitation curtains partitioned the interior waiting room to prevent ailments from infecting the injured. They waited for an available healer, with those hunched over and coughing or trembling from fever chills on one side while a few dockworkers clenched bleeding wounds on the other.

He approached the long desk at the far end where a healer in a sterile smock perked up and smiled widely. "Welcome to Merribellith's Healers Clinic! What ails you today?" She eyed him up and down in his armor, trying to ascertain the reason for his visit. "Did you get cut?"

"I'm not… I just have an inquiry—" He caught himself with a sharp breath, "Two inquiries, actually."

"Inquiries?" The healer motioned to another desk. "Try the information desk."

Lonn followed her lead and trailed across the room as

she helped the next patron. At the information desk, another healer sat hidden behind a stack of parchments. He cleared his throat to draw nis attention. "Need something?" the muffled voice asked.

"I'm… looking for a Healer. I was told he worked here… Baurin?"

"Baurin?" The healer tapped nis teeth, "Baurin." and gasped, "Oh, yes. Odd fellow. Works in the low down… Old Archives."

"And that would… be?"

"Stairs across the way." Nis arm stretched over the parchment pile and pointed. "All the way to the bottom. End of the corridor to your…" Teeth tapped again. "Oh… a while since I've been down there. Left, I think."

"I'm sure I'll find it." He lingered a moment. "Actually…"

"Was there something else?" nhe asked.

"Yes. Just wondering… do you have anything better than healing salve that would help for… older wounds? And… scars?"

"So… something stronger…" Teeth tapped again while nhe thought about it. "There's verliniment, I suppose. Might require multiple treatments depending on the wound and the amount of scarring. But it's not cheap… around five hundred gilvers per treatment."

Lonn blanched. "Seriously?"

"Verlith fletals are pretty rare, you know."

"Of course. But just knowing there is something out there is helpful. Thank you." Sighing, he headed down into the clinic depths, going round and round, passing five levels on the spiral steps until reaching the bottom. There was no indication where Old Archives was, so he followed the left path as directed, hoping the healer had remembered correctly. Passing a number of rooms, he finally stopped in the first open doorway.

Inside, a mortician hunched over and sewed up a cadaver for burial, pausing his work with an upward glance. "Help you?"

Seeing the half naked corpse of a min, skin like slate with her cold eyes staring at the ceiling, Lonn stammered, "I… looking for… Old Archives?"

The mortician pointed with a slender needle. "End of the hall."

He took one lingering last look at the corpse before continuing on. A shiver ran down his spine, which surprised him. He had seen dead bodies before, but they were always from the heat of battle. It was odd that sight affected him more, the idea of his body one day being laid out like that, wounds sewn closed to make him look presentable.

Shaking off the eerie feeling, he reached the door and pushed it open with some effort. Its hinges creaked and cracked from disuse. The air inside was thick and musty. And a withered voice spoke out, "Eh? Who's there?"

He squeezed through the doorway and stumbled over piles of parchment. "Are you Baurin?"

"Who wants to know?"

"My name is…" he hesitated a moment with a cough, "Lonn. I was told to speak with you."

"Speak with me? Told?" A small figure with wiry grey hair looked over a stack of books. "About what? By whom?"

Stepping closer, he reached into his pocket and set down the bottle his mother had left behind in his chambers. "By a… mutual friend. About this. "

Baurin creased his eyes and leaned forward, looking at the bottle intently. "Looks like tillup extract." He popped the top and took a whiff. "Smells like tillup extract."

"It is."

"Then, there's your answer." Baurin nodded. "Don't know why you needed to bother me about it."

"What is tillup extract, exactly?"

Baurin tapped the top back on and gave it a moment's thought. "Nothing much, really. Typically five tillup berries to one bursanthemum fletal, crushed into a fine paste and distilled from moonrise to sunfall. Add water, shake well, and then… tillup extract." He patted the bottle top. "Didn't have to come all the way down to visit the dead to learn that. Any first bloom healer knows how to make it. Great for sedating patients while they undergo more severe procedures… or… nah!" He drifted off with a wave of his hand.

"And just how do you deal with… complications?"

"Complications?" He looked the journeymin up and down in his armor. "Who told you about me again?"

"A… mutual friend."

"Mutual friend, huh?" He shook his head. "Don't have any."

"Someone with a… common interest."

"If I did have one of those… when you were told about me… did this so-called mutual friend with common interest know you were a… knight?"

"I'm a journeymin."

"Oh! Yes!" Baurin huffed, "That… must make all the difference, I'm sure."

Frustrated, Lonn pleaded, "Baurin, I need your help!"

"Just what do you need my help with, Sir Journeymin?"

"Finding a cure!"

The old healer reared back, laughing nervously, "No. No cure needed. No complications. Safe. Yes. Perfectly safe for all humins."

"You know bloody well I'm not talking about humins!"

"Do I?" He slid from his seat and pushed Lonn toward

the door. "I'm sure I do not, Sir Journeymin! Now, out!"

"I'm trying to find a cure for aelfins."

"Aelfins don't have complications either. They have an addiction. Yes. It will do horrible things." Baurin stopped pushing and sighed, "No cure— treatments, for them. Ask anyone here until you're out of breath. All inquires will fall on deaf ears, I'm afraid," before motioning emphatically to the door. "Yes. Well. Thank you for the visit. All very interesting. Nice to meet you, Sir Journeymin, but I must get back to work. Much research to do. I really have no time to waste on such frivolous endeavors."

Lonn stood his ground. "Baurin, has any aelfin ever resisted tillup's effects?"

"What? Resisted? No. Never." The healer stared at him for a long moment, pondering. "Is… such a thing… perhaps? Natural tolerance over time? Through the… bloodlines, perhaps?" Clearing his throat, he caught himself with a wave of his hand. "No. No! A frivolous introspection. Waste of time, you coming down here. Good day to you, Sir Journeymin."

"I hate the way they've been treated, Baurin." Lonn slumped his shoulders. "It's not right. And I thought maybe… if there was a way to help them… but no one wants to. No one cares enough. When I was a child, I thought those in charge treated everyone fairly, but it's not true. And now that I've seen it, I wonder… why has no one done anything about this?"

"Policies. Tradition. Excuses," Baurin sighed heavily, "so many excuses."

"I've heard plenty. And I'm sick of them."

The old healer studied the journeymin intently. "Why? The idea of anyone wearing that caring about them. What makes you so intent?"

"An aelfin saved my life, and I… I can't see my life with-out her."

"You…" he gasped, "love her?"

"I do."

"It's a hard thing, admitting what you just did. This aelfin… she must be young. Is she passing? Has she begun showing signs? Slurred speech. Loss of coordination. Loss of memory. A tremble in the extremities."

"No, Baurin. She…" he hesitated but pressed on, "she's taken tillup, but it doesn't affect her like it does others."

"Doesn't…" Wide-eyed, the healer scurried to his desk, flipping through parchments and books. "No. No! Not there either." He peered up. "Details, Sir Journeymin. I need details!"

Lonn took a hesitant breath, "Her… eyes cloud white. It dulls her sense of pain, and… it makes her… *very*… angry."

"No. No! Nothing!" Baurin swept through his papers, shaking his head. "No record. Nothing I can find. A new development? Something undocumented?" He stared at his books, panic in his eyes. "Sir Journeymin… you can't let anyone learn of this! And… you need to bring her to me. Immediately."

"She's… in the Palisum dungeon."

"Disconcerting. And… disastrous if they find out."

"Now you understand why I'm trying to find a cure."

"Treatment!" Baurin corrected with frustration. "Too few of us believe strongly in it… to lessen the Scourge our ancestors unleashed. The work is slow… too slow. Fortunate this… what ever *this* is… is not widespread. The panic it would create if aelfins rose up in riot?" His voice trembled, "It would start a purge so horrid… so violent… there'd be no stopping it."

"Unless they overpowered us and put us back in bondage."

"Subjugation. Revolt. Reprisal." The healer nodded.

"Always back to the endless wheel rolling."

"What would it take to finally develop one?"

"Plentiful test subjects in the wards. But, time… coin, certainly." He shook his head sadly. "But that would only address normal tillup addiction. No guarantee it would restrain this new… variation you've seen. And, of course, no patron would dare openly fund us."

"Tell me what you need."

"Very well, Sir Journeymin." Baurin stared, silent for a long while. "But, I'm risking a lot."

"We all are," the young journeymin agreed.

Caetriona huffed as she pushed up from the edge of the bench and went down again. The door behind her whined open, but she had grown so accustomed to it, it no longer affected her. Philla entered the cell and sat on the edge of the bench with the tray between them. "You spend too much time training."

"Gotta stay in shape. Besides, what else am I gonna do while I'm stuck in here?"

Philla looked at the open cell door. "Hardly stuck."

"Until I'm properly released, might as well be." She rose to her feet and tugged on her tunic, wiping the sweat from her face.

Philla cringed, averting her gaze from the scars marring Caetriona's back. " Oh… still can't get used to seeing that."

Turning red, she stuffed her tunic tails into her striders. "Sorry, Philla."

"Not your fault. But it must've hurt."

"That was the point." She draped herself in the blanket Philla had found for her to keep off the cold and collapsed beside the handmaiden, eyeing the half-filled tray.

"Slim pickings today."

Philla stiffened. "Some rotten little micat's been at the pantry. Sneaking food at night. So far, none's been able to figure out who… or… what."

Caetriona scrunched her nose as she popped a handful of purp berries in her mouth. "Well, don't look at me. Don't even know where the kitchens are. Not that the kitchens would be my first visit." She finished off the last and nudged the tray toward Philla.

Snatching up a handful of iunna berries, the handmaiden shook her head. "Still won't try any?"

"Nope." She watched as Philla popped them one by one into her mouth, ensuring she really was chewing and swallowing. "My mother told me never to eat them. Poisonous, she said."

"Well, I'm still fine," Philla goaded, sticking out her red-stained tongue.

"Can see that. Still think you've built up an immunity."

"More likely your mother was teasing you."

"Don't know. You weren't there. Found one when I was barely old enough to wobble along the deck, and she was on me so fast… never seen her run faster, smacking that berry so hard it sailed right over the bulwark and landed… who… knows… where?" She froze as a thought took hold and laughed so hard she doubled over into Philla's lap.

"What's so funny?"

"Found… a stray iunna berry bush… in the Ciration Forest. Not one for…who knows how many oktivals. Nothing but… purp berries. And this… one… fecky… bush! What if that was it? The berry my mother knocked from my hand? Grew into that all these blooms later?"

Philla thought about it for a long moment. "If she thought they were so poisonous, why were they transporting them in the first place?"

Caetriona caught her breath. "That's… a good question, Philla. Never… thought of that. Someone paid them, of course. And merchants don't ask a lot of questions as a habit. But, it was a big barrel."

"Must've told you that so you wouldn't scarf their stock before delivery."

"That…" she sat up, wiping at her eyes, "actually makes sense."

"Enough to make you try one?"

She looked at the berries that were left and still found herself hesitating. "Nope."

Philla popped another handful in her mouth. "Can I… ask about those scars?"

"Not much to tell. Punishment I deserved."

"Can't imagine you doing anything to deserve that."

"Only because you don't know me. That me. The old me. I hurt people, Philla. Some worse than others. A lot worse."

The handmaiden tilted her head, blinking in surprise. "Have you… killed anyone?"

"A min." Caetriona fell silent for a long moment. "Some blooms ago, now."

"Did nhe… deserve it?"

"I thought so, even when I wasn't myself. Tried to force himself on me."

"Oh." Philla lowered her head and bundled her kirtle in her clasped fingers, her voice falling to a whisper, "that's okay, then."

"Philla?"

"i… wish i had your strength."

Surprised, she hugged her tight. "Oh… Philla. I'm so sorry."

The handmaiden sniffed, "it's okay, Caetriona. i've…

gotten used to it."

"It's still happening?" Alarmed, she drew back, looking at the young handmaiden. "That's not okay. Have you… told… her grace?"

"Her Highness has always been most kind, but…" Eyes darting about, Philla fluttered her head. "no." Her mouth struggled to say the words, until she bit the side of her finger. "i… can't."

She frowned, taking Philla's hand. "Let's drop it then… for now."

Philla wiped at the tears in her eyes. "Thank you, Caetriona."

"It's nothing, Philla. Go on and have the last few berries."

It was after midsun when Lonn walked along the edges of the docks, watching the progress made to the flotilla. He lingered along the edge like usual, staying out of everyone's way, and heard the sound of clashing blades up on the moored steamrunner serving as the training platform for new cadets. Sir Malvek's voice called out, sounding pleased. "That's it! Thrust and parry!"

He was about to climb the gangplank to the deck when Soreign drew his attention, standing across the dock with Zhanne pressing close beside him. He raised his hand, pointing to something obscured behind all the steamrunners lined up, and the hefty dockamster waved dismissively. They debated between themselves, but at such a distance, it was unclear what their concern was. Certainly it had nothing to do with their relationship as he kissed the knight when they parted "And just where have you been all day, journeymin?" his taskmaster asked as he strolled up.

"Seeing to some business, Sir Soreign."

The knight looked him over and sighed, "Have you been getting any sleep, My Prince?"

"Very little. I had some… unpleasantness… with my mother… some… or many days back?" He glanced up at the steamrunner and shook his head absently. "I've completely lost track."

"Ah. But that's not the whole of it."

"Not in the least." He slumped down, groaning, "Didn't expect coming home would be this difficult. It's… not the home I thought it was."

The knight eyed the young prince sympathetically, "It was difficult for me, too, coming home after the war," and settled down beside him on the ground. "After being exposed to the real world out there… all that violence… all the pain and suffering that I saw and… did myself. They expect you to come back to your village… town… or the city and just pick up where you left off like nothing happened. But I saw everything differently. I was more aware of things I wasn't before. All apart of growing up, I suppose."

"Did you…" He covered his mouth briefly, unsure if he could ask. "There was a purge, Soreign. Just ten blooms back. And I never knew."

"Reason for that. You were only three, after all, and your mother didn't want you getting even a whiff of it. All a black stain." Gazing at him for a long moment, he confessed, "Didn't have any hand in it, if that's what you wanted to know. My focus was on protecting you, and you alone. Even if it wasn't… well… I have no love for fins, but I don't hate them either. They did what they did. We did what we did. It was too many blooms before my birth to much matter. I'd have no part in slaughtering the helpless. That *would* be a violation of the Knightly Order, far as I'm concerned."

"I'm sorry for…" Lonn shook his head, shamed that he

even thought it possible.

"Nothing to it, My Prince. Now, if you put me in a room with a Commonlander..." he laughed, "But I know that's on account of the war. Riles me up some, even still," and slapped his journeymin's knee. The armor clattered. "Now, how're you coming on with all this?"

"Getting used to it."

"As you should."

He nodded to the steamrunner. "And it sounds like they're getting used to those raider blades. I appreciate you considering Caetriona's advice."

"Don't make too big a point of it, My Prince. I'd've gotten there myself... eventually."

Watching, Lonn let out a labored sigh, "I remember having problems on the deck. I even sparred with Caetriona on the top of a caravan trailer. All that shifting ground... she always had the advantage because she'd lived on a steamrunner all her life." He grew concerned. "They won't be ready for the real thing. Need to get them in the air for real."

"I admittedly never saw any steamer combat during the war. Spent plenty of time traveling on them... but all my fighting was on the ground... footing it or on zorbaback. But I was right there with you on that steamer. I know." He gripped Lonn's shoulder reassuringly. "Just like we don't train knights on zorbas right away, let them get used to the blades first. We'll get them in the sky soon enough. And by the time they're actually deployed, they'll be well prepared."

Lonn smiled. "I heard something about you keeping the forgemin busy."

"Just a few little projects, My Prince." Soreign's face reddened faintly. "Preparations to make. Much like your own, I imagine."

"Slow fits and starts, I'm afraid," he groaned. "Everything takes more time than I have."

"Begging your forgiveness, My Prince, but you need more patience. Know that's not much coming from an old knight who has little left, but patience in all things. From preparation to… parents."

"Thought I was… where my parents are concerned, anyway. But with everything I've seen recently… not sure I can maintain that for much longer."

"So… you're set on freeing her?"

"Soon. Not fully prepared yet."

The old knight nodded faintly. "And how goes all that?"

"Challenging," he admitted. "The best plan I have is to return to Alisard. Find the body merchant's records and pick up their trails from there. They must have them. An operation like that… they'd want to keep notes on their patrons. For new merchandise. For leverage… and… if anything were to go wrong… extortion."

"Ahh." Soreign shook his head grimly. "Learning about all that certainly wasn't on my agenda, but you seem to have a firm grasp of the nefarious mindset."

"Wasn't with them long, but it certainly was an education."

"Well, it was never my intention to hide things from you, My Prince. But…"

"My parents," he sighed.

"His Highness and My Queen… well, they wanted something different for you," Soreign laughed, "And you certainly are that. But you're doing things they might not understand."

Lonn eyed his old taskmaster. "Do *you* know what I've been doing, Soreign?

"You are… doing what you think is best. That's all I need to know, My Prince."

"Thank you."

"You shouldn't. Because I must do what I think is best." With a grin, the old knight jabbed his thumb over his shoulder. "Ten laps around the docks, journeymin, and then we'll put you up against some of these cadets... see if they meet with your approval."

"Very well, Sir Soreign." Lonn clambered to his feet and huffed off in a clatter of metal.

Watching him go, the taskmaster sighed, "If this doesn't tire you out so you can get proper rest... don't know what will."

After exerting himself for the rest of the day, Lonn did exhaust himself and, for the first night in many, slept soundly. A faint breeze wafted through the open window of his chambers. The drapes fluttered. As light from the brighcrescent moon streamed hazily along the length of his bed, a shadow fell over him.

21 Catacombs

Caetriona pulled her blanket back and sat up, ears twitching to the familiar whine as the jail door opened. Her nose twitched, smelling something different than her usual fare. "Is it dinner time already, Philla?"

"It is," the handmaiden replied, scuffling in with a heavy tray and sliding it under the cell door. "Can't stay long to keep you company, I'm afraid."

"Is that… meat?" Staring at the plate for a moment and salivating at the thought of having a proper meal, she then remembered, "So… my last meal before my execution, is it?"

"Oh! No!" Philla stiffened. "Her highness gave me permission to use any kitchen scraps I could find before they disappear."

"How kind of her grace." She tore off a chunk of chickuck leg, chomping on it avidly. "Still haven't caught the midmoon kitchen raider?"

"Nhe's a sly one, for certain." The handmaiden knelt, her hands pressed nervously into her lap. "Caetriona, why do you think you're scheduled for execution?"

"Just something his grace said before his guards hauled me down here."

"Well… there's been no idle chatter. Not even a public posting of such a thing. And they do draw a crowd. Min come from oktivals away to see it." She tilted her head, "If I can be honest… hardly a person knows you're even down here, or why," and hesitated. "But…"

"Philla?" she eyed the young handmaiden.

"Her Highness has visited, hasn't she? Several times now. Alone."

"Suppose she has."

"Well… it's odd, don't you think?"

Giving it a moment's thought, she shrugged. "Couldn't really say. Kings… queens… they do as they like."

"That is true, as is their right." Philla twisted her kirtle in her hands. "I've never known Her Highness to imprison someone for no reason… and in such a manner."

"Ahh… but there is a reason, Philla." She hesitated a moment. "Can I ask… have you seen Prince Lonn? Is he… doing well?"

"The young prince? Well…" Her brow rose up. "No. Not often. Haven't seen much of him at all since his return. But he does seem… different… than before going to tourney… in a good way, I suppose. More serious. Determined. Been quite busy, actually. All very odd. The first night back, he remained locked away in his chambers, not to be disturbed. Spent the whole next day wandering around the Palisum, going this way and that as if he'd lost something. Don't think he found whatever it was because that night he went down to Palisity, even though he knows full well he's not allowed."

The handmaiden continued, considering with a tilt her head. "Though, Sir Soreign accompanied him… at least on the first night… so perhaps he finally is. Not sure how often he's gone now, usually at night, after training. Oh! And he spent quite a long stretch in the library. Searching for something quite frantically. Talk of riddles and all manner of unpleasant things. And you should see the state of his chambers. Filled with old maps and books. An unsightly mess, it's become. Strict orders not to tidy at all."

Caetriona listened until she gnawed nothing but chick-uck bone. "So… not often."

"Oh, my!" Philla's face turned crimson. "I must seem so forward."

"Suppose it's… only natural. He does have that affect."

"Doesn't he, though?" The handmaiden smiled, swooning, "Oh! He's always been ever so kind! Not like his sister or… brother."

She jerked in her seat, startled by the revelation. "Sister? And brother?"

Philla carried on, undeterred. "—just so… adorable! And now that he's come of age… I only hope Her Highness has made a good match for him… one deserving of such a prince." She looked at Caetriona sitting red-faced as her hands gripped the edges of the bench tightly. "But I didn't realize you knew him."

"Quite… well, actually."

"Oh?" The handmaiden gasped, "Oh! Is that why…" and her cheeks flushed red. "Oh, my!" She sighed, "But to have his favor! I'm certainly ever so jealous. Oh, but you'll be the envy of so many. You're so lucky!"

A shadow fell over her. "It really isn't."

Startled, Philla gazed up and gave a shriek as a heavy metal hand smacked her cheek, sending her sprawling to the floor.

Inside the cell, Caetriona tossed the tray and leaped to her feet. "Who're—"

"Oh, don't start that again." The Head Merchant stepped out from the far dark recesses of the jail hallway. His legs looked different after being crushed from their last encounter, and he sported a new armature to replace the one she shattered.

Clenching her teeth, she looked him up and down. "You!"

"Took a while to track you down after you left me crippled. Had to get myself fixed up for a proper fight before picking up the trail. Must admit… you two've given me quite the hunt. Finally found Journeymin Lonn. Expected you at his side. But finding you here of all places?" Drumming his metal hand along the bars, he laughed. "Most fitting for a fin beast."

"Where is he?! What did you do?!" Caetriona glared at him, seething, "What happened to my Lonn?!"

The Head Merchant grinned. "Come quiet and I'll let you see him one last time."

She shot a look to the bottle of tillup resting on the sack and lunged for it, but he swiped it across the room and grabbed her by the neck. "Oh, no! Won't repeat that performance!" The bottle shattered against the door while she choked. He squeezed tighter and appraised the sack curiously, blinking in surprise by its contents. "Oh! But I will take this along with your filthy fin hide. Payment for everything you cost me."

The door whined open as a guard, drawn by the noise, stepped through. "What's all the—" His eyes shifted from Philla laying motionless on the ground to the large figure reaching through the cell bars choking the prisoner. "Alarm! Ring the bells! Alarm!" he shouted over his shoulder before tightening his grip on the pike and advancing forward. "Unhand the prisoner and stand to!"

The Head Merchant grumbled, "Always getting interrupted," and flung Caetriona against the far wall of the cell. He turned to face the guard, deflecting the pike blade with his metal armature. Sparks flashed, and the two struggled over the pole until it was thrown aside with a clatter. The Head Merchant lunged and buried his dagger in the guard's side. He gasped, spitting blood, and fell beside Philla while the hunter snatched the keys. "Now… which is it? Finish this business."

Coughing, she swiped up the tray, bracing it against her arm like a shield, and staggered to her feet. Her eyes darted around, seeing the pike rolled against the far wall. The Head Merchant laughed, "Never reach it from in there, beast," but his face fell, startled, when she threw the cell door wide and snatched it up. "Ah. Unexpected."

The weapon was unwieldy in the narrow corridor as she swung and thrust. He clutched it and pounded his metal hand down, shattering the shaft. She stumbled back, and he was on her, his metal hand jabbing out and splitting her lip. "Pathetic without your daggers or your tillup. But fin've always been weak! To think! A beast like you trying to pass as one of us min!"

Wiping the blood from her lip, she lunged in again. He swung out with his leg, and his boot unexpectedly sprung to close the distance, knocking her back with a grunt. "New legs. Real kick to them." Clutching at her stomach, she wheezed. "Must be killing you, not knowing what I did to him. See him one last time as I butcher you like the filthy piece of fin meat you are." He swung the sack of gilvers over his shoulder and gripped her by the hair, dragging her along behind him into the deep recesses of the jail, with a laugh, "Nice of them to just leave all this coin laying about."

At the top of the protectorate tower high above, the hollow ding of the bells rang out, echoing along the corridors throughout the Palisum and down into the city below.

Before the clanging bells awoke the residents throughout the whole of Palisity, Lonn slept soundly. But it was short lived as his eyes shot open and his hand went to his throat, feeling it tighten. Heart pounding in his chest, he sat up and searched his chambers for a threat. Only himself. Alone. He stared through the open window. Had he left it open? Then the pressure faded.

He rubbed his throat, breathing easy again, but knew something was dreadfully wrong. "My lady!" He tore out of bed and hastily dressed before snatching her sword belt from where it dangled. The chair toppled over as he charged out the door heading for the protectorate tower and the jails below.

Two guards stood watch in the yard on either side of the tower door. One yawned tiredly. The other perked up when he saw the young journeymin approach, face enshrouded by his hood. "Halt. Who goes?"

The other shook her head, seeing he was undeterred. "Ain't stopping."

"Prince Lonn." He cast his hood back. "Let me pass."

"Apologies, Your Highness, but we're under orders not —" It was then that the bells rang out. Both guards gripped their pikes, tense. "What's that about, you reckon?" He risked a glance upward to the top of the tower. Lonn took advantage of the distraction, sweeping in with the hilt of her blade, striking upward, under the guard's helm. He slumped against the wall as the other swiped her pike around.

"Why, Prince Lonn?!"

The journeymin ducked and pushed the pike hard along its arc, knocking the guard off balance. "Sorry about this." In that moment, he swung hard, knocking the guard's head back. She slumped beside her fallen companion as the young prince entered and descended to the bottom. He pushed through the jail door, its old hinges whining loudly in his ears, and took in the sight before him in an instant.

Philla, the side of her face bruised pink and black, pressed her hands firmly against the bleeding wound of the fallen guard slumped against the stone wall. She glanced up, eyes wide with fear and panic. "Oh, Your Highness! He took her!"

"Who?"

She shook her head in a flutter. "A stranger! He had but one eye and a strange gauntlet."

A cold chill tore down his back as the realization set in. "oh no. Head Merchant! Here?!" Hoping they had seen the last of him in Fizzpot as their trail went cold, Lonn had to give the hunter more credit and cursed himself for not expecting it. Considering he had somehow tracked them across the whole of the Ciration Forest, he was certainly determined in his revenge.

Tightening his grip on her sword, he turned to retrace his path, but Philla pointed a blood-soaked finger, "No, Highness! Through the catacombs!" She called out behind him, "Careful! Protectors went after them!"

The catacombs sprawled out across the lowest level of the Palisum in a network of chambers. The Youta crypt took up a sizable potion in the center where the family's ancestors rested going all the way back to Merribellith herself. The most recent occupant was Lonn's grandfather, who passed during the Easter War blooms before his birth. Many of the Knightly Order and those who served the kingdom with great distinction were also entombed in smaller vaults along the fringes.

Lonn himself had never visited before, but his focus was elsewhere as he passed those vaults and gave chase down the dimly lit corridors after the Head Merchant. The dust and dirt on the ground was so disturbed and the air still, it made it difficult to know if the tracks were recent or ancient. But the sound of clashing blades guided his path more decisively. Through the dark, he saw flashes of lantern light, and then the clash of swords ended with a cry of agony.

Tightening his grip on her blade, he surged forward until the floor grew slick with blood. A protector lay sprawled out by a vault door, groaning. Lonn crouched to check on her. "How bad is it?"

"Who—" The protector flinched at the sound of Lonn's voice breaking the silence.

"Prince Lonn. Which way were they headed?"

The protector's eyes fluttered, "Garden… Highness…" Her body slumped still.

The young prince shook his head, "I'm sorry." There was nothing to be done except blame himself as he took up the trail. He knew the old gardens well, but there was no access— he cursed himself. There was the old door… tucked away and hidden by overgrowing vines… a service shed where the groundskeepers kept tools, or so he had always been told in his childhood. It was clear that narrative was to keep him disinterested.

But the Head Merchant had discovered its true purpose. An entry to the catacombs. And a path to the dungeons themselves. How long he had been in the Palisum or how he learned of Caetriona's presence there held little importance. He accomplished it, and Lonn set his course to stop him.

Behind him, the voice of Commander Henatore echoed through the corridors, "Fallen protector! Fallen protector here!" More reinforcements had joined the hunt. "Spread out! Ensure they don't double-back! Handmaid Philla said Prince Lonn came down here, so watch your strikes."

"What about the escaped prisoner? And that… one-armed min, was it?"

"One-eyed! One-eyed min!"

"Shush up!" The commander grew insistent. "A bloody head merchant! We'll sort it all out later! Just find them! Detain them all!"

At that, Lonn grew more determined, unwilling to be held back, and pressed on through the dimly lit corridors. A cool breeze grazed his skin. Even the lanterns set along the walls wavered. The trail led him to the way out where the ground grew damp, runoff from the gardens. He burst through the doorway and scrambled up the steep steps. Suppressing his breath, he listened intently. "Quit struggling, beast, or I'll hit you again!" It came from the far side of the Verlith enclosure.

The great plant that bloomed once every eight cycles was only just beginning to regrow its stem as the cloistered tenders diligently cared for it. Despite its importance and knowing full well to injure it, even accidentally, was among the highest crimes of all the kingdoms, Lonn still took the chance to close the distance by crossing the enclosure. The tenders yelled at him as he hopped over the exposed roots, careful not to step on any that stretched out and sunk into the dirt. He left them behind, furious as they scrambled to ensure he truly had not injured the plant, and listened again.

The sound of Caetriona's struggles guided him to the dock path. Bruised and bloodied, she clawed her nails uselessly along the hunter's improved armature while he dragged her behind him. She kicked and did everything possible to hinder him. Lonn felt his heart pounding as he closed the distance, his grip on her sword firm. "Head Merchant!"

Caetriona's swollen eyes went as wide as they could to the sound of his voice. "my Lonn?!"

"Ah! There you are, Journeymin Lonn!" The Head Merchant staggered to a stop and turned, dropping the sack of gilvers at his feet. "Wondered when you'd finally catch us up. Just about to perform a one-act play, as it were. Some public butchery. And I certainly need you in the audience.

No ribbons for blood this time."

"Let her go!" Lonn leaped, slicing at her taught hair to set her free from the merchant's grip, and barreled forward. Released from his burden so suddenly, the hunter stumbled back, and the journeymin took full advantage of the distraction, striking upward as hard as possible to the hunter's jaw. His fist impacted and knocked him off his feet.

Caetriona rolled over, gasping, as the young prince delivered one blow after another. Her sword clanged against the merchant's armature as he held it firm to shield against the assault. The blade bit deep into the metal, and the hunter twisted his arm until the metal screeched and the blade shattered.

Lonn stumbled back, and the Head Merchant gained his footing once more, pinning the journeymin down with his armature and pounding with his bare fist. "Why fight so hard, *Prince* Lonn?" The merchant seethed, "Consorting with such filth! A disservice to your station! To your kind! Should be ashamed!"

"Never!" Defiant, Lonn stared at him through the blood trickling down his face and took another blow. Fighting through the pain, he drew his breath and strength, kicking the merchant off of him. He rolled and scrambled to his feet, wiping at the blood before pulling his dagger. "She's worth fighting for!"

The Head Merchant fell back a step, goading Lonn to press his attack. When he did, the hunter kicked out. Caetriona tried to call out in warning, but it was too late. The spring boot unexpectedly closed the distance, knocking the journeymin off his feet. Pulling his own dagger, the hunter laughed, "Only have yourself to blame for losing here, Lonn. You and that beast of yours made me what I am."

Hoping to help, Caetriona crawled forward, flinching

as a sword dug into the dirt an okt-span from her face. "Feck!" She searched for another attacker, wondering if the Head Merchant had more of his henchmen but then looked up. Sir Soreign leaned over the upper garden terrace and nodded curtly. "Ah… never thought I'd actually appreciate that old knight." Dragging herself to her feet, she yanked the sword out and hefted it up with a groan.

The young prince struggled to his feet, readying his dagger as the Head Merchant fell on him using the overpowering weight of his armature and boots. The metal of their blades screeched against each other. Gritting his teeth, he was losing his grip along with his strength. The merchant's blade moved ever closer to his neck.

"Too bad, Lonn. Wanted you to watch me slice her—" he gave a labored gasp as the sword blade pierced through his chest. "See? Nothing but… a… fil… thy… back… stab… bing… beast."

Caetriona twisted the blade with a grunt, "This… better… kill you!" The Head Merchant slumped to the garden path, coughing blood while it drained from his wounds and seeped into the dirt. "Aimed… for his… heart. Missed," she laughed, collapsing to her knees, "Bloody… heavy, that!"

Lonn struggled to her side, hugging her tight with a cry, "My lady!" and kissed her. "I'm sorry. Never should've let this happen."

She wiped the blood from his face, crying herself, "Not your fault, my sweet prince," and kissed him back.

Soreign huffed down the garden path, skittering to a stop. "Oh. Ah-ha!" He turned away, letting the two have their moment, "Got it all sorted then? Good," he huffed, nodding his head curtly. "Very good."

When he turned back, Caetriona held her out arm, wavering and unsteady. "Thanks for your help back there, Sir

Knight."

Soreign blinked, trying to suppress his surprise at seeing her ears through her disheveled hair, "Ah… well… looking out for his interests, same as me." Clasping her arm with a nod of appreciation, he glanced to the Head Merchant. "So, this the one's been giving you all that trouble?"

Caetriona jostled him with her boot. Bloody mouthed, he coughed, "Fin beast!"

"Tough brute. Give him that."

Soreign nodded in thought. "Made a bit of a mess, but it'll get sorted. I'll… speak with His Majesty on your behalf… as much good as that'll do."

"Appreciate that," she nodded.

"Best get you cleaned up and… back to your cell, then."

She glanced at him with a frown, "Yeah," and took a hobbled step forward.

But Lonn grasped her hand tightly. "No. I… I won't let you go back to that."

"My Prince?" Soreign asked, hardly surprised, as they both looked at him.

Glancing at the Head Merchant, the young prince knew he was not the only threat. "We can't stay here." Frowning, he turned to Soreign. "And I'm afraid I no longer have the right to require your services."

The old knight stiffened. "I… see."

Lonn studied his taskmaster cautiously. "What will you do?"

"Well, I suppose I knew this time would come eventually." Soreign's hand went toward his empty scabbard before remembering his sword was lodged in the Head Merchant's chest. "Didn't expect it quite this soon, though." He stooped down, and Lonn tensed, hoping it would not come to a riot. But instead of reaching for his sword, the knight picked up the sack of gilvers and held it out. "As I understand it, the *Merribellith's Favor* is fully kitted and ready to fly."

"Sir Soreign?" he asked, surprised.

The knight grimaced, holding the sack out insistently. "Get going now, Lonn. The protectorate'll be here any time."

He hugged him and took the sack. "Thank you, Soreign."

"Yes," she nodded in appreciation. "Thank you."

"Can you fly, my lady?" he asked Caetriona, concerned.

"Fly?" She smiled and slumped in his arms, "Just get me there, my love. I'll fly us… anywhere you want." She hobbled a step and groaned. "Heal… later."

Lonn propped her up and helped her down the path. "For us both, my love."

Soreign watched the two disappear and wiped at his eyes with his sleeve. "Blast her."

"Shoulda… killed… that… oof!"

"Shush up!" Soreign knocked the merchant unconscious with a kick to the face. "Spoiling the moment."

The *Merribellith's Favor* was a steamyacht of sizable length and stature to accommodate the king and queen as well as guests on any number of diplomatic or leisure trips. She had three main propellers and four navigation props, with streamlined sails that helped maintain a sleak profile. Since her recent refit, she had also received a fresh coat of blue paint along the length of the hull with shimmering yellow trimmings.

Caetriona looked it over through her swollen eyes. "So… third generation, huh?"

"Fast as a steamscout, so I've heard."

"Hopefully faster," she commented as Lonn helped her up the gangplank to the mideck and along the ramp to the bridge. It was more spacious than any steamrunners either of them had seen, with a wide viewport offering a clear view all around. He got her to the central pilot station, and she grasped the wheel to support herself. "Oh. *This* is nice." She gave the controls a quick perusal and gave a faint nod despite the pain throbbing through her.

"Can you fly it?"

Despite a few unfamiliar features, the primary layout remained. "I'll get us up, my love."

As she prepped the steamer to sail, Lonn busied himself on deck pulling in the gangplank. His attention was quickly drawn across the dock to one of the observation platforms where his father waved frantically to get his attention. His mother stood beside him at the balustrade.

But any thing they yelled was drowned out as the propellers revved up. "Mother. Father," he sighed, turning away. "I'm sorry." He hopped up to the bridge and took to Caetriona's side, steadying her at the controls. "We should leave before the protectorate arrives."

"Going now, my love." The *Favor* lurched and strained. "I… think." Caetriona's brow scrunched as she looked over the controls and brought all three rotors to full. "Are we snagged on something?" The Favor gave a shuddering jerk forward, and they both steadied themselves as the steamyacht pulled away. "Huh. Must've been nothing." She peered out the viewport, seeing the king and queen as they passed them by. "Lonn. Your… parents." He nodded silently. "Are they…" The king shook his fist wildly. "Oh. They look quite fecked."

"I know." He turned and kept his focus forward. "Can't worry about that now."

Across the distance, King Youta leaned over the balustrade, squinting to see the far end of the dock where the royal steamers were moored. "Lonn! You fool boy!" He shook his fist frantically as his son reeled in the gangplank. "What does he think he's doing?!"

The queen tilted her head thoughtfully. "Staging a dramatic rescue and daring escape, it would appear."

"And the *Favor*! He's taking *Merribellith's Favor*!"

"You have four others, dear."

"But… that's my favorite! He knows that's my favorite!"

She reached out, patting his hand reassuringly. "I know, dear."

King Youta winced as the *Favor* strained to pull away. "Oh! No!" He waved frantically, shouting, "The mooring line, fool! Unlash the mooring!"

The deck planks groaned loudly as the steamyacht strained and broke free. Shattered planks flew about while the loose mooring line scratched at the fresh paint along the length of the hull. The king buried his face in his hands. "Oh! Can't look! He's ruining it!"

"A bit of paint will fix it right up when you get it back… eventually."

"But my docks!" His shoulders shuddered as jagged fragments of wood clattered along the ground. "My lovely docks!"

"Just a bit of flare to impress his lady," she swooned, "Oh, to be young and impulsive again."

"He gets it from you."

She smiled. "I'm sure he does."

Suspicious, he eyed her. "Did you have anything to do with this, My Queen?"

Bringing her hand to her chest, she gasped, "Me, My King?" As *Merribellith's Favor* rose up, her sails lowered awkwardly, giving a sway to her hull before leveling out. "Most certainly not. All far too flamboyant.”

“Well, I want answers!” He leaned on the balustrade, shaking one fist in the air while shouting, “Proper bloody answers!” before stalking from the observation deck.

Queen Youta lingered, watching the steamyacht fade from view. “Oh. She’d better ravish him well and proper tonight.”

King Youta, glancing over his shoulder, lingered in the doorway. “What was that, My Queen?”

“I said,” she blinked a few times, smiling. “I’ll inform the dockmaster to get repairs underway, My King.”

Aboard *Merribellith’s Favor*, Lonn stood beside Caetriona, his arm wrapped around her waist. Her head rested against his. She gazed down at him with a wavering smile. “Where to, my love?”

“Alisard,” he said with confidence, looking out the viewpoint. “Have some unfinished business with the body merchants.”

“That we do.” She gave him a kiss and set course.

Despite their trials and recent injuries, and whatever faced them in the future, at least they were together again. At that, Lonn beamed brightly.

About the Author

Born British-American in East London, Gavin Cash Brown currently resides mostly behind a computer screen in the occasional comforts of southern California. He holds several degrees in English, Creative Writing, and British Literature. Naturally, he works partially as a professor and admittedly can be accused of professing too much, such as here. He has interests in linguistics, history, and popular culture which heavily influence his writing.

In Light of Moon and Sun is his first published novel, inspired by the planetary romances, fantasy, and science fiction he read in his younger years.

For updates, short stories, poetry, and more, visit his website:
gavincashbrown.com

www.ingramcontent.com/pod-product-compliance
Lightning Source LLC
Chambersburg PA
CBHW031205310726
48969CB00001B/226